OLD MONEY

Books by Lacey Fosburgh

Old Money

Closing Time, The True Story of the "Goodbar" Murder

OLD MONEY

Lacey Fosburgh

DOUBLEDAY & COMPANY, INC.
GARDEN CITY, NEW YORK
1983

All of the characters in this book are fictitious, and any resemblance to persons, living or dead, is purely coincidental.

Library of Congress Cataloging in Publication Data
Fosburgh, Lacey, 1942-
    Old money.
    I. Title.
PS3556.0754S04   1983   813'.54
ISBN: 0-385-15310-4
Library of Congress Catalog Card Number 82-45246

To H.W.F. with love

Prologue

W hat's that sound?" Whitaker Stylus Rushing, the financier and philanthropist, asked as he lay along the ground.

"A river, sir."

"What's its name?"

"Doesn't have a name."

"Sounds like it's licking," he said.

He was her great-grandfather, and he sat in the shadows of the campfire and stared into the darkness of the clearing beyond. He had a house in New York one block long and half a block wide, but here in the northern country the world went as far as the eye could see, black almost, with the grasses blowing and birds calling. The wind moved ever so slightly, as if it had barely a thing to do, and there was a moon above, a sliver of light was all it was, hinting at what lay below, mountains, a lake and a running stream.

But all day and all night, his eyes kept returning to the willow tree. Or so he always liked to say. It spread far and wide, he said, its branches hanging this way and that, climbing to the sky, and already then, in 1878, on this his first visit to the place, it seemed a million years old. Sometimes it bent and shivered in the air, turning its leaves silver or green to tell of the coming wind and rain, but at others, it rested and grew still, not a leaf moving or a branch swaying, a powerful monument to what earth and land could do.

"I'll have the house right here," he told the others, local men all, lying on the ground, their horses tethered in the grass. "Right alongside the tree. See?" He had pointed at the tree. "See how it moves? See how it reads the weather and the sky?"

But nobody answered and he fell quiet. He rarely talked that way, financier and city man that he was, and they didn't know what he meant, and he never did say. But he must have had the notion that if a tree could reach that high, it must reach that deep as well, the roots, that is, for how else could it stand and sway and bend and be?

And so the house was built, an enormous thing, and for Whitaker Rushing it always seemed that they were mighty equals, the house, the tree, the land and he.

He said one more thing that night before he went to sleep, lying on the ground. "This will be good for us," he said. And later he added in a letter that was handed down: "I knew right away it would be good for us, this land and the wilderness. It's what we need. The family. A place where money doesn't count."

He called it Weather Tree. It was forty thousand acres in all, high in the Adirondack Mountains of northern New York State, meadows, lakes and forests, rivers, caves and peaks and a century later, it was still wilderness.

She was his great-granddaughter, Abigail Rushing Boar- chards, the fourth generation down. For after Whitaker Stylus Rushing came his children: John, who died; Florence; Bostrine; and little Max. The only offspring in the third generation were Florence's children: Sam and Andrew and Rushing. And their two heirs in turn were Andrew's son, Charley, and Rushing's daughter, Abigail Rushing Boarchards.

Sometimes it seemed odd to Abigail that all these people had come down to only two, she herself, a photographer, and her cousin Charley, who said he "traveled." She'd think of

Florence, her grandmother, whom she'd never met, a beautiful woman with a necklace she'd seen in the Metropolitan Museum of Art. It had three hundred pearls offset by diamonds, rubies and emeralds. And then, she'd think of Rush, the son, her father, born in the house in New York with a ballroom and a fountain, who loved nothing more than the woods and wilderness of Weather Tree, hearing owls and tracking deer, no regard for money or things.

But if he was different, Abigail thought, so was she. She, too, like all the Rushings and the Boarchards, had been born in New York with enough silver and china for twenty-four as a gift at birth; but she alone, of all of them, had spent her childhood at Weather Tree, and that had linked her to her father in a way that nothing else could match.

Year after year, summer, winter, spring and autumn, ice and floods, northern lights and west wind. But if he saw the weather tree, she never did—it died before she was born. Of rot, they said, the kind that seeps in along the branches above and the roots below, doing its deed in secret, so no one has a way to know.

April

Alvah Germaine was listed in the Manhattan telephone book under "Alvah Germaine, Services." There was no address, just a number, and it all started when he heard Mary on the phone downstairs. "Just a minute," she was saying. "He does that himself."

"Who is it?" he called down.

"I don't know. She wants an appointment."

"Tell her I'm busy."

"But she sounds nice."

He came to the top of the stairs, his hair gray, his tie too wide for fashion. "What shall I do?" he asked.

"Talk to her, at least," Mary said.

He picked up the receiver in his office upstairs. "This is Alvah Germaine. What can I do for you?"

The woman said her name was Abigail Boarchards, and right away Alvah was interested. He knew the name from newspapers and history books, museum halls and hospital wings. "I get a lot of calls," he said, "and I like to screen them as much as possible. Is it missing persons? Divorce? Industrial espionage? Murder?"

"None of those."

"What is it then?"

"I want you to investigate someone," she said intensely. "But we'd have to get everything done in three weeks. That's all the time I have. I put it off until the last minute. A lot's at stake," she added. "Money, land. Something else."

She didn't say what that something else was, and before he could ask, she had started talking again. "It's a legal matter too," she went on, "and the deadline is only three weeks away. May sixth is the deadline. Three weeks from yesterday." She sounded a little frantic.

"Who are you investigating? Someone you know well?"

"I don't know. But that's the point. That's the issue. It's my father, Rushing Boarchards. I thought I knew him better than anyone in the world, but now I know I was wrong."

Alvah frowned.

"He did something terrible," the woman was saying. "I know it's not a crime. I mean, it's not against any code of law. But I want to know why he did it even if I have to go back over his whole life. I think something happened to him, something that changed his life, maybe. I don't know. But it's possible. Very possible. I just realized it yesterday. It never even occurred to me before, and I have to find out what it was. Before it's too late."

"I met him once," Alvah interrupted. "There was something magnetic about him. Something special. He was one of the heroes of my generation. . . ."

"Yes," she said.

"But what did he do?"

"It's complicated."

"Then start at the beginning."

"It didn't happen at the beginning," she said. "It happened three months ago, in January. I got a telephone call. It was after midnight. I was in Paris working. . . ."

Picking up the receiver, Abigail had heard a click, and then the vast vacant sound of a transatlantic call coming over the hotel switchboard.

"Is this Abigail Boarchards?" a man had asked.

"Yes."

"This is Luke Reider," he had said. "I'm one of your father's attorneys in New York with the firm of Wynne, Wynne and Pine."

Her heart had started pounding immediately, and in a sudden rush she felt herself trying to get through to her father, trying to persuade an invisible thing to let her through to him. Please. Let me see him again. Please. I love him. I have to.

But the lawyer kept talking. He told her what had happened. He was very direct and didn't evade the issue. He just said her father had done it with a .32 caliber deer rifle and been found at Weather Tree that morning on the floor of the kitchen. Outside she'd heard taxis and the long wail of an ambulance.

"He had been drinking coffee," the lawyer was saying.

"What?"

"I said he had been drinking coffee."

"But I haven't seen him," she said. "I haven't seen him in a long time. You know how he doesn't like to talk."

"Yes."

"How he doesn't like people."

"Yes."

"How he just wanted to be alone." Abigail was crying. "It was hard. But he used to like people." She pressed a pillow over her nose to try to mute the sounds, but she knew the lawyer could still hear the crying in her voice. "He used to love people," she blurted on. "Love to play and laugh."

She had always kissed him good night the last of all.

Suddenly she remembered it.

Long ago, when she was three feet high. Or four. Last, after her mother or the other relatives or Pollibeaux, last so the memory would be strongest for later, to protect it from the ambivalence she felt for everyone else. The lawyer was still talking about the funeral, but she was back at Weather Tree, saying good night, kissing him last, and waiting for the squeeze he always gave her hand every time he took it.

"Sometimes he left a quarter in my hand," she said aloud.

"What?" the lawyer asked.

"Nothing. What were you saying? I'm sorry, I wasn't listening."

But other times, it was a little feather or a deer claw in her hand, a walnut or an almond. Once it was the key to a trunk he had left outside her room upstairs, a trunk full of every awful comic book she had always longed to buy.

"You give her quarters all the time and she'll just get spoiled," her mother had snapped.

And Rush broke out in uproarious laughter. "Oh, Grace," he exclaimed, "is that what you really think?"

But after that the quarters stopped.

"I wonder how she could be so fat," her mother said once as she crossed the room to bed.

"No one in the family's ever been fat," Uncle Sam said.

"Didn't you ever hear of baby fat?" Rush had replied, and they both shut up.

"Are you all right?" the lawyer asked on the telephone.

"No," Abigail said with an embarrassed sound. She blew her nose loudly. "I'm a mess," she added.

"Want me to call you back?"

"No, that's all right. I just hate this, that's all." She started crying again. "You said he was in the kitchen?" she blustered on, picturing her father sitting there in the dark, a world where time had stopped. She imagined him looking out into the night, across the fields and the mountains, feeling the despair and the lostness, and then, in getting his gun and doing it, the triumph. She knew absolutely then that he had felt a burst of triumph.

"Maybe it was a good thing," she said.

"That's what I thought," Luke Reider answered.

"And he's better off this way."

"Maybe."

She remembered liking the lawyer, wondering about him, then the odd part started.

"If it happened this morning," she asked, "why didn't anyone call me sooner? It's almost one o'clock at night now. And why didn't Uncle Sam call me himself?"

The lawyer didn't say anything.

"I should have been told as soon as possible." Abigail's voice was rising, alarm setting in. "Why didn't anyone call me sooner?"

"But we didn't know where you were," Reider had said.

Abigail had frowned. That wasn't true. The answering service had her number. She looked at the clock. It was Sunday. Almost a whole day had passed without anyone telling her.

Saturday, January 5

————————

Maybe Rush Boarchards never went to bed that night at all, but it was much more likely that he did, because he was never awake past nine o'clock and he usually got up before dawn. Sometimes the mere sound of geese migrating overhead would wake him up. Other times it would be the howl of far-off coyotes, the first light of dawn, or a single bird quacking at a nightmare.

Then, gaunt and tall, he'd get up and go down to watch the morning come in, light across the land. But that night, Friday into Saturday, early in January, no one knew exactly what he did. They only knew a wind moved in across the meadow and the mountains. Then a stillness came and in the quiet of the great north woods, it began to snow.

By morning, the snow was thick. Still falling, it blocked out all signs of the mountains and the sky and even the clearing itself. There was just the sheet of white moving slowly down toward the ground, and the land, thick and white and beautiful. There was no one but Simon Finney, the caretaker, and Rush Boarchards anywhere for twenty or thirty miles in all directions. At the farmhouse, Simon got in the jeep, just as he did every day, and headed for the courtyard a mile away.

There the five old wooden houses, shaped like mammoth chalets, were closed for the winter. In all but one, the water pipes were empty. Kerosene had been drained from the lamps, and even the shutters were pulled tight over the windows to prevent the weather and the cold, like thieves, from invading the interior.

Only one house, the first to be built by Whitaker Stylus Rushing and still the largest, was inhabited.

Simon's jeep inched its way slowly down the road, and gradually the man made out the signs ahead of the houses. The main one vaulted up in the center like a barn and had two long wings with a veranda that yawned deep like a giant mouth. Simon parked and got out. His dog, a collie mix, followed him. Any second he knew the door would open and Rushing Boarchards would come out.

But today the door didn't open. Reaching the entrance, Simon called, "Boarchards," but there was no answer.

He turned the handle and opened the door. A long hall fifteen feet wide, covered with Navajo rugs, pictures, tables and sconces for the lights, stretched ahead. The vast center room at the other end was out of sight, the door closed now, as it always was in winter.

"Boarchards?" he called. But there was still no sound.

Then he heard a dog growling in the kitchen on the left and he quickly opened the door. The big old room with walls of windows looked the same as it had for a hundred years. It still had a wood stove and a pump, and even now, of all times, Simon was struck by how most people wanted everything modern but these people wanted everything old.

For some reason he saw the dog first. The black Labrador was sitting on the floor, looking straight at the door, but not two inches from his paws, sprawled on the floor, was Rushing Boarchards. He was lying with his face up and his arms out. His eyes were open, legs bent at the knees, and thick frozen blood and excrement had oozed all over him and frozen solid. A rifle was not far away.

The smell was overpowering.

Simon gasped. The Labrador looked at him and began to whimper. Simon knelt down and embraced him. "There, there," he said, his voice breaking. The dog started to shake and Simon held him tighter, shaking too, as he stared at the body.

His own dog sat down in the hall outside and watched.

Boarchards hadn't weighed more than a hundred and ten pounds at the end, a walking skeleton, but he looked even thinner now on the floor. He was fully dressed, and the brown color of his eyes had started to fade and turn white. The skin, almost purple, hung from his bones like a rag. His gray beard was dirty, and the hair on his head stood out in clumps, like wet pieces of grass bundled together. He looked more like a bum than a millionaire.

Simon took off his gloves and laid his finger along the barrel of the gun. It was cold, made of antique steel and wood with curlycues from the past cut along the handle. A beautiful object, it was the hunting rifle Whitaker Stylus Rushing had given his youngest grandson his first day of school fifty-five years before, but Simon Finney didn't know that. He just recognized it from the rack in the big room, where it had hung for years with all the other guns.

Simon stood up and looked around the room. The man had fallen between the window and the table. There was a coffee cup on the table still half full, some letters to mail. He leafed through them. The ex-governor, the chancellor at Harvard. Others. He knew all the names. There were two that were different: a doctor and a bank. Simon shook his head. He knew what they were too. Payments for local people who couldn't make payments for themselves.

The Labrador, named Franklin after Boarchards' favorite president, started to whimper again. Simon bent down to him once more. He had to tell the family, he thought. And Pollibeaux, the old mountain man and trapper who was as much a member of the family as any brother could be. He got to the doorway. "Come on," he called sadly. But the dog wouldn't move. So he left him there beside the body and went slowly back down the hall, his own dog slinking along behind with his tail between his legs.

Outside he started the jeep. It was just eleven in the morning, and he knew the twenty-mile-long dirt road that led out to the highway and the little town of Licking River would be impassable in the snow. The only other link to the outside world, for miles and miles in all directions, forty thousand acres in all, was the one telephone in the farmhouse, way at the other end of the clearing.

In New York the penthouse was still. The gardener had arrived and was watering the plants. He was next door in the study now, and Samuel Stylus Boarchards could hear him moving around. He always wore big rubber boots, as if to make this interior garden in the sky a real spot on the ground.

He came into the morning room. "Oh, hello, Mr. Boarchards. How are you?"

"Fine." Sam looked up from the newspaper.

"Mind if I water in here?"

"No. Go right ahead."

The man went around, plant to plant. Sam paid him no attention. "Flowers come yet?" he asked when the man was about to leave.

"Don't think so, sir. Not yet. They usually don't deliver until around noon. Want me to ask Morris?"

"Don't bother."

The gardener left and the room was quiet. The morning room, they called it, because it got the sun.

He heard Ginny go by in the hall. "Oh, good morning, sir," she said through the open door. "I didn't know you were up."

"Have to rise and shine sometime."

"Oh, that's very true, sir." She wore a white uniform. "I'll do this room later, shall I, sir?"

"Yes, why not, Ginny. How's your daughter?"

"Oh she's much better, sir. Thank you for asking."

Wearing a three-piece suit and polished shoes, Sam went back to reading. He had coffee, plain. He always did, but the

silver tray was set with sugar as well. He drank slowly, reading
and turning the pages.

A man in a black coat and trousers came and knocked on the
open door. "Mr. Boarchards?"

"Yes, Morris."

"I have the Gristede's man here and he says the lamb really
wasn't very good today and so he took it upon himself to bring
swordfish instead. He says it's quite nice. I hate to wake Mrs.
Boarchards just to ask her. Do you think, sir, you would enjoy
some swordfish tonight?"

"How would Louis cook it?"

"Shall I ask him?"

"No, never mind. Swordfish sounds fine. And, Morris, now
that you're here, have the florist send roses up to Miss Bostrine
Rushing with my congratulations on the Opera Ball."

Morris coughed. "Mrs. Boarchards already took care of that,
sir," he said as he left the room.

Sam Boarchards had made it through foreign news, national
news, skipped financial and moved on to metro, when he saw
the first button on the telephone light up. Then Morris was
knocking at the door again. "Yes, Morris, who is it?"

"It's Simon Finney, sir."

"Tell him I'm not here."

"Yes, sir."

"Why's he calling? He knows Rush does everything up
there."

"Maybe the pipes froze, sir, something like that."

"Then he should talk to my wife or Mrs. Lurie."

"Shall I tell him you're not here and to call your secretary?"

"Yes, do."

Morris turned to leave.

"Oh, never mind. I'll talk to him."

Afterward Sam hung up the phone and didn't move. Goddamn, Morris, he thought. You'd think he'd have figured out it
was an emergency and warn him. The sun had gone and he felt
a chill. And Simon didn't even say he was sorry, God-what.
Then Sam remembered something and it calmed him down a

bit. "Run, Boarchards, run," the boys had screamed. He stared out the window at the overcast sky. It had been years ago. He could even remember the heat. God, it had been hot. Rush was heading down the stretch toward home and the boys were yelling from the stands. This was boarding school, long ago, and Sam was watching, so was Andrew, and there was Rush on the field below, winning the game, the championship and the kind of glory he had already come to expect.

But then, when he had stamped triumphantly on home plate, Rush had turned around, amid screaming applause, and looked up at his two brothers in the stands. Then he raised his arms, high and powerful, a stunning gesture for one so young, enveloping them in the victory as well. And now, to Sam, that gesture and the way it had made him feel, looking down at his brother on the field, said it all. People were right. Rush Boarchards really was special, and he always had been.

He dialed Mrs. Lurie, his secretary. "I want you to come in immediately. Something's come up," he said.

Then, without saying good-bye, he hung up and called the family lawyer Harvey Wynne at home. "You'd better get down to the office right away. Get Luke Reider too."

"Why? What's happened?" Wynne asked.

"Rush's gone and done it."

"What do you mean, 'Gone and done it'?"

"He shot himself, and I want you to call Finney and get the details. Find Diver too. He's always at the jail. You have the number?"

"Yes."

"Get him on it right away. Tell him we're counting on him to keep it quiet. He's our police chief, after all."

"Right."

"The family's."

"Right."

"Then get back to me. Tell me what's going on."

"I know he had a will," Wynne said.

"I know. He told me."

"Reider did it."

"Have Reider call me too."

"But he's leaving the firm."

"Send him up there."

"But he's thinking of leaving," Wynne repeated. "I heard he's looking around."

"Makes no difference."

"Does to me," Wynne said.

"Well, not to me," Sam retorted. "Get him up there. He knows his way around. Been up there enough," he added irritably. "Free vacation to him."

"Reider's not like that. He liked Rush, that's all," Wynne said.

"Just have him call me, will you, and don't bother me about it. I don't give a damn who Luke Reider likes."

"Has anyone notified Abigail?" Wynne asked.

"No time for that now. Simon says she's in Paris anyway. He tried to reach her. Got her service."

"Have we got the number in Paris?"

"You take care of it. Simon said the answering service has her number. I don't have time for that now. You know what it was, Harvey?" he said in an abrupt change of tone.

"What?"

"He was just too good, too sensitive. You have to be a son of a bitch today, and he was too good, too old-fashioned. That's why he changed. He just couldn't hold up anymore."

Sam Boarchards was tall and thin and balding, and of all the brothers, he was the most fashionable. He lived but a block from the forty-room house where he and Rush and Andrew had all been born in a second-floor bedroom decorated in silk. The house on Fifth Avenue was a school today, but once it had a courtyard and even stables, and in those days long ago, everyone had played and purchased as if New York was their very own, and the Rushings and the Boarchards had been no different. One century had ended and another had begun, but life went on the same. They all went off to weddings and summer palaces, chose gowns and heirs, and the three little boys, Sam and Andrew and Rush, were born one right after the other, while even the Romanovs and the Hapsburgs were still at play, wars and broken empires still a dream away.

Sam walked slowly down the hall to the library, to the alcove where the bucket and glasses were always set. There, with long silver tongs, he lifted one piece of ice, perfectly shaped, from the bucket and dropped it in a glass. He covered the ice with vodka, drank it quickly, poured himself another and sat down. He stared at the glass. It was paper-thin, the surface etched with delicate lines, leaves and grapes and a bird or two.

The room was dark, with paintings and cloth, color and shine everywhere. He finished the vodka, got up and filled the glass again. He drank it, filled it once more, his fourth, and then he sat back down.

It must have been twenty years ago, he thought. Rush was in his prime. He had done some dance in the big house at Weather Tree, squatting on his haunches, kicking out his heels. But he'd changed since then.

That was his fortieth birthday, and Weather Tree had been full. One hundred and thirty people, not counting help or the fiddlers, and Grace was still alive. She still loved Rush in those days, they were quite a pair, and that night Rush was a sight to behold. First he was laughing and carrying on, telling some god-awful story about the war, and then, lo and behold, Uncle Max, of all people, started dancing, and Rush joined him. They were kicking out their heels, the music was getting faster and faster. Everyone was laughing and clapping. Then Uncle Max collapsed, he should at his age, but Rush kept right on going. He still had the energy of a twenty-year-old. Sam had been amazed. "Didn't know you had it in you, you old fart," he had yelled above the noise.

Then Annie-Fey, more a sister than a friend, God-what, ran in and joined him, but it made Grace fucking mad, and why not, after all, the girl obviously had a thing about Rush, but all the girls did. Bostrine started to yell, "Enough, my boy," but Rush and Annie-Fey went on until they almost fell down.

Sitting in the darkened library, Sam found a button on the wall near him. He pressed it and not long afterward Morris appeared. "Do we have any olives?" Sam asked.

"I'm sure we must."

"Olives or cashews. And fix me a drink. I know it's early, but I think I'll have one."

Alone again, Sam leaned his head against the edge of the sofa and almost closed his eyes. The eyes were small, the lashes not a quarter of an inch long, and they stood out straight and little, like the lines of a delicate comb. Sam had never thought much about suicide, except as an intellectual proposition, and in spite of what had happened, he didn't think much about it now. It had never occurred to him that Rush or Andrew would die. They were younger than he, God-what, and it didn't seem possible any of them, much less Rush, would die before Aunt Bostrine or Uncle Max. For God's sake, Bostrine was eighty and Max seventy-eight, both strong as an ox. But now the order had been broken. The basic assumption that age determined the expiration of things was gone, and that was almost as disturbing as Rush's death itself.

In the dim light Sam could see a small photograph on a table nearby. It was a picture of a beautiful woman in white lace, his mother Florence. She was a cold, hard woman, he thought with the dispassion of having thought it many times before, a woman who'd put her husband in the grave. She had dark hair piled on top of her head, two little boys beside her, another, a baby, in her lap. The picture, no more than four inches square, was surrounded by blue enamel twice its size, and dozens, even scores, of seed pearls set in among the shine of the blue. Sam was standing on her right, Andrew on her left, and Rush was on her lap in his christening dress.

He was the only one looking at the camera. His eyes were round then and, staring at the camera, he looked stunned, fixed permanently there in an expression he would never have again.

He was all male, Sam thought, the real thing.

"What about the will?" Aunt Bostrine was saying over the phone.

"It's all right," Sam said.

"What do you mean, 'all right'?"

"He had one."

"Oh, I know that," she said imperiously. "The question is what did he do with it all?"

"He did just what he said he'd do."

"Oh."

They were silent.

The old lady lived two hours up the Hudson in a house she inappropriately called 'the cottage.' She also kept a flat in town, a house at Weather Tree, and another at Hobe Sound in Florida, next to the one her best friends Sara-Fey and Nicer had, but since they had died, she didn't use it anymore. It was boarded up.

"Do you suppose we should have done something?" Bostrine asked finally, breaking the silence.

"About what?" Sam asked, watching his wife Victoria, in bed with a broken leg. She was crying.

"The will. Everything."

"Oh, let's not talk about that, Bos. Let's keep everything on the up and up."

"But do you think this is a crisis or something?"

"Good heavens, no," Sam exclaimed. "He died. That's all. It has nothing to do with us anyway."

"I didn't think it did, really."

"He just should never have spent so much time in the woods," Sam went on. "That's all. It wasn't our fault."

"Yes. That's it. That's what Nicer and Sara-Fey used to say about Hobe Sound. 'You can't stay in Florida all your life.'"

"Well, of course," Sam agreed.

"Have you called Abby?" Victoria whispered through her tears.

"Simon did," Sam said absently as he held the phone aside. Bostrine's voice kept coming out of the receiver, filling the room with its sounds.

"What did she say?" Victoria asked.

"He didn't talk to her."

"Why ever not?"

"Let Wynne talk to her. I don't have time." He held the phone up quickly to his ear, but Bostrine was still talking.

"Where is she?" Victoria persisted, wiping her eyes.

"God knows. Timbuktu."

"Sam," Bostrine snapped. "What are you doing?"

"Nothing, Bos," he said hurriedly.

"Then pay attention. I'm talking to you."

When she finally hung up, Sam called her brother, his Uncle Max.

The butler answered.

"Get Uncle Max, will you?" Sam snapped.

"Relax, darling," Victoria said.

"Do you want to call Charley?" Sam asked her as he waited for Max.

"You're his uncle," Victoria said.

"But I hate these emotional things. You know how close they were. The whole thing will be bad enough as it is."

When Max came on the line, Sam told him the news and the old man got very subdued. "Well, it's all for the best," he said finally. That was one of Maximillian Fell Rushing's stock phrases, and its usage here did little to raise him in his nephew's esteem. It was the same thing Max had said when he drove up to boarding school years ago to tell the boys their mother had died. "It's all for the best," he had said when he took them out to lunch. The boys were orphans then, Max and Bostrine in charge.

Across town, Max hung up and started yelling at the top of his lungs. "Foster," he cried.

Foster, the butler, appeared immediately. He could not have been far away.

Max told him the news.

"Goodness gracious," Foster said, looking for a second as if he was about to sit down.

"Ring my sister. And find me a handkerchief."

Foster picked up the phone and dialed. "May we speak to Madam, please?" he said.

"I hope I didn't get you up," Max said when Bostrine came on the phone.

"Of course not, I bathed hours ago." It was a routine exaggeration.

"Have you heard the news?" This was another formality, because it was altogether unlikely someone would have called Max with such news without first informing his sister.

"Of course I've heard the news," she snapped.

"Now, Bos, don't go getting uppity just because you're upset."

"Well, of course I'm upset."

"Don't blame you," he said, sitting down heavily. "It's damn cold up there too. What a way to go. What do you suppose, it's the drink? Abby always said he'd end like this."

"What does she know."

"She's not so bad."

"Do you think it would have made a difference if he'd gotten into something?" Bostrine sounded worried and old.

"Of course not. Look at all he did."

"No. I mean really gotten into something," she said. "Like Nicer did. Have a business. I used to tell him that. Max, I pleaded with him, at least in the beginning. You know I did."

"Now, don't go getting upset, Bos. We have to stay calm."

"But he should have listened to me," she cried. "He should have let me help him."

"You know you can't interfere. . . ."

"Even Nicer talked to him."

"I know, Bos."

"Tried to get him to be serious."

"He was plenty serious. But he was like me. Adventurous, carefree."

"You're entirely different," his sister retorted, blowing her nose.

"I don't know about that. We were a lot alike."

"Don't be a fool, Max. He had a real skill for leadership. Look how people took to him. Everyone. He could have been anything."

"I hate to ask it, Bos, and I know I shouldn't." Max stammered suddenly. "But was Rush . . . you know . . . Was he your favorite too?"

"Shush, Max. Don't say things like that."

Neither Max nor his sister had ever married. The general assumption was that Max could never have found a wife, much like looking for a pill in a haystack, but Bostrine was another matter. She, at least, must have had a choice, because she had been courted by people far and wide. But she had refused them all and built a nest of a different sort, with her friends Sara-Fey and Nicer and their daughter, Annie-Fey, and all her errant nephews, Sam and Andrew and Rush.

But she was so old now, few, if any, could remember her as the exquisite beauty she had once been. Instead they knew her as the person, or institution, she had become—a magnificent if virginal dowager with a rolling chest, a million wrinkles, a tiny waist, and a long neck that rose up to a chin that had never held anything but a parallel relationship to the ground.

It was Max who brought up Abigail's name again. "I suppose someone's talked to Abby," he said.

"I suppose."

"How's she taking it?"

"I don't know."

"You should give her a call, Bos. Time like this."

"But, Max, what would I say? Really, what would I say? I wish I didn't have to ever look at her again." She paused. "That at least would make everything easier."

Across town in her bedroom Victoria was saying to Sam, "I'm not going up to Weather Tree. I can't bear it."

"You've been to lots of funerals," Sam said.

"That's not what I mean. . . . You know . . ." Her voice dwindled off.

"Well, just don't think about it. I'm not going to. After all, you don't have to think about something if you don't want to. I'm just going to dismiss the whole thing from my mind."

By night the story was in the evening papers and the telegrams had started to arrive. Sam and Victoria were reading them in the bedroom. Mrs. Lurie had arranged them in a silver punch bowl in order of their importance, with the ones from the most famous or the most loved closest to the top. Toward the bottom were some of the most familiar, and throughout there were many from people they barely knew. But they, too, like the Rushings and the Boarchards, belonged to the interlocking set of families that branched out along the upper crust of the earth like a tribe dispersed, and this honoring of death, as well as birth and marriage, was part of the ritual whereby they all kept together, and apart from the rest.

Morris was at the door. "Mr. Paine is on the phone for you, sir," he said.

Sam picked up the phone. "Where have you been, for God's sake?"

"Darling, be nice," Victoria whispered.

"I came back as soon as I heard the news," Jackson Paine was saying. "Had to charter a plane. You can never get out of Charleston when you want to."

"Damned fine time for you to take a vacation."

"For God's sake, Sam, how was I supposed to know he'd do this."

"The funeral's at Weather Tree. Monday noon. I want you to read. Ecclesiastes."

"Is that right?" Jackson asked.

"What?"

"Me? Ecclesiastes?"

"You're the closest friend he had. Except for Pollibeaux."

"True. But you know how he hated that stuff. Religion."

"It's still the only thing. I asked Pollibeaux, of course, and he agrees," Sam said.

"He does? Oh well, if Polly agrees, all right. He'd know. What does Abigail say?"

"I haven't asked her. She's away. Nobody seems to have her number. I've got Pollibeaux in charge of the body too. Somebody from the family has to pick it up."

"What 'it'?"

"The box," Sam said uncomfortably. "You know. Cremation and all. The box."

"Oh," Jackson said, understanding. "I don't suppose it could have been anything but suicide, could it?" he asked then. "I mean, his ticker didn't give out, did it?"

"Circumstances are somewhat confusing," Sam said.

"But there was a gun, I take it. I talked to Max."

"Yes."

"And there was a wound?"

"Absolutely."

"Well, then, it's not very confusing after all," Jackson said.

"No."

"Darling, hang up," Victoria said. "You're not making much sense."

Foster had prepared tweeds, cravat, watch chain and vest for Max Rushing to wear up to his sister's, but now Max couldn't find his wallet. His predilection to "collect," as he put it, had led to seventy years of accumulation, and even his dressing room, where he was on the telephone arguing with his sister, was piled high with books and maps and objects. Even the mirror itself was largely useless because it was dotted with photographs of "the family." To Max, "family" meant the Rushings, the Boarchards, Foster the butler, Foster's nieces, and even Sara-Fey and Nicer, their daughter, Annie-Fey, and their nephew, Jackson Paine. Jackson had come to live with Sara-Fey and Nicer long ago when his mother ran away, and he never left.

"Well, are you ready?" Bostrine asked.

"Of course I'm ready. I just can't find my wallet."

"But I want you to get here so we can go to bed early and take off first thing in the morning for Weather Tree. Has your car arrived?"

"Don't know."

"Oh, Max. Must you always be so vague?"

"*I'm* not vague. Let me find Foster."

Max and Bostrine, like their three nephews, had first made the journey north to Weather Tree as infants in the arms of Irish maids. They had been wrapped in cashmere in mid-June and had their faces covered to protect them from the germs. The trip required four days then, with a minimum of eight changes of clothes and twelve meals. In the cramped quarters of the private railway cars, children saw only a bit more of their parents than they ever did at home.

First the troops of servants, trunks and relatives all set out by steamer from the port of New York. The entire staff, as well as the family bankers, lawyers and physicians were on hand to wave them off. Once underway, they journeyed up the Hudson to a point above Albany, where they transferred to the railway cars, which were already stocked with food and drink and an appropriate selection of paintings. They chugged across the flats, sometimes stopping at the house in Saratoga for lunch or a rest, and then they went on up into the mountains. They traveled by train as far as the tracks went, and there, where the line ended in the middle of the woods, they disembarked and switched to a caravan of carriages and buckboards. The last lap, along the state road and then finally over their own road, twenty miles of dirt and rock, was always, even now, the hardest but most satisfying part of the journey.

It cemented the belief that the world ahead at the other end was not only wilderness, but theirs.

"You still there?" Max said, coming back on the line.

"Of course I'm still here."

"The limo's downstairs and Foster says I'm ready. He had my wallet all along."

"Don't dawdle. Remember, Max, we want an early start. I want to get there before dark. I don't want to drive at night."

She overlooked the fact that she and Max never drove. They never had and they never would. They were driven.

Sunday, January 6

After the flight from Paris, Abigail hurriedly bought a stuffed elephant and a box of crayons at Kennedy Airport. She told the taxi driver to take her first to New York Hospital "and wait." There she went up to the fifth floor, where little Bobby Altman, the six-year-old son of her best friend, Phoebe, was recovering from a tonsillectomy.

"I thought you went away," the boy said, hugging her tight.

"I did," she said, holding him close. "But I came back."

"Will you take me home, Abby? Please. I hate it here."

Abigail took off her suede fur-lined coat and sat down beside him. "You'll go home soon," she said, rubbing her hand over his damp forehead. "Just a day more. Can you wait that long?"

The boy didn't answer.

"Then it'll be over and you'll be home again."

"But I hate it here."

"I know."

He looked at the elephant, then the crayons.

"Will they help make it better?" she asked.

He shook his head.

It was almost six by the time she reached her apartment house on Central Park West. She dashed from the cab, her arms full of cameras and photographic equipment, and took the elevator up to the eleventh floor. When she unlocked the door, Eric was already in the hallway waiting for her, his feet prancing in animal excitement. His long gray tail curled up along her leg like a vine and, putting her things on the floor, she swooped him up in her arms and nestled her face against his fur. "Yes, cat," she said, heading toward the bedroom, "you love me, don't you. You're glad to have me back."

"He'll be good for you," Rush had said years before.

"But you know how I work," she had argued, not wanting the cat at all.

"But I have to give you something," he had said. "Besides, animals are better than people. They don't talk."

Passing a table, she noticed a letter. "Rushing Boarchards, Weather Tree, Licking River, New York," it said. She wondered why she had failed to mail it before she left.

As soon as she turned on the lights in her bedroom, she picked up the phone and called the answering service. "This is Abigail Boarchards," she said, throwing off her coat and starting to take her hair down. "Do I have any messages?"

"One moment, please."

Abigail was thirty-three years old, tall and thin, with dark hair piled on top of her head. She was a free-lance photographer, a job she sometimes thought required as much determination and grit as talent. Her pictures had appeared in newspapers and magazines all over the world. They had also won her awards. But although photojournalism had brought her enough money to make a down payment on the apartment, for example, it was no longer what she wanted to do. Now she specialized in long assignments and books, and, for the first time in her life she had begun to feel some of the peace and success that had intrigued her so intensely whenever she encountered it in someone else.

"We gave your number in Paris to a Mr. Finney and Mr. Reider," the operator said, coming back on the line. "Do you want their numbers?"

"No. Did my uncle call? Sam Boarchards?"

"No. But we have a lot of messages about your father. Saying they're sorry."

"Read me the names, will you," Abigail said. She listened. One of them was her friend, Phoebe Altman. "But none from my family?" she asked at the end.

"That's all I have."

"Are you sure?"

"Yes."

"Not Sam, or Charley, or . . ."

"No, miss."

Hanging up, Abigail went into the living room and tried to think. The room was warm and attractive, with antique posters, photographs, books, plants. There were pieces of sculpture everywhere, but only fragments of heads and hands, things she'd gotten in places like Mexico and India. She picked one up, then another, terra cotta and red stone, seeking a solace of sorts in their rounded shapes and broken ends.

She had to unpack her work from Paris, make arrangements with a neighbor again to feed the cat, and leave for Weather Tree for the funeral. But she didn't feel like doing anything. If she usually enjoyed her independence, now, in the silence of an empty apartment and the aftermath of death, being independent seemed painful, even a failing, a mask for loneliness and nothing more. If she rarely wanted her family, now she realized she did.

Still standing she dialed her cousin Charley's number, but there was no answer.

Suddenly the telephone rang and she reached out eagerly, but it was only Sally, a woman she rarely saw anymore, on the other end.

"I missed you last week," Sally was saying. "Why weren't you at Miss Rushing's ball?"

"What ball?" Abigail asked, but then she remembered. "Oh, my God. I didn't even answer the invitation."

"I know. I asked her if you were coming and she said, 'What that girl does is no business of mine. I wouldn't even recognize her if I saw her on the street.'"

"That's just her manner," Abigail said lightly. "They all like to disapprove of me and my work. But she understands."

"Understands what?"

Abigail changed the subject. "Did you hear about my father?" she asked.

When she'd hung up, she went down the hall to her office. "Dear Aunt Bostrine," she was thinking. "Just a note to apologize for not answering . . ." That was too casual. "Dear Aunt Bostrine. I want to apologize with all my heart . . ." Too hypocritical.

She sat down at her desk and, picking up the phone, dialed her Uncle Sam's house.

Morris answered. "He left this morning."

"I was afraid of that."

"Everyone did. Mrs. Boarchards is here. She has a broken leg, but now she's down with a sleeping pill."

"Didn't they know I was coming back for the funeral?" she asked. "I wanted to drive up with someone—Sam, Charley. . . ."

"I couldn't say, miss. I didn't hear one way or the other."

"So they didn't leave me a message or anything?"

"No, miss."

"Are there going to be a lot of people at the funeral?"

"Looks like everybody, miss."

"It'll be sort of strange," Abigail said. She sounded uncertain.

"Oh? Why is that?"

"I don't know," she said hesitantly. "I guess I just don't see everyone much anymore. You know how busy I am." She had never really talked to Morris before.

"Well, yes, miss, you're like a stranger to us now."

"Oh, my goodness, Morris. You don't have to be so dramatic," she teased. "It's not as bad as that."

When she hung up, she crossed the room and took a picture off the wall. It was an old newspaper clipping of her father as a young man. "He understands," she said to herself. "He understood everything." The photograph showed a handsome man with a spectacular smile. He was in uniform, a dog at his heels, and someone was pinning a medal on his chest. "Hero and his dog," the headline said.

The walls around her were covered with large blow-ups of her work, photos of victims of an earthquake, a Pope's hand, a president waving good-bye. Other photographs were valuable originals, Ansel Adams and Atget, the sepia tones of early French pictures and the later crispness of others, the stark romance of Canyon de Chelly caught decades ago, another of New York under fog.

But Abigail noticed none of these. Instead she stared at the picture of her father.

"Honolulu," the article began. "General Douglas MacArthur interrupted his duties here yesterday to attend a brief ceremony for an officer he described as 'one of the best our services, and perhaps our country as a whole, has to offer.'

"In awarding the Distinguished Flying Cross for Bravery to Lieutenant Colonel Rushing Boarchards of New York for the third time, the General said, 'This young man is an exceptional human being, but his valor represents everything the awfulness of war summons from all our troops, namely the courage and bravery that men never know they have until the moment of crisis arrives.

"'I first met Colonel Boarchards in the Philippines in 1941,' the General said. 'He narrowly escaped the Japanese Army in Corregidor and missed the dreaded Bataan Death March that killed so many of our men. He has since gone on to conduct an almost unparalleled string of bombing missions in the Pacific theater.'

"In praising the colonel for his recent action in the Pacific, General MacArthur said, 'Boarchards repeatedly took his B-25 bomber back into the thickest enemy fire, not only to drop more bombs but actually to be a target for fire and allow a number of our crippled aircraft to escape to safety. God only knows how many lives he saved.'

"'I only did what I could,' Colonel Boarchards said afterward, 'and I couldn't have done that without my crew.' He said his dog, named Abby, is a mongrel he picked up on Midway Island. 'She flies with us everywhere,' he said. 'She brings us luck.' "

Abigail stared across the room. She felt the memory of her father everywhere and yearned for someone to hug her and tell her everything was going to be all right. Just as her father had always done, she thought.

She remembered the day with him in the car long ago. She was getting all C's and B's for the third straight quarter her first year of high school in New York and she had written him a letter at Weather Tree that mentioned none of the strain of living alone with her mother. But the letter was full of despair and defeat and he must have taken the last line to heart— "I guess I'm just the kind of person who isn't interested in anything or good at anything"—because he showed up at school a few days later in a rented sports car and said, "Come on."

"Where?" she had asked, getting in.

"Anywhere."

She folded her wrinkled uniform down over her plump knees and sat mum. She hadn't seen him in weeks, just listened to her mother fighting with him over the phone. He drove through the streets of New York, smoking like a fiend and never talking, except at the edge of the island, when he suddenly stopped at a gas station, pulled a sack out of the trunk and, handing it to her, said, "Go change."

Inside she found clothes her mother had made her leave at Weather Tree, her favorite old blue jeans, sneakers caked with mud and a dirty sweat shirt that should have been thrown out long ago. She put them on and returned from the bathroom more comfortable than she had been since the day her mother stormed out of Weather Tree, taking Abby with her sullen in the back seat.

They drove on, headed vaguely north. They talked now, Abby as content as could be, stopped to eat cheap hamburgers and greasy fries and when she said she thought it would be "nice to be a photographer and work like you," he had laughed and said, "That calls for a drink."

Inside the nearest bar, she had Dubonnet on the rocks, he straight scotch, and they toasted her photography and his books. "To the woman of the future," he roared, hand up, clicking glasses with the bartender. Abby blushed with almost unbearable pleasure.

They came back late. He left her at her mother's door and she said, "But why did you do all this today, Pop?"

"You figure it out."

"Because you love me."

"Yes, but there's more to it than that," he answered, in a hurry to return to Weather Tree to sleep.

"Because I was depressed," she said.

"That's vague."

"Because you wanted me to have fun."

"You're getting warmer. How do you feel now?" He was suddenly serious.

"Happy."

"Is that all?"

She shook her head shyly. "Good. I feel good."

"And so what?" he pressed. "Good about what? The weather?"

"No. Me. School. Everything, I guess. I feel different, sort of."

"That's right," Rush had exclaimed. "And I don't want you ever to forget it. That's why you get bad grades. Because you feel unhappy. And so you don't work and don't try. But not because you're a bad person or stupid or dumb or uninterested. If you feel good about yourself, Abby, you have everything. Everything changes. Like now. The whole world goes from black to white. Don't ever forget it."

She hadn't. It was one of the longest speeches he ever gave her. Upstairs in the apartment, her mother yelled at her for seeing him at all. "If he looked at your homework every night, it'd be an awful lot better than popping in every now and then like a fairy godfather."

Later, her report cards came, but he didn't notice the grades had changed to B's and A's.

In her own apartment now, Abigail called out for the cat. "Eric," she said, and the cat came in from the bedroom and jumped up beside her on the couch. She pulled him into her lap and held him like a baby in her arms. Staring across the room, still in her black gabardine pants and loose sweater, she knew she should get up and get ready, but instead she remembered more. Ten, twelve years ago, and Pop calling. Saying now that she was graduating from college she could expect the money. What money? she had asked. From the family trusts, he had said. "It'll pay rent and utility bills, with plenty left over." But she said she wanted to support herself; money was for old age and having children. But he persisted. That was what the family "did," he said.

"Don't you want me to take care of you?" he had added, making it a joke. "Who else can I take care of?" She had sensed his loneliness more than ever. "All right, all right," he said finally. "I was young once too. I won't interfere. But this dream won't last. Photography. You'll get it out of your system."

Abigail stood up and put the war picture back on the wall. She saw another: she and her father walking down a mountain road—a tall man and a very small girl. She remembered the letter on the table in the hall. "Dear Pop," it said. "Just to tell you that I love you and don't let the bedbugs bite."

It was a letter from a little girl.

She glanced once more around the room before leaving to get ready, and stopped at the one picture of Weather Tree that was different from all the others. This had no lakes or forests. It was just a man. And, unlike the others, it had been published. In fact, it was probably the most famous picture she had ever taken. It was a picture of the killer Clovis Moran.

He came from the town of Licking River, of all places, and that was the only reason she had been assigned to cover the story in the first place. It was four years ago. "Go and take a look, Abby," the man at the agency had said. "You deserve a rest." She worked seven days a week in those days and she did deserve a rest. But she didn't get it. Up north the killings continued, and what had started as a local story grew into a national one. In the beginning Clovis Moran had killed four people, but by the end it was fourteen, and reporters showed up from everywhere. It was Man against Nature, they said, Drama,

Death and Tragedy in the Wilderness. But it was Abby's picture at the end that made it Literature.

The manhunt covered the whole north woods. The National Guard was called in. The snows were horrendous, helicopters hovered over the mountains, but still Clovis Moran could not be found. The tension became acute and his name synonymous with madness and terror. Every week he came forth from his unknown hiding place in the woods and ventured out to steal food from isolated farmhouses. He'd kill or injure anyone in his way, striking out blindly, as if his victims were interrupting some God-sent plan of his. But afterward he'd disappeared into the wilderness again, leaving no tracks, no trail, nothing.

After a two-month manhunt, it was Abigail of all people who found him. She and a childhood friend. And they found him, of all places, in the middle of the night at Weather Tree. He had come to look for food.

Her picture was remarkable. It was not the portrait of a killer, but of a man in agony. He looked like a bear or a monster. His beard was caked with ice; his arms were stretched out crazily into the blizzard and he was clearly screaming. But there was something in his eyes, and for all the terror of the rest of him, the eyes and the expression on his face made him look lost and sad, utterly vulnerable and real.

Abigail would never forget it. She had done that to him. She had hurt him. Clovis Moran had been screaming at her.

The thruway was covered with snow, and by the time she reached the halfway point, she had to slow down to forty miles an hour. She had made the journey many times—by car, bus and limousine, even by truck once, when Pollibeaux drove her. He hadn't said a word or let her go to the bathroom. "Have to learn to hold it if you're going to make your life in the woods trapping," he had said preposterously.

But she remembered watching through the bus windows as, the farther north she got, the more civilization was left behind. "Don't you want me to buy you a car?" Rush had always asked. "No, Pop." "You can't do it by bus." "Yes, I can." The higher up in the mountains she went, the more a rural world took over; the nearer she got to Licking River, the poorer the land became and the more she felt at home. This was a place of old cars and little houses, scrawny chickens and people who sat on their porches looking out. Only villages grew up around the crossroads here, and there were miles and miles in between, with nothing for tourists or skiers, not even much for people at all, no factories or work and only an occasional lumber mill.

Abigail turned off the radio in her car. She felt vaguely anxious about reaching Weather Tree. Night had fallen long ago and the snow was very heavy. A thick sweater came up high around her neck. Her blue jeans were old and faded. She looked at her watch. It was after ten.

"You won't let me give you cars or jewelry or an allowance," he had written. "You want to do everything on your own, even though you know it makes me mad as hell. So I've racked my brain about how to get around you and I've come up with something besides a cat that you'll have to accept. Your birthday is fast approaching, and I've figured out a way to beat you. I've thought of one gorgeous, expensive, lovely, outrageous thing that you'd never buy yourself, even if you had the money, but you won't be able to say no. Everyone, even you, has to wear a watch, and everyone, even you, will think this watch is too stunning to reject. Besides, just this once, let me have my way.

"One more thing," he had written. "If you ever acknowledge this or say anything to me about it, you know me, I'll never speak to you again."

And she never did acknowledge it. She sent him an unsigned postcard that said, "You win. I love you." And the next time she went up to see him, driving a secondhand car she had bought herself, she slipped her hand into his in a special way, and forever after she gave him the pleasure, or something, of seeing her wear the watch night and day, every single day, the watch her one and only piece of jewelry.

Solid gold, it was thin and flat and simple in design. Made by Rolex and sold by Tiffany's, it cost over six thousand dollars.

Abigail glanced at it in the dark and smiled. It was scratched now, and the gold had dulled. "Damn you, Pop," she muttered affectionately. "It never occurred to me I'd have to do without you."

She tried the radio again, but there was only static in the storm. The windshield wipers in her expensive German car were working hard, but even so the snow caked on the glass and made visibility hard. It seemed as if the weather was trying to keep her back, pushing against the car, and even now, she realized reluctantly, after all these years, and at this, of all times, she still felt ambivalent about going to Weather Tree.

She thought of that now, the ambivalence, not the lurking sense of something else, something askew, something not right. It was only the familiar ambivalence that was bothering her, she thought vaguely.

It had started when Grace took her and moved back to New York. "She's going to a good school and dancing school," she had yelled at her husband. "I'm going to control her now. This will teach you a lesson."

Whether it had done that or not, the move had further damaged her relationship with her daughter and instilled in Abby a different attitude toward Weather Tree. What had once been home, was, from then on, simply familiar, and she thought of it as not just the most beautiful place in the world but the most remote. If other families had summer places, few had worlds like Weather Tree to call their own—thousands of acres just the way God and the ice and the Indians had left it. But much as she loved it, she began to dread it. She didn't understand why exactly, but it was always the same: some part of her didn't want to drive north along the thruway hour after hour until . . .

She could picture it now—one turn, then another, and then the two-lane highway through the town of Licking River, and then, farther north, another turn onto an unmarked dirt road just wide enough for one car across. That was the road to Weather Tree, twenty miles in, but there was no sign on the highway, no mailbox, just a tree stump covered with moss. There was nothing to hint at what lay at the other end or even to suggest anything at all was there. It looked like a logging road that dead-ended somewhere in the middle of the woods.

But five miles down the road was a gate that marked the beginning of the property line. The boundary itself went up and over the fields and mountains, past peaks and caves and damp places where only the animals went. It curved and turned, in and around and through the woods, with Weather Tree on one side and the vast acreage of the state park that surrounded it on the other. And finally the boundary ended up back at the gate, making a shape, all in all, roughly square.

But here at the gate, too, there was nothing to mark the place. There was just a gate that was always closed. The road went on for another fifteen miles, past two lakes and a river, past Licking River Mountain and a couple of ridges, past steep cliffs and the old railroad tracks, which still existed, even though the train did not. The tracks went back up into the hills to an abandoned mine and some caves, and that was where, it turned out, four years ago the killer Clovis Moran had hidden in the dead of winter.

Finally the road came up and over a hill, and then suddenly the woods ended and the clearing lay ahead. It was a spectacular sight, looking out on a vast, rolling meadow, a lake that circled into the distance, the rooves of houses, the line of Licking River. Beyond, a range of peaks and hills and forest land touched the sky, and there was nothing but wilderness for miles and miles in all directions.

The clearing itself had stables and farms, quarters for servants and cottages for guests. There was one whole building just for dancing, honky-tonk pianos in the corners, closets full of drums. Other buildings stored food and ice. One building, long abandoned, was for the dressmaker. Another was where Pollibeaux and, before him, his father Marcel, the guide, kept guns and rods, cans of grease and animal traps. Another was for a blacksmith, another for a mechanic. There had even been a photographer's studio back in the days when cameras looked more like bar stools than little boxes.

But for Abigail, going to Weather Tree always felt like a journey to the isolation of the moon.

Every day, when she was a child, Simon had driven her down the road to the little schoolhouse, past the old brick building north of the town of Licking River. But it was the old brick building, the home for delinquent boys, that first made Abigail want to leave Weather Tree. Year after year she had watched the building on the side of the road as the shrubs grew taller and the weeds grew thicker. It became a hint of other lives, other worlds, things she didn't know. "That's what I want," she had said one day.

"What?" Simon asked.

"To see the world."

"There's plenty enough of that here."

"There's more than this."

But there was plenty here too, Simon was right; because night after night, after the servants had left, making their way back up the road to rooms at the farm, the fights began. Grace screamed and Rush sulked. Grace said he let her down and Rush said nothing. They all tried to get Rush to leave, Sam and Victoria, Bostrine and Max. "Licking River's no place to live," they said.

One summer night they were all in the dining room in the big house, Bostrine and Max, Sam and Victoria, Andrew and his wife who ran off with an English lord, Andrew's son Charley, and Abby, Rush and Grace. All these little families in one big family, seated around a table made of whole trees. Pictures as big as cars hung along the walls and big stuffed deer stood on four legs at both ends. Flocks of servants brought food on silver trays. Suddenly Grace said, "This is no place to raise a girl."

Sam agreed. "No one lives here, Rush."

"Sure they do. Don't they, Abby?" Rush answered with a wink.

But Grace cried, "Look at her." And everyone looked at little Abby with her fat face.

Abby's heart sunk. "She's just like you," Grace said. "She has no friends, no style. She's already a mess, and if she stays here, what will become of her? Don't you want your daughter to be a lady?"

"She's not as bad as all that," Rush had said, but Abby could tell he'd lost his nerve, the spark was gone. Leave me alone, she wanted to yell. All of you. Just leave me alone. I hate you all.

"Are you proud of her?" Grace persisted angrily.

I hate you.

"She's just a tomboy," he said.

"I told you I'd try it up here," Grace went on as Victoria tried to shush her up, "but I've had it. If you want to ruin your life, I won't let you ruin Abby's. Look at her." And again everyone looked. "She can't curtsey. She can't talk. She's fat. She's awkward. She's even mean."

"She's only a child," Rush said meekly, trying again.

Simon met her at the garage in Licking River with his jeep. It was after midnight, and he had to drive the whole way back to Weather Tree in four-wheel drive. Once a deer started to cross the road, but, seeing them, it leaped back into the woods. In another place, a brown owl swooped down out of the trees like a falling kite and then sailed off, high, afraid of the lights.

"There was something wrong with him, wasn't there?" she asked.

"Nothing you don't know about, honey. Just depression. Some people are like that."

"But why?"

"Who knows? Why does a tree stop going up and start to die?"

He told her about finding the body, and she asked, "Did he shoot himself in the head?"

"No, he did it right," he said. "He lifted up his left arm and shot himself in the armpit directly into the heart. Only one round was in the magazine and only one was needed."

He told her how people from Licking River had come in to open up the houses, which had been shut down like a resort in winter. And how, before that, the snow plows had come, and Diver too, the police chief, with the coroner and some deputies. They had gone from room to room, Simon said, from the basement to the attic, and had finally settled over on the north side of the house, in the room where Boarchards had really lived.

"What were they looking for?" she asked.

"A note or a will."

They found a will. It was four paragraphs long, handwritten and dated five and a half years ago. Diver had held it up in his hands. "Abby," he had told Simon. "He left her everything."

"I could of told him that myself," Simon said in the jeep. "Of course that was what he was going to do with it." He glanced at her and grinned suddenly. "Heir apparent. That's what you are."

"You won't leave Weather Tree, will you? Simon? Just because he's gone?"

"Where would I go?"

When they finally reached the clearing, it was almost two o'clock in the morning. The houses were black, with only soft, flickering lights turned low in a bathroom or a hall. The place looked very old and still, shapes from another time, and the scene, so quiet, filled Abigail with the sense of returning home.

Simon told her she was sleeping at Andrew's, but she said she wanted to "go ahead and look," so he drove on, left her alone, and she opened the door of her father's empty house.

The corridor was marked with the light of the fire—the door at the other end was open. She walked down the hall and went inside.

The room was enormous, a giant hall with beams and logs and a dome overhead. She was standing on a landing, and to her right and left were massive staircases, each broad enough for ten men to walk abreast, and they rose up on both sides to balconies and the second floor. Below and ahead of her, the room spread out so large even the grand piano seemed dwarfed in size.

She stepped down from the landing and crossed to stand in front of the fireplace. Orange light shot out into the room, showing couches, chairs and Navajo rugs, books, tables and a giant portrait on one wall of her great-grandfather, Whitaker Stylus Rushing. There were paintings as big as couches, rugs the size of small rooms, boxes inlaid with pearls, animals carved of alabaster and a Fabergé clock that no longer ticked.

In the wide V-shaped area above the landing, a painted mural spread forty feet long and thirty feet high, a pastoral mountain scene rich in golds and blues, pinks and greens and browns. If the room was a testament to wealth, the mural was not. It spoke of nature. Across the broad expanse was a lake, forests, and two men in a canoe. The painting was lush. Even at night, it gleamed with light as if a god were present. The mountains were high, the crags severe, and it was evocative of a time when people still believed in the desolate grandeur of the land and saw it as a link to God's perfection.

The fireplace was directly opposite the mural. High over the mantel was a moose. The animal was dark brown, with antlers that spread from left to right farther than any man could reach, and he had shoulders as big around as a tabletop. He was a huge prize of a beast and he had lorded over the room since 1880. Whitaker Rushing had shot him not long after he bought the vast piece of land and afterward, or so the story went, he'd told the architects in New York: "Make the room as big as you can. Make room for the moose. He had the land before me."

Now, standing there alone, Abigail looked up at the second-floor balcony that led down the corridor to her father's room. And then, not even knowing what she was doing, she threw out her arms, wide, as far as they would go, wide to embrace the ghost of a father past and to exalt in the notion of the future: that what had been his was now hers, and that she was no longer a relative or the heir but the owner, an adult in the place where she had once been a child.

Monday, January 7

In the morning Sam and Great-Aunt Bostrine were in seclusion. Andrew was too bleary with drink to notice her. Great-Uncle Max was holding court and her cousin Charley was up in his bedroom, too upset, he said, to do anything but get stoned. So she went outside alone, still troubled by the lingering anxiety she attributed to loss.

The snow was coming slowly down out of the pale-gray sky, as if it had years to do its work. The courtyard was full of jeeps and trucks, people coming from all over, but the large old houses, brown and shingled, stood out against the white like monuments or archaeological mounds that had survived. They were giant, hulking forms and they seemed impervious, as if they belonged to a different species and existed independently of the people's comings and goings. And it was true, they did. People are the intruders here, Abigail thought, the buildings a part of the land and the deep earth mulch. They had a silence whereas the people had none, although at least one among them had tried his whole life in vain to recreate a piece of that silence in his soul.

Now he was in a small tin can. It was five inches square and what was inside rattled.

In the big house the fire was going and the place was almost warm. She looked in the kitchen and remembered even now the time long ago when she had heard voices in the kitchen and seen a boy. But the next morning Pop had said there was no boy. It was one of those odd childhood memories that made no sense. "What boy? There was no boy." But there was a boy, she had seen him. He had escaped from the reform school. And so why did her father lie?

Now the floor was clean, no sign of blood, but the coffee cup was still on the table, still half full. The liquid inside looked opaque and solid, as if, untouched through the hours, it had hardened like the arteries themselves. She turned her eyes away and walked on.

In the big room with the moose and the mural, she mounted the stairs to the landing above, and there the smell began. She went down the long hall, past her own room, to her father's. The smell got stronger and stronger. His smell. As if he were still alive. Two days had made no difference at all. The smell was of sweat and smoke and alcohol.

She reached the doorway to his room. The room was enormous, with pictures and guns, books and magazines everywhere. Abigail sat on a couch and pulled her fur-lined coat tight around her chest. Up here it was cold. There was frost on the window and the dull white light of the snow filled the room. She hadn't been to Weather Tree in over a year, but she was struck by how much death was already here. There was a stuffed eagle by his bed, and beside his desk a stuffed bear, all four legs intact. There must have been at least a hundred skulls in the room. They were everywhere, white calcium surfaces with holes for eyes, no skin, hair, color or grease, just the clean white bone. Skulls of deer, mice, squirrels, bear and even little itsy-bitsy things that belonged to birds. Abigail looked around. Teeth and sockets stared at her, a gallery of death, but they were beautiful and she could understand his passion. Beautiful for the cleanliness of their line, she thought, as if death and decay had been a kind of improvement.

She got up. First she looked in the bureau, then the desk. Finally she found one whole cupboard up against the chimney filled three feet high with whiskey bottles. They were empty, just where he had thrown them, knowing one day a servant would find them and take them away without a word.

Abigail turned to the desk. It was covered with magazines and books, *Pepys' Diary*, *Boswell's Life of Samuel Johnson* and *The Military History of World War II*. His typewriter was an old black machine with long skinny keys and lots of wires. It was surrounded by his ever-growing collection of animal teeth, and cigarette ash, thick as dust, lay on everything. The ashtray, a large old ceramic salad bowl, was full to the brim with cigarette butts, short white things with stubby ground-out tips and broken backs. The hundreds, even thousands, of butts lay there like bloated, dead worms, disgusting.

She turned away and saw a letter on the floor. She looked at it, with no idea, of course, what it would mean three months later. In April, when she would call the detective Alvah Germaine.

She picked it up. It was bulky and sealed. There was nothing written on the envelope but one long name. That was all. No address, nothing.

"Joe Algodones," it said.

Abigail was curious. "Al-ga-DOE-ness," she said aloud. She had no idea who he was.

The file cabinets stretched across one whole end of the room. There must have been twenty or more, but there were others in the basement too, files as much a part of Rushing Boarchards as his skulls. He had made carbons of every letter he wrote and filed articles like a librarian. Long ago he wrote four books and called himself an author, but he bought carbon paper the way other people bought Kleenex, and through the years as he became more prolific at letters, the carbons and the files multiplied furiously, as if they in the end were to be his oeuvre, not the books. He had never given a thought to making them public. He kept them, Abigail had long ago figured out, at first because he viewed his every word and interest as important. But later, as he gradually ceased to talk, the habit became an obsession, as if while charting the path of his own self-destruction, he was accumulating proof that he had lived at all.

Abigail had never looked in the files, but now she pulled out one of the drawers, the B's, at random. But it was not hers. So she pulled another. This drawer had two headings: "F.R.B.," her grandmother, and "A.R.B.," herself.

It did not occur to Abigail to touch them, not at first, at least, the taboo against prying too strong, the respect for privacy too deep. But she saw old letters in her grandmother's files and pulled them out to read. This was history, she thought. "Rushing Mansion, New York City," said the heading on the stationery. "Dear Rush," began the first, a note to a boy at boarding school. "I've found a professor from Yale to do European History this summer at Weather Tree and an official from the French embassy for language. They'll serve as companions, instruct you in manners, thinking, whatnot."

The next was short too. "I'm off to London to buy some paintings and then to Paris for clothes. Hope the weather at sea is pleasant. Shall I dismiss the captain if it's not? Does my little boy think that's a good idea?"

But the next, from another year, was very different. "Browne tells me you never changed your unmentionables over the holiday," Florence wrote this time. "As part of her chores as governess she must see to your room and she says this is a sign I must still be strict with you in your father's absence. . . ." Abigail looked at the date. Edward Boarchards had been dead two years by then. ". . . I know we all have our lapses, but such behavior with regard to our unmentionables is not fitting to someone of your position."

The next letter continued on the same subject. "Browne tells me there continues to be this odd and disturbing contradiction between your outward appearance and what you wear underneath. She says you have made no improvement since your last visit home. I find this appalling and I am frankly at a loss for words.

"A gentleman is a gentleman through and through," Florence wrote on, "and I see it as part of my maternal, and now also paternal responsibilities to explain this to you so you never forget again. Being a gentleman is something that goes to a man's very soul. Otherwise he betrays his whole tradition and everything that is expected of him. Being a gentleman requires: (1) appreciation for cleanliness and appearance; (2) manliness; (3) protection of others; (4) restraint in everything; and, most of all, (5) sufficient respect for other people never to trouble them with your own affairs."

Abigail read that again: "sufficient respect for other people never to trouble them with your own affairs."

"But this matter of cleanliness," Florence continued, "is by no means as trivial as it may appear. A man's style tells the world what he thinks about himself, not that he is better than others, of course, but that he is quite well, thank you, and perfectly suited to take on any matter of responsibility or concern. It is not that you are better, I repeat, but that you are gifted at the very things other people usually are not, having to do with responsibility and leadership, and it is your manner, and a nobleness of purpose, that announces this.

"There must be no difference, my boy," Florence continued, "between what a gentleman does in private and what he does in public. We must never let ourselves forget and think we can fool people by slight, but secret, aberrations. Or think that what is not known does not count. It does."

Abigail read that line again. Something about it made her shiver. Maybe it was just the cold, she thought, or empathy for the boy who'd received it, the man who'd kept it. She read the line again. "We must never let ourselves forget and think we can fool people by slight, but secret, aberrations. Or think that what is not known does not count. It does."

She put the letter back and looked in her own file. She found report cards and childhood scribblings, a copy of the picture of Clovis Moran, but most of the space merely documented a teenage relationship, the hundreds, perhaps thousands, of letters from her to him and carbons of his to her. They all seemed to be in chronological order.

She traced her finger over the top of the drawer and abruptly came to a big gap at the back. She wedged it open and, looking down, saw a large bundle of letters bound together by a rubber band.

She lifted the bundle out and stared at it. It was heavy, all letters still in their envelopes, and she saw at once that the envelopes, from her to her father, were unopened. They were not opened. They had never been opened.

Without removing the band, Abigail looked at the postmarks. Some of the letters were six years old, others more recent, last year, last fall, last month, even last week from Paris.

She stuck the bundle back in the drawer, but then she took it out again, looked at it, frowning, and only as she put it back again and closed the drawer did the actual fact of the discovery take root in her mind.

The drawer clicked shut. She bit her lip. Her mind raced over the things she had written or might have said, all there, still glued shut by her own tongue. She had never even suspected, she thought. It had never occurred to her he hadn't read them. He talked so little, remained so quiet, how could she tell what he knew of her letters or didn't? Her anxiety turned to alarm and she saw her hands shake a little. She began to feel weak, hungry, and her stomach growled. Why hadn't he thrown them out? she thought. Just thrown them away? Then she'd never have known. Never even have known.

Suddenly she yanked the drawer open again and, starting near the front, leafed rapidly through the file. She didn't know what she was looking for. She glanced at the letters, reading lines, paragraphs. "I hate to admit it," he had written to Bostrine long ago, "but sometimes Abby is the only thing that makes life worth living for me. I don't know why, but that's the way it is. She can't go to sleep at night unless she's holding on to a stuffed animal named Fred. But at other times she is so grown up and mature it frightens me. She is an odd combination of very strong and very vulnerable."

I still am, Abigail thought, moving on hurriedly. But why didn't you read my letters? Why didn't you open . . .

She found nothing more of interest until the very end. The

last papers, out of order chronologically, were two four-year-old letters. They were stapled together. She lifted them out. They were both addressed to the lawyer Luke Reider, the man who had called her in Paris, but they were neither legal nor formal. Instead they seemed casual and friendly. Until the last paragraph.

"Somehow I've produced a monster," he wrote in the first letter, dated four years ago. "That's what Abby is. I can't ignore it anymore. I don't know how it happened, but I'd like to think my wife was responsible."

Abigail felt the room begin to spin.

The other letter was written a few days later. "Abby is vicious, cold, Machiavellian and tough," he said. "No wonder no man will have her. She doesn't have an ounce of decency, and if there is any despair that I feel, it is that my only child should turn out to be as complete a bitch as my mother and her mother. She has fooled a lot of people, but if there is one thing I do with my life, I don't want it to be said that I was fooled by her too."

She made it down the back stairs, but she barely reached the bathroom before she began to retch. She fell over the toilet bowl in the room off the hall and gagged. Behind her there were chairs, couches, even a carousel horse, but she paid no attention. She caught hold of her throat and gagged until nothing more came up. Then she straightened up, leaning against the sink for support. She looked in the mirror. Her face was pale against her black sweater, ghostly and thin. She saw the photograph of Great-grandfather Whitaker dressed in white linens holding the portable toilet they used to take on picnics.

Beside him was little Rush.

"Why am I 'vicious, cold . . .'?"

She splashed water on her face. It was stinging cold. I have to ask Bostrine, she thought. Sam. They'll explain. They'll tell me. But it was nothing. I know it was nothing. She headed down the hall toward the front door. When she saw it open, she thought, irrationally, it's Pop. I'll ask him.

Instead it was someone she'd never seen before. He walked

through the door. Dark hair, blue jeans, he wasn't much older than she, and the second he saw her, he stopped and stared at her as if he'd seen a ghost.

Suddenly she burst into tears.

"You're Abigail," he stammered, as if something about her was a great surprise.

She nodded, almost sobbing now; first death, now this.

"But what happened?" he said. "What's the matter?"

"My father. I can't . . . It's . . ."

"Are you sick?"

"Yes," she said, wiping her eyes. "I threw up." She looked down at her black sweater and little breasts, as if to check for vomit.

"Here," he said quickly. "Let me get you some water, or milk."

He passed by her, smelling of snow and air, and went into the kitchen. She followed, the long oak table, the coffee cup. She stared at the cup.

He glanced at the cup too, picked it up, and threw it in the garbage.

She heard it break. "I'm sorry," she said. "I'm not myself. I just . . . He . . ."

He handed her some milk. "Drink this," he said, watching her closely. He was tall and wore a navy-blue sweater, big boots and a parka. His face was dark and Jewish and handsome.

"But who are you?" she asked, the glass in her hand.

He didn't answer.

She started to frown. "Why do you know your way around so well?"

"I'm Luke Reider," he said.

"Oh my God." She started to back away. "Those letters . . ."

"We should talk," he said urgently.

"What did you do to him? What kind of a lawyer are you? He told you I was 'vicious, cold . . .' But I'm not. He didn't mean it. I know he didn't. He loved me. It was an accident. He wouldn't say that. Why would he say that?"

"I don't know."

"What?"

"I don't know."

"But what do you care?" She started waving her hands in the air irrationally. "It's just work to you. What do you care about anything? Client writes you a crazy letter, you probably love it."

The lawyer was staring at her, confused.

"Makes it easier for you to control them. That's it," she said. "That's all you want. Power. But this is my house and my father loved me. I know he did. Everybody knows it. We were very close."

"We should talk."

"I don't want to talk to you."

Then Abigail started to shake, and as the shaking got worse, she began to cry again.

"Let me help," he pleaded. "Please."

"No. Not you. I want my father. I want him to tell me . . ."

She pushed her way through the crowds at Sam's but she couldn't find him. She made it to the stairs and had started up when the ex-governor caught her with a kiss. "Remember the first time I saw you," he was saying, "we went out to visit that reform school with Rush and you took a fancy to some boy?"

"Yes," she said. "He had blue eyes."

She ran upstairs and knocked on her uncle's door.

"Who is it?" Sam called.

"May I come in?"

"I'll see you later, Abby."

"But I want to see you now. I want to say hello, and I have to talk to you." She opened the door and stared across the room at her uncle. He was looking at her over the top of a legal document with a blue cover. "I'm busy," he said. He seemed nervous.

"But something happened." Her hand was still on the door. "He said . . ."

"Really, Abigail."

"He said I was 'vicious.' . . ."

"Don't you ever care anything about other people?" he snapped.

Her eyes widened and she looked at the floor. "But . . ." she began.

"I don't have time now."

Her heart pounding, she closed the door and left.

She stood in the hall for a second, then turned around, raced through the house and crossed the courtyard to her Aunt Bostrine's. Inside she ran up the stairs two at a time and down the hall to her aunt's suite of rooms. The door ahead was closed. She tried to calm down and breathe more evenly, but she couldn't. "Auntie," she cried, knocking.

She heard voices and then her father's second cousin's wife called out, "Bostrine can't see you right now, Abby."

"But I want to see her."

"She'll see you later."

"But I've been here a long time. I already tried to see her this morning. I have to talk to her." Her voice was getting higher and higher. She opened the door.

Bostrine was sitting across the room wearing a wool suit and a fortune in jewels on her hands. There was a child at her side, one of sundry relatives filling the houses. "Tell me about school, dearie," Bostrine was saying to the girl.

Abigail held on to the door and stared. "I wanted to say hello," she finally mumbled.

Her aunt looked up at her as if she had just noticed her and then back at the child. "You were telling me about school, dear."

"I like it," the little girl said.

"And why is that?" Bostrine asked, her head turned away from Abigail.

Abigail stared. She felt a pain in her chest as if her breath was digging its way through concrete inch by inch to make its way. "But, Auntie . . ." she began.

"I like my friends, and we do things with frogs," the girl was saying.

"And what do you think of boys?"

"Not much, Auntie."

"But, Auntie . . ." Abigail said again.

"And what do you think of your teacher?"

"Please . . ."

"She's a nice lady," the girl said. "She reads us stories. . . ."

"I'm sorry I forgot about the invitation . . . to your ball. . . ." Abigail stuttered.

Bostrine looked up at her; so did the child and the other woman.

"I meant to answer, but I forgot. I was getting ready to go away. To Paris . . ."

They were staring at her.

". . . I was in Paris. I forgot, Auntie. I won't do it again. I promise. . . ."

"Dearie, what were you telling me about frogs?" the old lady said.

Abigail started to back up. "I'll be good . . . I promise." She closed the door and left.

Outside she made her way across the yard to Andrew's house and up the stairs to Charley's room. She went in without knocking and was greeted by the heavy smell of marijuana.

"Charley," she exclaimed, slamming the door. "Sit up."

A fire was burning in the fireplace and her cousin was lying on a bed, a silver fox throw across his legs, a joint in his mouth. "What's the matter?" he asked. "You look terrible."

She rushed across the room and sat on the other bed. "I have to talk to you, Charley. Something's happened."

"What?" He didn't move. Charley was thirty-six and single, and he used to be handsome, but now his skin was gray.

"Come on," she pleaded. "I need you."

He sat up a little.

"What's going on around here?" She leaned in toward him.

"Everyone's upset," Charley said. "What do you think? You expect this to be a party?"

"But Sam and Bostrine don't want to see me. Why? They were horrible. And I just went to Pop's room and found all these letters. He said I was 'vicious, cold.'"

"Relax, Abby. You're just upset."

"But the letters . . ."

"What letters?"

"They said I was awful and mean. And there was a whole bundle of my letters. He never opened them, Charley. He never opened my letters."

"Your letters?"

She nodded. "Something's going on."

"Nothing's going on. They're just mad at you."

"Why?"

"I don't know. Not mad. Bored. You rub them the wrong way. But you always have. You know that."

"But this is different. Worse."

He held the joint in her direction.

She waved it away. "No. Tell me. I want to know."

"But I don't know anything about it."

"But why won't they talk to me?"

"I don't know," he said. "I don't understand them any better than you do. I just know Sam didn't want you at the funeral." He looked at her. "I asked him Saturday if he'd reached you in Paris and he said he hadn't even tried and I said, 'What?' And he said, 'Well, who wants her there?' "

Abigail's head reeled back.

"And I said, 'What do you mean? What an absurd thing to say.' And he said, 'Well, Rush couldn't have cared less.' And I said that was crazy, and he backed off. I don't know what he meant about Rush. Don't think about it, Abby. Forget what you saw in the letters. Forget it."

"How can I forget it? It sounded like he hated me." She shivered.

Charley sat down beside her on the other bed. He was even thinner than she and he put his arm around her and tried to push her head down on his shoulder, but she pushed it back up.

"They should be proud of you," he argued. "They're just sick and drunk. All of them. Abby, listen to me." He looked at her, but she didn't look back. She was staring at the fire. "It's just because you don't toe the line," he said. "You're different. But so what? You're better than all of them."

She shook her head.

"It's true," he said. "Look what they've done to their lives. You're better off than all of them put together."

She shook her head.

"But what do you care what they think anyway?" he asked.

"Of course I care," she exclaimed. "Besides, I don't have anybody now. Nobody. Only them. You."

"Then just go off on assignment and forget it all."

"I'm not like that," she cried, standing up. "You make me sound awful too."

"You're not awful. Don't be silly. But you've never worried about them before. Your work's the most important thing to you. They've never bothered you one little bit. So don't start now. Don't, Abby, don't."

She went into the bathroom and locked the door, then sat on the edge of the old marble-clawed tub and stared out the window.

Rush said that he and she were exactly alike. She said she didn't know how to be and she got afraid all the time and insecure, and it was only going to get worse when she grew up. He said he was the same, and it was a good way to be. "But it's so hard, Pop," she had argued. And he had said, "Life's hard for people like you and me. We're too sensitive."

The water was running in the sink to prevent the pipes from freezing. She shivered. He had loved her. She knew it.

Look at the way he had talked to her. He never talked to anyone else that way. It was a fact, an absolute fact. Look at how he had talked about drinking. He said he liked it and he didn't want to be cured and he didn't care if he died. He wanted to live the way he wanted to live. And look at how he had talked about killing in the war. How he hated it. He didn't tell other people that. He only told them the good stories. With her he was honest. That was proof, real proof. He did love her. Look at how he told her about the man he killed in the war. "It's the worst thing that could ever happen to a man, to kill someone," he had said. "It was the worst thing I ever had to do. Don't ever do it," he had repeated. "It'll end up killing you. Killing a man is not like killing an animal. It's like killing some part of yourself."

"Do you ever talk to anyone but me about this?" she had asked, and he shook his head. "You should," she had said. "There's nothing wrong with what you feel."

"You don't change anything by talking about it."

Yes you did, she thought now. You changed the isolation. But already she could feel herself drifting off into it now, just like him, drifting off. . . .

She listened to the water dribble and far away a bell started to ring. It was time.

The Episcopal bishop of New York came down the stairs in purple and black. Even in his robes and splendor, the room seemed more splendid than he. He crossed to the fire, cleared his throat and lifted his arms. Then Pollibeaux came in, and they all turned to watch the tall old French-Canadian mountain man who lived in the woods and carried traps and equipment the way other people carried keys, dozens of things hanging from his waist, clinking as he moved. But now he walked down the stairs from the hall, silent in his big boots and red shirt, as much a part of the family as the Rushings and the Boarchards. He held the little box in his hands, down low near his belly, small and square, and as he walked, it rattled.

It rattled like a box of bones.

He set the box down in front of the fire on the table, and the bishop asked them all to bow their heads in prayer. Abigail stared at the box. The chairs and couches were now arranged in curves away from the fire. "Our Father who art in Heaven . . ." Why didn't you open my letters? she thought in panic. Her heart was pounding.

The rattle from the box echoed in her head, these not ashes, but the little bones of Rushing Boarchards, taunting her from the safety of death. Her mind blanked out. The next thing she knew, the bishop was saying, "He was a better man than most. A good man, an unusual man. . . ." She drifted off again.

Sam got up and went to the front of the room. He was still wearing his coat, protection against the cold. He talked and coughed from time to time and Abigail tried not to listen, but he sounded sick and she kept wondering if something was the matter with him. She glanced about the room—dogs, children, babies, people from Licking River and beyond. Her heart was thumping. I'm afraid, she thought. She saw Luke Reider in the back. Maybe he could tell her what happened. Sitting next to him, old Frank who owned the store in Licking River was crying.

"He took the sorrows of the world too much to heart," Sam was saying, and she saw the ex-governor blow his nose, and Jackson Paine, the family friend, wipe his eyes.

". . . and in the end, he was overburdened," Sam went on. "But his greatness lay not just in his bravery in moments of crisis in the war but in his kindness."

"Amen," said Pollibeaux.

"Amen," said Cloe, Pollibeaux's wife.

Then why didn't he read my letters?

"Even to the extent of his own self-destruction. He finally took no more care of himself than the poorest of the poor and . . ."

She didn't hear anything more until Diver, local police chief, got up. He was a short man, and the only one in the room wearing a suit. The sight of him softened her and she paid attention. She liked him. As he headed toward the front of the room he started to blush.

"Pollibeaux should be up here," he began. "Or Frank. But Frank, he shouldn't even be here at all. He should be in bed. He's sick. Nothing would get him out of bed but Rush." He stopped. "Rush," he said, cherishing the name. "Not 'Mr. Boarchards.' He was never 'Mr. Boarchards' because he belonged here with us as much as any of us do. He sent my nephew to veterinary school. He put my daughter through secretarial school. Sometimes he paid half the doctor's bills in town. But nobody knew. We just thought the doctor had forgotten. But he didn't go on and on paying the bills. Because that wouldn't have been right and he knew it. He just helped out when we needed it most. And never wanted anyone to know. He hated it if you thanked him.

"There was something uncanny about him," Diver went on. "He knew how to get to you. He knew what you wanted, what you needed, what you didn't. It was his idea my nephew be a vet, because he said he'd watched in here through the years how the boy worked with animals. And once there was a national conference of police chiefs, and he said to me, 'How'd you like to go?' It was in Las Vegas and I stayed at Caesar's Palace, had the time of my life. But he was a strange man too," Diver continued, looking out at the faces, his blush gone. "He sat in Frank's store with the rest of us, feet up on the stove, but hours went by and weeks might pass like that and he wouldn't say a word. I don't think he was ever too happy a man, but anybody who ever once had anything to do with him, they didn't forget it. He did something to you. But I don't know how to explain exactly what it was.

"I been thinking about that all day yesterday and again all day today," he went on, "and I still don't know if I can put it into words." He stopped and looked out a window as if the words were there. "The closest I can come is to say if there are differences between people, Rush Boarchards never knew it and he never felt it. He understood things better than anyone I ever knew, rich man, poor man, man of God, or not. And I think that what he understood he tried to help and what he didn't understand, he tried to fix. I think he wanted to make his mark on the world and I guess he didn't do that. Not the way he wanted to, at least. Instead . . ." The man paused and looked around the room slowly. "Instead," he said, "what he did was . . . he made his mark on us."

Diver walked back to his seat. He swayed from left to right. The room was silent. People were crying. Abigail was crying. Finally the bishop stood up. He cleared his throat, as if it were hard for him too, and he said, "Let us pray."

"I, Rushing Whitaker Fell Boarchards, of the state of New York, hereby make, publish and declare this my last Will and Testament."

Luke Reider's voice carried out into the room. Behind him the fire was burning. Darkness had come. The couches and chairs had been moved back to their normal positions. Max and Bostrine were there, Andrew, Charley and Sam, Pollibeaux, Simon Finney, Jackson Paine, Harvey Wynne and Abigail.

Luke stood in front of the fireplace holding the pale-blue folder she had seen earlier in her Uncle Sam's hands. On the cover was the Wynne, Wynne and Pine logo, its address and the four words of the dead man's name. Underneath was the date of execution of the will—four years ago. Reider had read the date and, listening, Abigail had noticed right away this was not the will done by hand the police had found upstairs on Saturday.

"First," the lawyer read, "I direct that upon my death my remains be cremated and my ashes be placed in the shallow waters of the lake there on the south side of the Back Bay, where the animals come to drink. My friend, Jean-Martin Pollibeaux, will know how to take care of this according to my wishes, and whatever he chooses to do is what I will wish.

"Next, I direct that my favorite gun, the antique steel-and-wood deer gun my grandfather Whitaker Stylus Rushing gave to me for my fifth birthday, never leave this place. That it remain here as a living symbol of me and the past and bespeak that the past lives, even if I do not."

Abigail sat in the back, her black turtleneck sweater stark against her pale face. Her hair was high around her head. She looked at the moose, the portrait of her great-grandfather and, from time to time, she looked at Luke.

The first section of the will dealt with bequests, the rest of his property, it said, to go en masse, with the bequest of the house itself. Certain paintings went to Sam and Andrew, Max, Charley and others, paintings by Eakins and Homer, Sargent, Whistler and Mount, drawings too, things from this room or that or even in storage someplace else. The Fabergé clock that sat on the grand piano went to Victoria, the Turner in the library to Max. The next section was for jewelry alone, all of it listed, one by one, brooches, bracelets, necklaces and rings, and they all, diamonds, emeralds, pearls and everything, went to the oldest person in the room, Bostrine Fell Rushing.

Bostrine's head was down. Her brother had his hand in hers and he mumbled to her from time to time.

The next dealt with more belongings, stocks and portfolios; the next with taxes, they to be paid from cash and the assets, it said, not Weather Tree or the land.

Then there were outright bequests of money, to Simon, Pollibeaux, others.

Luke was going slower and slower, and hearing the cadence of his voice, Abigail thought he wanted to stop altogether. Suddenly she felt frightened. He was nearing the end of the section and he looked up and his eyes met hers. She didn't look away, she just frowned.

Then he ended the section, took a deep breath and turned the page.

"Article Seven," he read. "All the rest, residue, and remainder of my property and estate, both real and personal, including money, land, the trusts and property, of every nature and wherever situated, of which I may die, seized or possessed, including, without limitation, all property acquired by me or to which I may become entitled after the execution of this Will, all the property over and concerning which I may have any power of appointment or disposition, I bequeath to one person.

"It is all to go to my brother Samuel Stylus Boarchards, to be held exclusively in trust for my nephew and his nephew, Charles Andrew Fell Boarchards of New York, until the time of my brother's death, at which time it shall go in its entirety, without exception or change, along with all rights and all claims, to my nephew. If my brother should predecease me, it shall all go directly, forthwith, without change or exception, to my nephew, Charles Andrew Fell Boarchards."

Luke turned the page.

"This shall include," he continued, "my share of ownership in the Weather Tree Land Corporation and all real property situated in or forming part of the Weather Tree Land Corporation in Licking River, New York, owned jointly and equally by me, my two brothers, my aunt and uncle.

"I therefore give, devise and bequeath all my right, title and interest here to my brother, to be held in exclusive trust for my nephew."

Reider paused. "To my daughter, Abigail Rushing Boarchards," he went on, "I shall give and bequeath no more and no less than four quarters of the United States Mint. It is a sum equal to one dollar, no more, no less.

"I hereby formally choose to disinherit this child and daughter, my only survivor, my one-time heir apparent. Abigail Rushing Boarchards is to have none of the land that is known as the Weather Tree Land Corporation, none of the residue or remainder of my property or estates, nothing of the property, of any or no value, of which I die possessed.

"I am cutting her off with the hope and expectation the rest of the family will in the future, or has already in the past, taken action to follow my lead and ensure she receives none of the inheritance that accrues to the Rushings and the Boarchards, be they now or in the future alive or living.

"From me she is to have four quarters and nothing more, and if it were not legally required to bequeath the amount of four quarters or one dollar to render the act of disinheritance legally sound and above dispute, I would not give her anything at all."

Luke Reider went on reading aloud, paragraphs about executors and costs, and Abigail stood up.

Her head was high, her back straight, and with all eyes turned in her direction, she walked out of the room that her great-grandfather had built a century before.

The dogs followed her to the bottom of the steps leading up past the great staircase and the mural, but there they stopped and watched her too as she went down the corridor and out past the kitchen where her father had waited and died.

February—April

The winter was hard and the animals ground down in an effort to survive. The trees were coated with frost, the land imbedded with pinnacles of ice. The air whistled and cracked. The lake itself froze over the day after Pollibeaux stood there with his boots on and opened the small tin can. Taking off his gloves, he had brought out the bones and held them in his fingers and tossed them out over the water, one handful and then another. They sailed into the air, dozens of hard rock things, little bits of fibula, metatarsal and teeth, and landed in the water and disappeared, the last sight of Rushing Boarchards.

The months passed, spring was coming. Rushing Boarchards lay at the bottom of the lake with the stones and weeds, tendrils of water life. Deer came to drink, and coyotes too, and who knows if bits and pieces of the late Rushing Boarchards not only disintegrated further and mixed with the underwater soil, but also got lapped up by some scratchy little tongue and swallowed with bits of gristle and berries, taken down into an animal's stomach.

In New York, Abigail stopped working. She even stopped talking very much. She took a lot of naps, watched television from her bed, and when she looked in the mirror, she saw the same hard glint in her eye and the meanness around the jaw that her father and his wife had seen.

She felt a lot of things during this time, but grief wasn't one of them. Death felt like rejection, and the fact that Rush Boarchards had died had not and could not penetrate her mind. Instead, day after day, month after month, the operative fact was that her father was simply unavailable. He could have been on a trip, visiting a friend. He was just forever unavailable. He would never explain.

She wanted to ask him, "Why did you do it? What did I do? Why did you leave me this way? Why did you leave me to wonder about it for the rest of my life?"

She never imagined him laughing at her, yelling or even being mean. Instead, in her fantasy, the worst thing he always did was just turn his head away. Indifferent. He hurt her to the core.

Abigail thought about something else too. Take the bathrooms at Weather Tree. How even they had maps and drawings, testaments to the will and the wish of the Rushings and the Boarchards to make every little piece of life as pretty as possible. Toilet bowls had taken the place of chamber pots, and sinks had replaced the water pitchers. But the back stairs were still there.

Little curling metal stairs that wound down like corkscrews deep inside the house, linking bathrooms to the servants' inner alleys, little, narrow stairwells meant for servants. They were built off bathrooms so servants could rush in and retrieve the nasty deposit in the chamber pot before anyone in the family ever had to face it.

To Abigail that was an omen from the past: the predilection of the Rushings and the Boarchards not to see what they didn't want to see.

From their point of view, she knew, sometime, somewhere, Abigail Rushing Boarchards had sort of ceased to be.

Late in the afternoon of Monday, April 15, a cab pulled up
to the building on the corner of Seventy-fifth Street and Central Park West. Dr. Phoebe Altman, a short, dark-haired
woman, got out. She identified herself to the doorman as a doctor with Columbia Presbyterian Hospital and, showing her staff
card, she said she'd appreciate it if he'd let her into apartment
11B to see her patient.

"You have an appointment?" the doorman asked as they
went into the lobby.

"Yes."

They got in the elevator. Upstairs in the hallway there were
weeks of newspapers and stacks of mail lying outside the door
to 11B. The doorman rang the bell and, without waiting for an
answer, turned the key in the lock and opened the door.

The woman thanked him and went in.

The apartment was dark and silent. It was also unbearably
hot and the heat reached out and enclosed her like a wrapping.
She opened her mouth to breathe. "Abigail," she said, but
there was no answer. The place smelled, a dense airless smell,
hot and wet, like a compost heap.

Phoebe blinked in the darkness. The shades were pulled
down in the living room on the right and the dining room on
the left and she stood there getting used to the dim light. She
took off her coat and started to pick up mail that was scattered
on the floor. From the dates she saw some of it had been there
for weeks.

"Abigail," she said again.

There was no sound in the apartment and no sign of life,
just the faraway noise of cars in the streets below. But the place
did not feel empty. The heat carried with it a sense of sickness
and fever, of something smoldering there. The temperature and
smell spoke of inhabitation.

Then she heard a cat meowing.

Phoebe looked around and saw a large gray cat with blue
eyes in the hallway ahead. "Eric," she whispered. He darted
away, tail aloft, back down the hall and disappeared into the
bedroom on the left.

The woman followed. In the doorway she was stopped by

the intense heat inside. Against the far wall Abigail Boarchards was curled up in the middle of a queen-sized bed. She was naked, covered only by a sheet, and even from the door, Phoebe could see she was sound asleep. She was perspiring heavily, her face shiny and wet. She lay on her side with her legs pulled up close to her body and her arms wrapped tightly around a pillow. Other pillows were all around her, at her back, her sides, her head, legs. It looked as if she had wedged herself in between them as tightly as possible.

Lying on top of the whole pile was the cat. He had stretched out in the curve along Abigail's neck, cradled between her shoulders and her head. His tail was draped over her hair and his head was in the pocket near her chin, resting against her face and the pillow.

They looked comfortable, and as the doctor stood there, the cat opened one eye slowly, as if he'd been asleep a dozen years, and then closed it again.

Phoebe tiptoed toward the radiator. It was turned on as high as possible, and steaming air sprayed up into her face. She turned the dial off and, careful not to make any noise, opened the window almost a foot wide.

The room was a mess. Empty food containers were strewn on the floor, and there were clothes everywhere, books and magazines. She looked for pills but saw none. There were glasses for liqueur by the bed, other glasses as well, wine glasses, tall glasses, and one little pint bottle of vodka that was almost full.

Phoebe went out into the kitchen. It was dark too, as if someone had methodically gone through the apartment closing every opening to the outside. She pulled up the shades and opened the windows. Breathing deeply, she wiped her sweaty face with her arm.

The kitchen was in the same disarray as the bedroom, dirty dishes and food everywhere. Someone had taped a piece of paper to the refrigerator. "Call me about the party April 15th," the message said. It was signed, "Michael."

This was April 15th.

For the next few minutes Phoebe worked in the kitchen, cleaning up and cooking eggs. Then, waiting for coffee to percolate, she went back out to the rest of the apartment. Wandering around, she noticed that all the photographs of Weather Tree and the family had been removed. There wasn't a one left, just empty spaces on the walls.

In the office she found Abigail's address book and the number for her answering service. She dialed. "I'm calling for Abigail Boarchards," she said. "Can I get her messages?"

She wrote them in a list. There were many, dating back weeks, from friends, her editor, a man named Michael Rutherford about the party tonight, his sister Sally, several from Phoebe herself and others, including someone named Nathan about a basketball game. There was also one from Charley Boarchards and four from a man named Luke Reider.

"I'm off to London to visit Mother," Charley had said. "I didn't know about the will. I promise."

Hanging up, Phoebe saw Abigail's appointment book on the desk. She immediately opened it to last January. On January 1, Abigail had left for Paris, and the days there had been full of appointments, all work, it seemed, but after her return on the seventh of January everything had been crossed out. The pages were blank. Nothing for the day of the funeral or the days that followed, just cancellations and blank spaces until the end of the month, when there was one item left intact.

"See Solomon Irving about the will," it said.

But the rest of the book was empty. In February, one date had been circled and the words "Book due" written in beside the name of her publisher. But that had all been crossed out too. After that there was nothing—no dates, none of the hockey games or basketball games Abigail liked, no theater, no exhibits, no gallery openings, no parties, no phone numbers jotted down in a hurry, no drinks at six, no weekends away or trips on assignment, no meetings with her editor or agent, no notes to jog around the reservoir or be sure to buy cheese, no reminders about someone's birthday.

Except for tonight. "Museum," it said in pencil.

Looking quickly ahead, Phoebe found nothing else written until May 6.

That was three weeks from today.

There Abigail had written, "DEADLINE. 10:00 A.M."
Deadline for what? Phoebe wondered.

Abigail opened her eyes and stared dully across the room.
She turned her head to look at Phoebe sitting beside her on the
bed. "What time is it?"

"Six."

"What day is it?"

"Monday, April fifteenth."

"How'd you get in?"

"Doorman."

"I've been here for weeks," Abigail said in a low voice, turning her head away.

"I know."

"I got tired."

Phoebe nodded.

"I just couldn't fight it anymore." Her hair was wet with
sweat, and matted around her face. "You don't know what it's
like. It's not like a divorce. Because I can't talk to him, Phoebe.
I can't ask him why he did it. 'What did I do? Pop, tell me.
What did I do?' You know what I wish?" Abigail looked up at
her.

"What?"

"I wish I knew why he left it secret. He could have told me.
Let me know before he was gone."

"Maybe he wanted to leave you this way," Phoebe said.

"You think?"

"High and dry. It's worse."

"You think that's why?"

"I don't know. It could be." Phoebe pushed some of the wet
hair off Abigail's forehead.

"He didn't even read my letters."

"I know."

"He didn't even open them."

"I know."

"Why didn't he just throw them out? He could have thrown
them out. Then I'd never have known. He must have wanted
me to know."

Eric started moving slowly up the bed. He stopped to inspect Phoebe and then, going farther, curled up under Abigail's chin on the pillow. The woman smiled a bit. "I haven't seen anyone," she said, holding the cat. "Just some men."

"Nobody special?"

"Nobody."

"Drinking?"

"I tried it, but I don't like it. Maybe I should become a drug addict or a gambler." She sounded sarcastic. "Find an addiction of another sort."

Phoebe started to reply, but stopped.

"I don't mind about losing the money," Abigail said. "I don't need money. I don't care about money. But Weather Tree . . ." Her voice drifted off.

Phoebe had moved down to the end of the bed. "Don't you think you should start taking care of yourself?" she asked.

"What hurts," Abigail went on dreamily, "is that he obviously wanted to hurt me. A lot. It's like murder."

"Yes. Yes, it is."

Abigail looked at her, alert. "You don't mind that word?"

"No."

Abigail paused, looked away, a strange expression on her face now. She started to giggle. "I mean, what if he hated me?" she said with false lightness. She giggled again and looked at Phoebe. "Really hated me?" Then abruptly her face took on a look of fright.

"I think he probably did," Phoebe said seriously.

"Oh no, you're wrong," Abigail exclaimed, shaking her head violently. "He loved me. I know he loved me. . . ." Then she stopped and stared at Phoebe, her mouth hanging open, no longer trying to maintain a pretense. "You think he hated me?"

Phoebe nodded glumly. "I think it's possible the love he felt for you as a child changed."

"But . . ."

They sat in silence.

"I know it's terrible, Abigail," Phoebe said kindly, "but I think you should try to start coming out of this."

"The alcohol changed him," Abigail said. "That's why he did it. It made him crazy."

"That's too simple an explanation for what happened."

"What'd you say?"

"Nothing. Never mind." Phoebe handed Abigail coffee and the eggs. "You have some mail."

Abigail shook her head.

"And messages. Your editor, Charley . . ."

"I don't want to think about it." She started eating.

"And a party tonight at a museum."

"I don't want to think about it."

"You should go out, Abby. Go to the museum. You've done enough of this. Hiding in here. It's been long enough."

"I don't want to go out."

"But you must," Phoebe said more firmly.

"Michael's terrible. Just like his sister Sally."

"That doesn't matter. You've done enough of this."

"Of what?" Abigail put the tray on the table and slid back under the sheet.

"Lying around. Hiding. Moping."

"I'm not moping."

"It was a terrible thing he did, Abby, and it always will be, but you can't let it stop you. That's really self-destructive. Just as bad as his alcohol. This isn't the way to live, and you know it. You're behaving just like him. You've withdrawn, retreated, gone into hiding. It's the family pattern, Abby. You've always said that."

"Maybe I can't help it. Like father, like daughter."

"That's absurd," Phoebe said. "Besides, you can break that pattern. You have to. Remember how you always say you can do anything you want to if you just put your mind to it?"

Abigail didn't answer.

Phoebe sighed, then gritted her teeth, as if trying to think what else to say. She held up the list of messages. Abigail didn't look. "The telephone messages," Phoebe said firmly. She started to read them off. Abigail slid further down under the sheet. Phoebe said the names more emphatically, as if this was a physical battle as well.

"I don't want to think about it," Abigail mumbled. "I'm trying to forget."

"And Luke Reider," Phoebe said at last.

Abigail looked up. "What did he want?" She sounded suspicious.

"He just left his name. How are you going to deal with him,
if you can't go to this party?"

"I don't want to deal with him."

Phoebe picked up the letters and started going through
them. Most were work-related. One, unexpectedly, contained a
royalty check for over thirty thousand dollars from sales of her
last book.

But Abigail didn't react.

"Your attitude is just stupid," Phoebe finally said, angry all
of a sudden. "There's two letters left and I want you to listen."

Abigail sat up. "Okay."

"One is from Harvey Wynne at the lawyer's office and the
other is from someone named Solomon Irving. I'm going to
read his first. I want you to listen.

" 'I am writing,' " Phoebe began, reading aloud, " 'to remind
you that legally you only have until 10:00 A.M. Monday, May
sixth, to decide whether to challenge your father's will. That
will be exactly four months after the will was filed for probate,
and after that you cannot contest. That is the legal deadline. I
will have to file papers with the court before noon that day and
I will need at least two hours to prepare the document. Any evidence to support the suit can be developed afterward. In order
to contest, you don't need evidence or even a hint of a case.
Your contesting may be as capricious as his writing of the will.

" 'What gives you this right to challenge,' " the letter went
on, " 'as we discussed at our initial meeting, is that there are
two wills in existence and the first, eighteen months earlier,
made you, the heir apparent, the sole beneficiary.' "

"I don't want to think about it," Abigail interrupted.

" 'The only way you can eventually win, however,' " Phoebe
read on, " 'is by showing that your father's frame of mind had
so changed during the intervening year and a half since the first
will that he no longer understood what he was doing. The fact

that he was an alcoholic and semi-recluse is not sufficient. It would have to be shown instead that he had lost his competency and that the act of disinheritance was the product of a deranged mind.

" 'I must warn you, however,' " Phoebe continued, " 'that it is almost impossible to establish this in open court. You must file nonetheless, in order for any out-of-court settlement to be reached, if that is even possible in this case, given what you have told me of your surviving relatives. The law, however, is definitely on his side. The courts have ruled repeatedly that no matter how capricious or in error a man's will—or "will"—may be, excuse my play on words, it remains his absolute right to do whatever he pleases with his money at the end. Only very rarely do the courts interfere. Under the law, a dying man is entitled to his last wish, regardless of what it is, so that he may rest in peace assured he will not be robbed in death of his final whim.' "

Phoebe put the letter down. "What are you going to do?"

"Nothing. I'm not thinking about it."

"Not even about the land?"

Abby rolled her head from side to side.

"You're going to let go of the land? That doesn't make any sense. It's your home, your roots. Come on, Abby." Phoebe stood up. "You're being ridiculous." Her voice was harsh.

Abigail looked at her.

"I don't care what you do or don't do about the will or the money, or even the land, but I do care about you. And I'm not going to allow you to go on like this."

"Like what?"

"I love you, Abigail," she said, her voice suddenly soft, "and my children love you and my husband loves you."

"They do?"

"Yes, they do, and they'd be sick if they saw you like this. You have to find the strength, Abigail. You're very strong and very vulnerable, but right now it's time for you to be strong."

"I'm tough and hard and selfish."

"That's bullshit. That's the product of your father's sick mind, and I don't want you repeating it."

"But it's true."

"No, it's not. You can be tough and relentless sometimes, and you could probably drive anyone crazy for ten minutes, but that's all, and anybody who says you're that way all the time is crazy himself."

"You think so?"

"I know so. Now sit up."

Abigail pushed Eric away and sat up. "Read the other letter," she said, "and I'll go to the museum. I'll do what you say."

"Good." Phoebe opened the envelope. "This one is short."

"Is it from Luke Reider?"

"No. Harvey Wynne. Luke Reider's name isn't even on the letterhead. 'This is to notify you,' " she read aloud, " 'that the processing of the last will and testament of the late Rushing Whitaker Fell Boarchards is under way.

" 'When the accounting of the estate is complete, your bequest of the four quarters will be distributed in full.' "

At nine o'clock people in long dresses and black ties were backed up onto the sidewalk waiting to get into the museum. The street was full of honking taxis and limousines, chauffeurs standing around with their caps on and photographers everywhere. Abigail held on to Michael's arm. A flashbulb went off and she jumped. She watched Michael's gold cigarette lighter move and wondered vaguely why she was here at all. She knew she'd never have said yes to him before.

They moved ahead in line. She could hear music inside the museum and the night air was cool against her chest. She wore a long silk gown cut low in front and no jewelry but her watch.

"Hey, buddy, you're blocking the street with that car," a taxi driver yelled somewhere. "Just because you can fucking afford a limousine doesn't mean you can stop traffic."

They moved again. The smell of Michael's cigarette reminded her of her father.

"Isn't that the Boarchards girl?" someone said.

Near the entrance she recognized photographs from *Women's Wear Daily*, the New York *Times*, *People* and the *Post*. Michael handed over their tickets to "Three Hundred Years of American Art—Gala Opening" and they went inside. He took her elbow. "I've decided to get into show business, you know," he said, leading her.

"Oh," she replied. She spotted an elderly woman way ahead in the main gallery and vaguely recognized her as Annie-Fey, the childhood friend of her father.

"I'm backing a musical," Michael went on.

The woman disappeared from sight.

"Probably make a bundle," he said.

"Probably."

They pushed their way through the crowds. Abigail found herself wishing the exhibition featured anything but American art. The pictures started to remind her of all the things she was trying to forget. The museum was very crowded, with everyone in long gowns and dinner clothes. There was a bar in every room, tables of food, and a band was playing somewhere. The noise level was high, and nobody seemed to be paying much attention to the pictures.

"Be sure to remind me to look at the paintings before we go," Michael said.

Catering crews passed champagne and liver wrapped in bacon. She drank one glass, then took another. "Is that a Galanos?" she heard a reporter ask, and watched as a woman with a notebook conducted an interview. She felt envious, work now something she did not do.

They walked and talked to people, and Abigail didn't notice clothes or fashion, faces or even men who looked at her. She was in an inner fog, becoming more and more conscious of the pictures. They bothered her, Whistlers and Eakins, Homers and Sargents, still lifes and landscapes. They seemed closer to her than people.

A young man suddenly stepped in front of her. "Aren't you Abigail Boarchards?"

"Yes."

"I just want to say I really like your work."

"That's very nice. Thank you."

"I have both your books. Do you have another one coming out?"

"No," Abigail said grimly.

"But I still like one picture the best."

"Do tell us," Michael interjected.

The man looked at him. "The killer," he said, moving away uncomfortably. "Clovis Moran."

"Why did you like it?" she asked after him.

"Just something about him."

"How can you stand that?" Michael said, handing her another glass of champagne off a passing tray. "It's so rude, really. And you were always so quiet. Well brought up, certainly." Michael spotted his sister Sally. "Come on."

"I'll just wander around by myself and look at pictures."

"Don't be a spoilsport."

Then Abigail saw Annie-Fey again and this time her heart jumped in excitement. The woman, gray-haired now, wore a big dress with puffy sleeves and looked enormous. "But she wouldn't even know me now," Abigail murmured. "She moved to Colorado."

"Who? Sally?" Michael said. "Don't be ridiculous. Sally lives on Park."

Then Sally was giving her a kiss. "So glad to see you, darling. It's been ages."

"But she wants to run off by herself," Michael said.

"Well, we won't let her, will we?"

Abigail watched Annie-Fey across the room. She hadn't seen her in twenty years. The woman had heavy braids wrapped around her head and looked dowdy but rich, but her very ungainliness made the sight of her all the more a relief for Abigail.

"Because she's different," she said aloud.

"You're absolutely right," Sally agreed. "American art is different."

Michael and Sally moved with the crowd, pulling Abigail in their wake. Silks and chiffons pushed up against her. Suddenly she spotted a Winslow Homer that belonged to Sam and a little Eakins of Bostrine's. "I'm going home," she said.

"But I absolutely must talk to you." Sally took her arm. "I'm thinking of opening a boutique. You simply must give me advice."

Abigail felt trapped. Then she saw Annie-Fey again and her husband Hunt. "I can't stand these paintings," she said.

"Oh, they're not that bad," Sally said. "What's the matter?"

Abigail was rubbing her forehead. "I have a headache."

"Well, let's just stand here and think of pretty things and it will go away."

But the paintings, with their big skies and feel of the land, kept plucking at some inner part of her mind. Abigail knew they were all part of the stuff of America tradition had meant for her. These paintings were supposed to be hers, the land hers, the jewelry hers. "I have to talk to them," she said aloud.

"Who?" Sally asked.

"They'll understand." Suddenly Abigail lifted her dress off the floor and started to run across the room. "Excuse me," she said, pushing couples aside. "It's an emergency."

She passed people and paintings and stopped finally when the two old people were in front of her. She stuck out her hand. "Mrs. Symington?" she said.

"Yes?"

"I'm little Abby Boarchards."

"Look at her eyes!" the man exclaimed.

"Look at her hair!" she cried. "Her figure. She's beautiful."

"She looks just like Florence!"

"She even wears her hair the same."

Abigail beamed. Annie-Fey gripped her hand, Hunt had her by the arm. Abigail could tell that by taking hold of her, they were taking hold of themselves as well, of the years and even decades when they were tied to the Rushings and the Boarchards—until they had moved away to Colorado and a ranch and a different life and the connection was severed. But now all of a sudden they were back again amidst the Eakins and the Binghams and one little piece of the Rushing-Boarchards too.

"I can't tell you how good it makes me feel to see you," Annie-Fey exclaimed, but the minute the woman mentioned Rushing and his death, Abigail pulled back.

"I have to go," she said, abruptly looking over her shoulder. Annie-Fey took her by the arm. "I know how you must feel. What a terrible loss."

"He committed suicide." Abigail loosened herself from the woman's grasp. "And he turned into an alcoholic too."

"No," Annie exclaimed.

"He drank three bottles of vodka a day. . . ."

"Impossible," Hunt said.

". . . he could barely walk."

"I can't believe it," Hunt declared. "He was a real figure of a man if there ever was one."

"He was pathetic."

"Then he must have changed remarkably." Hunt shook his huge body. "He must have changed a lot."

"When we knew him," Annie-Fey said, "he was happy and carefree, just like the rest of us."

"I know he didn't ever sink himself into anything that worked," Hunt said with reluctance. "But he didn't need to."

"Because he had money?" Abigail's voice was crisp.

"Lord, no," Hunt said. "Everyone has money. But he had ideas, projects, plenty to do, always."

"It must not have been enough."

Hunt rolled his eyes and behind them somewhere the loud-speaker was talking about tickets to Sardinia. "Save your tickets in the raffle for a free trip to Sardinia."

A woman in a ruffled dress asked them to move aside. "I want to have my picture taken in front of that." She pointed to a painting by Whistler. "It's mine."

They moved, talking in the flow of the crowd. The light was bright and Annie-Fey said she was searching for a calmer spot. "My mother and father just adored him," she added, as if that would prove Abigail's story untrue.

Abigail looked away.

"Everybody just loved him."

"He disinherited me," Abigail said abruptly.

"Oh no," Annie-Fey replied matter-of-factly. "Nobody does that."

"But he did."

"He did what?" Annie-Fey looked back at her. They were pressed in by people on all sides.

"Disinherit me."

"Are you serious?"

Abigail nodded. "He hated me." She sounded shrill, bitter. Beside them two men started arguing.

"But he adored you," Annie-Fey said, putting her hand on Abigail's arm and drawing her closer. "More than anything in the world. It was perfectly obvious to everyone. It drove Grace mad."

"I could tell you what he did. Do you want me to?"

"Yes, of course."

And so, talking through the noise, with Annie-Fey still holding her arm, Abigail told them about the will and the letters, both the mean ones and the unopened ones.

Then Annie-Fey started looking around. "Come on," she said. "Let's find someplace to sit down." She took Abigail's hand and led her through the crowd. "I'm worried about you."

"There's no reason to be worried." Abigail knew she was lying. She knew there was something wrong with her.

"I've never heard of anyone doing this. Have you, Hunt? Come on over here."

"Never," he said, following along. "It isn't done."

They pushed their way through the galleries until they reached a secluded area lined with poster art. It had been set up like a night club with tables and chairs, low ceilings and candles. It was darker here and quiet. They found a place to sit. The band, farther away now, was playing old songs from *Oklahoma* and *South Pacific*. "I'm going to wash that man right out of my hair," one began.

Annie-Fey, sitting down, moved the flowers and put her elbows up on the table. Then she reached out, picked up Abigail's hand and put it in the middle of the table. "There," she said, holding it tight. "You're not at all like your mother, are you?"

"No." Abigail looked at the woman's braids and her breasts, large like pillows. Her heart was pounding. She felt excited and shy but almost safe. She wanted to tell them everything, all that had happened, but more than that, she wanted them to tell her things.

Why her father had done it, what had gone wrong.

"Hunt, go get us some champagne." Annie-Fey gave her husband a sidelong glance. "I want to talk to Abby."

He looked back and forth between the women. "Right-o."

As soon as he was gone, Annie-Fey gave Abigail's hand a final pat and said, "Now tell me what happened."

"It must have been the alcohol," she said. "I think he got so sick he just lumped me in with his mother and my mother."

"But his mother was marvelous. Ahead of her time."

"He didn't think so," Abigail answered. "He thought the three of us were alike, all tough and mean."

"But that doesn't add up to disinheritance." Annie-Fey was frowning. "That just isn't done. Hunt is right. Disinheritance is a complete breakdown of everything. There must be something else. It's hard for me to understand this," she went on, "because the man you're talking about isn't the man I knew." She looked off, distracted, and Abigail worried she had lost interest. "You just can't imagine what he was like, Abby," she said then, almost dreamily. "He was wonderful, really wonderful, and so alive. He loved animals, people, books. He loved to have a good time. Stay up all night talking. Go to the theater. Give parties. But he could also sit and look at birds for hours. And then, a minute later, be the life of the party." She stopped and looked at Abby. "What are you doing about it?"

"Nothing."

"You aren't contesting?"

"I'd like to forget about it."

"You mean you can forget about a place like Weather Tree?"

Abigail didn't answer.

"I was always in love with him," Annie-Fey went on. "Did you know that?"

Abigail put her elbows on the table and leaned in.

"But no one ever knew. Not even him. After all, we grew up together, all of us and Jackson Paine. Mummy and Daddy and Bostrine were inseparable, and so we were always together. How was anyone to know?"

But Grace had known. "Stop paying attention to Annie-Fey," Grace had said one summer.

"She's only a friend," Rush had said. "She's not my type."

"So now you admit you like them pretty and soft . . ." Grace had sounded vulgar. "Like Melanie."

Melanie.

"Did you ever know a woman named Melanie?" Abigail asked aloud.

"Who?"

"Melanie."

"No," Annie-Fey said, "but women were always falling in love with him."

"Did he have affairs?"

"I don't know. I don't think so. But maybe. Women loved him. He was attractive and dynamic, but there was something untouchable about him. You couldn't have him and that made you want him all the more. Do you know what I mean?"

But she didn't wait for an answer. "He loved his grandfather," she rushed on. "I remember Rush used to sit with Mr. Rushing when people came to sell him paintings and he'd ask, 'What do you think of that one, Rush? Should I buy it?' But later Rush began to hate everything we had to do. He hated dancing school and riding lessons and the French tutors. He said he wanted to be different. He had a mind of his own. He was always special."

"But why?" Abigail asked. "Why was he so special?"

"It wasn't money. Everyone had money. Everyone had the first automobile and the first this, the first that. I remember this little plane that used to land on the lake at Weather Tree. It came every other day, late in the afternoon, bringing the lobsters. People rowed out in boats to meet it, came back with crates of lobsters from Maine. Can you imagine?"

But she didn't wait for Abby to answer. "Fresh lobster packed in ice every other day."

Abigail looked at her watch. Fifteen minutes had passed.

"And every day servants came to your room. They lit the fire, brought fresh flowers and fruits, asked what you wanted to do. If you said 'ride,' they'd make arrangements for a horse. 'Fish,' and there was someone to row the boat. 'Take a walk,' someone to show you the way."

"That's all changed."

"What?"

"My father didn't allow things like that. Everything had to be natural. He wouldn't even let Bostrine bring her hairdresser."

"I remember there was a box with a slot in it in the hall. You put money in there for servants, and whatever he counted out, he doubled and divided among the staff. Did he still do that?"

"Yes."

"He was just wonderful, Abby. Funny. Interesting . . ."

"Was he kind?"

"Kind?" Annie-Fey stopped and thought. She seemed to come back to the dark place with tables lit by candles. "I suppose he was kind. He was certainly generous."

"But he wasn't kind to me," Abigail said bitterly. "He was sadistic and cruel. For years he stared me in the face and knew he hadn't read my letters, knew he had disinherited me, and yet he never said anything."

But Annie-Fey didn't respond. "Did you ever have a dream?" she asked. "Well, he was mine." Then she was talking about a group of people, young and wealthy, who played and laughed their way through depression years and college years, wars and marriage, until one summer long ago, when Rush was forty and fiddlers had come to play. They would never come again, all these people, Annie-Fey said, nor would they celebrate birthdays so well again. After that Rush "settled down," she said, and the next year the day came and went with no notice at all.

And the year after that and the year after that, and by then Annie-Fey and Hunt had long gone as well, to Colorado, and little Abby and Grace had moved to New York.

"But why did it end?" Abigail asked. "Why did those good times end?"

But Annie-Fey didn't hear. She was talking about that last summer, and Abigail saw her in a red bathing suit with a pleated skirt and white trim. The woman was lying on a pine raft floating offshore near the boathouse, her neck thrust high in the air, her head back and laughing. Grace in blue was far more beautiful, and Rush was tall and tanned, and she, Abby, was just a little girl, chubby and awkward. And the picture came back, waves lapping at the edge of time.

Listening to Annie-Fey, Abigail sensed that they were all enchanting then, those people—too enchanting—and that the woman's memory was embued with the lushness of youth and what people in hindsight do to their youth. It was that feeling of the past she heard coming from Annie-Fey, of older people with their sense of who they've been before romanticized and turned into something just a bit more wonderful than the present, and just a bit more wonderful now than it ever really was.

Suddenly Abigail wanted to see it all without the distortion of time or illusion.

She wanted it cold and hard and real, a grainy photograph, black and white and full of lines and edges.

"I haven't thought about this in years," Annie-Fey was saying. "You're bringing it back to me."

"Remember that last summer you were talking about?" Abigail said. "Tell me something. I remember something about a big book he was going to write, but then he never did."

"Yes," the woman said. "It was to be about the Adirondacks. It was going to have pictures and history and maps, be the kind you put on a coffee table. The publisher wanted to give him a lot of money because no one in the world could write about the north woods better than Rush Boarchards."

"But he didn't do it."

"No."

"But why not?" Abigail pressed with an urgency that surprised her.

Annie-Fey didn't answer. "I even remember the day he left for the war," she said instead. "It was '41. Before Pearl Harbor. He came to our apartment on Sutton Place to say good-bye. Grace wore a little thing by Mainbocher and kept excusing herself to go to the bathroom. I could tell she was crying and didn't want Rush to know. We were scared out of our wits. War was coming. We knew that, and Rush had signed up for training as a bomber pilot. He was determined to be in the thick of things. We had this giant pot of caviar, but no one ate a thing, and Hunt said, 'Oh, Rush, you always have to prove yourself,' and Rush nodded. I was terrified. I could see him getting into the worst fighting on purpose, just to show he was a man. They were all like that then, you know," she added. "Everything was 'honor' and 'manhood.' I was in a panic. I was thinking, I can't bear it if he gets killed. I can't bear it. But all I said was, 'Oh, Rush, what a silly thing for you to think you have to prove yourself.' We had a penthouse overlooking the river, and he was standing in front of the windows. There were ships out there, and he said, 'That's what war is. When men go out to prove themselves. It all comes down to that.' He said that every minute you were facing death, and there was no better way to find out who you are, for better or for worse. And he was right, I guess. Because everything about Rush was different after the war. . . ."

"Different? How?"

". . . Hunt even remembers the first time he saw Rush, ever. I don't. I was too little, but it was the first day of school. They were all in the same class, he and Rush and Jackson, and Hunt saw this boy outside with his driver. He had a gun, of all things. . . ."

"It was the gun he used to kill himself."

". . . and he was telling the driver he was going to bring it into school and the driver was saying no, he wasn't. But the boy said yes, and they had this terrible argument. Rush lost, of course, but the thing was, then he said, 'My father will get you for this.'" Annie-Fey looked at Abigail. "And you know what?"

"What?"

"Mr. Boarchards died the next day of a heart attack. He was playing croquet. Nicer, my father, went round to the school to pick up the boys and bring them home, but when they got there, Florence told them their father had gone to Washington."

The band had finished and the staff was cleaning up. Hunt came back and said they should leave, but Annie-Fey said just a few more minutes. She started to fix her braids and Hunt sat down. Abigail was looking through the shadows, staring at the painting of fur traders on the Missouri. There was a low canoe, men reclining, and a black cat looming in the bow. There was ease and peace and more than a bit of menace there. Melancholy, too. She felt it and she could feel a change coming, suspense even, as if all these memories of Annie-Fey's had stirred up too much and the talking had punctured not just the beauty of the past but something else as well.

"It was an awfully frivolous life," Annie-Fey was saying. "Even by the time the war came we were getting tired of it. Hunt said there had to be more to life than staying up all night. But then the war came and we forgot about it, and when the war was over we still forgot about it. Life went on the same as before."

"But what about Rush?" Hunt suddenly said.

"What about him?" Annie-Fey asked.

"Now you'd call it a depression," he said to Abigail. "Then we just thought, 'Oh, Rush is acting strange.' "

"He certainly changed after the war. You're right," Annie-Fey said. "We all noticed it. Or rather," she corrected, "we all sort of noticed it."

"You were probably relieved to be alive," Abigail said.

"That's exactly it," Annie-Fey said. "Because, you see, none of our friends died, and it was such a miracle, really. We never talked about it, it was too tricky, in a way. But we couldn't believe it. Jackson had been a glider pilot over France. Sam and Andrew ended up in Italy, of all places. Rush in the Pacific . . ."

"I was on a PT boat," Hunt added.

"And somehow," Annie-Fey went on, "the exuberance of being so lucky kept us all together for a while. Then Rush wrote his book about the war, *Men of War* . . ."

"About heroism, really it was," Hunt said.

". . . and of course it was a spectacular success and that filled us all with an even greater sense of how lucky we were. But then, soon after that, he was the first of all of us to say he'd had enough."

"That's when he moved to Weather Tree?"

"Yes, more or less. He went to California for a while first, to Hollywood, to make movies. But we all followed his example. We all began to settle down and get more serious."

"But maybe, for him," Abigail said, "going to Weather Tree was just the beginning of his gradual retreat. That's what the family does," she added bitterly. "Retreat."

Annie-Fey wasn't listening. "I guess it's nothing important," she said slowly.

"What?" Abigail noticed again that tension had seeped in somewhere along the line.

"Maybe he didn't *change* after all," Annie-Fey said. "Maybe there was always something strange about him."

"Don't be foolish," Hunt said.

"Maybe we were so wrapped up in how wonderful he seemed, we never stopped to look any deeper. Maybe he changed a long time ago and we never noticed."

"You said the war made him 'strange,'" Abigail said. "I'm confused. Do you mean he was different after the war? Changed?"

"I don't know exactly what I mean," Annie-Fey said slowly. "All I know is I'm wondering for the first time now if something didn't happen to him along the way somewhere and we just never noticed."

"Alcohol certainly changed him," Abigail said.

"But maybe alcohol just made everything worse, Abby. What about that?" Annie-Fey asked. "He did something really strange once."

"What?"

But again the woman didn't answer. "He was different after the war," she repeated, and then she started talking about the house parties again, but now her voice was tense, even hard.

Even Hunt heard it. "All right, dear," he said. "Don't get carried away. The girl's had enough."

"No, she hasn't," Annie-Fey countered. "Why don't you walk around for a while."

"Guess I will." He got up and lumbered off.

Annie-Fey barely noticed. "We always had steak and caviar," she was saying. "Thirty, forty of us all the time. We went for walks in the woods, swimming, fishing . . ."

Abigail sat up straight. She started rubbing her arms as if she were cold.

". . . and at night the shores of the lake were decorated with hundreds of lanterns and there were bonfires, but nobody ever made much noise. It was like none of it belonged to you, or even to them, but to nature itself. Maybe God, I don't know. But the thing was you tried not to make too much noise or run too fast, and if you didn't want to fish, you said you did anyway. Or if you didn't want to climb a mountain, you went anyway."

"But why?"

"He made you. That's why. He hung over everything. Sam wanted to get electricity, but Rush said no. For the first time he began not to make sense. After the war, this was. He talked all the time about how money was unimportant and how the individual has to be true to himself. But the way he meant it, he meant that man didn't have to do anything he didn't want to do—not ever—and he didn't have to pay attention to anything but himself. And all the while he wasn't doing anything. He dabbled at writing and he collected all those goddamn magazines and papers. I never saw so much stuff. But everything was beginning to bottle up inside him. But instead of being honest about it, he turned it into philosophy and used it to be better than the rest of us. I didn't like it. He said Hunt was a fool and who on earth wanted to mess with cows. He had this thing about decency and he talked about it all the time. 'Decency' and 'integrity.' One night we were in the big room in front of the fire and he began to criticize Jackson for being in business. He said all business was corrupt. Max tried to get him to calm down, but he went on and on about how business was corrupt and businessmen had no creativity, no depth, and were nothing but greedy. He laughed at Jackson. Said he was a money-grubber, and it was awful, but Jackson didn't seem to mind. Then he even started to ridicule the memory of old Mr. Rushing. He got like that all the time, after the war.

"He said integrity meant having principles, and he did have principles. But we all did. He was no different. He just talked about it more. He kept saying he was a Democrat, but we were all Democrats. He said he didn't hate blacks, but neither did we. He was the opposite of what his parents and all our parents had been, but as far as I could figure out, it didn't go any further than that because he didn't do anything. He just talked more." Annie-Fey frowned. "And once he did something so strange, it took me a long time to forget it. I kept asking him what he meant and he just said to forget it. Forget it. So finally I did. But I never knew what he meant . . . if he was actually trying to tell me something, confide in me, or was just letting off steam."

"What did he do?" Abigail asked impatiently.

"We were sitting on the veranda at Weather Tree . . ."

"This was after the war?"

"Yes. And out of the blue, he suddenly stood up and said, 'I'm not what you think I am, Annie.' He laughed. He was nervous, and that's why I took it seriously. I said, 'Of course you are. You're the best of all of us.' But he protested. He said no, he'd done something terrible once. 'I'm no hero,' he said, 'like you all think I am.' 'Of course you are,' I said, but he insisted, said he wasn't, said he had gotten very afraid over there in the war, and he looked so miserable, I smiled. I remember that because I thought he was so dear, really, and I loved that anguish in him. 'This only makes you all the more a hero, Rush,' I told him, and of course he wanted to know why, why, and I said, 'Because you're so human. You're so real.'"

"But that all sounds marvelous," Abigail interrupted. "Intimate and wonderful. There's nothing strange about it."

"Wait. I didn't finish. I didn't tell you what happened. Suddenly he stood, kicked the chair, broke its leg, even, and almost screamed at me to forget it."

"Forget what?"

" 'Forget I ever told you that,' he yelled, and I said, 'Told me what? What did you tell me?' But he kept saying to 'forget it, forget it. Nothing happened,' and finally he stormed back into the house."

"I wonder what he meant."

"That's it," Annie-Fey agreed. "I don't know. Maybe something. Maybe nothing. Because if anyone was a hero in the war, it was him." She paused. "But remembering that now," she went on, "and thinking of all the horrible things you've told me, it makes me wonder if I ever knew him at all. I mean, who was Rushing Boarchards? What was going on inside him all that time? I frankly have to say I don't know. The man I knew, or thought I knew, would never disinherit you or even hate you. You were the most precious thing in the world to him."

"Imagine how I feel," Abigail said with a nervous giggle.

"And take all his talk about money," Annie-Fey rushed on intensely. "About how money didn't count and money didn't mean anything and money was just corruption. I didn't understand that."

"Why?"

"Because he couldn't have lived without it. That's why. And as far as I could tell, he never made a penny. Do the checks still come four times a year?"

"What checks?"

"The ones from the bank. The ones he lived on. I know they used to come four times a year because he used to pick up the envelope and say, 'Shall I tear it up?' But I bet he never did. They're all like that."

"Like what? Why?" Abigail asked.

"The Rushings and the Boarchards. They never worked. None of them. Except for old Mr. Rushing."

"But my father wrote books," Abigail argued.

"Only one was a success. The rest never made a penny."

"But that's still work."

"Is it, Abby? If he didn't make any money? Is it? Or isn't that just something he can afford to indulge himself in? He never put himself on the line like other people. He was never forced to survive. Compete. Fend for himself. There's nothing wrong with that," she went on, "except that he never admitted it. He was a hypocrite. Always pretending money didn't count when he couldn't live without it and when what he had was never his. All he did was inherit it. Sam's the same. Florence was the same. Once there was a big scene when Florence refused to eat with the bankers. She told Mr. Rushing she and Mummy would go upstairs to eat. He apparently got whopping mad and told her she'd better learn something about money or she'd be sorry. But she still refused and that made him even more furious. He said money was something she had to respect. Enjoy it and respect it. She said it only brought out the worst in people and she was going to ignore it, and he said she was a frivolous, stupid girl and money was nothing to sneeze at and only fools thought the way she did."

"What happened?"

"Nothing. She took Mummy upstairs and had the servants bring them lunch. Just the way she said she would."

Abigail couldn't sleep. Her mind was full of a million pictures and the room above Central Park was aswarm with lanterns and fires, a lake, a war and women in bathing suits. There were bankers for lunch and boys in knickers and they circled the ballroom and said they were going to be hunters instead.

For three months she had tried not to think about Rushing Boarchards, but the man in all these stories from Annie-Fey was someone else. He wasn't a father or a friend, and Abigail was wide awake, even electrified. Taking shape inside her head was the notion that Rushing Boarchards was a stranger and that she had never known him and maybe no one ever had.

But that somewhere in all this information about a family and a past was a reason for what he had done to her.

Tuesday, April 16

She got up. The clock read five past three. She put on her robe and went to the office. She turned on the light, got out a sheet of paper and started writing.

"What happened to him?" she wrote. "What went wrong? Why did he deteriorate? Why did he change? What went wrong? Could something actually have happened to him? Something no one knew about?"

Abigail pushed her long hair behind her ears and bit her lip. She was so intent her head was but a few inches from the desk. She started writing again. She felt herself moving a million miles an hour along some giant causeway in her mind, her brain finally freed to think again. She heard a siren in the distance, ambulance, fire, but the emergency here was hers. "Why did he change from loving me to hating me? Why did he disinherit me? Why didn't he write that book? Why didn't he read my letters? What couldn't he face in them? In me? Find the exact reasons."

She was writing so fast, she didn't realize the implications of her word, "find."

"What happened to him in the war? Why did he change from a social person to a recluse? Is there any of his tendency toward isolation in me?"

Abigail stopped writing. Suddenly she was not just excited by her activity, but frightened. Frightened by what she sensed were similarities between herself and the negative characteristics of her father. They were too much the same. If he sought safety in isolation, didn't she as well?

Sitting there at her desk, staring at the sheet of paper, Abigail felt as if she were driving along a high cliff, too close to the edge. She wondered if she was turning out like him and if this was only the beginning: alone, withdrawn, unable to work.

Suddenly she slapped her hand so hard against the desk it hurt, but the stinging cleared her mind, and she began to think again. To analyze. Maybe something traumatic, something like this had happened to him, she thought. Maybe it was something just as severe as disinheritance and rejection. Or maybe it was just a cluster of things going wrong all at once. But the point was, maybe something specific had set Rush back and maybe he never got right again.

But what was it?

She pulled out another sheet of paper and started writing again. The words were almost illegible, she was writing so fast. "For three months I have tried to get over it by not thinking about it," she wrote, "but it hasn't worked and I feel as bad now as I did then. I can't work. I don't see people. I'm always depressed. I must find a way to get over this or I'll end up just like him."

She got up from the desk and started walking up and down the room. Eric watched her from the couch. She stared at the walls; so many spots were bare. She remembered her grandmother's letter she had read at Weather Tree, the definition of a gentleman, "not that he is better than others, of course, but that he is quite well, thank you, and perfectly suited to take on any matter of responsibility or concern."

Abigail sat back down at the desk and started writing again. "She trained him to think he was special, but what did that do to him? I'm not the way I was supposed to be," she wrote. "But was he? That is the question. Was he? He was 'different,' 'unusual,' 'eccentric,' but was he something even more as well?"

The little clock on her desk ticked away, but Abigail didn't notice. It was still dark outside. She looked at her list of questions. She added more. "Who was Melanie? Did he ever have a successful relationship with a woman? If not, why not?"

Suddenly Abigail hated the last three months. She was disgusted by herself. She stood up and paced some more, but then abruptly sat down and started writing again. "Maybe I have to pit myself against him," she wrote. "Maybe that should be my strategy. Because that's what it is—him versus me. It's a contest of strength. He's done this to me and he set out to do it. So far he has succeeded. Look at me. Look at how far I've fallen. So maybe I have to fight him back. Smoke him out and find out exactly why he disinherited me. I can't get him in person, but maybe if I find out why he did it and understand, I'll get him another way. But maybe at least I'll get myself back in the process. But I have to learn everything," she wrote on, bent intently over her desk. "If he retreated, I have to advance. If he became a recluse at Weather Tree, I have to face him and face myself. I have to find the answers and the reasons and I have to be strong. The key," she wrote, "is confidence in myself. He lost it and so have I. But if he committed suicide, I have to get it back and survive."

Abigail stood up, started talking out loud. "When I decided to try to be a photographer, I didn't know if I had any more talent than a dishwasher. All I had was the willingness to find out and the willingness to work and the willingness to fail." She looked at the picture of Clovis Moran screaming. "Can't I do that now?"

The question hung in the darkened room.

"Can't I?" she asked more firmly.

She sat down. It was almost four o'clock. I have to do the same thing now that I did in the beginning, she thought. I have to work. Her face was reflected in the window in front of her. It showed long hair falling around her shoulders, the line

of her cheek unclear, undefined, a picture taken from a long
way away.

"I have to find out everything I can about him," she wrote.
"I have to answer all my questions. I have to track him down
and flush him out. Real and grainy, black and white and hard."

Abigail was awake again before seven. She went straight to
the office, found the letter from the lawyer, Solomon Irving,
and looked at the date. May sixth. That was the deadline, two
weeks and six days away. She got three more sheets of paper
and wrote the dates of the two wills across the top of one. On
the next she wrote, "People to See" and on the next, "Things
to Do." Under that she scribbled, "1. Hire a detective. 2. Decide about the will." But she crossed that out and wrote instead: "2. Be ready to think about the will in a week to ten
days and then decide whether to contest it. Specifically, decide
if I want Weather Tree enough to contest the will or if I want
to give it up instead."

It took her a couple of hours to map out her strategy. When
she was finished she had a long list of plans, but she had made
almost no headway in filling in the dates of events between the
two wills. In hindsight it was all just a collection of weekends
at Weather Tree with Rush and often Pollibeaux, none seem-
ing any different from the others. The list of people to see,
however, was long. It included Esther McCrea, their former
housekeeper, Isabel Daltenburgh, Rush's friend and lover after
Grace died, Sergeant Bud Krajewski, his gunner in the war,
Luke Reider, Jackson Paine, others.

But Abigail was unable to add the most important things of
all. She had thought of them and left them out. Going to
Weather Tree was not on her list. Nor was looking at her father's voluminous files. Nor were the names of Simon Finney
and Pollibeaux there, and "Victoria, Sam and Bostrine" appeared only at the very end, things to be done last, as if they
had the least urgency of all.

Abigail had written down some dates between the two wills,
but they were more notations to jog her memory than anything
else. They all involved Clovis Moran, who had been caught

just days before Rush wrote the second will. She had spent the duration of the manhunt in the town of Licking River and visiting Rush at Weather Tree.

"January 17," four years ago, was the first date. "Moran kills wife, her lover and their two daughters. Manhunt begins."

"January 27. Moran reappears, looking for food. Kills again."

There were more dates of more killings. His victims at the end numbered fourteen, and writing, Abigail remembered the climactic end when he had appeared at Weather Tree, without a gun, and she and a childhood friend named Josh had found him.

"Didn't your father tell you about the cave?" Moran had screamed as she clicked picture after picture, going in closer and closer, the man drooling, liquid frozen to his chin. "Didn't he ever tell you about the cave?"

"What cave?" Josh had yelled.

Moran's eyes were blazing in the glare of flashbulbs, but she found him strangely unfrightening for someone who had killed so many people. And then suddenly, like an animal more afraid of man than man of him, he had turned and run off toward the creek, arms flailing, heading back up into the mountains.

"What cave?" Pop had asked, sitting up in bed when she and Josh barged in to wake him.

"He kept saying, 'Didn't your father tell you about the cave?'" Josh had said. "There must be caves in the mountains where he's hiding."

"Did he say anything else?" Rush had asked.

She saw her father only once more that spring, but he had already written the second will by then. He wasn't there the next morning when the search party set out at dawn from the town of Licking River with Pollibeaux in the lead, headed for the caves in the mountains of Weather Tree. She and the throng of reporters and photographers waited in town, and that night they covered the arraignment in the county seat to the south.

Boarchards wasn't at the arraignment either.

Moran was so tired he could barely move. They'd given him jail clothes in place of the other things he had worn, cold and wet from two months in the woods, and he was thin with sad

eyes and long fingernails. The eyes were blue and they never
focused on her. Someone had found him a lawyer and the lawyer steered him in the direction he needed to go. In court he
looked at the judge as if he had no idea who he was or what
was happening. He blinked and never turned, and his defeat
and silence made her quiet. Somebody said he looked drugged.
Abigail said no.

"Flipped out," someone else said.

"How do you plead?" the judge asked.

"Guilty," the lawyer said.

The next time she saw Rush was two weeks later. He had
called her the night before, hoarse and depressed, and said he
needed a ride. "What for?" she had asked, and he'd said, "I'm
going to Connecticut." Out of the blue, it had come, his decision to go to Connecticut. She was surprised, pleased, no idea,
of course, he had just written a will disinheriting her. "Four
quarters and nothing more."

"I'm going to Blue Clipper Farm," he said. "Dry you out in a
month, and all I want to know is if you can give me a ride
tomorrow."

"Of course," she said.

"They do it cold turkey. Won't even let you have cars.
Won't even let you drive yourself there."

"Oh," she said, no inkling then, or now, that all this talk of
cars wasn't true at all, just a lie to cover up something worse.

"And Simon is sick."

"You don't have to explain, Pop. I'm delighted to do it."

In New York she was up before dawn to get there in time,
and the farther north she drove, the warmer it got, as if all the
heat and steam was caught up north for once, unable to reach
the plains. When she arrived, it was just a little after noon, and
as she drove toward the house, she saw Rush on the veranda.
He saw her too, picked up his suitcase and the typewriter, and
by the time she had stopped the car, he was coming down the
steps. "Let's go," he said.

"Right now?"

"That's what I said."

She put her arms around him, smelling the smell. She remembered thinking it was the first time she'd ever noticed it. "Come on," he said. "Let's get the show on the road." But then he stopped and looked her full in the face, and got that look that was the beginning of a smile. Then he reached out and patted her head and then the shoulders, as if she was a dog or something special, and the very slightness of it lessened none of its intensity. It was the way he always was and always had been, intense but tentative in any show of warmth.

"Let me go to the bathroom first," she said. When she came back out, he was in the driver's seat. They started on their way. "I thought you weren't supposed to drive," she said.

"I'm not."

On the road to Licking River, she asked questions. Pollibeaux, Jackson Paine, but he barely said a word. She asked if he'd heard anything more of Clovis Moran, in jail two weeks by then.

"No," he said.

She never thought to ask, of course, "Have you called Wynne, Wynne and Pine, or done anything about your will?"

They drove the rest of the way in silence. Even though the windows were open, she could smell him. He looked straight ahead, with two hands on the wheel, and smoked. The cigarettes burned so far down the ashes fell off and landed on his lap. He never seemed to notice. Just started up another, holding his head too close to the match, as if daring the flame to catch his hair and eyes. She peered at him from time to time, curious where the smell came from, and she finally decided it was the pores themselves. They secreted a kind of liquid potion that gave his face and even his hands a sort of shine. But the face was thin and the cheekbones stuck out underneath his skin. He was only fifty-six then, but he looked old and ill and the pockets around his eyes were gray, mauve.

In Connecticut the sign on the narrow macadam road said, "Blue Clipper Farm." Rush pulled over to the side and stopped. "This is it," he said. A driveway ahead circled up and around through trees and a meadow to houses at the other end, and it looked as if there should be children and bicycles there, not psychiatrists and men who liked to drink.

"I don't want you coming any closer," he said. He opened the door and the smell of spring rushed into the car. "It's up to me, not you." Without a word, he got out and reached into the back seat to get the suitcase. Then he slammed the door and walked away.

She watched him go up the driveway, stumbling, steeped in alcohol, the old Mark Cross suitcase covered with steamship labels hitting against his knee. The suitcase was a thing of history, bought for an ocean voyage while he was still a boy.

Now he kicked at stones in the road and never did look back, although she was waiting to wave, and it was only later that she realized he had left the typewriter in the back seat. She saw it on the way back to New York and pulled over to the side of the road. Lifting it up off the seat, she put it beside her and opened it.

The machine inside didn't have a ribbon. The handle that turned the spool was broken and the pouch at the back where paper belonged was empty.

Abigail was stunned. It reminded her of the time when she'd heard voices in the kitchen and seen a boy, but later Pop had said, "What boy? There was no boy." Reality askew.

She had turned the handle on the typewriter and listened to its broken sound. Why had he gone to the sanatorium? He not only had forgotten the typewriter, but it had no paper and no ribbon, so why had he brought it to begin with? The typewriter was just as much a key to his life as the alcohol. He took it everywhere, just as he took the bottles, but if the bottles were defeat, the typewriter was hope. So why had he left it in the car and why had he started out in the first place with only a broken machine? And why was it broken at all?

Abigail was confused. And to make matters even more confusing, all during the hunt for Clovis Moran only weeks before, he had drunkenly insisted he was writing a book, something he hadn't done in years. Not that she had believed him anyway, but that he should have a broken typewriter now made it all the more peculiar.

He stayed in Connecticut for two months, at two thousand dollars a week. She had the typewriter fixed and sent it north, and the afternoon Simon brought him home, he opened a case of vodka, took out a bottle, Simon said, and drank it halfway down.

One week later the final draft of the will was done, all typed and bound by now: "Four quarters and nothing more."

After Abigail was dressed, she called her lawyer Solomon Irving. She told him she wanted the name of a good private detective.

"You don't need a detective," he said.

She said she did.

He said they could get the information after they filed the notice of intent.

She said that wasn't the point.

"But your father has nothing to do with it," the lawyer said after she explained her plan. "Whether you contest or not is your decision. It should not be governed by his intentions."

"I may end up agreeing with you," Abigail said patiently, "but I want to know what those intentions were before I decide."

"Suit yourself, but it's unorthodox."

"What he did was unorthodox."

"Just so long as you let me know by Monday, May sixth, at ten A.M."

The brownstone was three stories high. Inside, the long corridor was lined from floor to ceiling with shelves of tapes, recording equipment, splicing machines and movie cameras. A woman with frizzed hair came out of one of the rooms and looked at her. "Boarchards? Go on up. He's waiting."

The stairwell had a framed poster of Nixon as a car salesman and a diploma from a midwestern law school. Abigail had almost reached the top when a big man with gray hair appeared. He didn't smile. "I'm Alvah Germaine," he said. "We can talk in here." He led her into a room in the back overlooking a garden. It had started to rain. "You want something to drink?"

He wore a suit that was an off-shade of green and a tie with shiny geometrics.

"No, thanks." She looked around for a place to sit.

He pressed a button on one of the four phones. "Mary," he said. "Bring some coffee. So Solomon Irving sent you to me?"

"Yes."

She sat down on a brown corduroy couch. She was nervous but in her high slim boots, tailored pants and silk blouse she didn't look it. Nobody she knew had ever hired a private detective, she kept thinking. There were bookshelves, magazines, a small computer. The man picked up a yellow legal pad and sat down across from her. Behind him on the wall was a picture of Eleanor Roosevelt at a radio microphone.

"Why don't you tell me what's on your mind," he said. He had a vague midwestern edge to his voice. "I know something about your father, but let's see if there really is anything I can do for you."

Abigail took a Xerox of her list out of her purse. "I've outlined an investigation with my father as the subject," she said. "I've figured out what I want to know and what I'd like you to do. For example, he wrote four books. I'd like you to get the reviews."

"Why don't you just tell me about the situation in general and then I'll tell you what I can and cannot do."

So Abigail proceeded to talk and Alvah listened. Occasionally he asked a question, said something, but at the end he put down his paper and looked at her. "Don't you want the money?" he asked.

"I don't know. The more difficult question is whether I want Weather Tree." She handed him her list.

"So you really are serious," he said, looking at it. "I'm expensive, you know. Fifty dollars an hour, all expenses. For three weeks, that adds up."

Abigail took the royalty check for thirty thousand dollars out of her purse and held it up for him to see. "This is from my book sales," she said. "I'm prepared to spend every cent of this money to find out what happened to my father. I know he loved me once, but that turned to hate. I want to find out why.

I want to know what triggered his flight into isolation and hate, and I'm going to spend every waking minute for the next three weeks trying to find out too. If you want to help me and are prepared to take me seriously, fine. If not, I'll find someone else."

Alvah looked at her in silence. Then he tossed her the yellow pad. "Take notes," he ordered, grabbing another for himself. "There are three main areas I can get into. Public records is the first: Department of Motor Vehicles, voter registration. Old newspaper files, court records." As he talked, they both made notes. "Tax records, law suits, property ownership."

"There weren't any law suits."

"None you know of," he corrected. "If you don't know about someone, you don't know what's back there. Do you?"

"I suppose not."

"Are you prepared for what you might find? You may be sorry."

"Then I'll face that too."

"The second thing is talking to people who knew him. Friends, servants, lovers . . ."

"That's what I want to do," Abigail said. "I want you to concentrate on getting things. Records. Accounts. Like the D.M.V. Obviously he had a driver's license, but maybe it'll turn out he was blind in one eye or lied about his birth date. That's an absurd example, but . . ."

"You never know."

"I want you to get facts. I want as many facts as possible."

"The third thing I can do," he said, "is all the illegal things. Like it costs me fifty dollars for an unlisted telephone number. About twenty-five to run a check on a car. Most of this is routine, and I've got sources—banks, government offices, military, IRS. But the first thing I'll do is get his back telephone bills."

"He rarely used the phone," Abigail said. "He did everything by letter. He even kept carbons."

Alvah showed a glimmer of excitement. "That could be a gold mine," he muttered.

But Abigail shook her head. "No," she said, "we won't be looking at the letters."

"Why not?" he asked.

"Because they're in the Adirondacks and we're not going there. Besides, we have plenty of other sources. We don't need the letters."

Alvah raised an eyebrow, but didn't argue. "You're the boss," he said. "Business records," he went on.

"You don't have to bother with that either. He didn't have any."

"There you go again."

"What?"

"Didn't he work?"

"No."

"Not at all?"

"No."

"But he wrote checks?"

"I suppose," she answered.

"And had bank accounts?"

"The lawyers took care of all that."

"But he had checks," Alvah pressed.

"I guess."

"All right. The point I'm making is everyone has business records of some kind. You'd be surprised how much you learn from a checkbook. It tells how someone spends his time. Whether he pays for golf lessons or has a season ticket to the opera. What kind of food he eats. Fish or the meat market. If he buys books . . ."

"But . . ."

"Goes on vacation, cheats on his wife, has motel bills, bar bills, medical bills . . ."

"But the lawyers have all his checks. How are we going to get them?"

"Do you know the lawyers?"

"Yes, but I don't like them."

"We'll work on it." Alvah scribbled something on his pad. "IRS records," he went on, "are usually impossible to get. They're kept in government warehouses for twenty years, but I've had some luck. I know some of the right people. Banks . . ."

"What do you actually do as a private detective?" Abigail interrupted.

Alvah leaned back in his chair and smiled at her for the first time. "Everything," he said.

"What's everything?"

"Surveillance, trial work, corporate investigations, SEC investigations."

"So why do you take a case like this?" she asked. "You're going to find out a great deal about me, aren't you?"

But then the woman with frizzy hair came into the room. "Here's your coffee, Alvah."

"Mary," Alvah said, "this is Abigail Boarchards. We're going to be doing a lot of work for her the next three weeks. Mary does everything for me," he explained to Abigail. "I've got six others downstairs to help me."

"You're not like Sam Spade at all, are you?" Abigail said when the woman had left.

"Don't be absurd," Alvah said.

"But you're not."

"What'd you expect? Me to peer in windows with a camera?"

"I didn't know what to expect."

"I develop high-class legal cases," he said bluntly. "Against an aircraft company, for example. Proving a certain plane design is unsafe and they knew it all along."

"But you own a gun."

"I haven't had a gun in years, and if I need something like that, if I even need a stakeout, you can be damn sure I hire someone else to do it."

"Then why do you take a case like this?" she pressed.

"I'm still a normal human being."

"You're curious, I bet," she teased.

He grinned. "Let's just say I have more than the normal share of curiosity, and I have a good deal of it about Rushing Boarchards and his very attractive, and probably very confused, daughter."

Abigail blushed.

He winked at her and picked up her list off the table. "Let's keep going," he said, looking at it. "You don't have a lot of time to waste. Who's Melanie?"

"I don't know, but I want to find her."

"What if your father was a homosexual?" he asked.

"He wasn't."

"You talk about his drinking problem. Was he ever arrested for drunk driving?"

"Of course not."

"Assault?"

"No."

"Could anybody have a hold on him? Blackmail?"

"I doubt it."

"Shall I get school stuff? Records, yearbooks?"

"Yes."

"Medical?"

"Yes."

"Military?" He took notes rapidly.

"Yes. Everything. Anything."

He asked a lot more questions. When they had finally finished, Alvah stood up. He put his hands in his pockets and went over to look out the window.

Abigail watched him, waiting. It had stopped raining. She heard a church bell somewhere strike six times. She decided to walk home afterward. She used to walk all the time, but the last three months she hadn't done that either. Go across town and up Central Park West . . . streets wet, air cool. She remembered being a young teenager, walking down Fifth or Park in the middle of the night, getting farther and farther away from her mother's anger. Running away, for the night. The streets of New York safer than her home. Despite what she was feeling, she had always looked self-assured and unapproachable, and it had worked. She had never been hassled, and somehow, on those nighttime sojourns, she had managed to carve out a world for herself, a spirit of independence, or at least the allusion of one, she thought now, for who was to say her running away had been any different from what her father had done. Abigail gritted her teeth and felt that rush of panic again.

"What's the matter?" Alvah asked, watching her.

"Nothing," she said hurriedly.

"I have just one problem with all of this," he said. "I don't want to scare you, but people do very peculiar things."

"I know that."

"But I don't think you do," the detective said. "You never know what you're going to find out in something like this, and I don't want to be party to something that's just going to end up hurting you all over again."

"I'm tough," Abigail said, sitting up straight.

"No, you're not. If you were, you wouldn't do all this to begin with. You wouldn't care."

"Just because I care doesn't mean I can't handle it," she said defensively. "I'm prepared to face whatever I have to. Unlike my family. They prefer to pretend something doesn't exist."

"But have you considered the fact he could have been involved in criminal activities or done something that could involve scandal?"

"That's absurd."

"Don't be naive a second time," he said severely. "You have no idea what you're going to find out, and you'd be damned foolish if you weren't prepared for that. If being naive or blind or stupid got you in this situation in the first place—or at least let it take you unawares—you'd be damned foolish to let it happen again. I just want to make sure you know what you're doing."

Wednesday,
April 17

⟨❦⟩

Suddenly the phone was ringing. She jumped up in bed. She'd been dreaming she passed her father on a staircase headed down, but when he saw her, he kept on going, and when she rushed after him, he ignored her.

"Did I wake you?" a man was asking.

"What time is it?"

"After nine. This is . . ."

"I know who it is." It was Luke Reider. She pulled the blankets around her and gritted her teeth.

"I need to talk to you."

"You've got a lot of nerve calling me," she said bluntly.

"I waited three months. But it's important. I have something to read you. Will you wait while I get it? It's in the living room."

"Why aren't you in your office?" she asked when he came back on the line.

"I left Wynne, Wynne and Pine."

"Why?"

"I didn't want to execute the will."

"Couldn't handle your own dirty work?"

"No," he said lamely.

"What changed your mind?"

"I didn't understand about you."

"I'll say you didn't. What'd you do? Realize I'm not as bad as he said?"

"It's not my job to decide if you're bad or not," the man said hotly. "Lawyers execute decisions. They don't make them."

"Is that the kind of person you are? You weren't even curious? You didn't even care?"

"I cared about him. A lot," he said intently. "I liked him a lot. Almost as much as you did."

"Sure," she said sarcastically, but the remark made her stop and listen.

"It wasn't until I met you that I questioned him at all," Luke was saying. "I thought he was eccentric and sad and wonderful, and I wasn't one goddamned bit surprised when he killed himself. But you could have knocked me over with a feather when I saw you."

"Why?"

"You want me to tell you?"

"Yes. I said I did. And I meant it. I apologize, too," she added. "This has affected me a lot. Please tell me what you were going to say."

"It's just that I happen to believe a man's ability to make sound judgments and deal in truth, not delusion, is the most precious thing he has. And it had never occurred to me your father was as sick or twisted or deluded as he obviously had to be to arrive at that opinion about you. I mean, I never even thought he was twisted at all. Just depressed. And cantankerous."

"All that hate and you never thought there was something wrong?"

"No." And with that Luke's voice suddenly became quiet. "And that's what I'm sorry about," he said. He sounded tired. "I really am, Abigail. I should have known, or sensed it, maybe even done something about it. To help him, not you."

"Why?"

"Not as a lawyer. That's none of my responsibility as a lawyer. But as a person. As a friend, even. I went up there all the time. I even began to feel I was one of the family. I was just kidding myself, of course, but I loved it there."

"Then why . . ."

"And I really believe that if you get involved in something, you take on its responsibilities too. I believe that."

"So do I."

"But I didn't do it here and I don't know why. I didn't want to see what was wrong."

"So you think something was wrong?"

"Of course there was. I see that now. But I was too caught up with him to see it, and now it's all I can think about. I can't get it out of my mind. I'm trying to finish this goddamned article for the *Harvard Law Review* and I have a big meeting in three weeks, and I'm having the damnedest time concentrating on anything." He paused. "I mean, did you ever have a fight with him or something?"

"No."

"A bad one?"

"No. We never had fights. But I know he didn't like my mother or his mother. That's part of it. Misogyny."

"I've thought about that," Luke said, "but it doesn't go far enough. It doesn't explain this. This is the deterioration of a mind and body. Complete deterioration, in twenty years' time. That's rare. I mean, do you know anyone else that happened to?"

"No."

"Did it ever occur to you something might have happened to him?" he asked. "Actually happened to him. Something you don't know about?"

Abigail caught her breath.

"What?" he asked.

"Nothing. Nothing at all. What's this letter you were talking about?"

"It's one more thing about him I can't figure out."

"Can I call you back?"

"What?"

"Can I call you back in five minutes? I just woke up and I'm still in bed. Can I wash my face and call you right back? What's your number?"

"Did you ever hear of a man named Joe Algodones?" he asked a few minutes later. He pronounced the name Al-ga-DOE-ness.

"What was the name again?" She was back in bed wearing a white terry-cloth robe and holding a glass of orange juice. Eric was in her lap.

"Algodones," Luke said. "Joe Algodones."

"Who is he?"

"That's just the point," he said, "I can't find him. He was a friend, or something, of your father's, but nobody's ever heard of him. I've asked everyone. Pollibeaux, your uncles, aunts, friends, people in the woods. Simon remembers mailing letters to him, but he has no idea who he is. Your father left him a very large sum of money. It was in a letter on his desk."

Abigail suddenly remembered seeing the letter herself. She had picked it up in his room before opening the files. It had had no address. "How much money?"

"Ten thousand dollars in cash."

She gasped. "What's it for?"

"That's the point. I have no idea. I'll read it to you. It begins, 'Dear Joe. You left your sweater here . . .'"

"'Left your sweater'?"

"'. . . but it was so filthy I threw it out. I won't be seeing you again, Joe. I'm going to do what I should have done long ago. Take care of yourself and give my best to Sue Ann. There's not much more to say to you after everything we've been through. It's been a lot, but it wasn't all bad (although I hate to admit it), and sometimes I even wonder if it would have been worse without you. Bet that surprises you. . . .'"

"What an unusual letter."

"'But if you'll let me give you a word of advice, I think it's time you finally went home and settled down. Everything here is finished. So go home. You've had enough of this. Remember how much you like the shortwave radio? Why not do that? It will make you happier. Not that I know a great deal about happiness, but you deserve more than you've gotten.'" Luke paused. "That's it," he said. "It's signed, 'As always, Rushing B.'"

"Rushing B."

"What do you think of it?"

"I'm struck by how intimate it sounds. What have they 'been through'? Who is Joe Algodones?"

"I have no idea. That's why I can't help wondering if something happened to him. Or if this is blackmail. I doubt it. But then what is it? Who is he?"

Abigail got dressed in blue jeans and a sweater, then sat down at her desk to work. First she called Alvah to tell him about Algodones, but he wasn't in, so she studied her lists, arranged an appointment at the school in the old Rushing Mansion for that afternoon, other meetings for later in the week. Today was Wednesday. She had nineteen days left.

Then she called Esther McCrea, the housekeeper who had followed the little family, Rush and Grace and Abby, through the years from New York to Weather Tree and back to New York again.

"But Esther died three years ago," said her daughter, who answered the phone.

"But I didn't know," Abigail exclaimed, remembering the smell of her rose-scented hand lotion. "Why didn't you let us know?"

"I told your father," the daughter said. "He said you were away."

Abigail suddenly remembered one morning before dawn long ago running from the cab through the alley behind the apartment building. Avoiding the doorman and the front elevator and going past garbage bins and storage rooms to the back stairs. Up floor after floor, green walls and metal steps, must have been four or five o'clock, and ahead the apartment with Persian rugs and paintings that went to museums to be cleaned. Finally, her key out, coat undone, almost home, she saw Esther.

The woman was sitting at the top of the stairs, leaning against the kitchen door, eyes closed, asleep. She had her hat on, pieces of velvet hanging off the brim, and her knees were drawn up under her coat. A newspaper lay folded in her lap untouched and her mouth was wide open, but as soon as Abby turned the corner, she opened her eyes and saw her.

"I've been waiting for you," Esther whispered, rousing herself. "Where've you been? Where'd you go? You can't go out at night like this."

"But I don't do anything bad."

"I never thought you did, honey."

"She doesn't mind." Abby nodded her head toward the apartment, where Grace was asleep.

"Does she know you do this?"

"I don't know."

"Well, I don't think she does. Nor him either. Or wants to know, if you ask me." She put the newspaper on the steps beside her. "Here," she said, patting it. "Sit down."

Abby sat down.

Esther rubbed up against her, their shoulders touching, and the smell of rose-scented lotion, the stubby fingers and the soft voice whispering in the stairwell made Abby feel at home. Garbage down below and the night outside, one parent asleep, another up north alone.

"Where do you go, honey?" Esther put her arm around the girl's back.

"Down Park Avenue. Or Fifth."

Esther looked at her watch. "I got here at one and you were gone. Now it's almost five. You walk all that time?"

Abby shook her head.

"You see somebody?"

"Not really."

"What do you mean, 'not really'?"

"I saw one woman."

"Where?"

"Waldorf-Astoria Hotel." She looked at Esther's little feet. "In the bathroom."

"The bathroom?"

"Well, it's not exactly the bathroom. It's the lounge. The women's lounge."

"What were you doing there?"

"Sleeping."

"Sleeping?"

"On the couch. And there's this cleaning lady, she puts newspapers over my legs."

Esther started to rock her.

Abby was rigid at first, resistant, but then she started moving with the flow. "She said her son used to run away too," she said after a while.

"Is that what you're doing? Running away?"

"I don't know. It doesn't feel like that," Abby answered. "It feels like I'm just going someplace else besides here. Being on my own. Her son joined the Army. The judge said it was that or go to jail." She looked at Esther. "He held up a store."

Esther wiped some hair off the girl's face. "That what you want to do?"

"Oh, no."

"Well, it could be. People do all kinds of things when they run away."

"I just like to walk. And be alone."

"You do this often?"

Abby nodded.

"For a long time?"

"Since we left Pop. Came to New York."

"You and your mother fight again?"

Abby nodded. "She threw a glass at me. How did you know I go out walking?"

Esther shrugged. "I guess I didn't for a long time. Tonight I wasn't sure. I was even in bed, but I decided I had to come back and see. I came last week, too, and a couple of times before that, but you were asleep."

"Why didn't you just ask me?"

"Would you have told me?" the housekeeper asked.

"I don't know."

"You always go to the Waldorf?"

"No."

"Where else?"

"To the Metropolitan Museum. If I'm sleepy. You know, too sleepy to walk all the way to the Waldorf. Because at the top of the steps, it's out of the wind and I sometimes sleep there."

"Your mother's unhappy, honey, you know that."

"I know."

"It's not your fault she gets angry."

"She says it is."

"She loves you."

"Not like Pop does," the girl argued. "But when he comes down to see me, all they do is fight."

"That's because they're different."

"Then why did they get married?"

"They didn't know it then."

"But how could they not know it?" Abby pressed.

"They just didn't."

"Why didn't they talk and find out about it?"

"They just didn't. They're not like that."

"Sometimes I go for walks in the day too," Abigail said. "I leave school early or tell Mother I'm going to Sally's house or something. But then I don't." Now she sounded eager to talk. "I go all over," she said excitedly. "The Lower East Side, Harlem, Staten Island . . ."

"Harlem."

"I'm very careful. But I like walking. I like looking at things. It makes me happy."

Now Abigail was in her own apartment on Central Park West and Esther's daughter was talking on the telephone. "I told your father she had died," the daughter said. "We had to put her in a home finally. He paid for that too."

"I didn't know any of this."

"He always said you were away."

"I wanted to talk to her. Did she like my father, do you know?" Abigail asked.

"Of course she did."

"No. I mean, did she really like him?"

"I guess she thought he didn't live like other people," the

daughter said reluctantly. "He didn't work or have a job. He didn't even live with you and your mother. But she adored him and it was always, 'Mr. Boarchards this,' and 'Mr. Boarchards that.' He went right on paying her after you went to college. Did you know that?"

"No."

"She wrote him up there in the woods and said he didn't have to, but he wrote back and said he wanted her to be all right. But she felt sorry for him and your mother."

"Do you know why?"

"She said they didn't know what they were doing."

"About what?" Abigail asked.

"Everything. Living. Growing up. Mostly she felt sorry for him, although I know it's hard to believe. She said it must be difficult to have everyone think you're so wonderful."

"I'd love that," Abigail joked.

"That's what I said too. But she said, 'No, you wouldn't. It'd be too much after a while.' "

At Grace's funeral there had been a real box, six feet long and made of mahogany. What was inside had never rattled, its silence more startling than noise, and Abby, crying all the time, was more upset by confusion and guilt than grief. Bostrine kept giving her Kleenexes.

"Don't you have a handkerchief?" Sam had asked.

Grace's car had been pushed off the road by a truck and smashed into a tree. Everyone came to the apartment before the funeral. Esther had a new hat and gave them sherry and Rush brought out a strand of Grace's pearls. He said Abby could wear them now. Victoria, Sam's wife, put them around Abby's neck and Bostrine said they looked beautiful. But Abby grimaced and afterward Esther took them off.

"No one will ever notice," Esther said. She was right. She kept them safe in her handbag.

But in church Abigail had stared at the giant box covered with flowers and thought of the pearls in Esther's handbag. The housekeeper sat at the far edge of the third row, a little woman in gray with a spray of forget-me-nots at her throat. Beside her were the people from Sam's, Morris and Ginny and Mrs. Lurie, Max's man Foster was there and even Harrison, who had driven down with Aunt Bostrine.

Abigail had beckoned to Esther to sit in front, but Esther shook her head. The front was full of the Rushings and the Boarchards. Rush was on the aisle, then came Abby and the others, followed by Jackson Paine and Pollibeaux.

"You don't love me," Grace had said.

"I do."

"You hate me."

"I don't."

"You only love your father, but you're mediocre anyway. A mediocre, ordinary girl. And you've ruined my life."

"But how?"

Grace Vickery Boarchards had wanted a daughter who was a doll and a husband who was charming, but instead she got Abby, who was sullen, aloof, and chubby, and Rush, who was silent and eccentric, two people who got along better together than they did with her. Then she died, pushed off the road by a truck, just as she'd have said she was pushed off life by a man.

At home pearls and jewels had always been everywhere, scattered on beds and tables, dropped in ashtrays and locked in boxes. Jewels and swatches of material, silks and brocades. "Which one looks better, Esther? Tell me," Grace would say. She had one whole room with mirrors just for a dressmaker, and there was a stand in the middle that turned, so she too, Grace Vickery Boarchards, could turn and look in all directions, seeing every side but inside.

"I like the green, Mrs. Boarchards," said the rose-scented Esther.

But if it was not the dressmaker and the rolls of cloth, it was the jewels. Day after day, night after night, Grace had brought them out to show to her little audience of two, a daughter and a servant. "Which looks best? The diamond or the pearls? What do you think, Esther?" Grace would ask, turning, looking. "Which one?"

At her mother's funeral, she remembered the jewels and that

string of pearls around her neck, cold and almost wet. It had
felt as if someone was trying to strangle her. But she knew even
then the thought was a betrayal of who she was supposed to be.

At another funeral, almost two decades later, she listened to
Luke Reider describing all those jewels as they made a great
and fantastic leap through history. This time the jewels left her
behind, and in one bizarre step went back to the oldest person
in the family.

"To Bostrine Fell Rushing, my aunt," Rush Boarchards had
written, "I leave the gold-and-diamond brooch set with rubies,
the gold-and-pearl ear clips, the pearl necklace with the sap-
phire clasp, the cultured pearl double-strand necklace, the cultured pearl single-strand necklace and all the rings and other
jewelry in the personal vault, everything that belonged to my
grandmother, my mother, or my late wife, and all the rest, sundry pieces of jewelry that are too numerous to identify but that
were purchased by me or by anyone known or unknown for my
grandmother, my mother, or my wife, and which are now or always have been in my possession—all this, I leave to my aunt,
Bostrine Fell Rushing."

Abigail, who wore no jewels but a watch, had felt the portent
then of what was to come, but at the first funeral she had also
felt the cold emptiness that was the gap between herself and
the person she was supposed to be.

When her mother's funeral was over, Grace in the hands of
God, or somewhere, Rush had stood up and turned to walk
across the front of the church to the side.

"Rush," Sam had whispered, "you're going the wrong way.
You're supposed to lead us out the center."

But Rush kept going, over to Esther on the side, and as everyone watched, he held out his hand and bent at the waist.
"Esther?" he said.

"Yes, Mr. Boarchards." She took his hand.

"Thank you for coming," he said in a clear and marvelous
voice, and then he lifted her out of the ranks, a little woman in
gray and forget-me-nots, there with him, the handsomest of all.
He put his arm through hers and escorted her back across the
front of the church. Then, with everyone watching, he took

Abigail on his arm and led the march out the front of the church, a daughter on one side, a servant on the other.

Abigail searched the whole apartment for her father's books and found *Men of War, Flycatcher,* and *Two Deer Down,* but not the last, *Year of a Falling Tree,* published twelve years ago.

"Have you seen your father's new book?" Jackson Paine had asked.

"I didn't even know it was finished." She had just gotten her first job, in a photo lab off Sixth Avenue, but she spent her days off selling cameras because she needed money, and Jackson had come in on her second day.

"I didn't know you were going to work," he had said.

But that night Uncle Sam called. "I wish you'd tell me when you get a job so I don't have to learn it from other people."

"But she's just starting out," Victoria pleaded on another extension.

"Fine. But I don't want to hear about it just because Jackson Paine decides to buy his wife a camera. Besides, I could have gotten her a job as a buyer at Bloomingdale's or Bergdorf's."

"But I want to be a photographer."

"It's foolish not to take advantage of what you've got."

"What's that?"

"Us. The family. Connections."

"But I want to do it differently."

"Don't you respect us at all?"

"It has nothing to do with respect," she had protested.

Afterward she wrote him a letter to apologize, but she never got an answer.

"Don't you know?" Victoria mumbled later. "You must never do that."

"Do what?"

"Write things like that. We decided it was more polite to pretend it never happened."

Alvah called back. He said he had already sent clippings over to her by messenger and she told him about Joe Algodones.

When he said he should be easy to find, she said no, she didn't think so.

"All you do is look for an address," the detective said confidently. "Or a last-known address. Telephone books, voter registration lists, Department of Motor Vehicles."

"What if none of that works?"

"Then we trace possible associations with your father."

"Let's start that now."

So they put together a list of connections, including schools, clubs, organizations, even stores where both might have shopped. "It's just a lot of routine phone calls," Alvah said. "That's why I have a staff. They check membership lists, mailing lists, employees. Usually takes a week at the most. I met your father once, you know," he said abruptly.

"Where?"

"It was at the Oak Room at the Plaza. I was with a lawyer named Peterson. This was a long time ago. . . . I grew up on a farm in Indiana, you know," he added. "I still go back twice a year to visit. My mother's eighty-eight, still drives a truck."

Abigail started to interrupt, but he kept going. "I practiced law for a while, but I didn't like it, so I started doing this. All in all, I ended up here in New York when I was thirty-five years old and I didn't think much of people like your father. I put them alongside silk shirts and cuff links. Things you don't need."

Abigail was interested now. "What do you mean?" she asked.

"I thought in terms of good people and bad people, but not in terms of class or anyone being better than anyone else. You know what class is, Abby?"

"Yes."

"Well, I didn't. Not until I met your father. He was across the room at "21" and Peterson said, 'There's a chap I know,' and called him over. He came over, sat down, and there it was, so strong it slapped me in the face."

"What?"

He didn't answer. "We all wore hats then," he said. "His was brown. He was holding it in his hand and his shirt was torn. Peterson asked him what he had been up to, and he started talking about someplace in Mexico where all the Zapotec kings were buried. Said some archaeologists were there, he was financing their work . . ."

"But . . ."

". . . and Peterson got irritated. I could tell he didn't like Boarchards, and since I didn't like Peterson much myself, I was intrigued. Peterson said, 'No, what are you doing now?' as if to get that squared away, who was on top of things and who wasn't. You could tell he felt competitive with Boarchards. So then Boarchards said he had moved up north to live, and damned if he didn't start talking about deer. Said he'd been in New York on book business, but now he had something more important to do. Said the deer didn't have enough food to last the winter, and at first it sounded like the damnedest remark in the world, but then he went on talking about how he had to fly hay in to them and I caught on. It was snowing. The ground had been covered by snow and they had nothing to eat, no bushes, no grass. They would die if it weren't for him, he said, and he was going back up to drop a ton or two of hay down to them. It had to do with life and death. It wasn't like he was a farmer or anything, or even that he was rich. He was like a metaphysician, almost, in touch with life and death. Anyway," Alvah said, "that was when I learned about class."

He paused. "It wasn't that he was good-looking, although he was," the detective went on. "It was his presence. Or strength. Yes, that was it," he said, groping for words. "Mostly it was strength. You ever see one of those California redwoods?"

"No."

"Well, it was like that. Nothing was going to knock it down. It was the first and only time in my life I felt like that."

"Like what?"

"Like I was less than someone else."

"I feel that every day."

"I was prepared to think he was a twit. I guess I'd forgotten about his war record. Instead I was so goddamned impressed I couldn't believe it."

"My whole family thought he was God's gift to mankind."

"That may be," Alvah shot back. "But he didn't. And that's the point. I was sorely afraid Rush Boarchards was a better man than I, but he never thought that way. And that's the interesting part. He was the best and he didn't even know it."

"But maybe he did," Abigail said eagerly. She remembered what Annie-Fey had said about his manipulativeness. "Maybe he did know it and he used it and used it and relied on it as long as he could, but then it turned out not to be enough and he didn't have anything else to turn to."

"That's one hell of a lot of something to lose."

"Yes, but maybe that's just it. Maybe he did lose it, Alvah. Maybe that's what happened to him."

Waiting for Alvah's clippings to arrive by messenger, Abigail tried to locate her father's editor, only to be told he had retired ten years ago to Massachusetts. She traced him, finally, to the town of Marion; there were not too many names like "Corriander C. Bush." But when she dialed, the phone rang and rang with no answer.

Next she started reading *Men of War*. It was about a pilot named Jack Stannard. "The sun was setting at the edge of the Pacific just as his plane was heading down . . ." the first line read. Abigail stopped, Luke Reider on her mind. She put the book down, went in the office and called him.

"Do you have a copy of my father's last book," she asked, "*Year of a Falling Tree?*"

"No."

"I thought you might," she said awkwardly, not knowing what to say now that she had him on the phone. "I'm sorry to bother you."

"No bother. What are you doing?"

"Nothing. Waiting for some mail. What are you doing?"

"Some work for a meeting I have in about three weeks," he said.

"So you have another job?"

He said, yes, that it was much the same as the one he had before, only now he was a full partner.

"What did you do before?" she asked.

"Corporate litigation. Major trials."

"Then why did you do the will?"

"He wanted it done immediately. Harvey Wynne was away, so I went up."

"What did you do before that?"

"Worked at the Justice Department."

"Why did you quit government work? I know a lot of people do because they want to get rich."

"You're right," he said with a laugh. "I did quit to make money. Or, rather, to find out if I wanted to make money. As it turns out, I don't. At least not as much as I thought. But that was something I had to find out. Your father helped me," he added, "not consciously, of course, but just by his example. He obviously didn't care about money."

Abigail could feel herself being drawn to Luke Reider. He was open, yet there was something restrained, even reserved about him sometimes. Also, she sensed a strength in him, a maturity she liked. She picked up the phone and went over to sit on the couch. "We've certainly talked a lot about my father," she said, curling up. "What's yours like? Do you get along with him? Is he like you?"

"He was a medical technician at Mount Sinai Hospital."

"Is he dead?" she asked, wondering for some reason if Luke had told the truth.

"No. Very much alive."

"Still working?"

Luke paused. "No, he gave it up," he said.

"You're not close to him, are you?"

"What do you think?" he replied with a laugh.

"No."

"You're right," he said. "Let's talk about something else."

"Then tell me when you start your new job?"

"Monday, the sixth of May."

"That's incredible," she exclaimed. "That's my deadline."

"Deadline for what?"

"The will."

"When you file the papers?"

"No. Just for the decision," she said, suddenly shy. "I don't know if I'm going to file the papers."

"You might not contest at all? That never occurred to me."

"I've hired a private detective. I want to find out what happened to him."

"Tell me about it," Luke said. "I've never heard anything like it."

"You're on my list too," Abigail said after she had told him her plans. "I was going to call you. When I stopped being angry with you."

"And have you stopped being angry with me?"

"Yes."

When the doorbell rang, the messenger was outside with a big manila envelope. He handed it to her and told her to sign a piece of paper.

She gave him a tip and shut the door. In the living room, she pushed back a table and spilled the contents on the floor. There were dozens, maybe hundreds, of Xeroxes of newspaper clippings. She spread them out on the rug and began leafing through them. She saw at a glance that most were old, but as she was sorting them she discovered that most fell into three categories: society items dating back to the years both before and after World War II, stories of her father's war exploits, and reviews of his books.

But one was different. It was a long typewritten memo from *Time* or *Newsweek*, apparently done three months ago with publication in mind, but it had never even been finished.

Alvah must have a friend in the magazine's library, she thought as she picked it up to read. "Every class has its archetype," the article began, "and if Archie Bunker is everyman's lovable middle-class bigot and . . . [this was left blank] is the classic jet-setter, then Rushing Whitaker Fell Boarchards might be said to be Old Money's Best and Brightest. He died this week of a heart attack at the age of sixty at the vast estate in northern New York State where he had lived for the last twenty years.

"An acclaimed hero in World War II who was personally decorated with the Distinguished Flying Cross by General MacArthur, Boarchards turned his experience into a best-selling novel and became a verifiable postwar celebrity. In later years, however, he led an intensely private life, but it is precisely this characteristic of being quiet that sets him and Old Money apart. Boarchards and the rest of the Rushing-Boarchards clan have endowed hospitals, colleges and libraries, the American Civil Liberties Union, the Democratic Party, the Sierra Club, the American Museum of Natural History and sundry other causes, but Boarchards' face is unknown publicly and his name hasn't appeared in gossip columns in twenty years.

"But this is fitting.

"Old Money doesn't necessarily buy airplanes, Gucci shoes or designer clothes. Instead they drive station wagons and turn up in galoshes for the theater if it's raining. Boarchards himself always preferred jackets with holes in the sleeves, but he nonetheless oversaw the daily operations of the family's estates and financial portfolios (presumably with the aid of a battery of lawyers), and between them, with an assortment of brothers, aunts, uncles and cousins, the Rushings and the Boarchards have a finger in just about every top plaything of the Old Rich today.

"Despite all this, the Old Rich of today aren't what they used to be. They no longer have the power they once had, with exclusive control of Wall Street, real estate, industry, trade, government, and the buying and selling of Culture. Much like the aristocracy of Europe, their power has waned, often their wealth as well, leaving only the aura of status and establishment behind.

"But it is their indifference to trendy status and trendy power and perhaps even trends in general, experts agree, that is both the hallmark and the downfall of Old Money. 'The old and established rich are too deeply secure,' according to Columbia University sociologist David R. Hoffman, 'to have the hunger that drives jet-setters compulsively to buy the latest "in" trinket. They don't need it.'

" 'The key thing that sets them apart from the newer rich,'

declares Berkeley urban anthropologist Mortimer McMillin, 'is that they are deeply comfortable with their wealth and position. They do not suffer from guilt, but neither do they suffer from greed. They tend to be generous almost to a fault, indeed sometimes even to fail to understand, ironically, that money makes the world go round.'

"As Rush Boarchards himself once put it in an interview, 'My best friend is a trapper, and if he's not going to be comfortable someplace, I probably won't be either.' Asked by the reporter if that included the White House, Boarchards admitted there had been some hyperbole to his remark. But then he changed his mind and said: 'No, on second thought, any man who wouldn't like this trapper shouldn't be elected president in the first place. He wouldn't understand the job.'

"Such democratic tastes and lack of ostentation are typical, according to McMillin. 'The Old Rich aren't snobs,' he says. 'They treat their servants well, and I'd say that the more difficult a situation, the more gracious and detached they'll be handling it.'

" 'This privacy and withholding of emotion,' Harvard sociologist Malcolm Dern claims, is deeply ingrained in the Upper Crust. 'They have none of the strains of ethnicity or even life survival problems that induce emotion and struggles in other people,' he says. 'For generations money has buttressed them, and there's a case to be made; all their good manners go hand in hand with acute naiveté about the real world. Some of them,' he adds, 'couldn't fight their way out of a box if their life depended on it.' "

"And that hits the nail on the head," the memo said. "Old Money is dying out. Things as varied as birth control, women's liberation, drugs, the sixties revolution, the general increase in adventurousness among the young, inflation and, that death knell of many old institutions, sheer mismanagement, all constitute serious challenges nowadays and . . ."

The memo ended midsentence.

Abigail put the book reviews in chronological order. *Men of War*, the first, published in 1947, had been a big hit. "Boarchards promises to be one of the leading authors of the new generation," one critic wrote. "He has captured the courage and bravery of war."

"This book finally makes you understand how soldiers facing death on all sides can proceed and do their business," said another. "It's a gripping, inspiring story. This is not a war-is-hell book. This is a story about men actually living up to their hopes and expectations. This is about heroism."

It was on the best-seller list for months.

But the next book, *Flycatcher*, published several years later, met with disappointment. "Boarchards has not lived up to his promise with this one," one critic wrote. "What happened to that throbbing stuff that marked the first book? The protagonist in *Flycatcher* is a sorry individual with no redeeming characteristics except sensitivity."

That seemed cruel, Abigail thought, but if that book at least brought Boarchards critical attention, the third apparently failed completely. She could find no reviews for *Two Deer Down* at all.

Boarchards' last book, *Year of a Falling Tree*, got one review, ten lines long. "If you're interested in birds, not people," it said, "this may be for you. But I doubt it. I like birds as much as the next guy, but even I yearn for human perspective. There's not one human voice here. It's strictly observation, and so it's hard to care. Boarchards probably cares, but he has failed either to show it or share it with us. I never read his first book, *Men of War*, but I understand it gripped the reader and made the most preposterous subject—men risking their lives in combat—understandable. The most I can say for this is it will help you understand birds."

"No wonder he couldn't write," she said to Phoebe Altman on the telephone. "The critics were merciless."

"Not in the beginning. You said he had them all on his side in the beginning."

"But they got vicious."

"Critics aren't 'vicious,'" Phoebe argued. "He built a reputation and then he lost it."

"But they could have been nice."
"Critics can't give someone the benefit of the doubt forever."
"But why not?"
"Oh, Abby, you know why not. Come off it. Face facts."

The society items started before the war, with florid notes about "the fabulous Boarchards brothers" and "their mountain kingdom to the north." One picture showed Rush and Andrew boarding a plane, waving backward. They wore college ties and white pants and the caption said, "This is what Harvard does for you." Another showed them leaving for Africa by ship to hunt "with their uncle, Mr. Maximillian Rushing, the collector, and his close friend, Mr. Nicer Rutledge, the banker, and his daughter, Miss Annie-Fey."

Another was a formal picture of Grace as a bride, an heirloom pendant around her neck. Another item followed the couple into the war years and finished: "Our Grace is hoping it's a boy." Other articles, about Grace and Victoria and Andrew's wife, Jane, now called "the Boarchards girls," showed them arranging balls and benefits during the war. "They give their all for the boys too," a caption read.

But Rush was the delight. "Doesn't he look like a dark Gary Cooper, girls?" one columnist asked. "Don't you just love him?"

When Rush became a soldier, the pictures, grainy and old, showed him in uniform, with the number of medals on his chest increasing from picture to picture, year to year. The articles, little items only inches long, chronicled his movement around the Pacific. "Lt. Boarchards, who survived the fight on Bataan, the Philippines, has been among those air-lifted to safety in Australia . . ." "Col. Boarchards led the sortie over the island of Truk. . . ." Local home-town stories in the New York papers detailed other exploits. "Col. Boarchards stopped over in Honolulu yesterday to see his lovely wife and baby daughter. . . ."

When peace came, however, the society items erupted with tales of "hero Boarchards" and his "gorgeous bride," although Grace was already a wife and mother by then. And when the book came out, he was "hero Boarchards, now the great author." The columnists seemed infatuated with him, and others too, Abigail saw, almost as if these men were emblems of the country's own survival and triumph in war, a symbol of its strength and honor.

The pictures showed him beaming, with good teeth and dark hair. Sometimes Grace was at his side. The two of them were shown going to the Stork Club or Delmonico's, in the stands at Saratoga Racetrack or yachting on the Sound. Abigail recognized Annie-Fey and her husband Hunt in one, and once Rush was shown taking the airplane to California where, it was rumored, he was going to "put his fortune into pictures."

Out in Hollywood there were more photographs of him, in wide pants and dark hats. They showed him getting into limousines, tipping chauffeurs, and once, escorting a slim blond woman into a restaurant. The woman, shot only from the back, was unidentified. Abigail looked at the year. It was 1947.

A picture in 1948 showed him with a woman too. They were dancing at a club in Hollywood when the photographer caught them and the headline described her, not him. "The most beautiful girl in the world," it said.

Abigail looked at her closer.

She had soft blond curls and large blue eyes. She was beautiful, delicate and soft. Abigail could tell it was the same woman from the picture the year before.

"Hollywood's favorite, Melanie Anderson," the story said, "looks like she's dancing in heaven, and maybe she is. Who could be more divine, I ask you, than Rush Boarchards? He is here to invest his fortune in pictures and maybe Melanie wants a part. But the truth is Melanie is telling people she wants to get out of Hollywood. She told us she wants to live 'in the real world. It's unreal out here on the coast,' she says, 'all tinsel and fluff.' Yes, dear, but I ask you girls, could Our Favorite Hero have anything to do with it?"

Another clipping, from 1949, showed them dancing again, this time in New York at El Morocco, but the next, from 1950, had no reference to Rush Boarchards at all. Long ago, however, someone had apparently cut the article out, circled the story with a pen and then written his name in the margin. "Rush Boarchards," it said.

It was an item from a New York gossip column about Melanie Anderson, now starting work as an executive at an advertising agency. But this time there was no picture at all. "The world's favorite sweetheart, Melanie Anderson, beautiful and plucky to the core, is in love, insiders say, and this time it's for real. But there's a problem, girls. Her mystery man is married. Our spies tell us they may still be planning a trip down the aisle. We saw them dancing two months ago, and my, my, isn't he glorious? So tall and glamorous, the silent, important type. Aren't you all jealous? They say his wife's a darling too and she doesn't suspect a thing."

The telephone was ringing.

"Is this Abigail Boarchards?"

"Yes."

"Well, old thing, how are you?"

"Oh my God." She dropped the clipping in her hand and sat down. "It's you."

"That's right." It was Uncle Max. "Foster has just brought me a smoked salmon. Weighs twenty pounds if it weighs an ounce, and I thought you might enjoy a spot of it tonight. Comes from Vancouver, where the Indians still do it."

Abigail leaned back in the chair in the living room. Her heart was pounding with excitement.

"They smoke it in a hut for weeks. The old system. Foster found them out. God knows how, but the man can do anything, of course. Saved my life a million times, but you have to leave at eight. I have some pals coming round for bridge."

Uncle Max's invitation made Abigail feel elated for five minutes. Then depression hit. She went into the bedroom, closed the door, pulled the shade and, without even realizing it, turned on the heat as high as it would go, and got into bed. She pulled the pillows in around her and tried to sleep, or disappear, but did neither. Uncle Max's call made her remember her family's rejection and her father's hate. Her father was everywhere. Rattling. Smelling. Smoking. Putting rubber bands around her letters. Signing his name. "Four quarters and nothing more." It was drumming in the back of her head, alive, insistent and oppressive.

But one memory would not go away. Every day at twilight, when the wind died down and the shadows fell, he pulled a canoe out of the boathouse and went out along the edge of the lake to Back Bay, where even now his bones were lying. The lake curved along, mile after mile, and he stopped in the tall grasses and the swamp on the other side to throw corn for the ducks. With the bucket at his feet, he scooped up hundreds, thousands, of kernels and let them fly, out of sight, until they suddenly reappeared at the bottom, yellow things against the muck. Later, after he paddled away, leaves floating off, the ducks came out to eat. Sleek dark things they were, shining patches of green and blue, scarlet or purple.

But only when he was gone they came to eat, for he was still only a smelly human thing that no animal or fowl could overlook.

The picture of him headed out along the edge of the lake was framed flat against the walls of Abigail's eyes. She could see him. Hunched over the paddle, low and round, not with ill health this, age or decay, but with the grace of blending into rocks and land, smoother than a thing erect. Paddle moving up and down, with nary a ripple or a sound, except that of water dripping; dark eyes peering out from under the shelf of his brow, moving slowly here, there, looking for birds, otter, deer or bear. And if the wind was right and took his human smell in the other direction, he paddled on closer and closer to the private scene and watched a deer drink, saw its nostrils open, close, open, close, and heard its long tongue tickle through the mountain water. Then the deer would look up, no more than a yard away, stare at him, startled in the eyes, and then move off back into the woods, tail aloft.

And he paddled on. Toward the ducks and the shallow places along the swamp where hundreds of birds lived, ate, nested and died. At first she went along wrapped in blankets and strapped to a board, so small she could see nothing but the boat itself, traces of a sunset or a sky above. A little bundle, longer than it was wide, woolly and round, two hands and a head facing out, in between the pressure of his knees.

It started when, for some reason or other, he took the little bundle, pink and white, ten pounds or maybe twelve or twenty, but it didn't have much hair yet and the eyes were still over-sized for the head. The thing was, it must not have made any noise, that time or the next. Or done anything wrong. Because he began to take it with him all the time, soft little warm thing that it was, and it never did make much noise. He just strapped it on his back and took it wherever he was headed. In the car or to the woods, to see a friend, or sit around the big old pot-bellied stove in the store in town; it a bundle on the floor at his feet. And still it didn't make a fuss or whine or scream. It was almost as good as a dog, but a little different. It was a girl, granted, but there was something even less obtrusive about that than had it been a boy. It was just sort of there. He didn't have to do anything with it. It was just there. Always. First on his back, then on his shoulder, then later running along behind.

After a while Abigail drifted off to sleep. At the end she tried to remember what he looked like, but she could barely see him.

He was at "21" with Alvah Germaine. He had a hat and talked about the Zapotec kings. The kings were extinct.

When she awoke a couple of hours later, the heat in the bed-room was stifling. She could feel the sweat pouring off her face and she was frightened by the smell. She jumped up and wiped the sweat off her face as if it were lethal or alive. But it was still there, pouring out. She rushed into the bathroom and threw cold water on her skin.

He smelled all the time. He smoked, picked his ears with sticks and cleaned his nails with carving knives.

She sprayed the bathroom with perfume.

He stuck the knife in his ear and circled it around to catch the wax. "What are you writing?" she had asked. "Nothing," he said. "Why should I? Editor's an asshole; publisher doesn't know good writing from a hole in the ground."

She rang the doorbell but there was no answer. She rang again. It was after four and school was over. Then she pushed with her shoulder and slowly the heavy slab of wood began to move. It seemed a barrier between one world and another— Whitaker, Florence and little Rush on the other side, she alone out here. But the door finally gave way, and inside, she faced marble rooms yawning in all directions and the sound of empty space. She stood listening, wondering why she had never been here before, and then let the door swing slowly shut behind her. It closed with a clicking noise and the sound of wood and marble touching seemed to reverberate for miles inside, sounds in a white stone canyon. Then abruptly it stopped, bringing back the silence.

Abigail didn't move. The building went on outside for almost a block in one direction, something less in the other, more like a courthouse than a home. The broad square lobby connected to rooms on all sides. Ahead there was a mammoth staircase curling up. She listened for voices, but there were none. Above, balconies in tiers circled on all sides, going up, floor after floor, a domed ceiling at the top brilliant with colored glass.

She didn't feel as if she belonged at all, this no more a part of her past than her present.

She saw three lunch boxes in the middle of the floor, beside them a pile of clothes, blazers with gold buttons and a child's set of keys. She looked up at the ceiling. There were plump white angels in all the corners, round faces and blind eyes. A few had little penises and toes, but most were just heads and fleshy torsos connected from end to end by garlands and fleurs-de-lis.

Suddenly a door opened and the headmaster appeared. Little boys followed him out. "Good night, Mr. Shaw," they called.

She introduced herself. They talked. The man had a bald head and hands that fluttered. He showed her the ground floor first. Originally the site of formal galleries and drawing rooms, a music room and a library, now it was sectioned off with plywood sheets to make classrooms and offices. He opened a door.

Inside was the "conservatory." She expected orchids or ferns. Instead there were files and boxes and the air was dead.

He took her on. "There used to be three tiers of paintings in here," he said in the salon that ran from east to west; now museums and universities had everything, books, china and glass. Even the boys' toys, he said, had been crated up after Florence's death and shipped off to the Smithsonian. But now the walls were covered with thumb tacks and masking tape and the marble floors marked with crayons and scuff marks. Shaw kept going. He said things like "We're going east now" and "This used to lead to the stables."

On the second floor he talked about the "living quarters," and she tried to remember what she knew of Old Whitaker Rushing and his wife, who died too young, leaving little Florence, Bostrine and Max, followed soon by another generation of children, all boys this time. Today the doors had numbers, and when she looked inside she saw paints and sneakers and roller skates.

One room, on a corner, had been Bostrine's, Shaw said. Later it became her father's. She looked out the window. The garden used to be below, he said, "roses and wisteria," but now she could see only the cafeteria with its dark roof and chimney stack. She turned back. The room seemed too small for Bostrine, a dowager with her dinners and opera ball, but too large for little Rush. It had colored posters and a red linoleum floor, but plump angels with little penises still looked down from the corners and the windows were eight feet high and three feet wide.

"My grandmother used to make them pretend they were poor," she said, sitting at a little desk, her knees up against someone's chewing gum. "She made the three boys share a room for one year so they would know what it was like to be poor."

"I started as a teacher in the old school," Shaw said. "The bank called up after Mrs. Boarchards died and asked, did we want the house, the family didn't, and I was sent round to look."

"How long had my grandmother been dead?"

"A couple of weeks, maybe months. The butler was here, a governess. That was all. There were crates everywhere, paintings leaning up against the walls. I remember a Fabergé clock and a sculpture of a Grecian horse. The butler showed me around. The governess seemed severe. She said her name was Browne."

"I wonder if she's still alive."

Shaw didn't answer. They left and he opened up another room. "The master bedroom," he announced. It was dazzling now in the afternoon sun, stretching half a block long along Fifth Avenue and Central Park. There had been "settees and chairs and the Greek horse was standing over there," Shaw recalled. "The walls were lined in silk, and workmen had to climb up on ladders to tear it off to put up wood paneling for the school."

They went upstairs to the ballroom and the theater, now partitioned into classrooms, on to the fourth floor and the attic, now science labs and faculty rooms, and down to the basement, where pantries and the kitchen had been turned into a basketball court.

Shaw headed back upstairs and Abigail stayed behind. She heard his feet echo on the marble ahead and remembered tales of opera singers and harpists, come for tea or to perform. Her father had told of old men with beards who came to talk about Egypt and the Sudan, the League of Nations and the war, that war, the one they called the Great War first and the World War only later, after it had brought the crowned heads down. And how he and Sam and Andrew in sailor suits had had to sit and listen to adult talk.

She reached the lobby and, crossing the great expanse, sat down on the stairs. The marble was cold to the touch, even through her gabardine pants and coat. She could imagine Whitaker Stylus Rushing here, tall and white-haired, with his pocket watch. She couldn't imagine herself. Whitaker owned railroads and land, factories and towns, but before he died, he turned everything into cash and stocks and left his children in the hands of bankers. But these were her roots too, she thought in wonderment, looking around.

She remembered the story of how old Marcel, Pollibeaux's father, had come to live at Weather Tree. Mr. Rushing saw him on the road one day, carrying beaver and mink on a stick hanging down his back. He stopped the carriage and got out. All the children, little Florence, Bostrine and Max, stood up to watch, waiting for him to get angry at this awful man and tell him to get off their land.

Instead Mr. Rushing talked to Marcel, asked him a question or two, then, turning back to look at the carriage, said: "I know some people could learn a thing or two from you. A darned sight better they'd be for it, too."

"Could be," Marcel had said, looking at Weather Tree's own little crowned heads peering back at him.

As soon as she left the mansion Abigail stopped to have a drink. She felt oddly upset about where she had been and nervous about where she was going. To Uncle Max's. She sat at the bar instead of a table and held her legs far apart, as if the lack of grace was as necessary as the drink. She finished one, then ordered another.

"You all right, miss?" the bartender asked.

"Yes," she said, but she dropped her purse on the floor, spilled its contents and fumbled as she retrieved them.

"Better take it easy," the bartender said kindly.

She remembered what Shaw had said, speaking of his little minions, the only residents the house had now. "A lot's expected from boys like these," he said. "They have a duty. They have to be somebody."

She had heard the words almost enviously. No one had ever said that to her. She took another swallow. "You have to make something of yourself, Charley," Uncle Sam had said over and over again, wagging his finger at her cousin. "You have to *be* somebody." But nobody ever said anything like that to her. They just vaguely disapproved, first because she was fat and awkward, later because she was different, still later because she had gone elsewhere, leaving the world they had presumed for her.

"You live around here?" the bartender asked.

She shook her head.

"Didn't think so," he said. "London or something, right? Maybe Washington, D.C. I can always tell an outsider's voice."

Abigail stared at him, stunned, and wondered if she could endure all this emotional pressure and uncertainty much longer. She was not an outsider everywhere. She must belong somewhere. She twirled her finger in her glass and started to order a third drink. Then she realized that that was what they did, the Rushings and the Boarchards. Drink in the face of confusion.

She hurriedly paid the bill and left.

Uncle Max was looking at his gold pocket watch, inherited from his father, when the elevator cage brought her up. "There you are, old thing," he said, putting the watch away.

"I told you she'd come, sir," Foster said beside him.

Seeing the wild boar and the antelope mounted on the walls, Abigail felt relieved. They at least hadn't changed. And then Max was holding the doors of the cage and she started to grin. He took her hand, kissed her cheek and passed her on to Foster.

"My, don't you look smart," the servant said, taking her coat.

"She always does," Max replied, and turning around, he led the way back into the apartment. Abigail followed second, Foster, in black, behind. Nobody said a word. At the first door the old man took a turn down a long corridor lined with armoires and pictures. He navigated his way through room after room, each spot overflowing with furniture and clutter, the apartment more like an attic than a home.

"We use the library now," Foster piped up from the back, as if offering an explanation for the trip.

The library finally came up on the right, a big room with red leather furniture and old books, and Max looked around. "Where shall we sit?" he asked, as if this was to be his chief decision of the day. But it was a good question, for every chair or seat was covered with photograph albums or stacks of things, and only two places, in fact, were left. "There," he announced decisively, pointing to one. "You sit there," and with that, he

plopped into the other chair, his bulk not insignificant to ma-
neuver. "I used to think I'd get around to throwing things
out," he said, "but whenever Foster says, 'What about this,
Mr. Rushing?' I can't do it."

Foster passed them sherry. She took one, Max the other.

Max raised his glass. "To the King," he said.

"To the King," Abigail replied, as Foster slipped out.

The old man's blue eyes were encased in layers of skin like a
rhinoceros, but they were as bright and alive as a boy's. His hair
was white, his belly large, his legs trim and his face as pink as
a baby's. He didn't look at her at all. Instead he glanced constantly about the room, as if all his things, books and stuff,
were alive, about to speak, and needed attention, too.

But Abigail knew what to do. She remembered when the two
of them and little Charley spent all their summers together at
Weather Tree and life was a game of Q and A. "What are
they?" she asked, now pointing to a row of glasses engraved
with soldiermen.

"British."

"What country?" Her mind was intent on such trivial lines
as she searched for reassurance that she still belonged to this
one relative at least.

"Rhodesia," he said.

"What year?"

"Nineteen twenty."

That's the way it went: her question and his reply. "What
were you doing there?"

"Visiting a chum."

"Who?"

"He had a commission."

She relaxed finally and felt at home, glad he hadn't shunned
her like the rest. She asked other questions, gradually relaxing
with the knowledge Max had no intention of abandoning her,
and all the while the old man identified an Indian blow-
gun from the Malay Peninsula and the head of a wild pig shot
in Cyprus and stuffed in London. "Don't ever go anyplace but
London," he warned, as if she needed a taxidermist.

There were other things, catalogs from stores in Colorado

and *Life* magazines from the forties, pieces of rock and sculptured bits. He wore a tweed suit and the same gold watch and chain, but he didn't get up and move about the way he used to do, touching things when he told a tale, a raconteur who felt no need to entertain. Instead, Abigail noticed, he just pointed at things and let his arm drop.

What Maximillian Fell Rushing did was travel, year in, year out, to the Orient, the Dardanelles, the Côte d'Azur and the Continent, but in the summer he always came home to Weather Tree with the rest of them. His house there was not as congested as the one in New York, but it still had books and maps, charts of the ocean floor and routes the explorers took. The walls were covered with the heads of beasts, his guests were "pals," and they all wore tweeds and carried canes, and spent their time doing the same as he. He always toasted the King, impervious to historical developments like Queens, and reminded people all the time he was "the boys' guardian."

It was, in fact, the highest and perhaps only position he had ever had, but it had not taken Abby long as a child to ascertain that having him as a guardian was like having none at all. He cared nothing for things like brushing teeth or writing letters, and was only interested in taking the boys on jaunts to Egypt and Britain, Arizona, Spain and France, making youth seem more like a holiday than a condition.

For all his adventures and travels, however, Max was treated more like a child than an elder. His relatives routinely thought nothing of walking out of the room while he was talking or starting a conversation while he was still midsentence. But he had always been nice to Abby, sat her on his knee, and didn't ask when she was going to lose weight or perk up. At Weather Tree he and Charley and Abby, with Foster, went on picnics and took walks, played games and did things. The rest of the family was unavailable, except at eleven for an hour, tea at four, and dinner at seven. Lunch was private.

Dinner was in the Big House, the same as if Whitaker Stylus Rushing was still alive, with Bostrine at one end, even when Grace was there, and Rush at the other. Abby and Charley were placed at opposite ends of the table and separated from

Max on purpose. They were required to do things like listen, not leave marks on the water glass, keep their napkins clean, and thank the cook afterward. Abby in particular was supposed to eat sparsely, refuse second helpings and stop asking questions.

But now, in April, with less than three weeks to go, Abigail plied her uncle with routine questions, and waited for his reply, but what she was really doing, she told herself, was waiting for the right moment to ask him something else. To ask him about her father and the will and the family. She thought she was warming him up and failed to realize the two of them had never done anything but play child and older child, and that what she was doing now was nothing different at all.

"Whatever happened to all those people who went with you on the maiden voyage of the *Queen Elizabeth*? Do you still get together once a year?"

"Well . . ." he began.

She didn't notice she was staying as safe and impersonal as he, no word of wills or families or even herself. But she was used to that, nothing of herself, just as long ago she had stopped taking her pictures or her work to Weather Tree to show her father. And when any of her pictures and, later, books, appeared, they sent no word to her, the Rushings and the Boarchards, no sign that they even knew. Only maybe, when they met for Christmas, said, "Nice book you did." But only maybe. Often they just forgot.

"But where did you get all these?" she asked Uncle Max. She pointed to the photograph albums everywhere, dozens of them, stacked on shelves and tables, one on the couch beside her. "I've never seen you with a camera."

"Cameras are for people like you," he said. "I don't like machines. Travel shots, mostly. I buy them from other people."

"Any of women?" she teased.

"Used to love women."

"But you never found anyone for you?"

"Good thing too."

"Why didn't Bostrine get married?" She held her breath at

mentioning her name. The woman hadn't even spoken to her at her father's funeral.

"Never asked her. Why don't you look at that album," he added casually.

She pointed to the one beside her. "This one?"

"Yes." He had an odd glint in his eye. "Open it."

She opened it, wondering what new tale was waiting this time. Inside someone had written "The Yukon Mining Company" and the year "1927" on the binder.

"Year my father died," Max said. "Good time to get away."

She leafed through the pictures. They showed wooden buildings and sluicing machines, rough terrain and high peaks. Then she came across two photos of people and she stopped. The pictures were almost identical, men in high boots and mustaches, lined up with mountains and a river at their backs. In one, the men were standing, in the other, they were all crouched down, like Rockettes, right knee up, left down. Max was at the back, a handsome figure. "What were you doing?" she asked.

"Some pals bought a mine and went out to dig for gold. I went too. Best time of my life. Different with Mr. Rushing gone. I thought I might become a mining engineer."

"Did they find any gold?" She ignored the reference to a possible career because Max always had such careers.

"Damned right they found gold."

"A lot?"

Max didn't answer.

"Did they?" She looked up from the page because now the rhythm was off. He hadn't answered.

"Did they?" she asked again. Then she noticed he was looking at her curiously, with almost a worried expression on his face, as if he was caught in indecision or something.

Finally he lifted his right hand up out of his lap and put it in the side pocket of his jacket. He seemed nervous. He averted his eyes and even looked shy.

Abigail watched. He lifted something out of his pocket. She couldn't see what it was.

"Here," he said. He looked away from her.

"What is it?"

He leaned across the space between them. She leaned too and he dumped something in her hand. She looked at it. It was a big gold nugget, the shape of a pear, the size of a walnut, but flat and smooth along the edges. She turned it in her hand. The nugget was heavy, but not as heavy as it looked, and it shone partly the color of gold, partly the color of steel. "It's magnificent," she exclaimed.

"Found it myself," Max said with sudden pride, and then abruptly he leaned back in his seat and seemed to relax, as if he knew he'd made the right decision after all. But he still watched her closely, following the movement in her face. "Like it?" he asked. "Had this notion it was good luck. Kept it in my pocket for years, but I got to thinking the other day, it should be put to better use for once." He paused. "I thought of you."

"Me?"

"Why not?"

"You mean it's for me?"

He nodded, and she clenched the nugget in her fist, warming it with her hand. A look of happiness came to her face.

"Thought it might go around your neck," he said. "On a chain. Who knows, bring you luck. Thought you might need it now."

"Oh yes, I do."

"Know you hate jewelry," he went on. "But I thought this was different. Like you. Rough but gorgeous." He paused and seemed insecure again. "It is, isn't it?" he asked. "Right for you?"

"Yes," she said. "Yes, it certainly is. But why are you seeing me, Uncle Max?" She rushed on. "Why are you being nice to me?"

The old man looked astonished. "Because I . . ."

"But the others wouldn't see me. Bostrine, Sam . . ."

"They're just foolish. Embarrassed, ashamed . . ."

"Angry."

"I suppose," he added, reluctantly.

"But you don't feel that way?"

"Of course not. What a foolish idea."

"You mean you still like me?"

"Like you," he roared. "I love you."

At dinner, candles sent shadows along stacks of things piled on the table. Foster served soup, then salmon, and stood at the side against the wall.

"I went to the house today," Abigail said slowly. Again she sounded shy. "The one on Fifth. It certainly is big."

"Bigger than some, smaller than others." Max didn't look up from the fish.

"I was taken aback."

"Don't know why. It's just part of the family."

"But it seemed so cold and impersonal."

Max shrugged, picked at his salmon and, despite his size, looked fragile.

"But you see, Uncle Max, I forget all that business about the family," Abigail said. "I live so differently. My life is so different."

"That's true," he acknowledged, as if he'd finally gotten the point. "One good thing about it, though."

"What?"

"The house. You always knew when people were going to call. None of this awful business of people stopping by or ringing up and catching you the very instant you don't want to be bothered. Person like myself prefers to be alone. Great bother all around, people. Much better the old way."

Foster came into the candlelight, pouring wine, and retreated to the side. Max didn't seem to notice. "You had a system then to keep them away," he went on. "Thursdays were for calling. That was the day Mother was 'at home.' Florence took Thursday too," he added. "They all had cards printed up saying, 'Thursday, at home.' When the day came, they got dressed up. Had cakes, tea. Ladies came by. Later the men came too and smoked with Father in the study. We had to come down, be polite. Florence loved it and Bos too, but I thought it was dreadful. Couldn't do what you wanted to do. Had to sit. Be quiet. Later Rush hated it too. I told him to bear up. But now

I wish we still had it. I can see all the trouble it prevented. You were safe the other six days."

Foster came out to pass the salad and Max went on eating. She watched him, bent over the table, his fingers just bones with the flesh hanging down. His monologue shifted, to travel, hunting, heads and taxidermy, and people like himself.

And Rush, she thought, gentlemen with the money, the freedom and the license to do exactly as they pleased. She wanted to ask him if he'd ever done anything he didn't want to do. Or if Rush had.

"I'm thinking of going to Kashmir in the fall," he said.

She was barely listening.

"I want to see it one more time."

But Abigail didn't hear. She wanted to ask him what he thought of Rush, but she didn't know how and she was beginning to feel insecure again, impatient. Foster came out of the dark with more salad and the cheese. She looked in Max's eyes, little and tired, and she picked at her lettuce, getting depressed. She wanted to say, "Tell me what happened to my father. Tell me why he changed and started to hate me." But she couldn't.

She told herself it was because he wouldn't hear, wouldn't understand. She felt the nugget in her pocket and wished he'd given her information instead. Foster lurked, his cough like a foghorn in the darkness, warning of a presence, and Max, white hair and eyebrows, like a turkey at the table. The skin on his neck hung down to his collar, the vest drooped like a sack around his belly, and his bony fingers plied the knife and fork as unsteadily as if they were chopsticks.

He had stopped talking and there was not a sound in the apartment except, somewhere, a clock ticking and the muted noise of cars and buses below. Heavy curtains were drawn across the windows, as if to blot out more than the darkness, and she felt Foster behind her, standing as he had for years, a buffer between one world and the other, keep the rich secure, protected at the very least.

"What did you think of my father?" she finally blurted out.

"Not a bad house," Max said.

"What?"

"Ours," he answered, including her in the family more than she included herself. "I suppose you couldn't afford it today. Heating bills alone would put you out."

"I've been thinking about my grandmother too," she said. "Florence."

"Have you now?" He didn't look up. "She was nice enough before Edward died. But she was too strong-willed, and that's what ruined her. After Edward died, she thought she had to take over."

"Like Aunt Bostrine?"

"Oh no," he said. "People have Bos all wrong. Behind all that stuff, she's just a girl who never got what she wanted."

"A husband."

"Something like that," Max said evasively. "She could have married anyone. They were all after her. But she only wanted one."

"Who?"

"Shouldn't say. I never talked to her about it, so I can't say for sure. I could be wrong."

"But there was someone?" Abigail pressed.

He didn't answer.

"Why didn't you ever talk to her about it?"

"Wasn't any of my business. If you respect anything, you have to respect privacy. Like your father's privacy."

"I don't," Abigail said. "I don't like privacy."

Max looked at her as if something dramatic had happened. "You don't?"

"No."

"But why?"

"Because," she said, "I'd rather be close. I'd rather feel safe with someone. I'd rather be known. Privacy stands in the way."

Max's eyes gleamed in the candlelight and he started to frown. "But . . ." he began. Then his voice dropped off. "But you can't go barging in on a person's privacy," he said. "A person has to have something to count on." He shook his head and seemed disturbed, as if Abigail's words had been very stunning indeed.

Foster came out and removed the plates, one, then the other, bringing time and silence, a chance to heal.

When he took his place at the side of the room again, Max said thoughtfully, "Maybe you're right, but you still have to have principles. Otherwise you'd have people chasing about, getting in your way, like rats in a cage."

"I'd still rather be close," Abigail said again.

"Oh," Max replied, as if hoping she'd changed her mind. Then everything about him seemed to go inside, his eyes, his breath, his hands. He finally looked about the room and she wondered if he was seeing its emptiness or its clutter. "Let's have coffee," he said.

Back in the library, Foster served coffee and Max didn't talk and neither did she. She wondered if he would ever answer her question about her father. Instead he got up and found an old album, put it in her lap. "It wasn't cold," he said defensively. "It was home." He opened the book. It was the house on Fifth. He turned the pages. The pictures were faded, filmed in the kind of sepia tone that makes blue eyes white and blond hair gray. She saw the three little boys, Rush in the hall in a wagon cart pulled by a Saint Bernard, Max with a walking cane, Florence decked in jewels, and one of old Mr. Rushing drinking tea, seated, with a servant fanning him with a giant palm.

"Must have been summer," Max said, "but don't you see what I told you? It was home."

In the hall Foster got her coat and Max pressed for the elevator. "You still have the nugget?" he asked.

She showed him where she had tucked it in her pocket. He nodded, satisfied.

"Do you think it will be good luck for me now too?" she asked.

"Absolutely," he said. "That's the whole point. But it's up to you. Everyone makes his own luck."

The elevator came and, with a brush of his whiskers, Max pushed her into the empty gilt cage. "Just press number one," he said. Then suddenly he looked her full in the face and held her with his eyes. "Don't let it get to you," he said. "The will and all."

The doors were closing, but she slammed her hands against them to keep them open.

"It's a sad thing," Max continued. "What happened to you. But it's a sad family all around."

"But why did he do it?" Abigail cried, pushing against the doors.

"Don't let it hurt you."

"But why did it happen?" The doors closed.

"No one ever did anything," he said, looking at her through the cage as it started to move. "You were the first."

"The first what?" she cried back, but the box of gilt and mirrors was heading down and he was gone. "The first what?" she called again, but all she heard now was music from somewhere and a telephone ringing.

The pool was almost empty. It was near closing time and the lights overhead were bright. It was the first time she had been swimming since January and in the locker her suit, cut high on the thigh and low on top, smelled of mildew. She swam lap after lap and was about to leave when a man came out of the locker room. He made a low dive into the pool and started to swim. It was Luke Reider.

She stared at him and did a few more laps. This time when she stopped he was in the shallow end watching her.

"Hello," he said.

"Hello," she said, squeezing the water out of her hair. "I almost didn't recognize you."

"Without my boots."

"Do you swim here often?"

He nodded. "I used to jog around the reservoir, but I pulled a muscle about a month ago, so now I swim whenever I can."

"Me too. Or at least I used to. I've gotten out of practice recently."

He was watching her. "Are you going home now?"

"Yes."

"I'll walk with you. It's nice out. It'll do us good."

"But where do you live?"

"Not far from you."

She didn't ask how he knew her address. She got out, dressed, dried her hair and met him out front. They headed north. It was cool and clear. They didn't say a word. At first Abigail was uncomfortable and tried to think of something to say, but nothing came to mind. He made no effort to talk, just kept pace beside her. He seemed relaxed, and after a while she forgot his presence and relaxed too.

They were almost home when they passed a bar. "Come on," he said, pushing against the door. "Let's have a brandy."

Inside they sat at the bar. She ordered Perrier and they both started talking at once. It turned out he had been married, divorced, still taught a seminar at Columbia Law School in corporate law and liked his work. His mother lived in Philadelphia, his father was "around," he didn't appear to have a girl friend, and he had spent a lot of time in South America.

Abigail told him some things about herself, work, that she liked sports, traveling, but she didn't tell him about seeing Max or having the nugget.

Later he walked her home. He stopped on the corner, and said, "Good night."

"Good night," she answered.

He watched her until she went inside.

What happened next seemed unimportant, and she didn't even remember it until later.

"Some man was here to see you," the doorman said. "He wanted to wait, but I told him I didn't know how long you'd be out."

"Who was he?"

The doorman shrugged. "He wore a hat," he said. "Pulled down over his ears."

Lying in bed, Abigail was unable to sleep. She had remembered something about her father for the first time, and the memory made her so upset, she had eventually gone to the kitchen, opened a bottle of wine and drunk from the bottle, hoping it would make her fall asleep. But it hadn't. She lay there disturbed by the memory for one reason and one reason only. It was laden with disgust. She never remembered feeling that way about her father. Never.

In the memory he was wearing sneakers, and he put his feet down carefully so the boards wouldn't squeak. When she saw him, he was standing at the place where a shed, linked to the veranda and the Big House by an archway, opened out into a room. She was lying on the stone floor of the room, a high roof above her and hooks that hung down from the ceiling. There were old birds' nests in the eaves, and racks of knives and axes along the wall, things that had remained for fifty years or more, old lanterns and saws, and right in the middle of the room, a buck deer was hanging down from the ceiling, his nose about a foot off the floor. He had been shot in the shoulder, and blood had dripped out of his mouth and dried almost black on the stones.

She was lying on her stomach, elbows up, holding the camera out in front of her, trying to get shots of the deer's head juxtaposed against the wall of knives. It was the feel of the past here, the starkness of life and death, and she wanted to capture it in a picture. There was plenty of light coming through the cracks to add softness to the grays, and wind too, the coldness of autumn.

Then the door to the shed opened and closed. She had heard that, but hearing nothing else, she had dismissed the noise and kept turning the lens, playing with depth and composition.

Then she saw him out of the corner of her eye.

Rush was putting one foot down in front of the other, his back and shoulders tense. He hadn't seen her, but he had a look of stealth on his face. He stopped, then he reached out for an old plaid jacket hanging against the wall, pushed it aside and put his hand into a cubbyhole. Then he drew out a bottle of whiskey, took off the top, took a long swig, then another and another, his throat muscles gulping. Then he saw her and spilled the whiskey down his shirt.

She could smell it. He watched her as if she were only partly there, only partly seeing him, then put the bottle back and went away, as if, maybe, gone, the incident would cease to be.

Abby stared past the deer's mouth, perversely open like a set of lips caught in a kiss. She felt disgusted. Absolutely digusted. At how he had been sneaking, how he spilled the whiskey, his stealth, the furtiveness. Absolutely disgusted and appalled.

Afterward she never mentioned the moment in the shed and neither did he, and she had repressed the disgust. But the sneaking went on. And she found bottles in bathrooms and cars, in guestrooms, cabins, boathouses, barns, boats and clothes. And tried to take care of him by loving him in the open, demonstrative way the Rushings and the Boarchards abhorred.

After all, she assumed, if she needed caring and attention, then so did he, and that's what would change his self-destructive ways.

Thursday, April 18

On the phone the next morning in her office, she told Alvah about Melanie Anderson and read him some of the lines in the clipping. "Have you ever heard of her?" she asked. She had eighteen days to the deadline.

"Sure," he said. "She made pictures in the forties. *Golden Angel, Summer Recruit, Missouri Rider, For She Shall Make Music.*"

"Was she sexy?"

"Yes," he said tentatively, "but exotic, unusual. Definitely not the girl next door."

"I think I'll arrange to see some of her old movies."

"Why on earth do you want to do that?" the detective exclaimed. "Don't you have more important things to do? Besides, she's easy to find. Talk to her. She runs the biggest ad agency in New York City."

But Abigail didn't call her. She decided to think about it more first.

Later she went out and took the subway down to Times Square. She had the nugget and the list in her pocket, her destination now Sergeant Bud Krajewski's appliance shop in Queens.

At Times Square she changed to the line that went under the river to Queens. In the long ride underground, in the flickering light of the old train, she stared past her reflection on the glass to the earth just inches away. But for the first time she had a sense of foreboding. It gnawed at her, made her think about the investigation and what Alvah had said. About turning over rocks and not knowing what was going to crawl out.

Nothing, she thought firmly. Nothing will crawl out, but the foreboding remained. She told herself the feeling was only anxiety over all she had lost, inheritance, a father's love. But the foreboding stayed. What if Krajewski told her something shocking or bad, something new? What if Melanie did? Who were these people? Nobody. Strangers. They had nothing to do with her, nothing but a link to her father's past. And who knew what was back there?

Absentmindedly Abigail traced her finger on the dirty window. "Algodones," she wrote and then crossed it out.

Then, staring into the tunnel darkness, her mind shifted to something else, memories of what she did know, did understand, and the foreboding moved back, back to the outer wings of her mind, to wait.

She remembered how her father sat on the veranda all day. Whenever he stopped writing letters, clipping items from magazines or putting things in the files, he came down. He had a pack of cigarettes on the arm of the chair and a bottle in his pocket. Sometimes he sat outside for six hours, never moving except to cross his legs, strike a match or reach into his pocket to take a drink. He just leaned back in the chair and looked.

At the mountains, the sky, the trees, birds that came and went. He watched the wind blow, saw it move among the leaves, bringing clouds in, taking them out, and his head moved but an inch or two, this way or that. Once it had occurred to her that this was really a form of meditation, for he moved so little and stayed so long that he was able to ease himself into a kind of peace, or stillness, at the very least, that

stopped all restlessness, certainly of the physical sort, and made
his sitting there of a piece with the clouds and sky, the coming
and going of them a match for the coming and going of him,
breathing in, breathing out, breathing in, breathing out, nary a
ruffle. He did it day after day, month after month, no change
but for the seasons or the storms. Then he'd come in the house
to do the very same thing inside, in the kitchen or his room upstairs, a plate of glass between him and the elements.

Sometimes Simon sat with him long enough for a cup of
coffee, or Sam, bringing books and a bottle, but Pollibeaux
stayed all day long sometimes and Abby for an hour or two,
three or four. She felt as close to him as possible then, for it was
nigh on to impossible to share such hours when nothing happened and nothing moved, nothing was said and nothing was
done, and not feel close to him. When one person sat there, it
was solitary, but if there were two, it was intimacy of a major
sort.

But at dinner, Rushing Boarchards was different. He always
sat at the head of the table and he always talked. He did, after
all, maintain his charm and the ability to entertain. He might
say a thing or two, about politics or the news, civil rights, gay
rights, more rights—he was in favor of all of those—but what
he liked most to do was just sit.

"See that bird, Abby?"

"Yes."

"Wood thrush. Had six young this year, but two died right
away, one fell out of the nest and broke its neck, another got
taken by a hawk."

"What makes birds die?"

"Age, not enough to eat. Same as us. Only they don't have
the hearts we do."

"You mean their hearts don't break?" she asked with a smile.

"That's what I mean. Their hearts don't break."

"Bud's" turned out to be a discount-cum-repair appliance
store. Notices about bargain prices were slashed across the front
window, and inside gutted machines lay everywhere, the place a
mass of broken fans and picture tubes. Abigail was directed

behind the counter to a glassed-in cubbyhole just large enough for a desk, where Bud sat, wearing a baseball cap with the visor turned up. When he saw her, he jerked back his head and looked startled.

Abigail was startled herself by his reaction and wondered if she should leave, forget the whole thing. She paused for a second. But then Bud, shaking his head, came out and took her back inside. He removed invoices from a chair and told her to sit down. Sitting, she watched him closely as he put a dirty ashtray in a drawer, shut the drawer and sat down himself, all the while still shaking his head. "Strange," he said, frowning.

"What?"

He looked at her. "You. Him."

"I don't understand."

"You look just like him. Didn't anybody ever tell you that?"

"No. Not in a long time."

"Strange," he repeated. "Spitting image."

"Is that why you looked at me that way?"

He nodded. "You're like a ghost." Then he went out and brought her back some coffee. They talked about the appliance business, and all the time he kept looking at her as if she really was only an apparition after all. But finally he began to settle down and she suddenly realized his reaction was only a measure of his regard for her father.

"So you really liked him," she said kindly.

His eyes took her in. "You've got his same expression too," he said. "Never knew a man could look so sweet sometimes. I mean, you think of girls as sweet, like you, but not men. Know what I mean?"

She nodded.

He stared through the glass walls of the enclosure. "Some of the guys said the only reason MacArthur picked him out was . . . well . . . you know . . . all that money. But I said they were wrong, all wrong. And they were. Seeing his obituary in the paper, I didn't know what to do," he went on. "I showed the guys his picture and said, 'I knew him. I was his gunner,' but they said, 'Huh?' I didn't know what to do except write

you a letter. I mean, thirty years is a long time to remember
somebody."

"Why did you feel so strongly about him?"

"Why?" He stopped. "Because," he said, looking at her.
"Just because."

"No, really. Why?"

"Because he brought us through. That's why. Our plane
should of gone down a hundred times. I can't make anybody
understand it," he said, pausing, "but he made it fun."

"Fun?"

"I know, I know. That's what people say. 'How can war be
fun?' But we were a team, the four of us. We did everything together. It was good. Sometimes, thinking back, I think maybe
it wouldn't of been so bad, say, the war went on a little longer.
I mean, we had a good time. 'It was the worst of times and the
best of times.' Churchill, wasn't it? But your dad made it the
best. Sounds crazy, I know. But it's true."

"But you never saw him again. That's what you said in your
letter."

"I know," he said. "It used to bother me. But now I understand. Things change. He had other things on his mind. I
wrote him a letter once. He didn't answer. But I never stopped
thinking about him."

"But why not?" Abigail leaned in across the desk. Bud
looked at her and blinked, as if she were still someone else,
coming too close again, her father.

"Some people are like that, I guess," he said. "You can't get
them out of your system. He sure was a handsome son of a
bitch. Had a real way about him. Same as you, kind of. Quiet
one minute, intense the next. You're two of a kind, you two,
aren't you," he said proudly. "Aren't you?"

She laughed, embarrassed.

"See," he said confidently, "I even remember the dog he had.
'Abby.' After you, he said. Said you were the best thing that
ever happened to him."

"But tell me why he meant so much to you," Abigail said. "I
feel silly, keep asking you that. But I really want to understand
why you liked him so much. Like you said, thirty years is a long

time to remember someone. But he seems to have affected people a lot. But what was it?" she asked. "Because he brought you through? Because he was such a good pilot?"

Bud shook his head. "That had nothing to do with it. It was because he made it happen. Because he made us believe. I know, I know," he added rapidly, "sounds crazy. But it was like there was this goddamned shield around us. Like the plane was protected. And it was. He was so intense about it, we got caught up in it too. He said we had to do the goddamned best we could do, like there was some competition out there between us and God, and we did. The best. The absolute best. The best any of us has ever done, I bet." He paused. "Danger meant nothing to him," he continued. "He'd do any damned thing with that plane he could. It was like he was riding a bird. Japs be damned. And we got to thinking nothing could hurt us. It was kind of foolish flying around up there the way we did, always going back for more. Thinking we were the best. But that was the thing. He never quit. He kept going back with that goddamned piece of tin. He saw a Jap and he wouldn't head for land till he got it. Bombs left in the plane and he wouldn't land. He wouldn't leave a fight."

Bud leaned back in his chair and stared at her silently. "Bet he had a good life," he said confidently.

She nodded.

"Lived well. Died well . . ."

She nodded.

"Good." He drifted off and she didn't interrupt. "Sure made up for the beginning," he said at last.

"What beginning?"

"The Philippines. Worst place in the world. Hotter than hell. Worse than Florida." He put his feet up against a dirty wall and took the ashtray out of the drawer. Then he got out a cigar and lit it. "Biggest defeat of the war, too," he said, blowing out a long puff of smoke. "Next to Pearl. We arrived in Manila November seventeenth—my birthday. Cloudy, hot, and we found this café where they had American beer. It was the first time I let him buy me a drink. I had a thing about that," he went on. "I didn't like guys buying me drinks if they were twerps. So he and I got loaded, talking about the war. Everyone knew war was coming and the Army was putting together some kind of strategic force to hold the Philippines. That's why we was there. We were supposed to hold the Philippines for America. Course it didn't work out that way, but we didn't know it then. This was two, three weeks before Pearl Harbor, and we was all gung-ho. And green. Thing was, our planes never arrived. We was waiting and waiting for them. Then came Pearl. Then, within a few days, the Japs was bombing us. They took out Clarke Field right away, only two planes got off the ground. The rest was destroyed. It was chaos. All the other flying units were sent south, but we were still supposedly waiting for those planes. But a group without planes isn't much of a group, so somehow we got turned into infantry reserves and in the general evacuation of Manila on Christmas Eve, we pulled out with everyone else.

"Pulled back to Bataan," he went on, shaking his head, "You ever see those pictures of Vietnam? Every goddamned peasant, chicken and grandmother on the road heading somewhere? Well, that's what it was like on Bataan. Everyone heading for the Bataan Peninsula because they thought they'd be safe there." Bud spit out a piece of his cigar into the ashtray. "Biggest defeat of the war," he said with disgust. "But your dad and I was lucky. We got out in time. I got out first. . . ."

"Got out?"

"Off to Corregidor. Then a week or so later, he found this old boat and got off too. Then we went to Australia and the fun began."

"I don't understand," Abigail stammered. "I'm totally confused. I'm sorry."

"By this time they had decided the war was only going to be won by planes, and so suddenly guys like us that could fly got real popular. . . ."

"I'm sorry," Abigail interrupted again. "But I don't understand any of this. The names, places, it doesn't mean anything to me. Do you mind explaining?"

"After the defeat of Manila in December 1941," Bud began

again, "the American troops evacuated Manila and pushed back onto the peninsula . . ."

"The Bataan Peninsula."

He nodded. "But it wasn't safe there either because the Japs just continued their advance on the Philippines and they ended up pushing us farther and farther down toward the tip of the peninsula. They had us under siege. It was hell. The only safe place to be was Corregidor. . . ."

"What was Corregidor?"

"Island off Bataan. In the mouth of Manila Bay. MacArthur made it his headquarters immediately after the fall of Manila and thought from there he could regain the peninsula and the Philippines in general."

"But it didn't work."

"That's right," Bud said. "Corregidor was shelled too, and in May it fell, Bataan in April, but in the meantime, before Mac-Arthur moved on to Australia, taking your dad and me and others with him, thank God, it was the only safe haven. Every-one who didn't get off Bataan and reach Corregidor ended up killed or captured. You ask a guy where he saw action, and if he says the Philippines, or Bataan, then you know he's had some real nightmares. Probably worst episode in the whole war. Except for the Jews, of course."

"You mean, because there was a lot of killing?" Abigail asked.

"Worse." He chewed on his cigar. "See, everything was evac-uated from Manila except food rations and medical supplies. Stupid, of course, but that's what the Army did. So there were the Americans, pinned down on Bataan by the Japs from De-cember to April, with nothing to eat but rice. If they were lucky. And constant fighting. The Japs bombarded us all day long and all night. Sounded like a train overhead. You couldn't believe the noise. But it got even worse, because then the Japs came in by land too. I must of lost ten, fifteen pounds," he said, taking a deep pull on the cigar. "Your dad lost more. GIs were strung out all over the place, and at the end even the units were gone, no order, no command. It was chaos there, every man for himself, and if you had a buddy, you were lucky.

Because that's all you could count on. Your buddies. But everybody that didn't find a boat or a dugout and get to Corregidor —and of course a lot of the brass went there in the very beginning in PT boats—was killed or taken captive."

"But why?"

"Because they literally had no place to go. It was the tip of a peninsula and the Japs rounded up must have been ten thousand GIs and Philippine soldiers."

"I photographed this man once who had been taken captive there during the war."

"At least he lived to tell the tale."

"But he went crazy. He ended up killing people."

"You ever talk to him about it?" Bud asked.

Abigail shook her head.

"Ten thousand set out," he said, "maybe half made it. They were walking over bodies. Literally. The road was human pulp. A guy would fall and they just kept going. The Japs shot at them for fun, did things like make them stand all day in the sun by a water hole, not let them take a drink. And the worst was yet to come. Prison. But, see, we missed all that, your dad and I. Day I left Bataan," he went on, "he was sitting in a foxhole. Must have been a hundred and twenty in the shade, eight million mosquitoes, no food. It was so stinking hot, your face running with sweat, and he was sitting there, clothes hanging on him like a bean pole, looking like he plain fucking didn't believe it. The next time I saw him, he was even worse. Must have been a week later, and he showed up in Corregidor by himself. He had found this dugout and paddled across. It wasn't far. He wasn't wounded, but he was shell-shocked or something, and they had him in the infirmary. I asked him, was it rough? He couldn't even answer."

"But what happened to him?"

Bud shrugged, took another chomp on the cigar. "Who knows? Japs were killing, torturing, taking prisoners right and left. He must have done something right. Because he got out. But he lay in that hospital bed for days. Didn't say a word. He didn't even hear me talking to him. I never thought he'd pull through. Psychologically, I mean. Then one day, just before we got shipped to Australia, he just snapped out of it."

"What do you mean?"

"He just stood up and told the nurse he was ready to leave. Just like that. And that was it. A few days later we left for Australia, got our bombers and he never let up till the war was over."

"But what happened to him on Bataan?" she pressed.

"I don't know. Maybe nothing. Maybe he just got psyched out. War does that to you."

Outside the sun was bright, and heading back to Manhattan Abigail bought four pencils in the subway from a blind man. When she came aboveground again, back in Manhattan, she stopped to have coffee in a shop and ended up eating two hamburgers, cake and ice cream.

"How do you eat so much and stay so thin?" said the man next to her at the counter, leering.

Abigail shot him a cold look, but wondered herself. Usually she didn't eat like that at all, but the last few days she had gorged continually, and now she remembered the feeling of foreboding she had felt earlier.

What had she started, she thought as she got up and paid the bill. What was all her questioning going to lead to? Anything?

Her next appointment was in an art gallery on Madison, and she walked slowly uptown in the warm spring sun. The air was fresh, the sky almost blue. The stylish but casual lines of her jacket and pants made her look attractive, but Abigail was unaware of it. She went in and out of stores, browsing, looking at things, not in any hurry to reach her next destination.

She bought a silk scarf for Phoebe, a silly ashtray shaped like a tiger's mouth for Max and something for a friend's birthday. At an expensive import shop she spent a long time trying on T-shirts and finally bought a sweater instead. It was big and thick and pretty, but that it was perfect for Weather Tree she only realized when she walked out the door.

The art gallery was in a huge old brownstone between

Madison and Fifth. Inside, the owner was waiting for her, and with a warm embrace, even though he hadn't seen her in years, he took her up in the elevator to his office on the top floor.

"Of course old Mr. Rushing himself was before my time," he said as he served her sherry in an exquisite old glass, "but my father knew him well. He was one of a kind. That's what everyone always said. A true gentleman. Pity you never knew him, Abby. You'd have been proud. But he and my father had a very close relationship. My father knew exactly what he liked. Knew his taste down to a t, and helped him look for everything. Not just paintings, of course, but furniture, sculpture, old books. Your grandmother was very keen about art too," he said. "She took it very seriously, but I would say Sam is more concerned about it than your father was." He didn't mention Andrew. No one ever did. "Sam has always wanted his collection to be one of the best in the country, and we do the best we can for him here in the gallery, of course, but unfortunately a lot of new money has gotten into the field the last few years. It's harder to stay on top now. Your father bought naturally, but not aggressively."

"Do you remember seeing him after the war?"

"The war?" he asked, surprised. "Now that's an odd question, but as a matter of fact, I do. It was six months or a year later. Maybe more. We had lunch. It was quite funny, really, because we could barely have a decent conversation—so many people coming over to talk to him, shake his hand. He said he was looking for an impressionist painting. Not his usual sort of thing, of course. He preferred American. But he said, 'Maybe something with flowers.' I said I'd keep my eyes open."

"Who was it for?" Abigail asked.

The man paused. "He said it was for a cousin."

"He had a girl friend then," Abigail said. "He was very much in love with her."

"Well, now that you mention it, that does fit my impression," the man said. "You see, I tracked down a couple of pictures but he didn't like them. He said they weren't 'pretty' enough. I remember one was a gorgeous Van Gogh. But then I found this marvelous Monet, in Venice, of all places, and he told me to send it to the Waldorf-Astoria. Of course, I didn't ask questions."

"Has the picture ever come on the market again?"

"I can't say for sure," he said. "I don't always know, of course. But I don't think so."

When she got home there were two messages on her answering service: one from Luke, asking her to call, the other from a man who'd left no message.

"He just said, 'Tell her I called,'" the operator explained, "but when I asked, 'Who is it?' he hung up."

"But if you liked him last night," Phoebe said, "why don't you want to call him back now? He said to call."

"I don't know why." Abigail twirled her finger nervously in the telephone cord. "Something about him makes me uncomfortable."

"Because he did the will with your father?"

"No. Not anymore. I don't know what it is."

"But you said you liked him."

"I know. I do. Sort of."

"Then what is it?"

"He makes me uncomfortable. He sees too much. He's sort of uncanny."

"But that sounds good," Phoebe argued.

"Oh, no," Abigail exclaimed. "It's just the opposite."

She called Jackson Paine instead, and despite the unusualness of her call, just asked if she could see him and didn't explain.

"But I'm off to Geneva Sunday for a couple of days," he said. "International monetary conference. Be back Tuesday."

"Can't I see you before you leave?"

"Don't know how, Abigail. I'm off to Washington tonight, won't be back until Saturday. I have a dinner that night."

"But I have to see you," she said, growing more urgent.

"What's up? You going to contest the will? Everyone's wondering. Bostrine's in a tizzy. Says nothing like that's ever happened."

"Like what?"

"Law suit in the family. She's shocked, of course, says it will bring nothing but publicity. Sam's outraged. The other night at dinner he said you made a terrible scene at the funeral. Barged into his room. I said, of course you were going to contest. Anybody would."

"I don't know whether I am or not."

"They think their only chance is that since you've never had anything to do with the family before, why should you start now. I say, do you like boats?" Jackson asked.

"What?"

"I'm going to this awful party Saturday on a boat in the harbor. You'll probably know more people than I, the way you get around. Why don't you meet me there? We can talk there. Be nice to see you. Now that you're all grown up and all," he added warmly.

"Fenway and Anderson," the operator said.

"Melanie Anderson, please."

"One moment, please."

"Mrs. Anderson's office," said another woman.

"May I speak to . . ."

"She's on the coast. She won't be back for maybe a week, or more."

"But I have to talk to her before May sixth. It's terribly important."

"I'm afraid that's what everyone says."

"But this is urgent. Do you know if she owns a Monet painting, by the way?"

"You'd have to ask her."

Abigail left her name and number and asked for Melanie Anderson to call her back.

When she hung up, the phone rang again right away. It was Luke. "Do you want to have dinner tonight?" he asked.

"I'm busy," she lied.

"Then let's have a drink."

"I don't really have time."

"But I have something to show you. Shall I come by?"

"What is it?"

"I'll explain when I see you. It's complicated."

"Then I'll meet you at the Oak Room at the Plaza," she said reluctantly. "My dinner party is nearby."

He stood up when she came to the table and she took the seat beside him on the banquette. She was wearing a dark designer suit with lean lines and a soft sweater, but he didn't seem to notice. He already had a scotch. She ordered Perrier and noticed the peanuts were almost gone. He asked her how she was, but she could tell he was preoccupied, even a little nervous. "What is it?" she asked kindly. "Something's the matter. Isn't it?"

He shook his head. "I don't know," he said. "But look at these." He took a bundle of papers out of his jacket pocket and put them on the table. "They're checks," he said, "made out to Joe Algodones by your father."

Abigail stared at them. They were held together tightly by a rubber band and they stood over three inches high.

"They add up to $989,878.54," he said grimly, loosening his tie and then putting his arm back up along the top of the banquette reaching in her direction. "Almost a million dollars."

Abigail was stunned. She stared across the room and remembered what Alvah Germaine had said about Rush. The best there was and he never knew it. She picked up the checks and looked through them. "How'd you get them?" she mumbled.

"I said I had to use the library. There's nothing wrong with that. Harvey Wynne wouldn't mind. I didn't go back to the old files until the cleaning woman left."

"Why didn't you tell me that's what you were going to do?"

"I'm like you," the lawyer said, smiling briefly. "I don't say everything on my mind. Besides, I had no idea what I'd find or if I wanted to get involved in what you're doing. I'll take them back tonight," he added. "I've already made Xeroxes. Most of the checks are for two, three thousand dollars, but toward the end they go up to five, six. Some are little—fifty dollars, twelve dollars." He was frowning.

"When was the first?"

"It looks like it was April 1947, and the last is September. Last September."

"It's not necessarily blackmail."

"That's true. I looked at the records. The accountant had him down once twenty years ago as an employee, but I called Simon. He said he never worked there."

Abigail took one check out of the bundle and looked at the Algodones signature on the back. It was up at the very top, little tiny letters in black ink along the edge of the paper.

"You want another round?" a waiter asked, bending over the table.

"You have time?" Luke asked.

"Yes. Another Perrier."

"Nothing stronger?"

She shook her head. "I don't like to drink."

He laughed. "Now there's a good family lesson for you. I'm the same way."

"What way?"

"Different from my father too."

"What's he like?" she asked, remembering Luke's reticence last time the subject arose.

He shrugged. "Hard to explain," he said. "He doesn't sit still much, he's always out."

"Different from my father, then," Abigail said, wishing he would open up and talk. "Was that one of the reasons you liked my father?"

"Yes. He seemed so stable." Then Luke changed the subject. "One more curious thing about the checks," he said. "Algodones used a lot of banks. You can see all the bank stamps on the back of the checks. New York, New Jersey, Westchester. That will make it hard to find him. If he only used one, you could trace him easily. He must have a bank account at one of them. Do you mind? I was thinking of giving these Xeroxes to Alvah Germaine so he could try to find him."

"No," she said, "it's a good idea. But why do you want to find him? Why do you care, Luke?"

"Don't you think anybody can be interested in your father but you?" He started eating peanuts again.

"It's not that. I'm just curious about why you care. You have other things to do besides spend all night going through old files looking for checks."

Luke lifted his glass and clicked it against hers.

"What's that for?"

He smiled broadly, his brown eyes almost green. "A toast to the new Abigail Boarchards."

"Who's she?"

"The one you're going to be when you get over this. Your father said you were a lot of things, but he never mentioned insecure. Have you ever studied much history?"

She shook her head.

"You want to know what happened to him?"

She nodded. "I'd love to know."

"The world changed on him. That's what. He was caught in the middle. Caught in a time warp. When he was born, you were who you were just because you were born."

"If you were in the upper class, that is," she interrupted.

"But you didn't have to do anything to be Somebody," he went on. "You didn't have to prove yourself. There was no notion of 'identity' or 'struggle' or 'psychological growth.' But then World War One came along, and then the Depression, and taxes and World War Two, and all that changed. He ended up in a kind of no-man's land. Probably resenting the old world that let him down and the new one that had no place for him. That's why he could identify with someone like your cousin Charley who didn't do anything, but not with you. You represented the new world," Luke said, looking at her. "Does that make any sense? You were everything that was competitive and aggressive and totally at home with the whole idea that what a person 'becomes' is what he 'is.'"

"But that doesn't explain what he did to me."

"It does in a way. It explains why he felt weak. You sure you didn't have a fight with him or something?" Luke asked.

"No."

"Do something nasty or awful?"

"I certainly can't remember it if I did."

"He taught me how to fly cast," Luke said abruptly. "Did you know that?"

She shook her head. There was a smile on her face now, watching him next to her.

"I never knew how to fish in my life. But he took me down to the river and stood with me day after day teaching me how to throw the line, holding my wrist and showing me how to make it loose."

"And you loved it," she said warmly.

He nodded his head.

"He stopped fishing years ago," she added.

"I know. I know," he said. "That's what made it so amazing. I don't know why he wanted to bother with me. I never even told him I'd always wanted to learn. I'd always wished my own father would teach me to fish. But one day Rush just said, 'Want to go fishing?' And I said, 'But I've never done it.' He said there was nothing to it, he could teach me in an hour. But at the end of the first day, when we were walking home, he said, 'Tomorrow we'll take some sandwiches and if you keep doing what I tell you, you'll be damn good. All it takes is grace. And confidence.' He let me use the rod his grandfather gave him and I said, 'But what if I break it?' But he just said, 'Don't worry.' Afterward, he gave it to me."

Luke suddenly turned to her full face with a big grin. "Isn't that a nice story?" he said.

"It is," she agreed.

He settled back on the banquette again and took some peanuts in his hand. "You know what I loved about him?" he went on.

"What?"

"I guess it sounds strange, but that he was at the end of a long, full life and he'd turned out weak and despairing, but that he knew it. He didn't pretend. I respected him precisely because he had tried to do something great with his life and failed, but he knew it."

"What did he try to do that was so great?"

"His whole life was one big experiment, Abby," Luke said, eating the peanuts from his hand. "He gave up everything he knew and everything he was supposed to be. He was just like you in a way."

Abigail didn't answer.

Luke paused, then said, "What he specifically did was give up everything he knew in the form of a normal daily life and exchange it for Weather Tree. He could have stayed in New York, did what everybody else he knew did. Work. Or not work. But go to parties, join clubs, see plays. But he decided to move up there. People didn't do that in those days. You have to remember that."

"But it didn't work. He just ended up unhappy."

"But he had all the glory of having tried," Luke argued. "He wrote books—some were successful and some weren't, but at least he tried. Don't you understand what I mean, Abby? I mean, what is life worth if we don't try?"

"But he stopped trying," she argued. "He gave up."

"But if we don't take risks, what is there? I always thought taking risks was a macho exercise in foolishness. Like gamblers who throw away their money and their life. And for what? For nothing." Suddenly he sounded bitter. "But getting to know your father, I decided the only real option in life is precisely to take risks. Otherwise we just plod along, taking it safe, never exercising the one great . . ."

"My goodness."

"Yes," he said with sudden embarrassment. "I'm sorry. I get carried away. But it means a lot to me. You must understand. You've taken risks. By all rights, you should be sitting around in white gloves having ladies' luncheons."

Abigail grinned. "But I have a question." She put down her glass. "You said he moved up to Weather Tree as part of a big experiment to do what he really wanted to do?"

Luke nodded.

"But what if that isn't true? What if he moved up there because it was all he had? And he couldn't face the real world. What if it was a retreat?"

"You know the answer to that as well as I do," the lawyer said. "It was both, and I bet both sides of him fought right up until the very end."

"Then which one disinherited me?"

"Both."

Luke eventually got her a cab and waved good-bye.

She wished they were having dinner after all. She sank down in the seat and wondered why she had lied about being busy. But she knew the answer. She hadn't done it to appear unavailable. She had done it to be unavailable.

The cab bumped along heading north. She pulled the list out of her pocket and looked at it critically. I'm not taking many risks here, she thought. Not going to Weather Tree, not seeing Pollibeaux, Simon. And Victoria, Sam and Bostrine only at the very end.

And little thought about the will. None. Abigail sat up straight and hit her head against the ceiling. What was she going to do about the will? She'd given it no thought at all. Did she want money and trouble? Or no money and freedom? Weather Tree or no Weather Tree?

Somebody had emptied the ashtray on the floor of the cab and the cigarette butts smelled. She covered them with her feet, but the smell stayed. Why did you hate me?

If she contested the will, there would be a legal battle. Her relatives would never go against her father's wishes, especially Sam, who had always disliked her. Only the threat of scandal or publicity would eventually influence them to settle out of court. She felt the sinking, tight feeling of indecision overtake her.

On the other hand, to accept the will meant giving up everything, including the land. Worse, it meant giving in to her father. It spelled defeat. Accepting a guilty verdict—his indictment of her character—without a fight.

Abigail glared at the movie advertisement in front of her. "Happiest Show in Town," it said. "Fun for the Whole Family."

The letter was on the floor when she got home, pushed through the slot in the door while she was out. It had obviously been delivered in person—no stamp, no return address.

She tore it open and pulled out a big sheet of paper. She recognized it right away for what it was.

It was a letter from Joe Algodones.

There was no signature, but the message was written in little tiny letters, the handwriting the same as on the checks, squeezed along the very top edge of the page.

"I know where you are," it said. "Yesterday you went to the school, had a drink at a bar, saw your uncle, went swimming and walked home with a man. I can get you any time I want. And I will. See what your father says about that."

"You're sure it's Algodones?" Alvah asked over the phone.

"Positive. The handwriting is just like the checks. But he doesn't know Rush is dead. Do you think he's dangerous?"

"Hard to tell," the detective said cautiously. "He's a sinister bastard. But one thing's clear: he was blackmailing your father. Now he's turned to you."

"Someone came to the building last night too," Abigail said urgently.

"Who?"

"I don't know. Maybe it was him." She told Alvah what the doorman had said. "And some man called the answering service today and wouldn't leave his name. Maybe it was him too. What should I do?"

"Did you tell this to your lawyer friend? Reider?"

"No."

"Tell him."

"Why?"

"See what he thinks," Alvah said. "I want a second opinion. He knew your father. He's seen those checks. If he's so interested in this, or you . . ."

"Not me."

". . . then get him more involved. Call him."

"But I can't," she said suddenly.

"Why not?"

"Well . . ."

"Well what?"

"I pretended I was busy tonight."

"You what?"

"I'm not supposed to be home yet."

"You always do that with men?" Alvah asked.

"No. I never did it before in my life."

"Well, then, call him later if you have to. But see what he thinks. I'll sleep on it. I think I should put a man outside your place to talk to Algodones if he shows up again. Find out what he's up to. Why he's following you."

"What about someone to go around with me?"

"You want that?" he asked.

She thought. "No," she said. "I don't. Not now."

Friday, April 19

After telling Luke about the letter, Abigail double-locked the front door and left all the lights on, but in the morning she felt different. Even when the lawyer Harvey Wynne called she didn't get disturbed. He told her everyone had gotten letters from Algodones and he wanted to know if she had too. Bostrine got one, Max, Sam and Andrew, and one even went to Charley, although Charley wasn't there to receive it. They were all the same. Abigail was the only one in the family, it turned out, who got a different one. The others were typed, with no address or any other form of identification, except for a New York postmark and the name at the end signed in little tiny black letters.

"What did they say?" she asked.

"Some nonsense about your father. Absolute malarkey."

She told him about her letter and said she had considered getting a detective to watch her house.

"No need to be so hysterical," Wynne said irritably. "Cranks like these are a dime a dozen."

Ten minutes later Alvah called. He had set up a three-way telephone conversation from his office with her and Luke.

She said she had decided she didn't want a detective watching outside the building. "I don't think it's necessary."

"But he got a million dollars out of your father," Luke exclaimed.

"That's right," Alvah agreed.

"That doesn't mean he's dangerous," Abigail argued.

"But now he's fixated on you," Alvah said. "I've already decided about this. There's a definite pattern of harassment on his part that has switched to you."

"He doesn't even know my father's dead," she protested.

"Then imagine what he might do when he finds out," the detective warned. "I'm going to put a man outside your building, Abby. He'll keep his eyes open and if Algodones shows up again, follow him. Find out what he's up to. That's all. Play it safe."

"I agree," Luke said.

"But you read the letter my father wrote him, Luke," Abigail said. "He liked Algodones. Remember how friendly he was to him. He must have known he wasn't dangerous."

"That letter was a lot more ambiguous than that," the lawyer argued. "The situation is just unpredictable enough to warrant some concern."

"But I'm not concerned," Abigail insisted. "You are. I'm just curious."

"You started this investigation, Abby," Alvah said, "and who knows what unfinished business this guy has with your father or what he's up to. Who knows what may crawl out from under a rock. I'm going to go ahead and put someone outside. I don't care what you say."

"Oh, all right," she relented. "You've made your point. Go ahead."

Downstairs in the lobby a few minutes later, she stopped in the doorway. She started to frown. Everything had changed. An anonymous letter, threatening her, and Algodones, obviously intent on something, following her.

"Cab, miss?"

"No, I'm taking my car." She started heading outside and

stopped again. She noticed that traffic on Central Park West was normal; she saw a line of children headed toward the park, cars jammed in on both sides of the street. She turned back to the doorman. "Did anyone ask for me today?"

"No."

She went out onto the sidewalk again, still feeling troubled, and headed up the block toward her garage. She peered around, looking at every car, three vans, a pickup truck, but no one in sight seemed to be waiting for her, watching her or even aware of her.

In Connecticut buds had started to appear at the Blue Clipper Farm and the lawn was already green. Abigail parked her car and headed toward the big old house full of men and doctors. The air was so warm she took off her jacket and walked along in her silk blouse and skirt. The air smelled of spring, fresh and clean, the scent of trees and grass. Walking up the steps, she had a flash that she was going to see her father, surrounded by cigarette butts and empty bottles. "I started to hate you because . . ." he'd say.

The attendant took her down the hall to the doctor's office. Inside she saw a neat little man with trim hair and big ears, and she knew her father had confided no secrets in him. What am I doing here? she thought critically. I should be at Weather Tree.

"I told him the drinking would kill him," the doctor said once their conversation was underway. "I figured the only thing I could do was frighten him because I knew he wasn't interested in treatment."

"Then why did he come here?"

"I have no idea."

"But don't people only come because they want to stop?" she persisted.

"Usually. Sometimes a court sends them, or they do it to please a relative. I can't tell you what you want to know," he added kindly. "Why he became an alcoholic. Why he committed suicide."

Or why he hated me, she wanted to add. But she didn't.

Because I'm afraid he'll tell me, she thought grimly. But looking at him again, she didn't think he could.

He had a file on his desk marked "R.W.F.B.," and he read from that. " 'Patient caught in a prolonged state of rejection of his parents . . . trying to establish himself as an independent personality . . .' "

"What'd he do?" Abigail interrupted. "Sit in here and talk to you?"

"He sat right where you're sitting. But he rarely talked much."

"Just smoked."

"That's right."

"All hunched over? Right? And when the hour was up, he'd just get up and leave. Not even say good-bye."

"You certainly know him well."

"I don't know. I don't know if I knew him at all."

"He was a complicated person," the doctor said. "Much more complicated than most people I treat."

"Do you think I'm like him?" she asked lightly.

"I have no way of knowing, obviously, having seen you for ten minutes. But I surely doubt it."

"Why?"

"For one thing, you're a contemporary personality. You work, et cetera."

"Why was he so complicated?"

"Let me read more from the file. It's probably self-explanatory." He picked up the papers again. " 'Defiant of the class system, that and family synonymous to him . . . low self-esteem masked by arrogance and an elaborate system of blaming others.' " He looked up at Abigail.

"Keep going."

" 'Overcome with guilt and confusion when mother died . . .' " He looked up again. "Death always feels like abandonment and rejection to a child," he said.

"But they don't all grow up to become alcoholics or commit suicide. Why did he, do you think?"

"And they're not all orphans either and they don't come from such a monolithic family as yours or choose never to work. All those factors added to his complexity. Here's something," he added, bending over the file. "Something about a fight with your mother. He told her he wanted a divorce and she got so angry, she took it out on you and hit you. Do you remember that?"

"That's not what happened at all."

"What did happen?"

"He never said a word about divorce."

"He said he did," the doctor answered.

"Then he made it up. He had come down again to see us in New York. They were fighting in the living room. She called me in, like she always did, and started to fight with me, but this time she slapped me. I started to bleed near my eye. She got me with her ring and I went to the bathroom to wash. When I came out, I didn't see him. I thought he had gone to bed. Instead he had left. He went out the back door and down the back stairs. He never came back and she didn't even know he had left either."

"Then what did he mean about divorce?"

"The next morning the lawyer called and he was the one who told my mother my father wanted a divorce. My father never talked to her about it himself."

The doctor was shaking his head.

"Then she died before the divorce was final."

"People's capacity for distortion is a remarkable thing," he said. "We can control our memories, you know. We can make ourselves forget unpleasant things."

"I've been doing that." Abigail looked down at her hands. "Not remembering things about my father. Sometimes I can't even remember what he looked like. I know I've blocked out a lot of the past. It's gotten worse since he died." She looked up. "Much worse. It's like everything that happened before suddenly got fuzzy."

"That's natural," the doctor said. "Death is a traumatic event, and so is suicide. Assuming you feel some guilt or responsibility, which would only be natural in this case, that acts as a further force of repression."

"But what can I do about it?"

"Just be patient. Memories have a way of coming back when you're strong enough to face them. In a way forgetting is healthy. It's a way of taking care of yourself. As long as it's temporary," he cautioned. "As long as you eventually face the truth. That's the only serious issue: that you face the truth sometime."

They were silent.

"Did he ever say anything about the war?" Abigail asked then.

The doctor turned back to the files and leafed through the pages again. "See," he said, stopping. "I've written quite a lot about that, because it's the one thing he did talk about. He was a curious man," he added, "very strong. But I doubt he was a very good father."

"Oh, no," Abigail exclaimed, sitting up abruptly in her chair. "He was a perfect father. Until the alcohol took over."

The doctor didn't say anything.

"But wasn't he weak?" she asked.

The man shook his head. "Definitely not. He had too much tenacity. Tenacity and character. He was insecure, but not weak. See, here's something about the war," he went on, looking down at his notes. "I've written 'traumatized by war and killing . . . war very bad episode in his life, but in his cosmology, this trauma later becomes just another excuse for self-destructive behavior and self-abuse.' "

"But he was a hero," Abigail argued. "He was a hero in the war. The war was a triumph for him."

"Apparently not."

"But why not?"

The doctor shrugged. "Everyone picks his own failures," he said. "They don't necessarily have any relationship to fact."

All she could think of when she left was to talk to Alvah. She used the pay phone down the hall to call him. "You were right," she said as soon as he answered.

"About what?"

"I didn't think so at the beginning, but this is getting to be a lot harder than I imagined. It's making me upset. I even have bad dreams," she rushed on, "and I don't know if he's my father or a stranger anymore. I don't even know what I'm doing or why I hired you. It all made sense on Tuesday and this is only Friday, but I'm already in over my head. The doctor said I'm repressing things. I'm supposed to be deciding about the will. Instead I never think about it."

"Hold on, hold on," the detective said gently. "Just calm down. Everything's going to be all right."

"But I'm supposed to be deciding about the will . . ."

"Fine. Don't think about it. Just relax. You'll think about it when you're ready."

"But I don't have much time left."

"You have two weeks. You'll do it when you're ready. When you've sorted out other things first. Don't worry about these reactions. They're inevitable. Unless you want to stop the whole thing."

"Oh, no," she exclaimed. "Absolutely not."

"You want some advice, Abby? The best thing is not to worry. You still have that list?"

"Yes."

"Then just follow it. Like it's homework. And don't think about it too much. Besides, you're a good girl. You have a lot of spunk."

"Spunk." She grinned. "What kind of word is that?"

"Never you mind. Just believe me. Luke brought me those checks, by the way," he went on, changing the subject. "That's how we're going to find this guy Algodones. You'll see. Don't worry. My people have been calling all over the Western world looking for him. He hasn't shown up yet, but he will. He has to have a bank account for all that money. Mary's got two guys helping her call all those banks."

"Do you want to have dinner tonight?"

"Reider said you were having dinner with him."

"I'll cancel it."

"He said you see your father's shadow everywhere."

"I wish he wouldn't talk about me behind my back."

"You can't distrust the whole world just because of what your father did."

"I don't," she snapped, "and I don't have any interest in Luke Reider."

"He does in you."

"He certainly doesn't show it."

"Well, of course he doesn't show it." Alvah sounded irritated now. "You'd run the four-minute mile. He's smart enough to know that."

"I would not."

"All right, all right. Let's change the subject."

"I wonder if you could find any clips on Reider."

"Sure I could. That what you want?"

"Of course not," she said. "I can't stand lawyers."

"I never met too many photographers I liked either," Alvah responded. "Or rich people, for that matter."

Abigail started to laugh. "All right, you won that round. I get your point."

"Then stop being depressed."

Driving home, she remembered something else. The red brick building north of Licking River. It was the state reform school. It had bars on the windows and pipes up the walls. She remembered it often and always had, all her life, but driving back to New York, the memory came back with more intensity than usual.

She remembered the rooms that echoed with her footsteps and all the boys locked up inside. They sat along the walls reading comic books and didn't look at her, her father, or any of the visitors.

Then one did look up.

He looked right at her. He had freckles and blue eyes, and the blue eyes looked at her for a million years. They didn't see Pop or the governor or the other men. Instead they went on looking at her until finally she had to look away, but then down at the end of the hall when she turned back to look at him, he was gone. The chair was empty. She felt bad, as if she'd been rude or done something unkind, but then, as they were leaving, she suddenly saw him again, a second chance. He was lined up with all the others by the gate. The governor told

them to straighten out, their whole lives were still ahead, and
they snickered and swore, but the boy was there looking at her,
blue eyes, freckles and a pug nose. He wore blue jeans and a
sweat shirt and she wondered who he was and what he had
done wrong, and if he was thinking the same as she. About
how one person could be inside and another out, one lucky, the
other unlucky, and she wondered if there was something wrong
with her for that, not him.

She kept looking back at the boy as she walked to the road,
until he was out of sight behind the gate, and when she left she
felt different, as if something big had happened.

"Like all those boys, do you, Abby?" Sam had said.

Later Grace got furious, but Rush had said it was "real life"
and she had to see it sometime.

Abigail had remembered the boy in the red brick building a
million times, and on the road back to New York she remembered him again. She knew she'd recognize him anywhere, and
she had looked for him for years, on streets and in buses, in
Licking River and New York, in elevators, trains and gas sta-
tions, but she never saw him again, or knew his name or anything about him, except that he had looked at her and she at
him, and she had traveled in that instant farther from Weather
Tree and the Rushings and the Boarchards than she ever had
before. And somehow, she had always attributed it to him in
part, that she had set her sights on a journey then that would
take her into the real world and beyond. It was as if in that one
moment, the boy had everything and she had nothing, for he
knew how he had gotten here and she didn't. He had the
knowledge and she didn't. She just wanted it. Right then and
there she started wanting it.

When she got back to New York, she parked her car in the
garage and walked home. In the lobby, the doorman was excited. "That man was here again," he said. "But it was before
the detective arrived, so I didn't think anything of it at the
time."

"What did he want?"

"He asked where you were. I said I didn't know. I didn't."

"Where's the detective now?" She glanced out into the street.

"In that blue car, but he said to act like he wasn't here."

She had been in a bad mood from the moment she arrived at dinner, and now, at home again, she stared angrily at her television set, some old movie, and fumed. Luke had already been seated, reading the paper when she arrived, and when she walked up it was all he could do to stop reading. When he finally did put the paper down, he was still preoccupied and didn't hear one word she said about the doctor in Connecticut, or about going to Washington tomorrow. Not that she really expected him to be as interested in Rush as he pretended to be, but he obviously thought she should drop the subject and talk about something else just because he was taking her out to dinner.

But she didn't want to talk about movies or politics, she thought, turning channels. Everything was irrelevant right now, and if all he was interested in was movies and current events, they certainly didn't have a thing in common. She had dreaded the whole idea of dinner to begin with. Just because she'd liked him at the Oak Room at the Plaza didn't mean she had to like him the next day. She had nothing to say to him, and he obviously had nothing to say to her. Then he said he wanted to see a movie, but she said she didn't want to. She wanted to stay at the restaurant and he just got irritated. So why did he bother to pretend he was interested in what she was doing, if he didn't want to talk about it? And why did he bother to see her in the first place? If all he wanted was to talk politics, he should see somebody else.

She turned the dial on the television and knew she wasn't making sense. She knew she was being irrational and, worse, just like her father, afraid to talk, afraid of closeness, afraid of someone like Luke, who saw too much. She'd never spent much time before with a man like that and now, for the first time, she knew why. She'd done it on purpose, to avoid exactly what she was feeling now.

Abruptly she turned up the volume on the television until the sound hammered in her ears.

Suddenly the telephone rang. She turned off the television and picked up the receiver.

"I have to tell you something." It was Luke. "You made me mad. I've cooled off some, but not enough to forget it. I don't like the way you behave. If you're going to be with people, you should show a little interest in them, too. Or else say you're sorry. Apologize. Say you know you're all caught up in something. But don't just assume you're the center of the universe just because something bad happened to you."

"But I don't think that. I was just upset."

"Then why didn't you say, 'Give me a break tonight. I'm sorry. I'm having a hard time.' Instead you just acted bored and irritated."

"Why did you ask me out in the first place?"

"Because I like you," he said. "That's why."

"But why?"

"People can still like you, you know."

"But you make me nervous."

"Then why didn't you say so?" he exclaimed. "Why did you go out with me in the first place?"

"I don't know. And then when I got there, you were reading that newspaper. I thought you were bored."

"You know I like you."

"No, I don't. You liked my father."

"But that doesn't mean I can't like you too. I'm capable of liking two people at the same time, Abigail. You mean you're never going to be able to be friends with someone who liked your father too?"

"I don't know."

"You let that happen and you'll be worse off than he ever was," Luke said, and hung up.

Saturday, April 20

The telephone rang before she had barely woken up. She hoped it was Luke, but it was Alvah. He was breathless.

"I've found something!" he said excitedly. "Your father didn't have a driver's license. It was revoked four years ago in Licking River. On drunk-driving charges. You didn't know that, did you? Somebody in Albany pulled the records for me. He just called. It's all there in writing, but it doesn't explain what happened. Doesn't give any details. So I'm going up to Licking River to find out."

"When are you coming back?"

"As soon as possible."

"But . . ."

He hung up.

She sat holding the receiver. She wanted to talk.

She called Phoebe, but there was no answer. Then she called Max, but she hung up when Foster answered. What she really wanted, she realized, was to talk to Luke.

On the plane to Washington, she read *Men of War*.

The book followed the crew of a B-24 bomber fighting in the

Pacific as the American forces took island after island away from the Japanese during the last half of the war. There was no mention of the Philippines. Their adventures were engrossing, but the relationship between an overweight bombardier who gradually succumbed to cowardice and the pilot who tried to help him was the heart of the story. The pilot was the most interesting character, charismatic and strong, but always propelled toward absurdly dangerous situations. Abigail thought it was never fully explained what motivated him, and she couldn't figure out if the author meant his success at war to be luck or courage or what. He had a girl friend back home, but apart from being sexy, her main characteristic, Abigail noticed, seemed to be unlimited understanding and a complete acceptance of him.

The taxi from Washington National Airport took a long time because there was a lot of weekend traffic making its way into the city. At the door Abigail apologized for being late for lunch, and introduced herself, but Isabel Daltenburgh, well-known society hostess, waved her worry away and acted as if they were old friends. The house was a red brick mansion on an enormous piece of land in Georgetown, and Isabel led Abigail to a room that looked out over the garden and some woods.

"Mummy left this to me, you know," she said, putting Abigail across from her at the table. Outside the sun was shining and squirrels were running on the lawn, city life someplace else. "I just adore it, you know. I think it's one of the few places left in Washington where you can still raise children. Don't you think?"

Abigail agreed, but noticed Isabel had apparently found other uses for the house besides children because there were photographs everywhere of people recognizable to anyone who read newspapers or went to the movies. One showed Isabel in the library doing a card trick for Eisenhower, and in another Gregory Peck was on the lawn in shorts, and a secretary of state was eating a hamburger.

Isabel had story after story about Rushing B., as she called him, and Abigail took in this version of her father, Boarchards all wit and clever conversation. But when lunch was almost over, the woman's narrative took another turn. "When Grace died, I made my move," Isabel said bluntly. "I thought we'd make a perfect pair. It worked for a while, but I'm glad he turned me down. I was devastated at first, of course, but he was a broken man, you know, darling." She rang the bell for the maid to clear the plates. "Grace was too much for him, you know. He was all show by the time I came along. I never knew it, mind you; that's why I was head over heels in love with him. I remarried almost immediately, but of course it didn't last."

"Were you surprised he remembered you in his will?"

"I gave him a boost when he needed one and we did have a good time together. Naughty, naughty," she said, wagging a finger at Abigail. "I know what you're thinking. Sex, sex, sex. But men are all alike, you know. They pretend they're God's gift on earth, but if the truth be told, they'd rather read a book at night. Of course, he was so divine, I didn't mind. Besides, he was in love with someone else," she added. "But you know that, of course."

"Of course," Abigail said sweetly.

"So he told you?"

"I figured it out for myself."

"I always assumed I'd be fighting off memories of Grace, but then it turned out there was someone else on his mind. My, my."

"Did he say much about her?"

"No, but I think she turned him down cold." Isabel sounded slightly pleased. "He certainly worried about what would happen to you," she went on. "He seemed to think you were quite delicate, and I said, 'Oh, girls have a way of taking care of themselves. She'll find someone.' He said, well, at least you'd have money."

"But I was twenty years old then."

"Well, of course, darling, but you know how men are. They think they have to take care of everyone. Your father was like that. I finally had to propose to him myself. Here in front of the fire one night." Isabel took a little cookie, thin as glass. "He was marvelous about it," she said, studying the cookie before she ate it, "so I assumed everything was going like a house afire, but then, when nothing happened, I brought it up again. He said he thought I understood. 'Understood what?' I said, and he said you needed him. That the change wouldn't be good for you."

"But I was in college."

"I was too much for him," Isabel went on, ignoring Abigail's remark, "but at least he knew the truth about himself. Do you know what?" She leaned across the table.

"What?"

"I always thought he enjoyed it."

"Enjoyed what?"

"Rejecting me. I always had this sneaking hunch he planned it. To get back at someone. That other woman." She raised her nails and looked at them.

"But he wasn't like that," Abigail said.

"Sure he was. Haven't you ever really wanted to hurt someone?"

"No."

"Well, don't look so shocked. It happens all the time."

On the way back to the airport she thought about Luke some more and looked at the pictures Isabel had given her. She recognized actors, politicians, even Jackson Paine in one, wearing a three-piece suit. Rush was in most of them. He looked strong and attractive, his tie undone, the jacket missing a button, but his face was alive and vibrant. It looked amused.

There was one close-up of him sitting on a bench. He was obviously listening to someone, but a cigarette had burned down almost to his knuckle and a long ash dangled at the end. Another ash had already fallen on his pants and it lay there, whole and untouched, like a fat worm.

Abigail put the picture down.

She wondered if he had already started to smell too.

She read the book all the way back to New York. There was plenty about airplanes and airfights in the book, but no outright killing. Death and destruction was something unleashed from the air, but while dying lurked at the outer edge of the pilot's bravery, and plenty of people died, no one ever died in front of him. No last words. No killing. No blood, no wounds.

"Have you decided to go to Weather Tree yet?" Phoebe asked as she fixed Abigail tea in her kitchen above Riverside Drive. Little Bobby was still at school and they were alone.

"I decided that long ago," Abigail answered firmly. "I'm having dinner with Jackson Paine tonight," she said, changing the subject.

"I thought you said you'd never shared one word of personal information with him your whole life." Phoebe sat down at the table. "Shouldn't you be seeing people up there in the woods? Or get down to brass tacks and go see your relatives?"

Abigail hunched over her teacup. "I'll get to them," she said defensively. "But look at what I've already done." She pulled the list out of her purse.

Phoebe glanced down at all the items Abigail had checked off, stores where he'd bought guns, got fitted for boots, old roommates. "What's good about this?" she asked, frowning.

"I've got all kinds of information about how he gradually withdrew from contact with people."

"But this one," Phoebe said, pointing to one name. "Your headmistress at school. What did she have to say?"

"That's not a very good example. It turned out they'd never met. But I got a lot from the tax-reform people," Abigail rushed on. "They said he really believed the tax laws should be changed to help the poor and shift advantages away from the rich."

"But you knew that." Phoebe put down her teacup and leaned across the table. "Listen, Abby, I think you're being kind of a coward. If you say you want to find out everything about your father, you don't go to an art gallery."

"I came by hoping to be cheered up, Phoebe. This is hard work. Everybody's criticizing me. Luke . . ."

"But you're still hiding, just like you did for three months. Just like your father did. You're hiding from your feelings and you're avoiding finding out exactly why he turned against you.

You've got to go to the horse's mouth. See Simon, your relatives."

"But I've made lots of progress. And I'm not at all like my father."

"You're not seeing relatives. You're not going to Weather Tree. I bet you haven't even really thought about the will."

"I still have plenty of time to do that."

"But why aren't you doing it now, Abby? Right now? You only have two weeks left. Do you know what's preventing you from thinking about it now? Do you know why you can't decide?"

"I'm waiting until I get a picture of him."

"But what about a picture of Abigail? What's she going to do? I don't mean to be hard on you, Abby, but this business about the will is very important, and I don't think you're facing it. You're ignoring the fact that it's one of the biggest decisions you'll ever have to make."

Abigail averted her eyes.

"Money's part of it," Phoebe went on. "Millions of dollars are probably involved, I don't know. But the issue is what kind of person you're going to be." She leaned across the table. "What you do about the will is going to affect everything, Abby. Your feelings about your family, yourself. You may regret it later if you don't contest. You may wish you had the money. The land. What if you give it up and end up poor? No money? No roots? Photography's not the greatest profession in the world, you know." She stood up and started walking around the room, still looking at Abigail. "Do you want to be poor?"

Abigail was staring at the table.

"Do you want to work all your life? I mean, *all* your life? Do you want to end up seventy years old and wonder where your money's coming from? Maybe for you, giving up the money is like giving up your heritage. You ever think about that?"

"Yes."

"Like deciding to be an expatriate the rest of your life."

Abigail put her hands around the teapot to warm them. "So you think I should contest?"

"I don't care what you do." Phoebe sat down suddenly and

moved the teapot away. "Most people would contest without a second thought, and in a way it is the natural thing to do. But I understand your dilemma."

Abigail looked up. "You do?"

"Yes, I do. There are two sides to it. At first I didn't think so. But the other night, coming home from the hospital, I saw the other side for the first time. Now I can understand why it's a difficult decision for you. There really is a strong case for leaving it all behind. Of course the reasoning's subtle and allows for no greed at all," she said with a quick grin. "And, to be frank, I think it'd be wrong for ninety-nine percent of the people who had to make this decision, not to contest. But maybe it's not wrong for you. I don't know."

"See," Abigail said triumphantly. "It is a hard decision. I'm not crazy. But tell me," she added urgently, "what is the reasoning for not contesting?"

"Doesn't it have something to do with dignity and honor?"

Abigail nodded.

"And just being yourself? Letting the whole thing go? Poof. Gone. Clean. It's over. Done. Freedom. Independence. *C'est la vie*. But all I really care about," Phoebe said intently, "is that you face it, Abigail. I don't ever want to see you again the way you were last Monday."

They were silent.

Finally Abigail looked her straight in the face and said slowly, "Tell me exactly what I'm not doing."

"One," Phoebe began, "you're avoiding the will. And two . . ." She picked up the list and ran her finger down the columns. Everything had been typed, single-spaced, item after item—things to do, people to see—with Victoria, Sam and Bostrine at the very end. "First, look at what's not here." She tapped her finger against the paper. "Who you're not seeing. Where you're not going. And then, these three relatives . . ."

"I will see them at the very end," Abigail said firmly, her voice rising, "but I will not lay eyes on them again until I know I can handle it, and that's definite. Sam and Bostrine didn't even speak to me at my father's funeral. They didn't even give me a perfunctory hug, and I'm not going to see them today and I am not going to see them tomorrow. I am going to postpone it as long as I can and then, when I do see them, I am not going to have one single feeling in the world. I am going to be so strong and so in control that nothing they can say or do will affect me, and the only reason I am going to do it at all is that I want to have done it. I want to be able to tell myself on Monday, the sixth of May, when this whole thing is over, that I came out on top."

Nobody spoke. Phoebe poured tea. Abigail drank it. Finally Phoebe said, almost in a whisper, "There's still one thing. I hate to say it, but . . ."

"What?"

"It's what's really holding you back."

"What?"

"Your father again."

Abigail started shaking her head.

"You're afraid of him and his hating you."

"No."

"Yes, Abby. And by not seeing your relatives, not going to Weather Tree, you're trying to hide from it."

"No."

"To keep it as far away and as unreal as possible."

"No."

Phoebe paused. "Can't you just go to Weather Tree for a couple of days? See if you want to keep it? Or let it go?"

Abigail shook her head. "No."

The taxi bumped its way across town headed toward the Hudson River. Abigail wore a long slim silk dress and no jewelry but a watch. She lay with her head against the back of the seat and looked up. Buildings loomed overhead just as they had years ago when she made her way to the Waldorf-Astoria ladies' lounge to sleep.

People disappear in New York, she thought. She could change her life, slip into the crowd and vanish.

At the dock, voices from the yacht rose up in the night. She stepped on board and was caught in a swarm of people. The night was warm, with stars and a breeze, and soon the yacht, long and white, pulled away from the dock. It slid out into the rolling water of the harbor, the engine a rumble underneath. A man was playing the piano inside and music drifted out, mixing with the sounds of the night air passing. She stood in the bow and watched the New York skyline spread out across the water like a forest of lights. She thought about Luke. Maybe she liked him after all.

Later Jackson took her downstairs, where it was empty, and talked about Sam's health. Colds, he said, and coughs that wouldn't go away. Abigail watched him. He had baby-soft skin and manicured nails. "The doctors think maybe it's pneumonia," he was saying, "but they're not sure. They're putting him in the hospital for tests."

Short and fat, he didn't seem the sort of man to call Rushing Boarchards a best friend, Abby thought, but family linkage with Sara-Fey and Nicer had accounted for that. He had a town house in New York and children she had never liked, and he came to Weather Tree with expensive luggage, and loved it like his own home.

But tonight he was just like Isabel had been, Abigail thought, and she listened to him with growing irritation. Everything he had to say about Rush, when he finally got around to that, was glib and of no account—that he'd been great at school, the best friend a man could have, a terrific writer. But he told her one interesting thing about Annie-Fey: that she had been Rush's "first lay."

"He had her in the barn," was the way Paine put it.

Finally Abigail put down her Perrier and stood up. She had decided to be blunt. She didn't care if he liked her or not. "How can you not have any better insights about him?" she said. "You're supposed to be one of the best financial analysts in the world, and yet you have nothing consequential to say about a man you've known all your life. I asked you to tell me about him and you talk as if he had two kids and four grandchildren, and still played a great game of tennis."

Jackson rummaged in his pocket for a cigarette. "You've got a hell of a nerve."

"And you don't? Here he was, sick and self-destructive. He did an extraordinary thing to me and he committed suicide, and you have nothing more to say except that he was proud and iconoclastic. Don't you think there's more to it than that?"

"Of course there is. But why I should tell you, I don't know."

"But why not tell me?"

Suddenly Jackson's face looked tormented.

"He made fun of you for years," she said. "Called you a toadie and a fool behind your back. You had to know it. What did you think about that? What did you think about him?"

"I thought a lot about it."

"But what did it do to you?"

The yacht's horn was blowing.

"What did it do to you?" she repeated, her voice rising. "What's the point of keeping it to yourself? Who could understand better than I?"

"I thought he was probably the coldest son of a bitch I ever met," Jackson said. Suddenly he bent over and laid his head on his knees.

She went over beside him and put her arm around his back. "Why?" she cried.

"He was contemptuous of everyone. He called me Paine, Paine and Paine. Did you know that?" He looked at her.

"No."

His forehead was shiny. "Paine, Paine and Paine," he said, staring down at the floor. "He even began his letters that way: 'Dear Paine, Paine and Paine.'"

Abigail turned her eyes away. "Why didn't you ever tell anyone?"

"I didn't even tell myself. He even made fun of Mr. Rushing," he went on without a pause. "Said he was a crook, and he probably was, but that wasn't the point." Jackson got up and started walking around the room, his hands in his pockets. The boat swayed gently. "He didn't come to my son's wedding or my wife's funeral. I wanted him to see my first office and he said, 'I never go to offices.' I thought that was grand. He never told me he had a bad marriage or what happened to him in the war."

"He told you about me."

"I figured it out by myself. I figured everything out by myself. He never really liked me or trusted me. But . . ." He stopped in front of her and looked down at her. ". . . but that's what he thought about everyone, Abigail. Not just me and you. But everyone." Sitting down, he took her hand and squeezed it. "Except Pollibeaux," he said. "He liked Polly."

They didn't talk for a while. The yacht rolled and rolled and they sat holding hands. She wanted to interrupt the silence and ask his advice about the will, but she didn't know what to say. Do you simply ask, "Is money important?"

"But you know, Abby," Jackson said finally, "if Rush Boarchards said it, then I believed it. When he said the Nazis were bad, I decided the Nazis were bad. When he said he liked Roosevelt, I said I did too. I listened when he needed to talk. I went up when he wanted company. If he called and said, 'Paine, you son of a bitch, has work gotten to you yet?' I knew that was his way of saying he couldn't stand to be alone another second and he needed me, and I went up. But, goddammit, Abby, every single time he made me feel like he was doing me a favor. And you know what? I never questioned him or doubted him. Can you believe it? I saw everything in terms of how wonderful he was and how all of us did what we had to do, but he didn't. He dared to be different, and it's true, Abby, he did dare to be different. He didn't ever really want to do anything, as far as I could figure out, but he believed a lot of things and one of them had to do with people. That people were equal. Not him and me, we weren't equal. He was better, he had no doubt about that. But he didn't believe in 'class,' and that conviction meant a great deal to him. The way we all grew up made a profound impression on him. You've seen Rushing Mansion?"

She nodded.

"When the Depression came, all those tents were in the park. All those wretched people in their white tents. It was awful. Not for us, of course, but for them, and I remember him looking across the street at them once. It really got to him. And it got so he wanted nothing more than to live up there in the woods and be different, with all those people for his friends.

"But that took a lot of character at one time, Abby," Jackson went on. "You probably don't know that because now that sort of thing is common. But in our day, Rush was special. He had the courage and guts to go it on his own. To be himself. But I can't help thinking . . ." His voice drifted off.

"Thinking what?"

"I don't know," he said sadly. "Why did he have to hold it over us? Why did he have to act as if he was so special and we were all so ordinary? Why?" Jackson went over to the port-hole and looked out over the water, as if it held the pieces of a man or a friendship. "Where did it get him, Abby? You tell me. Where did it get him?"

Abigail woke in the middle of the night with a pain in her chest. It was between her breasts, deep and internal, something tearing her apart. She wanted to cry, but she couldn't. She thought about Jackson and herself, even Isabel, the deep dark pain he had brought to others, to her, but still the tears didn't come.

Sunday, April 21

Luke called. She was in the living room with the newspaper clippings spread around her on the floor and as she picked up the phone, she hoped it was him.

"So you're taking the day off for once," he said cheerfully.

Her heart leaped in relief. She could tell he had decided to forget their fight.

"Why don't you come to the movies with me," he said.

"I was thinking of going to Staten Island."

"Why?"

"They had a governess named Browne, and Jackson said she had a house on Staten Island, lots of relatives. Maybe the relatives are still there."

Luke didn't say anything.

"Maybe they can tell me something interesting," she said defensively. "It's not such a bad idea."

"Sounds absurd to me. If you want to know what I think, I think you should go to Weather Tree and stop horsing around. Any time you want help going through his files up there, I'll be glad to go."

"What movie do you want to see?"

"I want to see two. One at noon. The next across the street at two-thirty."

An hour later, when she spotted him up the block outside the theater, he was standing with a young man.

"This is my brother, Eddie," Luke said when she came up. "He's down from Harvard for the weekend. He wants to meet girls, so I brought him along."

Eddie blushed. He looked just like Luke, dark and handsome, except he had long hair and a skinny frame. "You went to Radcliffe," he said.

"But you'd have hated me." She laughed. "I was a mess. Awkward. Shy. Are you staying with him?" she asked as they made their way through the ticket line.

Eddie nodded. "My dad doesn't have much room."

"What does your dad do for a living?" she asked him.

"Just about lives at the tracks."

She bought her ticket. "I thought he was a medical technician, Luke. Why didn't you tell me?"

"I didn't want to bother you with extraneous information," Luke said, looking embarrassed.

"That's not extraneous," she said. "And I bet he's not a handler or a groom, is he, Eddie."

"He's a gambler," Luke said as they headed into the theater. They sat down in front, with Abby in the middle holding the popcorn. "He used to have two wallets," he continued when they were settled. "One for gambling, one for everyday expenses. But he gave that up a long time ago and now he just has one. . . ."

"And it's always empty," Eddie said.

"So he's a real gambler?" Abigail asked.

"A real one," Luke said, "complete with debts, flophouses . . ."

"Luke gives him money all the time," Eddie said. "He'll call up with no money to eat and Luke'll drive out to Queens to give him some."

When the movie was over at two o'clock, they bought hot dogs from a vendor's cart in the street and Eddie said good-bye.

Luke gave him a big hug. "Don't forget to send me that paper," he said.

Eddie gave Abigail a hug too and caught a cab to the train station.

"What paper?" she asked as they bought their next round of tickets.

"Something he wrote about South-American land use."

"Does that really interest you?"

"It does. I'd love to work there for a year or two."

"Do you speak Spanish?"

He nodded and they went inside. They were quiet now, more self-conscious, no laughing or joking without Eddie. In the middle of the movie, the film broke.

"Tell me more about your father," she said as they sat in the dark.

"I'll tell you about him another time," he said. "Tell me about your work instead. I'd rather hear more about you. Tell me why you like it so much."

"Lots of reasons."

"Give me one." They were leaning back, their heads against the seats.

"Financially, because it makes me independent. Professionally, because I'm talented and successful. Politically, because as a feminist, I believe in being a worker, same as I believe women should be allowed to drive trucks and climb telephone poles."

"What about the personal?"

"Because being a photographer lets me do what I like to do. Knowing about other people and their lives." She paused. "You want to know the real reason?"

He nodded.

"Because I really want to know how people work out their lives," she said, sitting up in her seat and looking back at him. "How they deal with night and day, fear, survival, love, wanting. I know it sounds silly, but that really interests me, and taking pictures allows me to be with people when things are happening to them, or maybe when nothing is happening, but I get to find out about them. And when all this will stuff is over . . ."

"And you're the new and different Abigail Boarchards. . . ." He grinned.

"Maybe," she said. "But then I can't wait to get back to work. This is the longest I've ever gone without working. You want to hear more?"

"Yes."

"Well . . ." Her eyes were flashing in the dim light. Luke was smiling a little, watching her. "People expose themselves in front of a camera," she said. "At least, if you make them comfortable they do. And I think of my pictures as telling stories, as finding moments when things suddenly happen and making them permanent. Because, you see, my memories are like that. Moments when things suddenly become clear. Do you have any idea what I mean? Does that make sense?"

"Sort of," he said.

When the movie started, he took her hand.

They went back to her apartment afterward. It was almost six and Alvah was due to arrive at six-thirty. She showed Luke her office, her filing system, the darkroom, the empty spaces on the walls where pictures of Weather Tree had been, the face of Clovis Moran screaming. She was about to tell him the story of Clovis Moran, when the doorbell rang. It was Alvah holding a batch of newspaper clippings under his arm. She gave him a quick kiss on the cheek.

The two men shook hands and she asked Alvah if he wanted coffee or a drink.

"That's a long drive up north," the detective said, loosening his tie. "Don't know how you do it all the time, Abby. Can I have coffee?"

When she came back with wine and coffee he was sitting on the couch in the living room and Luke was looking at her books.

"Let's get going," Alvah said, taking the coffee. "I want to get home."

As soon as she and Luke sat down, the detective started talking. "The upshot of the whole thing," he said, "is that your father tried to kill someone. I don't know who he was. All Diver could say was that he was small, dark-complexioned, and about fifty. It could be Algodones, or it could not be. There's no way to know. . . ."

"Maybe Algodones is a Spanish name," she interrupted.

"The only other thing about him," Alvah said, "is that he had only one ear. Just one ear. The other was cut off. Diver saw the whole thing. Boarchards shot at him, missed him, then tried to run him over with a jeep and ended up slamming into a tree."

"Was he drunk?" Luke asked.

"He was drunk. It was March, four years ago," he said and he added the date.

Just after Clovis Moran was caught, Abigail thought. The week her father called Wynne, Wynne and Pine.

Alvah's story went on for a long time. It had to do with the little town of Licking River that had grown up a long time back at the other end of the road that led to Weather Tree. It sat on the shores of the river itself and had a justice of the peace and a police chief, but no police force. Diver was all that was needed because the land was so poor, there were no people but old people—and young people who hadn't left yet. There was no crime or speeding, only tourists who had taken the wrong road to Lake Placid, and no outsiders except that winter when reporters had filled the diners and trailer courts for miles around because of the search for Clovis Moran. But that was all over now, and the town of Licking River, so small a driver blowing his nose would miss it, had slipped back into silence and routine. On the day in question, the police chief was doing one of the things he always did, year in, year out, just sitting in his own two-door Chevy sedan that could be described as an unmarked law-enforcement vehicle in the process of entrapment, except that it wasn't. He was just spinning the dial on the radio, content with the same small salary that meant he didn't have to work a farm or move his family south.

Alvah had driven up and found the justice of the peace, a man named Murphy, eating in the one place in Licking River that served meals, and together they found Diver down at Frank's store buying mosquito repellent. Alvah told them he was "from the family," and they went back to the jail where they told him everything they could.

"The one ear," Diver said, "looked like it was chopped off."

Diver said the day it happened he was sitting on the edge of town listening to music from Montreal when he noticed this guy standing where the New York–Montreal bus stopped. Diver wasn't paying much attention, he admitted, except to notice that he didn't know the man. Then he saw the man had one normal ear, but was flat on the other side of his head where the other ear should have been. "There was some kind of nubby stuff where the ear had been," he said, "and all kinds of scar tracks running up and down his neck."

That was when he saw the jeep. It was weaving along the road, with Boarchards leaning out the window aiming an antique hunting rifle straight at the man with one ear. He fired and missed, fired again, and the man started running up the road, trying to get away. Diver stormed out of his car, yelling at Boarchards to stop. "Are you crazy or something?" he screamed. But Boarchards aimed the jeep at the guy, stepped on the gas and went straight for him. But the guy jumped out of the way, and the jeep plowed straight on into a tree and stopped, the front end smashed all the way through to the steering wheel.

Diver managed to get the door open. Boarchards was draped over the wheel. Diver started to yank him out, afraid the thing would blow up. Behind him he heard a bus go by. Then Boarchards started vomiting, slid out of the jeep like a sack of grain, rolled over and passed out on the edge of the road.

Diver shook him by the shoulders, but he was dead to the world. He stood up, looked for the man with one ear, but there was no sign of him anywhere. He figured the man had taken the bus and disappeared. He stuffed Boarchards in the car and drove back to the jail. There he dumped him out on the bed in the cell and went right back outside. He found the judge having a beer and whispered in his ear he had Rush Boarchards in jail.

The judge paid up right away and left.

On the way back, Diver told him what had happened, but inside the cell, Boarchards was still dead to the world, the antique steel-and-wood hunting rifle beside him on the bed—the one he used to kill himself with, Abigail interjected—and Murphy said it looked like attempted murder to him, but since they didn't have the man with one ear, he didn't think they could make a case.

"But the thing was, they didn't want to anyway," Alvah said.

The judge told Diver to hold on to Boarchards until he sobered up and they figured out what to do. In the meantime, not to tell anyone.

"After a while," Alvah continued, "Boarchards came to. He looked depressed, Diver said, and he asked if he could borrow a cigarette. He wiped off some of the vomit with a rag and told Diver to go get Pollibeaux."

"He doesn't have a phone," Abigail said.

"Diver got Pollibeaux, and when they came back, he let Pollibeaux into the cell and sat out in the front room. He left the door ajar and tried to listen, but he didn't hear anything. Thing was, he said, they weren't saying anything. They were just sitting there."

Abigail nodded.

"Then, after a while, he began to hear voices, but he couldn't make out the words. It must have been midnight by then, and pretty soon the judge came over to see what was happening and Diver told him they were still in there talking and the question in both of their minds was . . ."

"What had happened?" Luke said.

"Exactly. Anyway, Pollibeaux came out after a while and Diver said he looked kind of shaken, like Boarchards had told him something. But Pollibeaux didn't say what it was. Instead he started to talk and he ended up working it out with the judge that Boarchards' license would have to be revoked. Pollibeaux asked was that all, and the judge said no, he'd have to be sure, if he wasn't going to press charges on something as serious as this, that Boarchards would go for treatment. Pollibeaux said your dad would never go for that and the judge said he just didn't say anything then, so Pollibeaux got the point and went back in and made your dad see he was lucky to get off so light. So then Boarchards came out and mentioned some place in Connecticut and said 'For a month?' and the judge said, 'No. Two.'"

"But what happened?" Luke asked, putting his wineglass down on the table and looking totally confused. "What on earth was it all about?"

Alvah shook his head. "I asked the same thing, and they said they didn't know. The judge said Pollibeaux told him something or other when he came out of the cell, but he didn't believe a word of it. He claimed Boarchards never saw the man before."

Alvah said the judge told him he looked at Pollibeaux and shook his head. "He's got weird eyes," he told Alvah. "You ever met him? Pollibeaux?"

Alvah had said no.

The judge took out a cigar. "He's something else. When we were after Clovis Moran, I swear to God that man can see a deer blink at a hundred yards. He just looks off into the distance and picks it up. I mean everything. It gives me the willies. He lies out there like an animal himself. You ever seen his house?"

Alvah had said no.

"Can't get him to say a word. Half an animal himself, must be. How he and Rush got so tight, I never could figure out. He would have found Clovis Moran in a hot minute," the judge went on, "but the snow covered up Moran's tracks so good, nobody could ever figure out how he got from the road to back in there in the mountains where he was hiding. We always figured he was someplace closer in because how in hell could he survive back in there? We never took him for smart."

Then the judge had returned to the story of Rush Boarchards and the antique hunting rifle, and he said when the trapper came out of the cell, looked him in the eyes and said it was all an accident, he just thought, Well, it could be true, and decided to let it go at that.

The next morning, he said, he and Diver filled out the papers about drunk driving, a tree and a wreck, but made no mention of the man with one ear or the gun. Then he sent the papers off to the D.M.V., category License Revoked, and that was that.

There was one other thing Alvah told Luke and Abigail. It had to do with Clovis Moran. Alvah said he stopped off to get newspaper clippings about Clovis Moran because he was curious about the coincidence of Moran hiding in the mountains at Weather Tree.

"But that's all it was. Wasn't it?" Abigail asked. "A coincidence?"

Alvah nodded. Then he moved his coffee cup and laid the clips out on the table. "Man Kills Wife, Her Lover, Two Children," said one headline. "Largest Manhunt in the North Woods," said another. "National Guard Called In."

"And he was hiding at Weather Tree the whole time," Alvah said.

"But my father didn't know that," Abigail replied. "Nobody did."

"What does Moran have to do with Boarchards?" Luke asked.

"Maybe nothing," Alvah answered.

"Then what's it all about?" the lawyer persisted.

"Moran was a local farmer," Abby explained. "He was on the Bataan Death March and spent four years in a Japanese prison camp. He came back with a hundred percent psychological disability. His wife, Joanne, had taken up with another man and they had had two daughters, but she brought Clovis home anyway and they all took care of him. He seemed retarded, but certainly not violent. Then he went crazy and killed them."

"Did you know him?" Luke asked.

Abigail shook her head. "They lived north of Licking River. The thing was, sometimes he took off into the woods and didn't come back for days. But later it turned out he was stocking this cave. . . ."

"What cave?"

"Where he ended up hiding. In the mountains. He had blankets, sleeping bags, things he had been stealing for years."

"How many?" Alvah asked.

"How many what?"

"Sleeping bags."

"Two."

"Like for two people?"

"Yes," she said. "I guess so. But he was alone. He had food, flashlights, matches. It started when his sister came to the house and found him hiding under the bed. He said, 'They're coming. The Japs are coming.' Joanne was going to move south and people were coming to take Clovis away to an institution, and so the sister assumed he must have heard Joanne talking and confused that with some incident from the war. She finally calmed him down, but that night when the family came home, he shot them and ran off into the woods."

"Diver told me one other thing about Clovis Moran," Alvah said. "He said he had a son."

"I don't think so," Abigail replied easily. "The girls were Joanne's and the lover's."

"This was another child," Alvah said. "Born even before the war. He died about fifteen years ago. His name was Robbie, and he'd be just a few years older than you."

Right then the memory came back.

Abby, peering over the cliff.

"The kid got lost in the woods and died," Alvah said. "On Weather Tree land."

Abigail started to nod.

"You know the story?"

"No. Yes. In a way."

"They found his body where it had gone over a cliff . . ." Alvah said.

"Yes. I saw it."

Little Abby looking down the steep incline, her sneakers in the mud.

"They told Moran, of course, when the boy was found, but Diver said they never did know if he heard them or understood."

Below her, outcroppings of rocks and trees, and then, far below at the bottom, a car with the side torn open. Leaves and tangles, a patch of red and a leg partially exposed in the under-brush.

Then Simon jerking her up by the collar and pulling her away. "Don't look there."

"Why not?"

He had her by the jacket and was dragging her across the road.

"Why not?"

"It's not nice."

"But what is it?" Trying to get away from him.

"Nothing. It's not for girls like you, that's what." Diver's car was there and her father's jeep, and a man on foot, a hunter from the village, stood looking over the cliff where Boarchards and Diver were making their way down the side. "I found him," the hunter said to Simon.

"Who?" Abby had asked.

"Get her out of here," Boarchards had yelled up.

"That's what I'm doing," Simon called back, and pushed her into the car.

But she had seen it.

The red flannel, flat, but not too flat, bunched out like there was something inside. And the blue jeans almost empty, but not quite empty. And up above the red shirt was a patch of something else, red too, a different color from the leaves, and it was only later that Abigail figured out it must have been the head, a mat of hair, separated from the skull, because there was no getting around that this was not a whole body, only the left-overs. Left over from winter and the animals.

It took her a while to notice the smell because she was so fixated in her mind on the red hair and the jeans and figuring out that it was pieces of a body, leftovers. But by the time Simon put her in the car, she could smell it too, an odor com-ing up out of the ravine like a balloon rising. She was ten years old, the first look and smell of death.

She didn't move. She stared straight at the dashboard, know-ing this was the biggest thing that had ever happened, and then she realized the red patches and the blue jeans were not only the leftovers of a body, but that the body was small and it was a child.

And that, she knew, made all the difference. That made it wrong. Not just sad, but wrong. Children didn't drive cars, go over cliffs, or die.

She also knew she had seen the boy before.

It was the boy in the kitchen. "What boy?" Pop had said. "There was no boy."

But there he was, the boy with red hair and a red plaid shirt, the leftovers.

"I'm going to leave you here, honey," Simon had said when they reached the crossroads. "I got work to do." But when she got out and started down toward the courtyard, he didn't go to the farm at all. He turned around and went right back out the road as fast as he could go.

She didn't tell her mother, but then her mother didn't ask. "Where's Pop?" she asked at bedtime and Grace said she didn't know and she could care less and Abigail said good night and went upstairs. But up there she took the flashlight and tiptoed across the hall to one of the bedrooms that looked out over the other side, to the clearing and the courtyard, and waited. There was no moon, and from up there, the meadow and the mountains were all dark, only the rooves standing out against the sky, and the sound of Licking River licking in the distance.

She already had her stuffed animal, the giraffe named Fred, but after a while she went back and got a pillow and a blanket, and with her chin resting on the windowsill and the window open so she could see out, she waited.

Downstairs she heard Grace move about from time to time, but there was no one else. The woman who cooked and the others who cleaned had left hours ago, walking back up the road to the farm. Now it was quiet.

After a while she saw the two headlights of the jeep and those of the truck behind. They came up out of the woods and into the open. They went slowly, one turning down toward the house and the other going on to the farm.

When the jeep stopped below, she pulled her head in. She heard the big door open, close, and then voices, and she tiptoed in the dark to the top of the back stairs, but they had gone

down the hall to the big room. So she ran lightly along the hall
to the door that opened to the balcony above the room and
carefully pulled it open.

Then she lay down on the floor, looking out over the balcony
and the room to the moose's glass eyes on the other side. Someone had laid a fire and its crackling now hid their voices where
they sat on the couch too far apart. She waited and waited, for
a word, at least. She was waiting for him to mention the boy
she had seen two months before in the kitchen. But nothing
filtered up, so after a while she crawled back out and went to
bed.

In the morning, she asked Rush what had happened.

"Nothing," he said.

"But I saw something in the leaves."

"What?"

"I don't know. Some old clothes. A car."

"That's all it was," he said. "Old clothes and a car."

On the way out to school, and then later on the way back in,
Simon wouldn't tell her anything. But then the next day when
she kept it up, he said, "It was a boy."

"What happened to him?"

"He ran away from the reform school."

"When?"

"Two or three months back."

"But I visited the reform school two or three months back."

"I know you did, honey."

"With Pop, and I saw a boy."

"Same place, honey. Lots of boys. This poor boy was probably there too."

"Then maybe I saw him?"

"Maybe."

She remembered all the boys who didn't look up and then
the one who did. He looked at her, freckles and blue eyes, and
the blue eyes looking at her for a million years. But she didn't
remember if he had red hair, like this one.

"Why was he in reform school?" little Abby asked of the boy
she had seen first in the kitchen and then over the cliff. "What
did he look like?" For she never had seen his face in the
kitchen, only his hair and a shirt and the back of his head.

"How do I know what he looked like," Simon said. "He stole stuff. Cars, radios, broke windows. Never went to school."

"That's not so bad."

"Not so good either. He broke out a couple of months ago. Punched a guard and stole a car."

She cooed like that was bad and asked how he got here.

"The car went over the cliff," Simon said.

"No. I mean, how did he get to Weather Tree?"

"He must have lost his way looking for a shortcut over the mountain," Simon said, knowing she knew, as everyone knew, that some mountain roads were shortcuts to the south.

"Oh," said Abby. She knew Simon thought he was telling the truth, but she also knew he wasn't.

He was the boy in the kitchen. She never saw his face, but it was not long after their visit to the school, and the boy was standing with his back to the door. He had red hair and a red plaid shirt and his arm was out, pointing across the room at Pop. Pop was facing her, his eyes wide and staring, and she was about to say, "Pop, I'm thirsty," but instead she pulled back into the hall.

Just as the boy, the one in the bushes, the leftovers, said:

"My father says you owe me."

Afterward Pop had come up to bed. He didn't leave the house or follow the boy down where he ended up off a cliff. He came to bed. Abigail remembered this now as she was lying in bed. Alvah and Luke had gone, and she lay in the dark and remembered. It had been winter then, cold and dry, and she heard Rush come up the stairs past the mural and the balcony. Then he stopped outside her door. Down in the courtyard, she heard a car drive away and she knew the boy was leaving.

When Rush came into her room, she had pretended to be asleep. He crossed over to the bed, bent down and kissed her on the cheek. Then he stood up. "Sweet dreams, little girl," he said.

And so she knew he was thinking of the boy, not her, and talking to him, not her, because he never called her "little girl" or said words aloud like that. She had the feeling, even then, he was saying them to her because he hadn't said them to the boy.

He left and went down the hall to the great big room with
the files and the typewriter. She heard his chair being pulled
out from under his desk, got up and followed him.

"You should be asleep, Abby."

"I know."

"Well, go back to bed."

"I just wanted to see you."

He laughed a little and patted her on the head.

"What are you doing?" she asked. The room was dark, looking out over the mountains. Grace was asleep next door.

"Nothing."

"You're thinking, aren't you?"

"Sort of."

"About what?" She didn't mention the boy because in the
glow of his cigarette, she could see his face and he was so ab-
sent, almost, she didn't want to disturb him. For the first time
she felt that her father was like something big whittling down
to something small. It frightened her, as if he was about to disappear, and she put her hand on his arm. "What are you thinking about?"

"Nothing."

"Remembering?"

"Sort of."

"What?" Waiting for him to mention the boy.

"Nothing much. You should be in bed."

"You remembering bad things?"

He didn't answer.

"Are you sad?"

He still didn't answer.

"I know you are."

"You do, do you?" He smiled.

She wanted to keep him talking, because there was something so terribly sad in his voice.

"You go to bed now," he said.

"But what about you, Pop?"

"I'm all right."

"I'll go if you go too."

"I will. In a minute," he said. "I promise." He patted her on
the head, and when she reached the door she turned back and

said, "Good night," but he was already gone, looking out the window. He had forgotten she was there.

The next morning he was slow and quiet.

"Who was the boy?" she asked.

"What boy?"

"I thought I heard a boy in the kitchen last night."

"There was no boy."

And when Simon came to get her to take her to school, Pop still didn't say anything about the boy, and so, for the first time, she had wondered what had happened. And worse. It wasn't very nice to send the boy away, mad like that, and two months later, when she saw the red plaid over the cliff, she knew her father had had a hand in letting him fall.

And so the thing was, she always knew that Pop had a big sad wondering all tied up, in part, with a boy he helped to die. But because her knowing was illicit, and his own doing illicit too, it seemed, she never made it real. She stashed it away and it got all covered over, never more than a second or a flash, "My father says you owe me." And it got locked off in time somewhere, almost gone, red hair and a shirt, more a speck than a memory.

But later it got distorted even more.

Through the years she had tried to remember a million times if the boy in the red brick building had hair like the boy over the cliff, the boy in the kitchen, but she couldn't recall. Nonetheless, in some faraway, magical way, she made them one and the same. She never knew the dead boy's name, until Alvah Germaine said it in her living room—Robbie Moran—and she still didn't know the other boy's name. She never would. But she had always given the dead boy the other boy's face, blue eyes and freckles, and so it was that there were two boys and two lives, one dead, one alive, but for little Abby or Abigail, they were one and the same. They had the same face. And the whole thing, so vague and obscure, was illicit at the core, a boy who was never in the kitchen. A boy she never saw. A boy who died anyway.

Monday, Tuesday and Wednesday

$\mathbf{D}$uring the next three days Abigail had lunch with Jackson Paine, dinner with Alvah and drinks with Max. She had a telephone conversation with Rush's editor, Corriander Bush, and countless other talks about her father. A detective was now stationed outside her building, but there was no sign of Joe Algodones, and between her continued uncertainty about the will and her concern over why this man was on her trail, she felt increasingly uneasy and adrift.

She knew periodically there was something important she wanted to tell Alvah, but she couldn't remember what it was or that it had to do with Clovis Moran and a boy. It was all part of falling asleep and dreams, too elusive to have words or talk about.

She had a headache, too, all the time now. It was as if someone were inside, she imagined, pounding on her skull trying to get out, get loose. But she proceeded steadily with her investigation, closed her mind when Phoebe prodded more about how she had to go to Weather Tree, and she spent a good deal of time thinking about Luke Reider.

She remembered Alvah's story about the boy over the cliff, but instead of trying to locate the odd memory that tickled around the edges of her brain, she fixated on the coincidence instead. That her life had intersected with Moran's not once, but twice. That those leftovers, the boy in the red plaid shirt, were pieces of his life too, not just hers. But that they were a part of her father, too, she had not quite realized.

Instead she remembered a lot of other things these three days.

Grace's voice yelling triumphantly at Weather Tree. "You're trying to take her away from me! She's no daughter to me, so I'll take her away from you. See if she wants your precious woods when I've got her in New York."

More. Grace again. "She's fat and awkward. It's your fault. If she had a normal father . . ."

More. She buying Grace presents, cards, trying to get her to like her more.

Another. This time an ashtray thrown across the room in New York. "Look at me," Grace yelled at him. But he didn't. She yelled at Abby, slapped her, but he didn't move. Abby in the bathroom, water running, blood dripping from her forehead, and then silence. A door somewhere opening, closing, a man going down the back stairs. Later the papers arrived, typed and legal, Wynne, Wynne and Pine. Dissolution desired.

More.

Blue jeans and fatigue jacket. Cameras, a name tag and a press pass. The sixties long ago, marches and demonstrations, she running in and out, getting pictures, Vietnam not far away at all right now. Then, at one demonstration, a limousine on the side. Washington now, and it had official plates, antennas, an official seeing for himself. He was on the sidewalk with aides and walkie-talkies, and she ran up, camera ready in case he was Somebody. And he was. Famous face and all.

But suddenly he glared at her name tag, grabbed her by the arm, and screamed, "What are you doing here? You bastard. Your father was my friend. What's the matter with you?" Then he got himself under control. "No better than the rest, are you?" he snarled, letting her go.

"Right," she cried, anger unleashed, and brought the camera up like a fist and clicked away until they pushed her back. "Fuck you," she yelled and gave him the finger for invoking a family to tell her who she was supposed to be.

Corriander Bush had said a lot of things. Yes, there was an unfinished manuscript, but no, it was not "the big one" about the Adirondack Mountains Annie-Fey had described.

"That turned into a real fiasco," he said. "It was supposed to be his comeback, and he kept telling me he was working on it, but when I finally said, 'Rush, I'll have to show them something,' he said, 'Oh, that.' He said the publisher didn't know anything and he, Rushing Boarchards, couldn't be bought and sold like toothpaste. I told him he was a fool, always wanting to write about the Adirondacks; now he had his chance and he couldn't do it."

Abigail asked him about the unfinished manuscript, but Bush didn't answer. "Your father had talent," he said instead. "But he could never get it out. Writing was torture. That's why he drank, of course."

"What was the manuscript about?"

"The war," Bush said. "Right after *Men of War*, he told me the next book was going to be about 'the bad side' of war, and I said great. But the next thing I knew he said he was moving to the mountains. He said he could write better up there; the city was too distracting."

"What happened to the war book?"

"He always said he wasn't ready to show me anything. About four years ago he called me up and said he'd finally started writing it. But I don't know what happened to it. I never talked to him again."

She had lunch with Jackson Paine at "21." She had shrimp, all he had was madrilene, and after their exchange the other night, she liked him now. They talked about Algodones and the will and money. Money, he said, could be liberating or stultifying, but it had been both to the Rushings and the Boarchards. "I'm sure they'll settle your suit," he said. "It'll never go to court. Bostrine will see to that."

Later, when Abigail rambled on trying to describe the maze of emotions that stood between her and any final decision about the will, he listened carefully. "I'm paralyzed with indecision," she said.

"I don't know how to advise you about it," he said afterward. "Except to tell you that I agree with one thing you say—that whatever you do will be right, because the issue is simply the doing and the deciding. The process itself. That's the way you tell it and I agree with you. Of course, half the world would think you were a fool to hesitate for one second going after this much money, but I don't. There is no right or wrong to this. Money isn't something one necessarily has to go after. There are other things in life, and besides, you're not going to be destitute if you don't contest. You still have the money Grace left you. It's certainly nothing like the Rushing-Boarchards money, but you'll never be a pauper. And I wouldn't be surprised, given what you say, if Max left you everything.

"But now that I've said that," he went on as a waiter poured wine, "let me say that if money is not an issue to you, then Weather Tree should be. It has to be. I know if I could never go there again, something would drop out of my life. I don't know what I'd do."

"But why?" she asked, toying with her glass.

"Why? For lots of reasons. Belonging, for one. Nature, another." He looked at her. "My Uncle Nicer first went there the year he married Sara-Fey, but I first went as a baby, like all of you—you, your father. And so I have much the same feeling about Weather Tree as all of you."

"What feeling?"

"That this magnificent, private spot—and the 'private' is as important as the 'magnificent,' Abigail—that it is mine. Belonging and owning," he said. "Those are the reasons. Those are the feelings. Because to own and belong to a place like Weather Tree can give you a depth of security and peace no visit to a national park can match. It's like having a piece of God or Time all for your very own. Trouble can come and go—wars, death, change—but all that land remains, Abigail. It survives. It lasts. Do I sound silly?"

"No. Not at all. It's very moving."

Later Jackson also had something to say about Melanie Anderson.

"She was pretty, all right, but I told him she was no good. He wouldn't listen. When she finally threw him over, he came to my place for a brandy one night and he said I'd been right. That's what made him pull up stakes and move to Weather Tree. She hurt him very badly. He was never the same again."

"Everyone says that. Isabel said it was Grace. A soldier said it was the war. A doctor said it was his mother. His editor, the book."

"But it was Melanie," Jackson insisted. "I saw them at El Morocco one night and everything was fine. He even got me into the bathroom with him and asked if I could come to Sun Valley with him, hinted he was going out there to get a divorce. But a couple of days later, he suddenly rang my doorbell one night and stood there looking like hell warmed over. I brought him in, sat him down, gave him a brandy and he said he was taking Grace to live at Weather Tree, and I said, 'Christ, why?' He said he wanted to be 'a real writer,' but I never saw anyone look so sad. 'Come off it,' I said. 'What happened with Melanie?' "

"What'd he say?"

"That she'd thrown him over. Out of the blue."

Things came from Alvah, clippings, Army records, credit ratings, bank statements. There was even an old article quoting "Whitaker Stylus Rushing, Esquire" saying he had given "a million or two" to the Liberty Loan.

"Get it off to a good start," he told the reporter.

On Wednesday Luke called for the first time since Sunday. He talked about his upcoming meeting on Saturday, May 4, but she knew right away something was the matter.

"I've been doing some work on your father," he said finally.

"I started going through old credit card receipts over at the office one night."

"What was it? Tell me."

"Well," he said with obvious reluctance. "He spent three months in New York last winter."

Abigail didn't say anything.

"I guess you were here then, weren't you?"

"Yes."

"And didn't know."

"No."

"You want the address?"

"I guess."

She wrote it down. The Jefferson Hotel on a seedy street off Times Square.

Luke asked if she wanted to get a hamburger later.

"I can't." She pressed her hand against the pain in her chest. "I'm busy." Her head throbbed. She'd had the pain in her chest for days. It hurt. Now this.

"We could go over to Ninth Avenue," he said. "Have a few drinks. Play pool. Do you play pool?"

"No."

"I'll meet you at the bar on Fifty-sixth and Ninth at eight-thirty."

She swung open the door. It was dark inside. Spotting him at the bar, she walked over and sat down. He was playing with a pack of cards and drinking a beer. He smiled at her. They were both wearing old jeans and sweaters.

"What do you want to drink?" he asked.

"Vodka tonic."

He placed the order. "Make it a double," he added. "That's a nice sweater."

"How do you know?" She laughed. "You barely looked."

"I have eyes inside my head." He did a card trick.

"I could do that one in the second grade," she said. "Don't you know any better ones?" She took the pack and pulled her stool closer to his. He looked at her as if he were going to say something, but then he didn't.

"Are these cards yours?" she asked.

"His." He nodded toward the bartender.

They did tricks and didn't talk much. They never mentioned the Jefferson Hotel or Rushing Boarchards. After a while he ordered her another vodka and she started feeling better, but the pain in her chest was still there. The jukebox played the Clancy Brothers and he said she should live in Ireland. It was nice and gloomy there.

"I'm not always gloomy," she said.

"I know. You're not gloomy now."

"You want to play fish?"

He dealt the hand, she won the first round, he the rest. The clogged feeling in her chest was beginning to go.

He ordered another round.

"Are you trying to get me drunk?" she asked.

"No. But it might do you good. Have you ever been drunk?"

"No."

"Didn't think so."

"Did you think of me at all?" She looked him in the eyes suddenly.

"Yes." They went on playing fish and ate hamburgers.

The next bar a few blocks south was mostly Puerto Rican and the Spanish-language radio was blaring loudly. He asked the bartender for cards again and this time they played rummy and drank more doubles. He was drinking vodka too now and Abigail knew she had drunk too much.

"What if I get really drunk?" she asked.

"You *are* drunk. So what? I'll get you home."

"But what if I get sick?" Her head was starting to weave.

"Then it'll be just like the first time we met. But do you want to go home?"

"No. Actually I feel great for once. All week long I've had this terrible headache, this awful pain in my chest."

But something was beginning to happen. Through the haze of alcohol, everything she had forgotten earlier was coming back—her father, the will, people who didn't talk to her. Knock, knock. Who's there? Please let me in. Please let me in.

The next bar had a pool table but they sat in a booth against the wall. Abigail held out her right hand. "How would I look with a diamond?" she slurred.

"Terrible."

"A big diamond?"

He shook his head.

"Emeralds?"

"Worse." He had his arm up along the booth near her head.

Weaving a little she pulled her sweater back to free the wrist and look at imaginary bracelets there. "I might want them one day. What do you think?"

His hand touched her hair.

"I might want the jewelry."

"I doubt it." He was playing with the hair, pulling out strands away from her neck and watching them fall lightly back in place.

"I might need the money."

He shook his head.

"Do you want to be my lawyer?" she mumbled. " 'S all right. I have a lawyer."

"You want to go home, Abby?"

"You tell me what to do about the will."

"Let me take you home," he said.

"You decide. Somebody has to decide."

"I'll get a cab."

She shook her head drunkenly.

"You're very beautiful," he said.

She got up from the table and started making her way toward the back. She bumped into a man with an empty tray. He put his hands out to steady her, but she dodged and kept going. In the back she headed down the hall to the phone booth, stumbled, made it to the door and then collapsed inside. She slumped over her knees, until she finally pushed herself up, dialed, managed to give her credit card number, and then let her head fall over again as she listened to it ring.

A man answered. "Rushing residence."

"May I speak to Miss Rushing?"

"Excuse me?"

"Miss Rushing, please. Abigail Boarchards calling."

She waited. The phone booth was dark, the bulb burned out.

"Hello." It was Aunt Bostrine.

Abby didn't say anything.

"Hello?" the woman said again.

"It's me, Auntie. I want to come in."

"Abby? I can't understand you. What's the matter?"

"Why did you do it?"

"Do what?"

"I want to come in."

"You'll have to speak up."

"You didn't talk to me. You didn't say hello. You went right on talking about frogs, and I wanted . . ." Her head keeled over and bumped against the wall.

"Are you drunk?"

"You took my things. The jewelry was mine, Auntie. Those diamonds, emeralds. They were mine."

"That's nonsense. Don't be ridiculous, Abby. I didn't take anything. It was what he wanted."

"He did not."

"If you're drunk, I'm not going to talk to you. I never talk to people who are drunk." Bostrine hung up the phone.

Abigail rocked back and forth in the dark. The jukebox was playing in the background. She found a dime and put it in the phone. She started dialing. "Victoria?" she said aloud as the phone started to ring. "You'll talk to me. I know you will. I . . ."

A man picked up the receiver. "Hello?"

Abigail suddenly jerked her head up as if she'd been slapped and dropped the receiver. It slammed against the wall, the voice of Sam inside. Abigail started shaking her head back and forth. The receiver kept knocking against the wall. "Hello?" came the sound of Sam's voice. "Hello?"

Abigail began to cry. She caught the receiver and put it back in the rack. Then, picking it up right away, she dialed again, still crying, tears rolling down her face.

"May I speak to Uncle Max?" She hiccuped loudly.

"Are you all right?" It was Foster.

"I want to speak to Uncle Max." Her head was still shaking from side to side.

Max came on quickly. "What's happened?"

Abigail got off the seat and crouched down on the floor.

"Why are you crying? Abby? What's the matter?"

"I'm having dinner with Luke," she said, through her tears.

"Who's Luke?"

"I called Auntie."

"Oh dear."

"She hung up on me."

"Oh dear."

"And Victoria. But Sam answered. Why did Sam answer? Jackson said he was in the hospital. He said he had pneumonia."

"He's going in tomorrow. What'd you say to him?"

"I hung up."

"You've had a few drinks, I take it."

"A few."

"This fellow, he'll take you home?"

"Uncle Max? Will you help me?"

"Anything."

"Why did he do it? Why did Pop . . ."

"Let's talk about it tomorrow."

"If I go to Weather Tree, will you come with me?"

Someone was knocking on the door. She looked up. It was Luke.

"I have to go." She hung up the phone.

Luke wedged open the door and crouched down on the floor beside her. "What are you doing?" He put his arm around her.

"I called Bostrine."

"Oh, Abby."

She bent her head down and pulled away from him.

"Come on," he said.

"Let me be."

"Let me take you home."

"I'm cold."

"Come on." He took her by the arm and lifted her out.

"They took my things."

"I know." He put his arm around her and steered her through the bar.

"They didn't talk to me."

"I know."

He got a cab and helped her in. She leaned against him and he put his arm around her.

"He never came to my school."

"I know."

"Or looked at my pictures. Or said good-bye."

"I know."

"He just left. She hit me and I was bleeding and I didn't even know he had gone. I even have a scar. See?" She sat up so he could see her better and lifted the hair off her face. "See?" She pointed to a thin line along her scalp.

He pulled her down against his shoulder and rocked her a little bit.

At home he helped her off the elevator and down the hall. He took off her coat and got her on the bed. She reached out for him with her hands and tried to pull him down, but he just took off first one boot, then the other, and then he lifted her legs, pulled off the jeans and slid her bare legs down under the covers. He pulled the blankets up to her face.

"Don't leave," she mumbled.

He fixed the pillows around her head and sat down beside her. Her eyes were shut and he put his hand on her head and started stroking her. She began to perspire. Then she got very hot.

"Do you want to vomit?"

"No."

"Shall I get you some milk?"

She shook her head.

"Go to sleep."

"My chest hurts."

"It'll be all right."

Suddenly she pushed her face down into the pillow and started to cry. Her body began to shake. He tried to lift her up to hold her against his chest, but she was a dead weight. She cried harder, face against the mattress, sobbing. He kept his hand moving over her shoulders and her hair. She cried and cried and cried.

"My father, he . . ." she sobbed.

"I know."

"He never had time for me."

"I know."

"Never. Even when . . ."

"You were little. I know."

A long time passed, she crying more, then falling silent, and Luke watched her, looking around the room, then back at her still form lying there. Finally her breathing got slower and slower, and she fell asleep.

Luke didn't move. He waited, watching her, and then he stood up. He looked down at Eric, lying near her face, then he put his hand on her head and moved it slowly down to her neck, along the top of the blanket and down her back to her fanny.

When he reached her fanny, he stopped. He felt the rise of her buttocks with his big outstretched hand. Then he moved the hand and squeezed first one, holding it firmly, and then the other. Then he turned, went down the hall and let himself out.

Abigail woke at once at the sound of the door closing. She sat up in bed and stared into the dark. A single powerful image was stamped in her mind. It was electrifying.

Little Abby Boarchards was holding her father's hand. Holding on and not letting go. For all the world, not letting go. But the thing was, the father's head was turned away. Unaware, preoccupied, he was gone.

The little girl just didn't know. She thought he was all there, all hers, but he was already gone, no need to wait for alcohol and decay. The girl just didn't know. She didn't want to know. He was all she had.

Thursday, April 25

⚜

She woke early, looked in the mirror at her red eyes and immediately got the list out of her purse. Then she tore it up, threw it away and got a fresh sheet of paper. Going back to bed, she wrote in big bold letters:

"Eleven days left." She underlined that, then she wrote:

"Go to Weather Tree. See Simon and Polly.

"Face his hate. Look at it. Feel it if I have to, but don't avoid it anymore.

"Talk to Melanie.

"Find Algodones.

"Visit Jefferson Hotel.

"Decide about the will.

"Talk to Victoria, Sam, Bostrine."

Finished, she went to the darkroom and pulled out one of the pictures from where she had hidden it months before. It showed Rush, tall and handsome, and she, little, running along behind.

She stared at it with new eyes and wondered how she could have overlooked for so long the power of her own devotion and its capacity to distort the truth.

Alvah said he could leave tomorrow.

Max asked what was going on and she said she'd explain "up there."

Simon simply sounded relieved to hear her voice and said he'd get a cook.

Melanie Anderson's secretary apologized for her boss's "delay" and wrote down the telephone number for Weather Tree.

"You have to get the operator," Abigail explained. "Just ask for New York State, Licking River One."

She called Jackson Paine to tell him her decision to go. He approved, then said, "I thought of something else after we left '21.'"

"What?"

"It will only confuse you all the more."

"Tell me anyway. I can't get much more indecisive than I am now," she added, laughing.

"Well," he began, "there's philosophy to all this, you know."

"Philosophy?"

"Yes. By being his only child, you are his heir. You are the heir apparent."

"Yes."

"And although the law may say you have the same right to his property as he has to disown you—that these two rights are equal legally . . ."

"Yes."

". . . philosophically they are not equal at all. You have a greater right to inherit than he has to disown. Because the heir inherits. It's a broader, more intangible right than the law recognizes. It's biblical. Historical. International. It's even mythical, for God's sake. A right that has no boundaries, no limitations. Every culture since time began has recognized the heir's right to inherit what is his. And that it *is* his," Jackson emphasized. "The son takes over where the father left off. His herd becomes the boy's herd. His land becomes the boy's land. The father's death becomes the son's fulfillment. The son can come into his own only when the father dies. To pass on and to inherit is an act of Nature."

"Is it the same for a daughter?" she asked.

"Of course it is," Jackson Paine said. "It's exactly the same."

She called Luke and told him she was going to Weather Tree. He asked her if she remembered much about last night. She said no.

"It made me start thinking about something, Abby. . . . No, hear me out," he insisted when she started to interrupt. "I figured something out. It began when I realized you were like a little girl crying. And first, I thought about the fact that you really were a little girl once, and that Rush was younger once too, and about how this whole thing between him and Algodones, whatever it is, goes back ten, twenty, thirty years. And, Abby, that's a long time," he said. "A long time. And I figured something out."

"What?"

"There's a connection between your father and Clovis Moran. . . ."

"Clovis Moran? But what about Algodones?"

"Hear me out. A connection that goes back a long time."

"I don't think so," Abigail said.

"Then why did Moran hide in the cave at Weather Tree?" Luke asked.

"It was a good hiding place."

"Why did he come to the clearing that night when you and Josh found him?"

"He was looking for food . . ."

"Why did his son die on your property?"

"He took the shortcut over the mountain."

"Why did they both, Clovis Moran and your father, end up in the Philippines? Two men from Licking River?"

"Coincidence of war," she said, but suddenly the memory snapped back.

Boy in the kitchen. My father says you owe me. Little Robbie Moran. And she knew nothing was a coincidence at all. It was an intertwining of lives, little Abby Boarchards just a witness from afar, leftovers too.

"What if the war was just the first coincidence?" Luke was saying. "And all the rest weren't? What if there's a connection between Clovis Moran and Joe Algodones and your father? Three men? And Clovis Moran is the missing link to Algodones . . . ?"

Little Abby Boarchards, witness from afar, caught in an intertwining of lives that had nothing to do with her. Three men, one who brought her professional success with his picture in the snow. Another who brought her "four quarters and nothing more." And the other? . . .

What would Algodones bring her?

"I think we'll find Algodones through Moran," Luke was saying. "That's how we'll finally track him down."

The man behind the desk in the Jefferson Hotel looked back in the register and found his name. "Come on," he said. He took her up in the elevator to the top floor. The room was the color of dirty beige. It had a bed, a bureau, a light bulb in the ceiling and no bathroom.

"He stayed three months and then someone came to pick him up," the man said. "Couldn't drive himself."

"Who came?"

"He was real tall, smelled like bacon fat or something."

It was Polly. "Did you ever talk to Boarchards?"

"Sure. Me and him and his friend . . ."

"Friend?"

"A little guy. Only had one ear. Said he lives in New York."

"You know where?"

The man shook his head.

"Did Boarchards ever say he had relatives here?" she asked.

"No. Didn't have a family, this man. This man had nothing but the clothes on his back."

"Did he go out much?"

"Saw him down at the corner a couple of times."

"The liquor store?"

He nodded. "You say he's dead? Well, I seen it coming. You might even say he was looking for it. Who'd you say you was?"

"I work for his lawyer," she answered.

"Oh," he said. "Too bad."

"What do you mean?"

"Too bad he didn't have someone like you."

"What do you mean?"

"That's all you need, you know."

"What?"

"To help you out. A pretty face. Company. Doesn't even have to be love. Just company."

Luke picked her up downstairs. His car was an old Mercedes, dating from the times when cars were more round than sleek.

The doorman showed her where the detective was parked, said nothing had happened, no one had come. "But you never know," he added. "Some people, you never know what's in their head. He might still be looking for you; he might not."

"That's right," Abigail said grimly.

"Where are we going?" she asked when she got in the car.

Luke pulled out into traffic. "Have you ever been to Montauk?"

"Yes."

"Jones Beach?"

"Yes."

"Oyster Bay?"

"What's this all about?" she asked.

"Where's someplace you've never been?" He looked at her.

"Lots of places."

"Nearby. Preferably with a beach."

"City Island."

"Now ask me where we're going."

Abigail grinned. "Where are we going?"

"City Island."

"Why?"

"This is the first outing for the new and future Abigail Boarchards."

"I see." She folded her arms across her chest. "And what's she like? Just in case I see her?"

"Oh, she's marvelous," Luke said. "You'd like her. She's got a wonderful sense of humor. Lots of confidence. Doesn't mind when her eyes are so puffy she looks like a sick Chinaman."

"Stop it."

"You'd never have liked the old one. She was touchy, suspicious. Only told the truth once a week. Rest of the time she lied and said she was busy. . . ."

He parked in the empty lot and they walked toward the ocean. Some fishermen were there, a couple of Puerto Ricans standing in the waves eating oranges and old blacks with long fishing poles, hair like gray cotton.

They headed toward the pier, side by side, kicking at driftwood brought in by the tide. A wind was blowing. The smell of salt and fish was strong. Abigail took a rubber band out of her pocket and pulled her hair back out of her eyes. Luke watched her and then, walking, he reached out his arm and put it around her shoulders and left it there.

They walked along the pier, their collars up against the wind. The shops were closed, wire nets across the doors until the weekend came. A few dogs lay in the sun and the signs said things like "Worms," "Tackle" and "Burgers." He asked if she wanted something to eat and she said, sure, but instead they stopped at the railing and peered out into the water. Boats were moored, dinghies bumping on the current, seagulls everywhere, swooping, calling, diving, floating.

"If I could be any bird on earth, I'd be a gull," she said.

"What if I wanted to be a hawk?" he said, but he didn't seem to expect an answer, so she didn't give one.

They watched the gulls and the water, a man below plying along the pier in a rowboat.

"Let's get something to eat," Luke said.

They wandered down the pier and found a little place with a counter along the window and the grill in back. They ate fried clams and tartar sauce, taste of the sea.

When they finished, the sun was going down. Luke took her

by the hand and led her across the sidewalk toward the beach.

Abigail looked down at his hand in hers. She knew what was going to happen. His hand was big and warm and its warmth seemed to extend up her arm and beyond. I'll be with him the rest of my life, she thought.

The sun was shining on the water and in the distance the boats stood out against the sky. They went along the shore, looking at the sand and waves, and she listened to the gulls, the wind, the water licking at her boots. His hand was strong, held hers firmly. Fishermen were packing up their things to go and some boys had started a fire on the beach. They walked slower and slower.

Then Luke stopped and turned to face her. He didn't say anything, just looked at her and moved his hands up along her arms to her face. Then his fingers moved across her cheeks as if taking information from her skin and he drew her head in and kissed her.

Their lips touched so softly at first, it was as if people were barely there. He closed his eyes, but Abigail kept looking, at his hair, his face, and she frowned for a second. But then he looked at her, and pushed his head harder against hers, her lips pressing against his, and she closed her eyes and wrapped her arms tightly around him, feeling his back, his arms.

After a while he stepped back from her, looked at her almost as if he were looking through her, as if she weren't there, weren't watching him. And he brushed his hand over and over her hair, as if for the first time he was getting to do what he had wanted to do for a long time. "Are you cold?" he finally asked quietly.

"No. Sort of."

He put his arm around her shoulder and led her away from the water toward a shack at the end of the beach. "Alfie's Snacks," it said. It was closed, had a porch, a door and a wall against the wind. He sat down, pulled her next to him, and they leaned against the wall, legs out in front, the water straight ahead.

"Warmer now?"

"Yes."

They sat that way, hand in hand, shoulders, arms and feet aligned, and sunset was a long time coming. Abigail felt things she knew she'd never felt before.

"I came here once as a boy," Luke said after a while. "It's funny you picked it. My father brought me out to fish. It was before he started going to the tracks all the time. He still had two wallets then. After that it got so he spent every weekend and every night at the tracks, then he stopped coming home altogether. He told my mother he couldn't do two things at the same time. So he took a room in Queens close to the tracks. She tried to get him to see us, but he said he was too busy. He quit his job. She found him in a flophouse once when I was thirteen, brought him home for a week, but then, one day, he was gone. He came back about a year later, gave her some money, came back another time when he'd been beaten up for nonpayment of gambling debts."

"Where is he now?" She was holding his hand tight in both of hers.

"In Queens. But I pay the rent now. He was the kind of person who never took a risk in his life until he started gambling."

"How often do you see him?"

"He's more stable now, with the rent paid. I take him to lunch every now and then. Eddie tries to see him more. It bothered me for a long time," Luke went on. "I wanted a father. Everyone else had fathers. They took them fishing, went to baseball games. That's what I liked about your father. He was always there. In the same place." He leaned his head back against the wall and looked at her.

She smiled.

"I used to go to your room," he said. "Wonder what you were like."

"Can I meet him sometime?"

"Don't you want to know what I thought up there in your room?"

She blushed.

"Doesn't matter anyway," he said, standing up and pulling her up into his arms. "Wasn't very interesting anyway. I was mostly confused."

They drove back to Manhattan. Outside her building he parked and took her toward the door, but at the last minute he pulled her around the corner and in the shadows they started kissing again. He pushed up against the building, his body along hers, their arms tight around each other, kissing as if the world was going to end. Then he started moving his fingers through her hair.

"You like my hair," she said.

"I do." Then he frowned a little. "I've been waiting for you," he said. "Did you know that?"

"No."

He was tracing her eyebrows with his finger. "Not at all?"

"Maybe yesterday," she said.

"But not the day before yesterday?"

"No."

"Not last week?"

"No."

"Or the week before that?"

She started to grin. "No."

"Not last month? Not February?"

She started to laugh. "Stop it."

"Not in January?"

She pushed her face against his chest.

"Not in the hall when I saw you for the very first time? You didn't know then? I did."

She went upstairs alone in the elevator. He hadn't mentioned coming up and neither had she. Go slowly. At the door, Eric was waiting. She scooped him up in her arms and, nuzzling him in the face, went down the hall to the bedroom.

She remembered Alvah: "Any man that wants you would be a fool to hurry you. You'd run so fast—the four-minute mile. If he really wanted you, he'd wait and go so slow finally nothing could keep you away."

Luke called when she was in bed. "Were you asleep?" he asked.

"No. Just lying here thinking."

"About what?"

"Everything."

"I'll see you Saturday," he said at the end. "At Weather Tree."

Friday and Saturday, April 26 and 27

At Licking River it was overcast and raining. The road through town was empty. A truck was parked near Frank's store and another by the post office, but except for a dog trotting along the highway with its head down, the place seemed deserted. She told Alvah where to pull into the garage, and when she unlocked the door and turned on the lights, the first thing he noticed, way in back, were the old cars, the Pierce-Arrow, the Bentley and a Duesenberg. He headed back along the concrete floor and said couldn't he take one of those instead, and she laughed and said they didn't work anymore. They parked his car on the side and took out a jeep. It sputtered, cold, then came together and, midafternoon, they headed on toward Weather Tree.

The rain came down in straight lines. It was cold and still, the snow gone, only a few patches left here and there. Once they passed a lumber truck headed south and, at the turnoff, she went down to second gear, then first. "This is it," she said.

The narrow road stretched out in front of them like a dream ending in fog and rain, and in places branches reached in toward the jeep like sleepers in a trance. The world was eerie in here, caught between winter and spring, and deep, hard ruts and shards of ice stuck up from the ground. Thick fog blocked off all visibility a few feet from the road but sometimes it suddenly moved laterally over the ground as if a force was rushing it along. The woods seemed even more closed than ever, a world apart, the road a mere path to the other side.

Later she pointed out the spot where Clovis Moran's boy had fallen, and later she said, "You can't see now in the fog, but over there's the mountain and the cave where he was hiding."

"I wonder if he was looking for his son," Alvah said.

"Thinking he was still there somewhere."

When they came up over the top of the hill and left the woods behind, fog had settled down close to the land so there was no sign of the clearing, or the lake and the mountains beyond, just an airy whiteness. The rain had stopped, but it was like heading along the edge of the earth, with only an occasional bush or rock for company. The houses came, dark monoliths in the fog, and Alvah made a sort of whistle under his breath.

The Big House lay like a ship along the land and, pulling up, Abigail felt the impact of what she had done.

She had returned.

Simon came out, the two dogs at his heels. He opened her door and, nervous, she gave him less a hug than normal, but when she went to introduce the two men, she kept ahold of Simon's hand.

"Pleased to meet you," Simon said.

"Heard a lot about you," Alvah said.

Inside, the lamps were blazing and the Navajo rugs seemed more red and bright than ever. She could hear a fire crackling in the room at the end and could smell the wood. Simon went ahead down the hall past the kitchen and the library, the dining room and the place where the back stairs headed up. He stopped when he reached the guestrooms. Abigail, following, didn't look to the right or the left, and she turned her head away when she passed the back stairs going up. But, behind her, Alvah stopped at every door.

"I've got you in here, Abby," Simon said, gesturing toward one room. "Alvah across the hall."

She nodded.

"And this one for Max. Put Luke and Foster in the other wing."

Abigail began that night by going through drawers and closets. She found empty bottles, photographs, ammunition and one notebook that had belonged to her grandmother, with only one sentence inside. "About money," it said. "Spend it, enjoy it and give away as much as possible."

Abigail had brought few clothes to Weather Tree, no books or cameras and only a simple plan. She would talk to Simon and Polly, do what else she could, but let Alvah and Luke go through the files. She had made one other agreement with them: she would not go up to her father's room if she didn't want to.

The first thing Alvah did was go upstairs with a flashlight and open Boarchards' files. He was looking for "Algodones" and "Moran," he said, but later he came down and said he hadn't found a thing.

The next day was Saturday, April 27. Nine days to go.

At breakfast she had told Alvah that Algodones made her more nervous than afraid. "But I hate him hanging around my life," she said, wiping her hands on her old blue jeans. "I wish he'd leave me alone. He's not my problem. He's not my doing. He has nothing to do with me."

Afterward, she went outside. She was headed for the icehouse, where she had found Clovis Moran, but she went down to the lake first and out along the quays at the boathouse. It was raining hard. His canoe was gone, the slips empty. She watched the water. Something tugged at her memory.

Back on land, she crossed the bridge over Licking River and stood in the middle, staring down at the current. The river came from a spring in the mountains, with marshy sides and a bottomless source. Before it reached the clearing, it ambled its way through forests and meadows, staying gentle and not so wide. Beyond the clearing it headed back into the forest again, going south toward the town of Licking River and beyond. There it mingled with a larger river of greater repute and went south to cities and the sea, mixed forever in bigger and bigger things.

Finally she tore herself away from the river and went on toward the icehouse. Passing the old dining hall, she peered in a window at the rows of tables stacked on top of each other. She could still see footprints in the dust where children had played last summer. Next she passed the kitchen and the pantry, given over to squirrels and mice, on to the woodshed and the stables, empty now, until she finally came to the icehouse.

Where she had seen Clovis Moran and played him right. Gotten the look and the picture she wanted.

The icehouse stuck up like a church or an A-frame and had a pulley on the side for loading ice. She and Josh, her friend, had waited out front in the car. Moran had come on the third night.

She opened the door and went inside. The temperature dropped dozens of degrees and her face felt the sharp rush of the cold. The walls were lined with shelves of milk and butter, food and cheese. For a hundred years people from the village had cut the ice on the lake, using horse-drawn teams and a saw, lifted chunks out with giant tongs and stored it here.

She opened the next door and went deeper inside. Here it was dark and windowless, and heavy with the scent of wood. Sawdust rose like a mountain to the ceiling, and buried inside were bricks of ice and hundreds of parcels of cow, deer, chicken, bear and pig. It was like a tomb.

Ironic, she thought. The promise of food and survival had lured Moran here. Instead he had gotten caught. If it hadn't been for her, he would have run away, no one the wiser about his hiding place. If she hadn't talked to him to get the picture she wanted, they woudn't have learned about the cave.

Old Frank lived outside of town in a square, fat house set up on blocks that made it look like a chicken on legs, with two front windows for beady eyes. Simon had said he knew something about Rush and Clovis Moran. There was an old bathtub outside in the yard, and the torn-out seat of a car leaned against the front steps. Inside Frank was sitting up in bed with a towel wrapped around his neck and medicine by his side.

He gave Abby a wet kiss, told her to sit down and, holding her hand, said he remembered when "Old Mr. Whitaker" gave him money to start the store. "He told me some good people had to stay up here with his children. But your dad, God rest his soul, he had too much money for his own good. He never knew what to do with it except give it away. But I loved him from the moment I saw him," he said. "Marcel brought him out to show me right after the family arrived from New York and we had to take off all these blankets to get at him. There he was underneath, in nothing but some diapers, and I remember he opened up those big brown eyes and looked at me and it was a wonder."

"A wonder?" Abigail asked.

"I loved him from that minute on," Frank said, looking at her. "Sort of like I had a little bit of a right to him."

The old man sank down lower in the bed and Simon poked Abby with his elbow. "Frank," he said, taking over, "did you ever hear of a fellow named Algodones? Joe Algodones?"

Frank shook his head.

"What about Clovis Moran? You told me once Clovis was in to the clambakes at Weather Tree once. You ever know him and Rush to be friends?"

"They both served in the Philippines. I know that. And Rush took a lot of the boys down to sign up. He took Fred." Fred was Frank's son. "Maybe he took Moran too. Ask Fred."

"But what happened at that bake?" Simon hurried on. "Didn't you say they were friends? Didn't you tell me once something happened?"

"It wasn't much. Everybody was in for a clambake and a group of us was standing over there by the boathouse. Rush, talking up a storm, you know, the way he used to, and Clovis came up. He looked real young then, all that red hair and those big blue eyes."

Abigail remembered the eyes, but his hair had been covered with ice.

"He was thin, like you could see through him," Frank said. "He'd lost weight in that prison camp, and this couldn't have been too long after that. When your dad came back, we had a sign up clear across the road. 'Welcome back, Rush, Licking River's Own Hero.' But at the clambake, Clovis was just standing there, staring at your dad. He looked kind of crazy to me, all happy or something. This weird grin on his face. He didn't say anything, but he started touching your dad's shirt, his face. It got embarrassing. His wife came up, apologized, said Clovis wasn't right in his head anymore. Rush said he thought Clovis had been killed in the Philippines."

"Why did he think that?" Abigail asked.

"I don't know, but Joanne said maybe he should have been killed. She had Clovis by the arm, pulling him away, but he was still smiling at Rush, like a baby, touching him, and Rush didn't like it. He was trying to get away. But Clovis wouldn't let go. Joanne said he didn't talk no more either and Rush said, 'What happened?' and she said, 'The war.'"

"Then what happened?" Abby asked.

"Nothing. She took Clovis and left."

They rode back in silence.

"You don't like what I'm doing, do you?" she asked.

"What's the point in stirring everything up," Simon said. "What's done is done."

At Weather Tree there were more jeeps outside in the courtyard, and Luke was in the living room talking to Uncle Max. "Hello," she said shyly from the top of the landing. The two men looked up.

"Hello." Luke took a few steps toward her and stopped.

"There you are, old thing," Max declared.

She came down, kissed her uncle and sitting beside him on the arm of the chair, looked at Luke. He didn't say anything, neither did she. Max watched them both.

"Did you have a nice drive up?" she finally asked Luke.

"Yes. Did you?"

"Yes."

Max cleared his throat and stood up. "He was telling me what you're up to." He held his jacket collar with both hands. "This investigation."

"Do you disapprove?"

"Don't know if I do or not. But you're not hurting anyone, far as I can see. And I suppose you have to do everything your own way. You always have, God-what; don't know why you should change now."

"Was she always a troublemaker?" Luke asked with a grin.

Max ignored him. "He says you don't know what to do about the will."

"What do you think I should do?" she asked.

"I never give advice," Max declared. "That way I never get in trouble."

Dinner followed, and by then Alvah had returned from the farmhouse, where he had talked to Mary, his assistant, on the telephone. "It doesn't look like Algodones has a bank account in three states," he reported, as all of them, Abby and Luke, Max, Alvah and Foster sat at one end of the enormous table. Mrs. Smith, the cook, was bringing in plates of meat and salad.

Moran's lawyer had never heard of Algodones either, Alvah went on, and a "contact" at the phone company was going to run a national search for Algodones on the computers. Extra costs for the investigation were up to a thousand dollars, he noted, and Abigail was saying she didn't mind, when, out of the blue, Max asked Luke a question.

"You ever go to Kashmir?" he asked pointedly, his eyes narrowed.

Everyone looked at Luke. "No, sir, I haven't," he said, "but I'd like to."

"You would, would you," Max said with a hint of approval. "That's very good. Why do you want to go there?"

"We've been there fourteen times," Foster interjected.

"You find much corruption there, do you?" Alvah asked Max. "Bribery?"

"Bribery?" Max repeated. "Foster, do we find much bribery?"

"We prefer to avoid that altogether," Foster answered.

"How?" Alvah asked.

"We prefer to pay rather lavishly to begin with, and we find that does wonders to avoid troubles."

"I can imagine," Alvah said sarcastically.

Suddenly the detective pounded his fist on the table and said angrily, "Goddammit, Abigail, I can't call a man 'Foster.'"

"But everybody calls me that," Foster said.

"It's damned ridiculous."

"I don't even know his first name," Abigail interjected, "and I've known him all my life."

"It's Bartholomew," Max said. "After my father's first cousin."

"Christ," Alvah said, shaking his head. "I don't believe it." He looked at Luke. "These people," he muttered, less angrily.

Luke broke out laughing. "I agree."

"I really do prefer 'Foster,'" the butler said.

"You do?" Alvah asked seriously. "It sounds disrespectful to me."

"That's because you don't understand," Foster said. "It doesn't convey the slightest bit of disrespect or inequality to me. It's just the way things are done."

"He and I are really great friends," Max said.

Alvah frowned in disbelief.

"They are," Abby piped up.

"That's true," said Foster, who, with his hair parted down the middle, looked more like a salesman or a bureaucrat than a servant.

"Couldn't get on without Foster," Max mumbled.

"Why do I need to know all this?" Alvah asked, turning to Luke again. "I've lived a long time, done a pretty good job. Why do I need this?"

Max cleared his throat. "I say," he began importantly, "if you fellows are finished, can we do some business? Foster, read the letter. Harvey Wynne—he's our lawyer, Mr. Germaine—he says this Algodones fellow is just a crackpot, but since you people seem so interested in him, maybe you should hear this letter. He sent it to all of us. Foster thought to bring it along."

Foster had pulled a sheet of paper out of his pocket. Abigail saw the little black signature. " 'Dear Mr. Rushing,' " Foster began. " 'You're goddamned lucky you got this far with no one knowing, but I've got all the information I need. If I write my book, you'll be exposed. All of you. You'll be sorry. If Rush doesn't come through, I mean business. Ask him what I mean. See how he likes being on the other end of a kill for once.' "

". . . of a kill," Abigail said softly.

Footsteps in the snow. . . .

She following, he far ahead with a gun. The others were talking about Algodones, but she was remembering. Sometimes she lost sight of her Rush, other times he waited for her to catch up. Sometimes sun glared, other times the sky was dark. But it was always silent, a windless day, because Rush wanted himself and the animal to be a perfect match—the woods at ease, no wind to hide a move or cover a sound. He hunted to track. To decipher the path from a broken twig or a sound, from a print or a spoor. This was proof of mastery, just two things going, he and the deer, one stalking, one free (she a third that didn't count). So that whoever saw or heard or smelled the other first was the winner, so perfect was the match between hunter and beast.

But the first time she heard the gun, she no more than three or four feet tall, she screamed.

The sound ricocheted off the trees and she saw her father start running suddenly, gun up, antique steel and wood, and she ran too. Crying.

Suddenly there was another shot and she slammed her hands over her ears and screamed.

He went out of sight. She kept going, out of breath, and then, over a hill, no warning, she stumbled upon him.

The deer was in his lap. He had wrenched its head back to break the neck. The deer's mouth was open, blood pouring on his clothes, and before he saw her, there was one loud terrible crack as he broke the deer's neck. Then he stretched the animal straight out from head to toe, plunged the knife in its belly, ripped it down the middle from neck to crotch, yanked it open. And saw her.

"For God's sake," he roared, wiping sweat off his face. "Don't you know enough not to cry?"

Then he pulled the carcass open until it yawned like a suitcase, miles of intestines and guts inside. Steam poured up, vapor to the trees, and as she uttered one last little whelp—the last cry Rushing Boarchards ever heard from his only child—he bent over the animal and yanked the innards out.

"Why are you doing that?" she asked, tears gone.

"Have to. Else all the shit backs up and poisons the meat." He pulled out guts and intestines with his hands, threw them on the snow. She felt the steam on her face. The deer's head was back like a freak shot of death, and he cleaned the cavern out until only the ribs were left, the rest red in the snow. Then he broke a branch over his knees and dug a hole in the ground and, lifting the guts with his hands, dropped them inside.

"So the animals won't eat it," she said.

"Right."

Then he covered the hole back over, pulled a rope out of his pocket and tied one end three, four times around the deer's feet, lashed the other end around his shoulder and gripped it in his hand. Then, together, the three of them headed home, Abigail, her father and the deer.

Kill complete.

How'd you like being on the other end of a kill, Algodones had said.

Abigail shivered.

Long after dinner the front door suddenly opened and Simon came tromping down the hall, the dogs at his heels, to the big room where Max and Foster were playing bridge, Alvah was reading, Abby and Luke looking through a chestful of old photographs. Simon stopped at the top of the landing. "Alvah," he blared. "Want a drink?"

The detective put down his book and went to the kitchen. In

a minute Luke followed. Abby stayed, looking at pictures, but then abruptly she got up and went to the kitchen too.

The three men were sitting around the table.

"What's going on?" she asked.

"Tell her," Alvah said.

"It's about some phone calls," Simon said. "First one came about a month ago and I didn't think nothing of it."

She sat down.

"This guy says, 'I got a message for you to give Boarchards.'"

"Nothing strange about that," she interjected.

"Except Boarchards was dead," Luke said.

"Then he says, 'Tell him I don't care if he misses one payment, but he better not miss two.' Then he hung up. It happened so quick, I didn't even have a chance to tell him Rush had, you know, died. But a few weeks ago he called again. I wanted to tell him, but he did the same thing. Just said Boarchards had better get on the stick and then he hung up."

"It has to be Algodones," Luke interrupted.

"And tonight he calls, says for me to tell him he knows how to 'get him.' 'I got his soft spot,' he says, 'and I know where she is. I can get her anytime I want, and I will.'"

Abigail shivered. The man was following her. "Did you tell him Rush was dead?"

"No. Didn't get the chance."

Alvah pushed the old oak table away and stood up. "All right," he said, "no more fun and games. We've got to find him." He headed out of the kitchen. The others followed. "I want everyone to be ready to go in the morning. And you, too" —he turned around to wag a finger at Abby. "Our deal's off. You work on the files just like the rest of us." He stopped on the landing. "You two ready to work?"

"Yes, sir." Foster stood up.

Alvah turned to Luke and Abigail. "You two start in the basement. Foster, you finish upstairs with me. Mr. Rushing, you work downstairs. We're looking for anything in the files that tells us where Algodones is or what this is all about. I mean," he added, "who is this guy? We need an address."

"An explanation," Abigail added.

"An address," Alvah retorted. Then he looked back over his shoulder at Simon down the hall. "What about you?"

"Not me," Simon answered. "If Rush had wanted anybody to know, he'd have told them. I wouldn't have told you about the phone calls, if he hadn't involved Abby. You go ahead. I won't stop you. But I won't help you either. I still take my orders from him." Then he turned, walked down the hall and left.

The others were silent. Abigail sat down on the steps, dejected. Luke sat down beside her. Alvah leaned against the railing.

"He's right," Max said pensively.

"I know," Abigail agreed. "If he'd wanted us to know, he'd have told us."

"That's bullshit," Luke said angrily, standing up. "Simon is not right. Why did your father save everything to begin with? All those files? Why didn't he throw out that letter to Algodones? Or mail it?"

Alvah was looking at him with respect and nodding his head.

"He had a reason," Luke went on. "Consciously or unconsciously, he wanted people to find them. To know him. If we can't find Algodones any other way, we have to do this, Abby. No matter what he thought about you, he never wanted any harm to come to you. . . ."

"That's right," Max said.

"And so if there's any validity at all to these threats, he himself would tell us to go ahead and look."

Abigail didn't say anything, but she was thinking that if Rush had slipped into isolation and enigma, she was coming after him. To find him. She stood up. "All right," she said, her hands on her hips. "Let's start."

With Luke's words, she felt the last prohibition to her search removed. This was a salvage venture of her own.

"There's just one problem," Foster said to Alvah. "Have you looked downstairs? Do you know what you're up against?"

The detective shook his head.

"He's right," Abigail said. "Come see." She headed down the corridor. The others followed. The sconces on the walls were lit, the flames bright and yellow. At a table, she opened a drawer and took out a flashlight. She turned left into a side hall and went straight until she came to a door. There she turned the handle and pushed with her shoulders, but it didn't budge.

Luke came up and pushed with her. Creaking, the door slowly started to move, and little by little, it opened, revealing a well of darkness below. Dust floated up through the door.

Abigail waved it away from her eyes and pointed the flashlight down. It punctuated the darkness and showed, far below, kerosene barrels, an old crib, and the edge of a file cabinet.

She went first, Luke next, then the others. As they descended, the air got damp. She brushed cobwebs away. Her flashlight shone on the stairs, great slabs of marble, and picked up more kerosene barrels, old chairs and, gradually, wooden pillars that rose from floor to ceiling and spread out like a forest. The place looked like an underground maze of catacombs. There were files everywhere, too numerous to count. Behind her she could hear Luke breathing. She glanced at him. He was frowning.

"My God," Alvah whispered.

There were so many files, in the distance they just blended into the darkness and disappeared. No one said a word. At the bottom of the steps, Luke took the flashlight. He started walking deeper into the darkness. They followed. The light seemed pitiful and weak, the space too great.

Luke led them this way, that way, files lining their path.

"What are you doing?" she whispered.

"It covers the whole house," he said, taking her hand. "The basement is one entire room covering the whole underbelly of the house."

In the dim light giant patterns of spiderwebs filled the space and the files seemed like wreckage, pieces of life broken off and sunk, settled on the bottom of the sea. Each cabinet had three drawers, but even the handles were covered with dust and crud, and the metal itself had acclimatized through the years so that, obscured by what had settled upon them, the files looked as if they had reverted back to nature and become part of a creeping underground ecology. It was as if the floor of the sea or the earth itself had grown back over the cabinets through the years and reclaimed them for its own.

It took them three hours to figure out that at some point, God knows how many decades past, Boarchards had obviously abandoned whatever plan he might once have had for storing the files in some order. Faced with too many cabinets to keep any plan at all, he had set about storing them the simplest way he could.

At random.

Afterward Abigail was so tired she went to bed without even washing the cobwebs off her face. She thought briefly about Algodones.

Whether he was dangerous or not, he was doing the same thing as she, she realized. They were stalking each other. He was trying to find her and use her, just as she was trying to find him, and they both had the same design in mind: to settle things with Rushing Boarchards.

Sunday and Monday, April 28 and 29

For the next few days they searched in the files from morning to night. Monday was no different from Sunday, and Tuesday no different from Monday. Their hands were covered with dust, their hair full of cobwebs, and Monday they wore the same filthy clothes they'd first worn on Sunday. They had lamps, knives, brooms and towels. They pried drawers open, only to discover that many of the folders lacked headings. Others were wedged in so tight they were almost impossible to move.

Abigail had positioned dozens of lamps around the chamber and turned the underground place into a forest of campfires, but the lights did little to dispel the forbidding nature of their task. With small glows, they lighted the ceiling and cast shadows over this, the internal world of Rushing Boarchards, and Rushing Boarchards himself still seemed very large and very compelling, but very hard to find.

Alvah went off from time to time to the farmhouse to make calls to Mary and others. There the telephone was a long wooden box on the kitchen wall, with two bells shaped like bowls in front that hit each other to make the ring and a voice box that stuck out in front like a petunia. Standing at the phone and getting more and more angry at "old-fashioned contraptions," he placed an ad in the New York papers. "Reward for information leading to the whereabouts of Joe Algodones. Address, identity unknown . . ." The number given to call was his.

He also made calls all over the country, trying to find this, that, working contacts in the military who could pull out records thirty years old for Algodones and Moran. All he really wanted, he kept saying, was a last-known address for the one.

Sometime later, Tuesday it was by then, Mary called back with the first response to the ad. A man in the Bronx said Algodones kept a 1972 Chevy pickup truck in his garage, took it out every three months or so, used it a day or two. Yes, he had one ear and paid in cash. But address unknown. A dead end.

As the days passed, Abigail was no clearer about what to do about the will, and the files themselves, thousands of them, seemed to mirror the confusion in her mind. The subjects covered everything from A to Z, but as she waded through them, their very bulk grew to reflect her own increasing uncertainty.

She went to the farmhouse once too. She tried to reach Melanie again, but without success, and she called Diver, the police chief, to ask him about Clovis Moran.

"Remember his boy?" she said. "The one over the cliff? Do you know if he had freckles, blue eyes and a pug nose?" The same as the boy in the reform school, she wanted to add. Was that boy in the school by any chance Robbie Moran? Was there one boy all along, not two?

But Diver didn't know. "There wasn't enough left to tell if he had blue eyes or red eyes," he said.

On Sunday she was alone with Luke for the first time. It was the day after he arrived, the day they started in the basement, and he said they should stop searching long enough to go to Licking River, she to see Pollibeaux, he to see Frank's son Fred. But at the edge of the clearing, the first thing they did was stop the jeep, get out and kiss, licking the rain off each other's faces and saying how, in a place so big, could it be so hard to be alone.

But back in the jeep, Abigail began to talk. "I don't know who I'm supposed to be," she said, so low she could barely hear herself. "That's why this decision is so hard. I don't know if I'm supposed to be rich or normal. I've never known that. From the very beginning I've never fit in anywhere. Living here, I was different from everybody else at school, but in New York I was even more different, just because I had grown up here. I never fit in anywhere until I had my work."

"Abby . . ."

"I went to France five times by the time I was fourteen, but I never walked down a street by myself. I slept in Central Park at night . . ."

"Abby . . ."

"But if I told my mother I wanted to go shopping, the driver had to take me in the car."

Luke stopped the jeep and pulled on the brake. "Abby, you're not a mass of contradictions and confusions." He pulled her across the gear box and held her in his lap.

She pressed her face into his wool jacket and he held her tight.

"Luke," she mumbled. "What's happening to us?"

"You know what's happening."

"But I'm too confused for that. I don't know if I'm coming or going. I don't know what I'm going to do about the will. I don't . . ."

"But that doesn't matter," he said, wiping the hair out of her eyes. "You will. All you are is hurt. And you're supposed to be. You found out a parent you loved hated you. What could be worse? You're working through one of the biggest things that will ever happen to you. But the thing is, you will work it out. You'll get over it. Because you're brave, kind, talented . . ."

"Maybe you're wrong."

"Is Alvah wrong? Is Max? Foster?"

"Max?"

"He says you're quite a girl."

She smiled shyly.

"Do you realize you've probably changed his life?" he asked.

"How?"

"He's a very lonely man, for all his manner, and getting involved with you is probably the most important thing that's ever happened to him."

"You mean, because he's not alone anymore?"

"Because he's not alone anymore and he knows it."

She left Luke with Fred at the store in Licking River and drove on past the reform school to see Pollibeaux. She felt trepidatious. She had never liked the trapper much or felt comfortable with him, and going to see him now seemed difficult. The old man's two-room cottage was set far back off the road and almost hidden in the trees. As she approached, the passel of dogs outside started jumping and barking, long, ugly things trained to follow smells. "Get away," she muttered as they leaped in the empty air.

She saw that Polly's jeep was gone, but she knocked on the door anyway and his wife, Cloe, opened it and peered at her in open dislike.

Abigail went around her into the kitchen. Smoke poured up from the wood stove. Fresh skins were stretched along the walls on nails, feet and paws sticking out in all directions, and she could almost see juices oozing from the pores.

"They're drying," Cloe said.

Cloe even looked like Polly, Abby thought as she sat down. The woman was tall and thin, with beady eyes and skin like bark. She wore a long skirt and a sweater that hung to her hips. Cloe sat too and picked up two cow hides that were spread across the table. "Sewing them to make a bedspread." She picked up a needle as big as a pencil. The ends of her fingers shone with suet.

"I was hoping to see Polly," Abigail said. "Is he around? I thought maybe he could tell me what happened to my father. Help me understand."

"He's not here."

"Where is he?"

"Camp Four." A cabin in the woods at Weather Tree, five miles from the clearing.

"When will he be out?"

"Month maybe. June sometime. Took his traps."

"I can walk in to see him."

Cloe gave her a hard look and then went back to her skins. "Long way for a girl like you."

"I can make it."

"None of my business if you do or you don't."

Abigail swallowed. "Did you ever hear of a friend of my father's named Joe Algodones?"

"Never did. But then again, he never had any friends except Polly."

"He had lots of friends," Abby argued.

"Well, you weren't one of them, the way you treated him."

Abby gasped. "I didn't like his drinking. He was killing himself."

"We all die someday."

"But that doesn't mean you should abuse yourself in the meantime."

"Don't know why not, if you feel like it."

"Well, I don't think that way."

"Maybe you should," Cloe said. "You wouldn't have caused so much trouble."

"I didn't cause trouble."

Cloe looked at her. "Is that right? What about the time . . ." But then she let her sentence die and went back to sewing.

"What time?"

"That time you told him off."

"I never did that," Abigail exclaimed.

"You did too."

"I'd never do anything as cruel as that."

"Huh!" Cloe retorted in outrage. "You sure didn't want anything to do with him."

"That's not true. That's not true at all."

"He thought so."

"How do you know? I was closer to him than anybody, and

that's why Polly never liked me. Or you either. You're jealous of anyone that comes between Polly and my father."

Cloe wiped her greasy hands on her skirt. "Did everything to be different from him, didn't you."

"I did not." Abigail stood up. "I wanted to work. Be on my own."

"He wanted you here. He was alone. But you said no, your work was more important."

"If I'd known Polly was away, I'd never have come today." She backed away, her voice rising.

"You think he feels any different than me, Abigail Boar-chards, you're wrong."

"I know exactly what he feels, and I always have," she said angrily. "He thinks he's better than anybody else just because he knows about the woods. But what's the big deal about stay-ing at Camp Four for a month? Weather doesn't talk back. It doesn't need food. It doesn't need attention. It doesn't need love."

"You're putting your father down, too, young lady, right along with Polly, when you say stuff like that. You know that?"

"You're darned right I know that!" Abby yelled and stormed out.

Luke jumped in the jeep as soon as she pulled up in front of the store. "How was Polly?"

"Fine," she said curtly, and got back on the road.

"What'd he say?"

"Not much."

"Fred said your father first met Clovis Moran when he drove him and some others down to Albany to enlist in the summer of '41. Moran was dim-witted even then, he said, and latched on to Rush like a puppy dog."

The jeep plowed up the hill into light mist.

"How was Polly?" Luke asked again.

"He wasn't there."

"I thought you said he was."

"He wasn't."

"Was Cloe?"

"Yes."

"How was she?"

"Fine. But I hate their dogs. They have the worst, ugliest, meanest dogs I ever saw."

"She say something bad?"

"No."

"Did she?"

"The first thing I'm going to do when I get back is cross Polly off my list. Nothing is ever going to make we want anything from him as long as I live. I can't stand that man and I can't stand his wife."

They rode in silence. Luke opened his window and fresh air filled the jeep. Abby finally calmed down. "You want to see where Clovis lived?" she asked.

He nodded.

She drove on, left the highway near an old sawmill and nosed the jeep into the closing darkness of the pressing trees. Traveling on a narrow dirt road, they went by a couple of farms until they reached a clearing with a barn, an outhouse and a little building on the side where people had lived and died. She brought the jeep up in front of the house and turned off the motor.

The house looked empty, no signs of people, just a flat roof held down by cement blocks.

"He shot them in the kitchen," she said.

Twilight was coming.

"Let's get out," Luke said.

They sat on the front steps of the house, looking across the fields. They were shielded from the mist by the roof. All around there were furrows in the ground where a garden had been planted before death and vacancy settled in.

"Do you feel like you're intruding?" she asked.

Luke shook his head.

Fog swirled down low around the trees and she watched it move, curl, rise and fall like something alive. They sat in silence a long time. Then she pointed above the firs and pines. "That's Weather Tree land right over there," she said, "and hear that water trickling?"

They listened to the sound of water flowing somewhere in the woods nearby.

"That's Licking River," she said.

"Your Licking River?"

She smiled. "It starts in the hills at Weather Tree, flows through the clearing, and at the town of Licking River, it turns south and heads toward New York City and the sea."

"Nice river," he said.

"Yes."

When they got back to the clearing, it was raining much harder. It had rained ever since they arrived, but Abigail thought of it as tears and imagined that when it stopped, she would be cleansed too—all the crying that could be done, done; now the living to do again.

She told Luke she was going on to see Simon. "I'm finally ready to talk to him. After all," she added with a grin, "nothing can be as bad as what Cloe said."

At the farmhouse Simon opened the door for her. "What do you want?" he asked sullenly.

"I want to talk."

"I don't have anything to say." He moved aside to let her pass. "I don't," he pleaded. "You know how he never talked."

Abigail realized suddenly this was hard for Simon too. "It's awfully cozy in here," she said kindly, sitting at the kitchen table and looking around at his prints of dogs and deer and firewood stacked in the corner.

"At least it's mine," he said.

She looked at the surveyor's map of Weather Tree that stood eight feet wide and six feet high on the wall beside the petunia-shaped telephone.

"You want a drink?" Simon asked.

"No, thanks." The map, dated 1878, had hair-fine lines for mountains, forests, lakes and rivers. In the middle of the clearing was a large drawing, three inches square, of a tree. It was high and wide and glorious, thickness spreading in every direction. "Did you ever see the weather tree?" she asked.

"Gone long before I got here." He poured himself a drink.

"Tell me what happened with my father, Simon. You can help me understand more than anyone."

He shook his head, drank some scotch.

"But I want to hear it. I want to know when he started to hate me. And why."

Simon downed one drink, poured himself another. "It was coming for a long time," he said slowly, averting his eyes.

"I can't hear you."

"I said it was a long time coming," he repeated loudly. "I could see him fighting it off. I'd tell him you called and he wouldn't say anything. I'd say, 'You got a letter from Abby,' and he wouldn't open it. It used to be every time I went out for the mail, he'd say, 'Anything from Abby?' and then he'd make me stand and wait while he read it."

Simon picked up the scotch bottle. "Chivas Regal," he said. "I learned that from you people. Nothing but the best. Why do you have to bother with all this?" He still looked away from her.

"It's my way of getting over it."

"Damned crazy way if you ask me."

"I didn't ask you."

"It got so all the time he was saying you were too big for your own britches."

"I'm not like that," she said.

"You can't have it both ways. You want to hear, you got to listen. I can't stand an argument."

"I'm not arguing."

"He said you were too full of yourself. He said you always had it easy and people like you always got their comeuppance sometimes. He said you'd get yours too, and you'd deserve it."

"So is that why he disinherited me?"

Simon didn't answer. "It got so he didn't even like your coming up. 'You go get her, Simon. I'm busy.' And so I'd have to go out and meet you at the bus."

"But that was a long time ago."

"That's right," he said.

"But . . ."

"You want me to finish? He said you didn't even like

Weather Tree. He said how could he have a daughter who didn't like Weather Tree. He said all you cared about was making money and showing off."

"Sounds like Cloe."

"Did you go see her, Abby? Now why did you do that? I'd never agree with one word that woman said. I'm just saying that you having it so good down there in New York was hard on him. Made him feel like he didn't count for much."

"Why wasn't he happy for me?"

"He was. He was so proud of you he couldn't see straight."

"That's not what you're saying. You're saying the opposite."

"Well, then, both was true," Simon said. "That's why it ate him up. Made him drink all the worse. Cause it was eating at him all the time."

"He told you this?"

"It wasn't so much what he said as what he did. Like, it took him a long while to get over your visits."

Abigail started shaking her head.

Simon turned away from her. "Your visits depressed him."

"No," she mumbled.

"Whenever I told him you had called or you was coming up, first thing he did was get a bottle. Right in front of me. He wouldn't even come downstairs, two, three, four days after you left."

"No."

"I had to go up, open the window, bring him a sandwich or something. I told you you didn't want to hear this."

"I do want to hear it."

"But why do I have to be the one to tell you? I can't stand it. I didn't like it then and I don't like it now. I don't even want to think about it."

"Did you know about the will?" she asked.

"Never. I never thought it had gone that far. Never dreamed. But it got so everything changed. It seemed like one day he just changed completely."

"When?" She suddenly remembered the feeling she had had at the boathouse, water lapping against the boards, and the presence of a memory she couldn't find. "Did I do something?

Did I do something to cause it all? That's what Cloe said. That it was all my fault."

"It was just you being you," Simon said.

"But that's even worse. That means he really hated me."

Simon looked at her and didn't argue.

"Go on," she said. "Tell me the rest." Her voice sounded resigned, sad.

"It seemed like one day he just stopped fighting it off and gave in. Like he'd had it with you. Didn't want nothing to do with you. Didn't even want to bother pretending to himself."

Abigail rubbed her arms. "I'm cold."

"Like all of a sudden he turned a corner and had nothing good to say about you."

"When?" she mumbled.

"After they got Clovis Moran and when he came back from Connecticut. From then on it just seemed like he had it in for you."

Back at the Big House she went right in to see Max. She found him in his bedroom sitting on the couch in a scarlet bathrobe pulling on his socks. He was getting dressed for dinner. "Where did Foster put my pants?" he asked as she walked in.

She looked around and then pointed at the hanger on the closet door.

"Right." He took the clothes and disappeared into the bathroom. When he came out he was fully dressed. She was seated on the bed looking glum. He peered at her. "What's this all about?" he asked, sitting down by the fire.

"I talked to Simon."

"And I suppose he told you everything."

She nodded.

Max sighed and the flesh under his chin sagged. "Well, that's what you wanted."

"It's still hard to hear."

"Yes. That it is," he said slowly. "But you'll get over it."

Abigail suddenly wondered what he had been like as a little

boy. Did he know he would be one of the few people in the world who would never work or have a job?

"I kissed Sara-Fey in here once," the old man said after a while. "This was before she and Nicer got married. She was a sweet little thing, you know, Abby, Sara-Fey was. Not like Bos or Florence. Had a way about her. Nicer was a lucky fellow, but I think his daughter was more to his liking than his wife. Annie-Fey had spunk. She had a mind of her own. Nicer liked that. Probably why he and Bos got on so well. Sara-Fey never did have much to say. But this one summer it was hot. No air, no rain. It was even too hot to go swimming, and Florence told the girls in the kitchen to make us something to drink. Mother and Father were in New York, and I brought her in here, Sara-Fey, and closed the door."

"I saw Annie-Fey last week," Abby said. She could hear the rain outside, and the smell of wood smoke was strong and sweet in the room.

"Rush should have married her. Annie-Fey."

"Did you ever meet Melanie Anderson?"

Max shook his head. "That was none of my business. Remember that, Abby. Never interfere."

"I don't believe in that, Uncle Max. I'm interfering right now. Everything I'm doing is one big act of interference."

Max looked at her and sighed, his eyes drifting off. "Sara-Fey sat over there." He pointed toward a wall. "There was a chaise then. I sat down beside her. I'd never done a thing like that. It isn't like nowadays. You and this lawyer, you can carry on, but then . . ."

"We're not carrying on."

"So I kissed her," he said. "And then all of a sudden cars started pulling up outside. It was Mother and Father, troops of servants, and Sara-Fey squealed and we rushed out. There was a great to-do outside. We could tell right away something was wrong because Father didn't shake anybody's hand or ask where Marcel was. He always did that. 'Where's Marcel?' Instead he just marched straight in, told us all to follow and went right to the living room. Sara-Fey said somebody must have died. Father made us sit down, and Edward, this is your grandfather, he said, 'Oh, Mr. Rushing, it's too hot to be serious,' and Father told him to shut up and have some sense for once. And then he told us war had started on the continent. But the thing was, we didn't understand. We kept waiting for the bad news. War meant nothing to us. Then he mentioned some place we'd never heard of, it must have been Sarajevo, and I remember little Sam, your uncle, piped up and said, 'What's war?' and Florence said, 'Does that mean we can't go on holiday?' because we were planning to go to the continent, and I said . . . you want to know what I said?"

Max looked across the room at Abigail. She nodded.

"I said, 'Of course not. Of course we'll go.'" He stared off again. "Imagine that. A war's going on, mind you, millions of people will die and all the crowned heads will go, the world change for people like us, and I say our trip will go on as planned. Nothing interferes with us. That's what I thought. Nothing can touch people like us."

He stopped talking. Abigail didn't say anything.

"But everything's changed," the old man said after a while. "People like us don't count anymore. They even make jokes about us. 'Let them eat cake.' I suppose it's true, but it used to be you'd go in a store and the fellow would drop everything to come over. 'How are you, Mr. Rushing?' 'What can I do for you, Mr. Rushing?' Now you're lucky if he even sees you. Takes its toll, things like that. How's a fellow supposed to know where he stands anymore? I told someone I was a traveler the other day and you know what he said?"

"What?"

"He laughed. He thought I was making a joke. Of course, doctors still come to the house, but only if you pay them a bundle. That's all that counts now. Money."

"You don't think money's important?"

Max didn't answer.

"Do you think I should contest the will?"

But he didn't seem to hear her. "Nobody cares who you are anymore," he said. "Used to be all you had to do, really, was mention your name and people respected you. Now, how's a fellow to know where he stands?" Max looked at her, as if she had the answer. He waited, eyebrows raised, but when she didn't say anything, he just looked away.

"You can't go around saying that, of course," he went on. "Everyone would think you were a frightful snob. No wonder Rush boarded himself up in here. Good idea, really," he added, "shut the other stuff out. But I suppose it's all for the good."

"What?"

"Change. Can't have people like us going around thinking we know everything." He stopped talking, the skin around his neck settled down over his collar.

She heard Luke go by in the hall outside. I even recognize his footsteps, she thought.

"Never should have happened," Max said.

"What?"

"The will." He looked at her and Abigail realized that what he was trying to do was tell her the changes were part of the reason for the will, that the changes had changed her father. "Terrible thing, the will," he said. "It shames us all. Shows how much we've lost. My father would never have done anything like that."

"Should I contest it then?"

Max looked at her. "Give it up, Abby. Let the act be over. Let his hate and confusion be the end of it. We aren't a bad lot."

"I didn't think you were."

"Sometimes you did," he said. "You were in such a hurry to grow up and be somebody, you got rid of everything in your way."

"I didn't mean to."

"No," he said. "I don't suppose you did. But you wanted to make a name for yourself. Made us feel the one you had wasn't good enough."

"I just wanted to be myself. I didn't want to be like any of you. Nobody's happy here."

"I know. I tried to explain that to Bos, but all she sees is that you never bothered to come for tea."

"But I was working."

"I told her that, but she said you could work at something else."

"But I love what I do."

"I know. But you were always in such a god-awful hurry."

"I didn't mean to be."

"Yes, you did, Abby," the old man declared. "And it's all right. But don't deny it. There's no sense to that. You were in a hurry, and it's a good thing you were." He paused. "You know, you're not a bad girl at all," he said, "and that's probably why you were in a hurry. Florence was a nice girl, too," he went on. "Until Edward died. Then she thought she had to run everything."

"I'm like her, aren't I?"

Max twirled his hands in the air around his head. "It's that thing you do with your hair. You see, none of us really liked Florence . . ."

"I liked her."

"Well, yes, but, you see, that's the whole point. Isn't it?"

That night after everyone had gone to bed, Abigail got up and, naked except for a big T-shirt, went down the corridor, across the room, up the other stairs and down the hall to Luke's room in the second wing. Outside it was still raining. She opened his door without knocking, and in the light of the burning fire, she saw him sitting up in bed. He was naked, looking at the fire, and his penis was back along his belly, halfway hard.

Before she could even close the door, he was standing beside her, and she felt his hands on her arms. She hugged him tight. "Oh, Luke," she whispered. He closed the door and pulled her to the bed, where he pulled her T-shirt off over her head. Then, lying beside her, he started moving his hands over her breasts and belly. He went slowly, as if there was something more marvelous to her than flesh alone. She felt her nipples standing up as he touched them with his fingers. "Abby, Abby," he said softly, as he licked them with his tongue and took her breasts farther in his mouth.

She started to moan and he slid down over her body. She felt him licking her stomach, her thighs, and finally he buried his face between her legs. She could hear the fire crackling and the rain outside and feel the tickle of his breathing into her little hairs, then his tongue going deeper inside her and his hands up her breasts.

She arched her body up, pushing it closer to his mouth and moaned. She ran her fingers through his hair. It was thick and clean, and his tongue kept moving inside her. Finally she pulled him up and felt his body move higher along hers. Shivering with excitement, she drew him up until he lay fully on top of her.

He pressed his mouth against hers, but she lifted her legs up around his back, her body aching for more, and then he slid into her, all of him, as if he was coming up through her belly to her chest and throat, she thought. She moaned in an extraordinary kind of pleasure and ease. It's so easy with him, she thought, and felt herself moving faster and faster. He lowered his head to her breast and sucked in hungrily. They kept moving, their bodies linked, and then he left her breast and lay flat on top of her. They were rising up and coming down, moving into each other, up and down, all the parts of her alive, electric. They went on and on and suddenly, too soon, they were ready, all this weeks or months overdue, and then, just a second after him, in the wake of all the stuff of him that flowed into her, Abigail pushed up against him and, crying, came too, in something that almost hurt it was so strong.

Luke collapsed on top of her, covering her body, and she held him as tight as she could. She felt him kissing her face, her ears, her nose, her eyes, and she smiled in the dark, knowing that if nothing else was ever right, Luke Reider was.

By midmorning on Monday, April 29, with less than a week to go, they had begun to discern a definite pattern to the files.

Going from file to file, one by one, they had found material on about almost every subject imaginable, but an even more telling list had emerged of what was not there.

Besides "Joe," "Algodones," "Clovis" and "Moran," they had found nothing in appropriate places in the alphabet for

"War," "Pacific," "Army," "Air Force," "Manila," "Philippines," "MacArthur," "Bataan," "Corregidor," "Bud," "Krajewski," "Truk," "Iwo Jima," "Kwajalein," "Killing," "Blackmail" or "Secret."

There was nothing about the war.

There was a file for Melanie, but it was empty.

Late Monday afternoon Alvah suddenly told Abigail to get her coat. Leaving the others in the basement, they went upstairs and out through the pelting rain and made it to the jeep. The road was almost ready to overflow with brown churning mud, and even the lake was invisible in the continuing storm. At the farm Simon had bolted the barn doors shut, and the single telephone cable swept wildly across the road in the powerful wind.

Inside Simon and the dogs were gone. Alvah went straight to the phone, dripping water all over the linoleum, and put through a call to Mary. "Stop looking for a bank account for Algodones," he declared as soon as she answered. "I've got a better idea. I don't know why I didn't think of it sooner. See if he's got everything squirreled away in a safe-deposit box. . . . Yes, a safe-deposit box. It's perfect for someone like him. Once a year," he hurried on, "banks get a computerized print-out with addresses of everyone who has a safe-deposit box. Get back to every bank he used, Mary, and get someone to look at those lists. See if Algodones is on one of them. See if we can find him that way."

Abigail pulled out her own list and looked at it. She still had a lot to do, she thought, feeling a little desperate. Pollibeaux was crossed out, but Algodones, Melanie, Victoria, Sam and Bostrine were still there. And I only have one week, she realized.

When Alvah hung up, she told him to go home without her. "I'm going to call Melanie," she said.

This time Melanie herself answered and, watching Alvah drive away in the jeep outside, Abigail introduced herself and told the woman she would like to see her, to discuss her father.

"I don't know a thing about him," Melanie answered quickly. "There's no point in seeing me."

"I wouldn't bother you if it weren't important."

"What can I possibly tell you?"

"Anything."

"But I don't have time for interviews."

"It's not an interview."

There was another silence. The wind was pushing hard against the little farmhouse.

"You're up in the mountains, aren't you?" This time Melanie's voice was low, almost sluggish. "He never took me there. He told me I'd like it, but, I don't know, how could it be 'the most beautiful place on earth'? That's impossible. No place could . . ."

"How could you be 'the world's most beautiful woman'?"

She heard the woman gasp. "How do you know about me anyway?"

"Will you please see me? I'll tell you everything then. May I call you when I come down?"

"All right. Yes. I guess so."

She took the trail that led off through the southern part of the clearing. It skirted the line of the woods, crossed the bridge over Licking River where the water widened out to about thirty feet across, and then circled around until it finally headed back toward the lake and the houses.

Walking, she went faster and faster. It was still raining hard. The field was wet, the ground soggy, and the woods seemed ominous, almost as if they might open up and suck her in, with branches reaching out, illicit hands ready to grab her.

She didn't like it.

Maybe her father was right, she thought. Maybe she didn't like Weather Tree.

At home she found Max and Simon in the big room. Max was agitated. "Bos called," he announced gloomily. "Wants to know what we're doing. But it's no business of hers. She just feels left out. But why does she have to go poking her nose in

my affairs?" He was sitting on the couch, pouting. Simon stood
in front of the fire. "Go ring her back, Simon, and tell her it's
none of her business."

"I can't do that," Simon answered as Abby took off her
poncho and sat down too.

"Sure you can," the old man retorted. "Tell her it's my message."

"Well, I won't do it."

"Then just don't answer the phone when she calls back."

"I can't do that either. Alvah's waiting for all those calls.
Besides," Simon went on, "she's already grilled me, about who
is here, what you are doing, where you are sleeping."

"Sleeping?" Abby asked.

"I told her I had you and the lawyer in separate wings."

"Why don't you just talk to her, Uncle Max," Abby said.
"We're not doing anything wrong."

Max grunted noncommittally.

Suddenly Abby grabbed her rain poncho and started out of
the room.

"Where are you going?" the old man called after her.

Outside she pulled the poncho over her head and ran across
the courtyard to Bostrine's house. Inside it was cold. She
walked quickly through the house and up the stairs. At the
door to her aunt's suite of private rooms she hesitated, then
turned the handle and went in.

It was silent, no little cousin or icy words. The great white
counterpane bed was made, the vases for flowers empty. It was
an old person's room, with portraits on the wall and china
boxes, photographs everywhere—men and girls now old or
dead. Abby sniffed the air. Perfume lingered on, a shade of
rose.

She sat down on the bed and realized she felt relaxed in here
now, not like the last time. She wondered if the peace augured
well for the future, if the ability of all these ghosts and people
to disturb her had diminished in the face of her growing
strength and resolve. She could hear the rain, close, hitting the
roof. She looked across at the pictures mounted on the wall by

the bed where Bostrine would see them last thing at night, first thing in the morning.

Pictures of Florence and Sara-Fey, Nicer and Rush. All dead. Florence boating, Marcel at the oars. Another, Florence and Marcel too, his arms around her, showing her how to shoot a gun, but almost like an embrace now. Florence, dainty and soft, her hair dark and wispy.

Abby stared. She and Florence looked exactly alike. It was her own face looking back at her.

Rush on the wall appeared many times—as a baby, a man, his foot on a Duesenberg, and boarding a plane. But, looking closely, Abby saw that the picture with Sara-Fey was more one of Nicer instead. Sara-Fey was almost in a carriage, but Nicer was outside, looking straight at the camera.

She opened the drawer in the table by the bed. Inside she found a little Fabergé egg, a string of pearls and a book of English verse inscribed, "To Bostrine from Nicer. Always." There was also a handkerchief trimmed with lace. It was folded over. Abby picked it up and turned back the edges. Inside she found a photograph.

It was a picture of Nicer Rutledge.

There was writing on the back. "Isn't he a dream? Our marriage is planned for the fall and I long for your congratulations. Your adoring friend, Sara-Fey."

Abigail looked at it. Nicer wore his hair parted in the middle and his eyes had a serious, penetrating look. He was gazing right at the camera. At Bostrine.

Abby folded it up tenderly in the handkerchief and put it back in the drawer.

Later that night, after dinner, Alvah asked her what she was going to do about the will and Abigail grimaced, shaking her head disconsolately. They were in the library, just the two of them. Down the hall they could hear Max in the big room playing the piano. "But don't you want this place or the money?" Alvah asked.

"I just don't know. I still can't decide. It's driving me crazy. One minute I think one way, but five minutes later, I think the other. I don't have any convictions about either course of action, and neither option seems emotionally right." She leaned far back on the couch, her legs out in front like a board, her arms folded across her stomach.

Alvah stood in front of the huge fireplace, one foot resting inside on the end of a log to get warm. "Contest, not contest. Do, don't do. I've never been hung up that way," he mumbled.

"Well, one thing has become clear, though," Abby said brightly. "I suppose that's something. I have a hard time thinking about it from a financial point of view. . . ."

"Meaning?" the detective interrupted.

"Meaning, I don't think money is what's at stake."

"But it is," he said, leaving the fire and going over to the liquor cabinet. "When all's said and done, that's the bottom line. Money, wealth." He handed her a brandy. " 'Oh, to be wealthy and blue.' Isn't there a song about that?"

"I don't know. I never heard of it. But I don't agree that money is the bottom line. Not for me, at least. It's part of it. One consideration. But that's all."

They swirled their brandy and stared at the fire, the lamps turned low, rain still falling.

"Too bad the weather's so wet," she said vaguely. "I like it this way, stormy and damp, but you . . ."

"Oh, nothing bothers me," he answered, looking down at the flames. "Long as I stay dry."

Down the hall Max had switched to some tune from the forties on the piano and the sounds mingled with the noise of the rain in the background.

"Maybe you're right," Alvah said after a while.

"About what?"

"Maybe you know better than the rest of us how little money matters." He shrugged and wiped at some dust from the basement that covered his pants. "It pays the bills, means a certain life-style. But you're in a better position than almost anyone I've ever known to understand what money doesn't bring. Happiness. Peace of mind."

She nodded.

"Would there really be a scandal if you contested?" he asked, glancing over at her. "Is that what you want to avoid?"

"Yes, partly," she answered. "Sam would fight tooth and nail. It would be hard, maybe impossible, to win in court because Rush certainly wasn't deranged. I wouldn't have much of a case. But eventually Sam would probably agree to settle, just to avoid the publicity."

"How much money is involved?"

"A lot, I guess. I don't know exactly. And land, of course. I always come back to two things," she said, suddenly sitting up straight and stretching out two fingers in front of her. "Wanting the land," she went on, bending back one finger, "versus, two, wanting just to end the whole thing. Just letting it be over. Finished. Ended. No more chapters."

"But you love this place," Alvah said, as she slumped back on the couch. "It's your home."

"Yes. But one thing is clear. Contesting will get me nowhere emotionally. I'll get no real satisfaction from it. It won't undo what he did, and the more I think about it, that's my main reason for not contesting. Sort of like, Why bother?" She glanced over at the detective. "Does that make sense, Alvah? You know a lot about everything. Does that make any sense at all to you?"

He nodded and gave her a smile.

"Because what he did is a fact, Alvah," she rushed on, sitting up straight again. "It happened. I can't make it unhappen. Certainly not by contesting its legality. And I can't make him regret it, or stop hating me."

"But all this is yours," the detective argued, with sudden intensity. "You're his heir, and the land and the money is just as much yours as it ever was his. He didn't earn it, Abby. He inherited it. No last will and testament should be allowed to break the connection."

"But the connection's already broken," she said. "That's a fact, emotionally, legally and in every other way. That's what happened. Now I have to decide about 'things.' Property, money, stocks, books, china, silver, paintings, jewelry, bedspreads, salt, pepper, sheets, towels, soap, shampoo. Things and the land. What do I get by contesting the will? And what do I lose?"

Tuesday, April 30

The next day they were still in the basement looking for anything that promised an address or an explanation for a connection between two old men—or three, for they still didn't know if Moran was involved or not. Then around noon Simon came to the top of the stairs and yelled down to Alvah, "There's a colonel on the phone for you. He says he has to talk to you right away."

Alvah rushed upstairs, Abigail behind him, leaving the others to go on searching. At the farmhouse the detective listened to the colonel on the phone for a long time, taking notes and asking questions. He looked excited, widening his blue eyes, squinting and winking knowingly at Abby all the time. She and Simon stood nearby waiting.

"Well, we got it," the detective said triumphantly when he finally hung up. "Luke was right. It did start in the war, and they were all in it together, just like Luke guessed." He suddenly sat down at the table, as if he were too excited to stand.

"What'd he say?" Abigail pressed.

"Moran and Algodones were in the same squad. It was just

about wiped out on Bataan. Massacred in April, 1942, seven-teen lives lost. The only survivors were Algodones and Moran." He looked down at his notes. "He's Sergeant Joseph Paul Al-godones. Tag number, D2114193. Moran was a private. Your fa-ther, of course, Abby, was in a completely different unit. The Air Force."

Alvah turned up the flame in the lamp on the table and started to read from his notes. Abigail looked over his shoulder. "Algodones' last-known address is 2141 Mesa Drive, Baran-quilla, New Mexico. . . . He and Moran were taken prisoner by the Japanese April 7, 1942. Same month your father es-caped to Corregidor . . . and both Algodones and Moran par-ticipated in the Death March. . . ." He turned the pages. "They were eventually transferred to the same prison in Japan," he mumbled hurriedly, reading, "and liberated by the Americans in forty-five. Moran was released," he went on, "to the care of the Veterans Administration in San Francisco, Cali-fornia, with a one-hundred-percent psychological disability, re-sult of hardship of imprisonment, the records say. He was even-tually turned over to his wife."

He flipped to another page. "Algodones was processed out in San Francisco, but requested travel accommodations back to New York City, not New Mexico. I'm skipping some of this," he said, glancing up quickly. "He's listed as 'single, brown hair, brown eyes, five feet seven, 185 pounds' when he enlisted. Weighed 115 when he got out."

"Christ," Simon said.

" 'High school dropout. Signed up in 1940, requested com-bat, expressed interest in career in the military, made steady progression through the ranks.' Colonel said according to the records he showed good leadership potential and was en-couraged to pursue a career in the military, but after his pris-oner-of-war experience, the subject was dropped."

"What'd he do after the war?" Abigail asked.

"No information on that. But he got a Purple Heart. Listen to this: 'Suffered the loss of one ear, complete, at enemy hands.' But that's better than being massacred, I suppose."

Alvah called information in Baranquilla, New Mexico, and

was told 2141 Mesa Drive was The Algodones Café. Then he
gave the operator the phone number and she put through a
call. "I'm calling from New York City," he said when someone
answered the phone. "I want to speak to Joe Algodones."

Then the detective stopped and repeated the whole thing
again, going slowly. "Spanish," he whispered to Abigail.
"Yes? . . . His father owned it?" he said into the telephone.
". . . You took it over when he died? . . . But what about the
son? Where is he now? . . . Do you know where he is
now? . . . No, there's no money unless . . . twenty years
ago? . . . She was his cousin? But where does she live? . . .
You don't know her name?"

He slammed down the phone. "Dammit," he exclaimed.
"They don't know anything, except that he went to live with a
cousin and they haven't seen him in twenty years. It's a dead
end."

Late that afternoon Max started to yell. His voice echoed off
the basement walls. "Hey!" he cried. "I've found it."

Abigail stood up.

"Alvah! Luke!"

Little flames from the lamps flickered all over the basement.
She started to run in the direction of Max's voice. She saw the
shadows of the others, heading for him too. They converged on
the old man standing at the point farthest from the stairs, right
up against a stone wall. He had an apron wrapped around his
waist and a pile of old yellowed newspaper articles in his hand.
A couch had been pushed up in front of a file cabinet that was
wedged in against the wall. Max had moved the couch aside
and gotten one drawer open.

"It's the whole thing," he said excitedly, pointing at the
drawer. "He's got it under 'Cave.' The whole drawer. 'Cave.'"

" 'Cave'?" Abigail said.

"Let's have a look." Alvah pushed Max aside and went back
in behind the couch and crouched down. Holding flashlights,
the others peered in over his shoulders.

The cabinet looked just like all the others. It was rusty, covered with cobwebs and dust. The bottom drawer, three feet in

length, was pulled out now and they could see it was crammed with pamphlets, letters, magazines, notebooks, sheets of paper, pages out of books.

"It has everything," Max was saying. "Algodones, Moran, the Philippines."

Alvah was running his fingers through the contents. "He's right," he mumbled. "Bataan, Algodones . . ."

"Let's take everything upstairs." Luke pushed the couch farther back. Then Alvah started lifting up stacks of material and handing them to Luke, who passed them on to the others.

A letter fell on the floor. Abigail picked it up. " 'It's your turn to take care of Clovis now,' " she read aloud. " 'He's your responsibility by rights anyway.' " It was signed, "Joe," the letter written two years after the war ended.

They filed upstairs, arms full. She and Foster were last, but suddenly, without a word, they glanced at each other and, laying their piles on the stairs, they headed back into the basement. Going together, they circled through the underground place, picking up every lamp, one by one, and gently blowing down into its chimney until the flame died. Gradually the underground place of Rushing Boarchards reverted back to shapes and darkness, old things hidden, life gone, back to spiders and mice and silence. Then, with just a flashlight to guide their way, they headed back toward the stairs.

"I'll be glad if I never come down here again," Foster said.

"Me too."

The others were by the fire. They had spread the files all over the floor and were down on their hands and knees sifting through it. Mrs. Smith was watching.

"Put everything in order," Alvah was saying, "according to subject matter."

Luke looked up at Abby. "The manuscript's here," he said.

She sat down beside him. He wiped a cobweb off her face. "It's about a killing."

"Is it about a cave?" she asked.

"I don't know. We'll have to read it."

"Put everything about Moran in one pile," Alvah was saying.

"Algodones in another. There's a lot on the Death March. Put that together. Remember, we're looking for his address."

"He's got a lot of letters from 'Joe,' " Max said.

"You people want something to drink?" Mrs. Smith asked.

"Very good idea," Max answered.

"But what's 'cave'?" Foster said to no one in particular.

"Clovis hid in a cave four years ago," Max offered.

"That's too recent," Alvah said. "The file goes back twenty, thirty years. Put stuff about the Japanese in another file," he went on, as he leafed through the material. He looked across at Abigail. "He had libraries all over the country sending him stuff. Did you know that?"

She shook her head.

He started passing things around the circle toward her. "Universities, history departments. Listen to this." He held up a letter. " 'I am a collector of war material relating to the Bataan Death March and the Japanese prison camps and I am writing to ask if you have . . .' "

"I never even heard him mention it," Abigail said. She picked up an old *Life* magazine. The pictures showed pitiful stick figures with sunken eyes and gaping bellies that made them look more like skeletons than people.

Luke found a doctoral thesis from the University of California at Berkeley about torture during World War II. He came to a section of photographs of Bataan reportedly confiscated from official Japanese files after truce was declared and started handing them around the circle.

The reproductions were poor, but they showed gruesome sights, American bodies dumped in heaps, GIs lined up in rows, the men so gaunt they looked more grotesque than real. "I wonder if they're here," he said, handing them to Abby.

She looked for the face of Clovis Moran; she didn't know Joe, of course.

One showed a young Japanese soldier watching a GI dying on the ground. Another showed dead bodies clearly discernible as the troops marched over them.

Then she started reading aloud from the thesis. Her voice had a dull cast. "Torture was not uncommon on Bataan. But it occurred largely when small bands of soldiers, of either side, came across stragglers. There is evidence of such occurrences on both sides, but the most grievous cases can be attributed to the Japanese. These situations largely occurred in early April just before the American surrender, when GIs had broken off from their units and were trying to make it on their own, hiding from the Japanese or trying to escape to the island of Corregidor. Japanese scouting parties proliferated throughout the peninsula looking for them. These parties operated largely on their own, with no officers present or in charge, and thus, with no control at hand, they were susceptible to the kinds of human breakdowns wars produce."

Mrs. Smith came back with wine and sat down on the floor to look too. She started reading Joe's letters too. Max found a stack of notebooks. Thumbing through to find an address, he mumbled, "accounts," "subscription to *Argosy,*" "one plane ticket to Albuquerque," "treatment for Joe's broken collar bone," "treatment for foreign object in eye." It was dark outside. They worked in silence.

"You want to wait on dinner?" Mrs. Smith asked after a while.

"Yes," Abigail mumbled, not looking up.

Luke read a letter from Algodones. " 'I got a call from Robbie,' " it said. " 'He ran away from the reform school, and said he was going to you for help, but then I didn't hear from him again. What happened? Did he ever see you? He had a car. I called the reform school and they gave me the run-around, but I don't think he's there. Let me know as soon as possible. I'm worried about him. Have him call me.' "

Then Mrs. Smith spoke up. "This letter's about Clovis too," she said. "Joe goes on about how he's been taking care of him for years. Says he drives up all the time to see him, give Joanne money and . . . here, he writes, 'You should be doing this, Boarchards, not me. He's your responsibility, not mine, and all these years you haven't even once been over there to see him. You wouldn't help Robbie and look what happened to him, and you've never helped Clovis. Not once. You've shirked your responsibility toward Clovis. Toward me. You won't even tell me if you remember.' Remember what?" Mrs. Smith asked, looking up.

"What else does it say?" Abby asked.

" 'Do you remember or have you really blanked it out? Which is it, you bastard? You're driving me crazy, you know. That's all I want. I want you to apologize. I'm sorry, Joe. Then I'll leave you alone.' "

"Apologize for what?" Luke mumbled.

Max read from another of Joe's letters, dated four years ago, about the shooting incident in Licking River. " 'You think if you shoot me, the whole thing will be over and you won't have a guilty conscience, but try it again. See if I care. You'll see. Nothing's going to make you feel better.' "

But the next letter Max picked up to read was entirely different. It had no date. " 'I'm going to bring you some of that cheese next time,' " it said, " 'so don't lock the door. I'll put it in the icebox. Leave my check in the kitchen if you want, but if I have to leave the cheese out in the shed all night, the racoons will get it. Also, I bought you this old chess set. It has the King a stag and the Queen a doe. I know you'll like it. Thought we could use it for a while, not the other.' "

They all looked across at the chess set on top of the grand piano and lapsed into silence.

Afterward Abigail silently read an article about Clovis Moran that quoted a psychiatrist. " 'This series of killings probably represents the crisis of a lifetime for Moran,' " he had said. " 'The psychiatric issue is what happens to all the feelings he has always repressed. They have to go somewhere. That's what these killings are all about, but they could either continue or he could finish, and just come out and give himself up. People often do things that make no sense to anyone else,' " the psychiatrist continued, " 'but they are perfectly understandable to them. Moran probably just couldn't hold it together any longer, even in the marginal way he was functioning before, and he finally broke loose. Who knows,' " the doctor added, " 'in his own mind he could be feeling triumphant, even though to the rest of us his behavior looks like a total breakdown.' "

He could be describing Rushing Boarchards, Abigail thought: disinheritance and suicide, his triumphant acts.

It was almost eight o'clock when they finally realized the truth: that, despite its bulk, the material had revealed no address and no explanation.

"But we do know something," Alvah mused as he paced up and down the room. "We have three men in a war—a private, a sergeant and one who became a famous lieutenant colonel. Two shared the march and the prison camp; one became a war hero. Two suffered terrible privation, one didn't. Two were victims. One was safe. Boarchards. He came out on top."

"Maybe you've got it entirely wrong," Luke countered. "Maybe it's just the opposite. After all, Boarchards isn't the one who's alive. Algodones is. And Algodones didn't become an alcoholic and commit suicide, Boarchards did. So maybe Algodones is the one on top and Rush is the loser."

Abigail shook her head. "I don't think there's any winner in this."

But at that moment something changed.

She felt it. It was a passing-on. It was as if something inside her had opened up, a tremor in the land, and the land had reshifted and then, in settling down afterward, a rearrangement of the pieces had taken place. All this had passed on to her.

It was hers. Not just her father's, a thing of three old men and the past, but hers. Now. In the present. Something very much alive. Something stalking her, a man. It was hers, even before he found her or she found him.

It was a legacy of another kind.

When they finally sat down for dinner, Mrs. Smith came in and, with her hands holding the back of an empty chair, she started talking. She sounded apologetic. "It's about that man," she said. "I wish you'd told me before he only had one ear. Because I saw him once."

"When?" Alvah asked.

"Before I got married. Long time ago. I was the housemaid

then, and Abby's mother and Sam had a terrible run-in with him."

"What happened?" the detective asked.

"He drove in," Mrs. Smith said. "I was in the kitchen and I knew right away he didn't belong here because his car was old and dirty, and in those days cars like that still went right on up to the farm. But he drove down here and Mrs. Boarchards was outside and . . ."

"Where was my father?" Abby asked.

"In New York. The war hadn't been over but a year or two, and this fellow got out of his car and he looked sick, Abby. He was thin, almost yellow. He looked around, you could tell he'd never been here before. Then he headed over here and I said to Valerie, she was the cook's helper then, 'Look at that.' He was limping and there were these scars on his neck and throat and he only had one ear. You couldn't miss it. There was a hole in his head. I told Valerie to go get Sam and this man must have come up on the veranda and seen your mother because I heard her scream. I don't know what they were saying, it happened so fast, but she started shrieking like rape or a house afire and came running inside. And he opened the door and was coming down the hall after her. He was hideous, the most terrible expression on his face, and he was screaming too."

"What?" Luke asked.

"Something about 'I found you, Boarchards. Come on out.' He must've thought Rush was in here hiding. Then Sam came out and said, 'What on earth do you think you're doing?' And it took the wind right out of the man's sails. You could tell that. But he said he wanted to see Rush, and Sam told him people like him didn't get to see 'Mr. Boarchards,' and the man said, 'Oh yeah?' Sam told him to get out and he was brushing the man out with his hands, pushing him back down the hall toward the door. Mrs. Boarchards and I were in the kitchen, peeking out behind the door, but then she went out and said, 'Yes. Get out of here.' Well, that must've done it, because the fellow just sort of put his tail between his legs and left. He waited around in the courtyard awhile and then Sam went out and told him to go away, that he couldn't hurt anyone if he wanted to anyway. Finally the man just got in his car and left, but I felt sort of sorry for him by then. They weren't very nice to him. I don't blame him."

"For what?" Luke asked.

"For being mad, you know. At the family."

"What did he actually want?" Luke pressed.

"I have no idea. He just said how he had found Rush and now he wanted to see him."

"Did he seem dangerous?" Abby asked.

"Of course he's dangerous," Max snorted.

"But maybe he's not," Abigail argued.

"Not then, he didn't seem dangerous," Mrs. Smith answered. "He just wanted something and he didn't get it."

"What did he look like?" Abby continued.

"I don't remember, really," Mrs. Smith admitted. "Except for the ear, he wasn't anybody you'd ever notice."

The story in Rush's manuscript took place on Bataan during the early days of the war against a backdrop of encroaching defeat. The Japanese had laid siege to the American troops, who were poorly equipped, starving and in total disarray.

Abigail kept remembering it had been written during the month of the manhunt for Clovis Moran, but that Rush had had it in his mind for over twenty years. She and Luke were alone in front of the fire. They were sitting on the couch. The others had gone to bed. Luke had the manuscript in his lap and after he read a page, he handed it to her. Outside the wind had died down and the rain had stopped for the first time in days.

The plot involved three soldiers, but their names and physical descriptions changed repeatedly. Reading, Abigail found it difficult to figure out who was who until, after about twenty pages, she realized that one was the hero, named variously Frank, Mark, John or Julius, and that the other two were not only not heroes, but they were really nothing. Called Hooper, Hupper, Murphy, Melvin, Clause and Amos, they were sick and weak, and totally dependent on the hero for their survival.

As characters, however, they were stick men, one indistinguishable from the other. Only the hero was different.

He was described as dark, but sometimes he was tall, other times short. But either way, he had all the attributes of a savior. He fed the others, took care of them, and protected them.

The manuscript was not only not good, it was weird. Abigail told Luke it was more like a puzzle than a book, because the action and the scenes changed repeatedly and without warning, midsentence, as if the author had no clear idea what he was doing, where he was going. The narrative, such as it was, constantly switched back to something that had been described pages earlier and was then redone in an entirely different way.

In reading, all that became clear by way of plot was that the three men, with the hero in command, were headed somewhere, that they were in great danger, and that something cataclysmic was going to happen. Significantly, however, what that was, or even that it was going to be cataclysmic, was never spelled out in the actual writing. Abigail only realized it herself when, totally confused about what on earth was going on, she stopped reading and tried to figure it out. She decided that the author, whether he knew it or not, was actually postponing something. Repeatedly he kept not getting his three men to something or somewhere, a climax perhaps, and most of his efforts, she realized, were directed at reshaping the prelude. She also noticed that all these ministrations concentrated on redoing the character of the main figure, progressively defining him as more and more heroic and important.

"This is nerve-racking," she said aloud.

"I know," Luke answered.

Finally, midway, the story actually began to take shape. One morning the hero, Frank, Mark, John, Julius, fled with two buddies in a jeep. It was every man for himself on Bataan, the story said, a nonstop barrage of missiles overhead, the Japanese taking prisoners right and left. Defeat for the Americans was at hand. Some had escaped in boats to the sea and made it to the island of Corregidor, just as Rushing Boarchards himself eventually had. But not these three. They had been hiding out on the peninsula, the story said, when suddenly the road they were on intersected up ahead with a column of Japanese soldiers and the men fled back into the jungle, retreating to high ground, away from the water.

In some versions the story started out on high ground and the three Americans were headed toward the water to look for a boat when they ran into the enemy column. Then they retreated back to high ground again. In others, they were looking for a jeep and never found one, or else saw a jeep and went for it, and then came across the column instead. But, in all versions, they always ended up on the high ground.

Up there it was all rocks and occasional trees bleached white in the sun, an almost unnatural landscape. He used the phrase "sun and bare rocks" over and over again. There was no wind or forest, no humidity, mosquitoes or sweat, just the endless glare of white on white. The two other men, Hooper, Hupper, Murphy, Melvin, Clause and Amos, were so depleted from the siege they couldn't move. They had quit. Frank, Mark, John, Julius, was breathing the very stuff of life into them to keep them going. He pulled them by the shoulder, carried their rifles, forced rice down their throats, and even spit into their mouths to give them nourishment. It was an androgynous role he had, larger than strictly male.

The very moment when the climax suddenly came, when an attack suddenly happened, he was keeping watch while they slept. He was sitting out there "in the sun and bare rocks," they sheltered behind him in the crevice of the stones when, out of the corner of his eye, he suddenly saw a Japanese soldier. The soldier was coming up the stark hillside. And he hadn't seen them yet.

Like hunting, Abby thought. The kill. Man and deer a perfect match.

But if Boarchards would have shot the deer, Frank, Mark, John, Julius didn't. He couldn't pull the trigger. He suddenly got afraid. Became paralyzed. He couldn't move.

Then the Japanese soldier saw him. Both their guns were down. Too far down. No position to shoot. And still the hero didn't move. The Japanese soldier started to raise his gun. Still the hero didn't move, something about the man's eyes. The Jap looked at him, straight in the eyes, looked at him and held him, controlling him, imploring him, hating him, and ready to kill him.

But then, in the last second, just before it was too late, the hero raised his gun and shot the man in the eyes.

The bullet blew his head apart. And the hero started to vomit.

Or else he had been vomiting all along. Ever since he was first paralyzed and couldn't move his gun. It was almost impossible to decipher the plot at the end. It was even unclear in some versions whether it was the Japanese's head that was blown apart, or, weirdly, the hero's. Sometimes the explosion was outside and the hero saw it, other times it seemed that he was feeling it himself inside his head and he himself was being destroyed.

One other thing was even more irrational. If, all along, the plot had focused on three men, suddenly, when the Japanese soldier arrived, in some versions there were still only the three Americans, but in others there were "more," "others," "many," lying on the ground too, asleep and wretched.

Abigail read and reread, she turned the pages back and started over, caught up and read on, trying to make sense of the thing. So did Luke. She kept remembering Rush had written this during the weeks the hunt for Clovis Moran went on, but that he must have finished it before he did the will and went to Connecticut, because then, she knew, the typewriter was broken.

"It's a complete contradiction," Luke said suddenly.

"What?" She went back, read it again, and this time she saw what he meant.

In some versions what the hero did—shooting the man in the eye and making the head explode in a million pieces—was an act of survival and courage, even triumph. But in others, with the explosion in himself instead, and vomit all over the place, it was a moment of self-destruction, self-disgust and disgrace.

"Look at what he does to the paralysis," Luke mumbled.

She read it again and again.

Each time she reached the ending she noticed more clearly

that what increasingly stood out in the writer's mind, as he wrote version after version of the climactic scene, was not the killing or the explosion of brains, but the paralysis that preceded it. The writing conveyed a monumental loathing for that single fleeting moment of weakness.

There was never any recognition of the fact that the hero finally triumphed, fired the shot and killed the man. "We pick our own failures," the doctor in Connecticut had said.

Luke stood up. "This doesn't make sense," he said. "There's no 'cave' in this manuscript at all."

In the distance they heard the jeep. Then Simon came stomping in, dogs at his heels, clothes pulled on over his pajamas. "Mary wants Alvah," he said. "Some man just called her and she says now she's got what you want. You're to call her right away."

Instead of waking Alvah, they went straight to the farmhouse, and there Simon and Abby listened as Luke talked to Mary. He wrote something down on a piece of paper and then he hung up. "It cost you a hundred and fifty dollars, Abby," he said. "A clerk at Seaman's Trust Bank in New York agreed to go though the files for Mary and he found out Joe Algodones has had a safe-deposit box in the Fourteenth Street branch for eighteen years. His current address is Pescadero, New Mexico, about one hundred and fifty miles north of Albuquerque. The clerk even gave Mary the phone number."

He waved the paper with the number in his hand. They stared at it in a mixture of relief and disbelief.

"Call him," Abby blurted out. "It's only nine-thirty there. Tell him we want to see him."

"But he's been in New York following you."

"Who knows. Call anyway. Maybe he's back in New Mexico. Find out who is in New Mexico. Say we want a meeting."

Luke turned the handle on the phone box. When he got the operator, he gave her the number in New Mexico. Abigail pulled a chair over near the phone and, standing on it, bent her head down near the receiver. She could hear it ringing. Simon moved in closer too.

A woman answered.

"May I speak to Joe?" Luke asked calmly.

"He's not here right now," the woman said. She sounded pleasant. There was noise from a television in the background.

"Will he be back soon?"

"I don't know."

"Is there someplace else I can reach him?"

The woman didn't answer.

"Is he in New York?"

She still didn't answer.

"Are you his wife?"

She laughed then. It was a strange, almost childlike sound. "I'm Sue Ann Crosby," she said, the name sounding almost as odd as her voice. "I'm his cousin. What do you want him for?"

"I'm a friend of a friend of his. My name is Luke Reider, and I want to get in touch with him as soon as possible."

"Who's the friend?"

"Rushing Boarchards."

Abby held her breath.

"Oh, yes," the woman said warmly. "Him and Joe are very good friends."

"Very good friends?" Luke exclaimed. "So you know Boarchards too?"

"Of course I do. I told Joe we had to reciprocate."

"Reciprocate? I don't understand."

"What?" Now the woman sounded confused too.

"Tell her we're coming out to see him," Abigail whispered urgently.

"But he may not be there," Luke whispered back.

"Maybe he is. Who knows."

Luke cleared his throat. "This is Tuesday, Miss Crosby. If you and Mr. Algodones . . ."

"Say we'll go Thursday," Abigail whispered, doing a quick calculation of the days.

". . . are going to be home, I'd like to come see you Thursday. It's very important. Abigail Boarchards will be with me."

There was a long silence at the other end of the phone. "But I don't know if Joe will be here or not. He comes and goes."

"But he might be there Thursday?"

"He might be."

"Is there someplace else I can find him?"

"No." She sounded hesitant.

"She's not going to tell us where he is," Luke whispered to Abby on the side.

"Just tell her we're coming," Abby insisted.

"Then he's not in New York?" Luke asked the woman.

She still didn't answer.

"Tell her," Abby ordered. "Even if it's a wild-goose chase."

"Is it all right if we come by to see you Thursday, Miss Crosby?"

"It's fine by me. I'll be happy to meet her anytime. Tell her I'll give her her father's favorite cheese."

"Yes, certainly," Luke stammered.

"Mary," Luke was saying, "we need three reservations for Albuquerque Thursday morning. Three, in case Alvah comes. And returns on Friday."

Abigail took the crumpled list out of her back pocket, where she had kept it for days, and looked at it. "Algodones," it said, "Melanie, Victoria, Sam and Bostrine," and now New Mexico, she thought, and only five more days to go.

Abby kissed Simon good-night and they left.

Luke drove home. The night was beautiful, the clouds going by fast, pushed by a powerful wind above. "It's clearing," he said, looking up through the window. "I didn't even notice. Did you?" He looked at her.

She nodded.

"You would." He grinned. Then he reached out and took her hand. "You all right?" he asked.

"Yes. Exhausted."

"Me too."

"And relieved. Now that we're seeing Joe."

"Maybe. At least we're getting closer to him."

"And to Monday," she added.

He turned down toward the courtyard. Her father's house lay

ahead like a ship along the land, but he stopped the jeep midway and got out. "Come on," he said.

Outside he took her by the hand and led her across the meadow toward the lake. They walked along the shore, the moon reflecting on the water. When they came to one of the guest cottages, he opened the door and lit a match to see. Inside there was a couch, a big stone chimney, and a bedroom on the side. He went over to the fireplace and got logs out of the woodpile. She knelt beside him and watched as he made a fire and the small flames traveled up along the paper to the wood. Smoke wafted out into the room and she inhaled deeply.

Luke went to the bedroom and came back with a big old quilt, star-patterned, and draped it over her shoulders. He sat beside her and they stared into the flames threading their way around the logs. Orange light with streaks of blue leaped toward the chimney and bits of steam hissed in the fire.

Then Luke stood up and pulled the couch over in front of the fire. He drew her down beside him and, with their feet at one end, heads at the other, they lay together with the quilt wrapped around them, looking at the flames.

He touched her face once. "You all right?" he asked again. "Yes."

After a while her hand reached into his pants and, taking down the zipper, she felt him inside, getting hard, then she bent down and used her mouth on him until he almost came. Instead, he lifted her up, yanked her pants off and climbed on top of her. Then, moving and moving, quickly and urgently, they came together strong as a train roaring through a tunnel. Afterward they fell asleep.

When the fire had died down and even the embers had lost their light, they woke up and went back to the house. It was almost dawn.

Inside, at the door of her bedroom, he said, "You can't go on hating him, Abby."

"Why not?"

"Because then you'll be the same as him. And the manuscript . . ."

"Yes."

"It's sort of pathetic. Isn't it?"

"Yes."

"Well, that's the same man who wrote the will, the same man who rejected you. He obviously didn't know what he was doing, Abby."

Wednesday, May 1

The morning sky was clear and the air electric with the sounds of birds. The rain had stopped and everything seemed polished and bright. Out on the veranda Abigail felt exuberant and lusty, as if her triumph had already begun, and for the first time she felt a presence of Rushing Boarchards that didn't smell foul. Instead he seemed part of the peace and silence of the land and she remembered him the way she used to, like a tree or something natural that had gotten old and decayed, the way all life is meant to decay. But then the feeling disappeared, the hint of triumph too, and she thought for a second of going upstairs to his room at last, but a rush of panic moved in and she knew she couldn't do it. It was the smell. She couldn't face his smell.

Inside, Alvah said he wasn't going to New Mexico. He'd been away from the office too long as it was, he said, and he had work to do. Then they all piled into the jeeps and set off, Luke in the lead, Max and Foster next, Alvah and Abigail last.

"Take care of yourself," Simon said, the two dogs at his heels.

"You, too," she said, holding his hand.

"And don't do anything foolish."

It was overcast in New York. Alvah dropped her off at her apartment. "That's Mike over there," he said, pointing at the van across the street. "But be careful when you go to see Melanie. Keep your eyes open. Algodones may not be in New Mexico at all."

"What do I do if I do run into him here?"

"Mike'll be behind you somewhere. He'll take care of it."

"But what if I lose Mike or Algodones just comes at me?"

"Then don't look afraid. Intimidate him. Same as rape. Get the upper hand. Remember how much you despise him and show it."

But upstairs there was another letter from Algodones. Abigail stared at the envelope, postmarked New York City, and dreaded reading it.

"Dear Abigail Boarchards," it said. "You tell your father I know where you are. He thinks he can give me the old one, two, but you tell him I know where you are. See what he says about that. See if he likes that. How do you like it?"

Abigail sat down. This time he had signed his name; he was coming closer. Suddenly she stopped breathing and listened. She heard a noise in the kitchen.

But when she got to the kitchen, it was water dripping and air pushing around a window.

She double-locked the front door and called Phoebe. "It's like getting obscene phone calls, over and over, from the same person. Only worse."

Hanging up, she went down the hall to the office and found the dictionary. She looked up the word "contest." To contest a will.

To "fight" or "compete," it said, "as in: The decision was contested by the loser."

She grimaced. Then she looked up the word "acceptance." Her other option. To "accept" what had happened to her. "As in," the book said, "assent, agree or consent."

"But I don't want to agree," she snarled, "and I don't want to be a loser. I want to win."

Abruptly she turned the pages of the book to "win." "To gain the victory in any contest," it said, "to triumph and prevail."

"That's it," she said. "That's what I want. To triumph and prevail."

The phone rang while she was getting dressed. "Have you made your decision yet?" the lawyer Solomon Irving asked.

"No."

"But it's five o'clock now. It's Wednesday. Monday's the deadline. What's holding you up?"

How'd you tell someone you were waiting to prevail?

She dressed carefully for Melanie, suit, blouse, hair up, thinking she was preparing for a woman with blond hair done in a page boy, still dancing at El Morocco. She was just about to leave when the phone rang again.

It was the lawyer Wynne. "I'm calling in the interests of the family to see what you intend to do," he said.

"About what?" she asked coolly, but suddenly she felt all the pieces falling into place.

"Your father's will."

"What about it?"

"You must know Monday is the deadline," he said uncomfortably.

"Deadline for what?"

He cleared his throat. "If you don't want to be cooperative . . ."

"Cooperative?"

". . . it's up to you. I just called to see if you wanted to discuss the situation and find out if . . ."

"You couldn't wait until Monday? You that nervous about it?"

"I'm not nervous at all. I'm just doing my job for the family, just like I've always done and like my father did before me."

"Who's the family, Harvey? Sam's in the hospital. Andrew's drunk. Charley's in London. Max is with me. Who's left? One eighty-year-old woman? A dead man?"

"The family is larger than mere individuals."

"Is it?" she said angrily. "I'll tell you, Harvey. I know what my decision is, but you're going to have to wait until Monday to find out what it is. You're going to have to wait for a sheet of paper, Harvey. You're going to have to read a document, all of you, to find out what your fate is, and it isn't even your fate, is it, Harvey? You've just latched on to it and you're out there swinging in the wind like a man with his pants down."

She slammed down the phone and dialed Solomon Irving back. She was spitting mad, ready to tell him to prepare the papers, but she suddenly realized she was late for Melanie and hung up.

I'll call him tonight, she thought.

Downstairs the detective's van was gone, and she looked up and down the block wondering what had happened. Where was Mike? Had Algodones come and Mike followed him, or was Algodones out there now, waiting for her?

"You'll be quicker going by subway, this time of day," the doorman said to her.

She finally headed for the corner, but after a few feet, she stopped and turned back to the street. Rush-hour traffic was heavy. She waved for cabs. They all sped by full. Her eyes went up and down the sidewalk, looking for Mike or Algodones, any certainty about the will evaporated in the greater uncertainty of everything else.

Finally she set off at a run toward the subway but kept looking over her shoulder, and once inside the train, she studied every face.

At Melanie's office Abigail gave her name and sat down to wait. She finally relaxed a bit. The search for Rushing Boarchards had taken her to familiar turf at last, a place where people had briefcases, cheap pens and no time for lunch. This was her world now. A world of work.

Then a secretary appeared, asked her to follow. Abigail set off down an aisle, curiosity mounting, looking for someone with a page boy, dancing, but instead she only spotted Melanie because the woman spotted her first. She was standing to the side, tall and blond with hair piled up on top of her head, blue eyes encased in wrinkles. The eyes were staring at her and Abigail missed a step. Her heart started pounding. She stared back. The woman was obviously stunned by her, but Abigail was surprised as well. Melanie looked strong and capable and even more beautiful than if she had been dancing, but she also looked old. Time had caught her and Abigail found herself mesmerized by the woman's neck. Even from a distance it draped down like overlapping pieces of cloth.

"What's the matter, Melanie?" she heard someone ask. People were showing her mock-up posters, but she saw Melanie shake her head and start walking toward her. Abigail tightened her hands and waited. She knew something had suddenly broken loose, but she didn't know what it was. The woman got closer and closer, but then, just as she reached her, she passed on without a word, down another aisle.

Abigail turned and followed. She watched the woman from behind, beautiful clothes, legs, and abruptly she realized they were alike, same size, same height, width, both in suits, hair up. Only one was dark and one was light, one young and one old.

Melanie went right over to the desk in her office and picked up a cigarette. "Anyone ever tell you you look just like him?" she said as Abigail shut the door.

The woman inhaled deeply and blew the smoke out. Her shoulders lowered with the exhale, but she still stared at her visitor and Abigail wanted to say, "I'm sorry," wipe away her face and start again.

Suddenly she thought maybe Harvey Wynne was right. Maybe a family is more than individuals.

The woman was asking her if she wanted something to drink. Abigail felt herself nod and the woman got up and went out, leaving the door open, and Abigail was still thinking maybe Wynne was right. Maybe a family was more than individuals. Maybe it was a matter of things, like faces, being repeated again and again, traits, beliefs, wishes, fears. Maybe she was not just a single thing at all, but pieces of Florence and

Florence's son all wrapped up in one, a package meant to trouble, haunt and remind. The same things repeated generation after generation, showing up in her, confusing first her mother, then her father, then all of them, as if she, Abby, like each of them in turn no doubt, was not just she herself, one little girl who couldn't frighten anyone, but pieces of all of them, past, present and future, a configuration of millions of things, a haunting, bewitching problem, the complexity of life itself.

"I never did see your mother," Melanie was saying as she brought in the Perrier and sat down again. "I understand she was very beautiful, but there's no doubt you're the very image of your father." Even old she was dazzling. Only the cigarette in her hand hinted at any vulnerability at all.

"Thank you for letting me come," Abigail said.

"It's my pleasure." The woman was pouring the Perrier, and for the first time Abigail noticed the room, and the painting. The Monet, water lilies and leaves, hung there along with ads and posters, but most of the room was mirrors. Whole panels of mirrors stretched from floor to ceiling, reflecting everything not once or twice, but dozens or hundreds of times, columns of images that extended down smaller and smaller into infinity.

There was no solitude here, Abigail realized with a jolt. The woman had designed it so she could never be alone. "Thank you," she said, taking a glass. "I'm sorry, showing up like this. I really am. But I'm doing something that's important. Otherwise I wouldn't bother you. Can I ask you some questions?"

Melanie smiled in assent, but the smoke from her cigarette curled up in circles, as if the tension had caught it too.

"Did he ever mention someone named Joe Algodones from New Mexico?"

"No."

"Or Clovis Moran?"

"No."

"The war?"

"All the time."

"What'd he say about it?"

"He was obsessed with it." Melanie leaned back, looking aloof.

"What did he say about it?"

"When?"

"Any time."

"He said things like, 'War is great.' 'It's the ultimate test.' 'The ultimate proving ground.' 'You can't understand; you're a woman.' 'Bullshit,' I said. 'Getting up in the morning and staring at yourself in the mirror is the ultimate test.' "

The telephone cut her off. Melanie picked it up, listened, then, still holding the phone, she stood up and started to walk around the room. Abigail watched her, partly fascinated, partly repelled.

"Well, I don't care, Harry," Mclanie was saying. "You're not cutting it any more. You're just not doing the job. And don't tell me twenty years is a long time, I owe you something. I don't owe you anything. I run a business, not a charity."

Abigail looked away. She stood up to leave, embarrassed by the woman's toughness, but Melanie waved her back to the chair and grinned at her quickly, as if to say, Who cares about these little things? It's business. You and I are the same. You understand life, same as me. Abigail felt confused, and turned her head away.

When Melanie hung up, she looked relaxed, almost refreshed. "Ask me more," she said conspiratorially. "This is fairly entertaining."

"I'm curious why you still dislike my father so much now." Abigail's voice had a hard edge now.

"I don't dislike him."

"You act like you do. I feel that I've intruded here."

Melanie turned and faced the mirrors, dozens of aging blondes. "He brought me flowers every day," she said abruptly. "We went to Santa Barbara, took a house with a tile roof and cactus flowers, ate breakfast in bed and read by the pool. We went to San Francisco and San Antonio and Cuernavaca. All over. Restaurants, hotels, by ourselves. Finally he said I had to find the thing inside me that made me what I was. I said, 'What is that?' And he said, 'Only you can find it.' And I said,

'Well, it certainly isn't in Hollywood'—because I already hated Hollywood by then. And he said, 'Well, maybe it's someplace else,' and I said, 'But I just want to be with you. I don't want to think about anything else.' But he said I had to."

She turned around and looked at Rushing Boarchards' daughter. "He made me what I am today. He made me come alive. That's the most important thing somebody can do for you. That's why I didn't want to see you. I didn't want to remember."

"Didn't you ever find anybody else?"

Melanie waved the question away.

"You must have had a very interesting life," Abigail said. "Two very successful careers."

"But men can't take it."

"Is that why you hate him?"

"I didn't like what he did."

So she did hate him, Abigail thought. "What did he do?"

"He talked about divorce. He said he wanted to make a break with the past. I believed him. But then he never did it. The more I changed, the more he pulled back. I came to New York, started in business, but . . ." She paused, looked distracted.

"But what?"

"Something happened to him, didn't it?" Melanie asked, turning to her. "I don't know what it was. I didn't want to know. One little dent in their shining armor and they can't take it. How do they expect to survive? What do they think they are? Perfect? I could take your mother, but not that. Don't keep looking at me like that," she said, laughing awkwardly. "You make me nervous."

Abigail averted her eyes, but she felt nervous too. She still felt both attracted and repulsed by this woman, empathetic and at the same time horrified by her bursts of harshness. I'm not like that, Abigail thought defensively. I'm not.

"He was talking about how he wasn't what he pretended to be," Melanie was saying, "and I said I didn't want to see him again. He got mad. He said I'd led him on, and the minute he opened up, pounced on him."

"So he did open up. He must have loved you a great deal. What did he say?"

"He talked about the war. How it got to him. How he had to kill some Jap in a cave and . . ."

"A cave?"

"And how he didn't like it."

"The killing happened in a cave?"

"Yes," the woman said impatiently. "I told him, 'So what? Killing is always bad. That's war, isn't it?' "

"You were awfully harsh with him, weren't you."

The woman didn't answer. "I said there was no reason for him to pretend or be ashamed of his own trauma, but he said I didn't understand. I said I understood perfectly and he should follow his own advice and be himself, just like he told me to be. Instead he was a phony."

"But why are you still so angry about it? Twenty-five years is a long time."

"Because he blamed me. He was a broken man, but he said I did it to him. Because I didn't listen. Because I didn't care. Because I . . . You want to know why I'm still angry about it? Because I believed him, Abigail. For years and years I believed him. I thought I destroyed him. That's why."

"But don't you think he was trying to establish real contact for once?"

"You weren't listening," Melanie snapped.

"I'm trying to."

"I don't care what he was trying to do or tell me. I had waited years for him, but all of a sudden it came to me he wasn't stringing me along, he was stringing himself along and using me to do it. It's not my fault what happened to him."

"I didn't say it was," Abigail protested.

"You act like you do," Melanie retorted.

"I don't mean to."

"Haven't you ever had an experience like that?"

Abigail felt herself pull back. "Like what?" she asked.

"When someone's doing something to you? Using you? You're strong. You're a woman like me . . ."

"No, I'm not," Abigail blurted out.

"Don't men do this to you? Use you, use your strength? Then hate you later. Didn't he do that to you?"

"Of course he didn't," Abigail said with sudden fury.

"I bet he did. Daughter like you."

Melanie looked ugly all of a sudden, Abigail thought, her eyes hard, cold, her face a thousand years old. "I'd have to think about it," she said aloud. There was something somewhere. . . .

"It's not easy," Melanie said.

"I didn't say it was." Something was gnawing at the back of her mind. She wanted to leave. She looked at her watch.

"He twisted people around," Melanie was saying. "He had people in Hollywood dancing on his fingertips, same thing in New York. I thought they wanted his money. Then I realized they wanted his attention. But he didn't give it. He held it back, played with it and worse. Sometimes I could see what other people didn't."

"What?" She was interested again, despite herself. That's what she'd wanted too. His attention.

"That he didn't even know they were there at all. They didn't count."

"Then what made you like him?"

"Because he made everything serious," Melanie answered. "And he made me laugh. I had more fun with him than with anyone in my whole life, but he gave everything its proper regard. I've never known anyone quite like that." She paused. "I guess I keep contradicting myself, don't I?"

"Sort of."

"One minute I sound like I hate him, next minute I love him." She sounded embarrassed, gentle for once.

Abigail liked her again. She wondered whether to tell her about the will and all.

But then Melanie picked up her lighter again and started another cigarette. She drew her lips tight and her eyes got cold, almost hostile. "You're trying to understand why he fell apart, aren't you?" she said harshly. "Why he committed suicide. Oh yes, I heard about that. And who did it to him. Who ruined him. Well, it wasn't me. I had nothing to do with it, and if

I've lived with the memory of his accusations all these years,
I'm not going to listen to yours."

"But . . ." Abigail protested.

"You want to know why someone ends up a failure?"
Melanie said, holding her cigarette like a clever little weapon.
"They do it in little steps all along the way. That's how. And
he did it to himself. All I did was get out when the going got
rough. That's spelled life, honey, L-I-F-E, and I bet you'd have
done the exact same thing."

"But I still don't understand why you didn't just forget him
if he was that bad."

"Because it was more complicated than that. You're the spitting image of him, you know that? You even sound like him."
She made it seem like an accusation.

"You're like him too," Abigail said coldly. "You took work..
He took the woods. But you did the same thing to each other.
You both ran for the hills."

"I find that slightly absurd."

The two women were silent. Abigail drank more Perrier.
Something was gnawing at her mind, pieces drifting in the
ozone, same as the boy in the kitchen, my father says you
owe me. "What was he trying to tell you that night about
what happened in the cave? Killing the Japanese," she said.
"Tell me more about that." But even as Melanie started
to talk, Abigail knew there was something else as well she
wanted to know. Just as those fragments about the boy had
been put away and forgotten because they spelled something
forbidden, a connection between her father and a boy who
died. "What boy? There was no boy." A connection he didn't
want, and so she didn't either. But now, out in the ozone, there
was the hint of something else, something she didn't want and
maybe Rush hadn't wanted either. . . .

She started to listen to Melanie. "He said he was trying to
tell me something," the woman was saying. "But I swear to
God I didn't believe him. I still don't. He was trying to do
something to me instead. It was wicked. He was supposed to
file for divorce, but he kept saying he was waiting for the right

time. For Grace. For you. And I finally realized he didn't dare
make the change, but that he couldn't admit it."

Abigail began to feel anxious. She had no idea why.

". . . so he had to find a way to make me get rid of him instead. What he did was find a way to blame me."

Abigail stood up.

"What's the matter?"

"Nothing." She looked around, women in the glass on all
sides, same size, same shape, some young, some old. "It just
bothers me." She sat down and laughed awkwardly. "I don't
know whether to like you or not. I want to blame you too, but
maybe that's so I won't have to blame myself. I don't know. I
better go."

Melanie was drumming out a cigarette. "Did I say something wrong?"

"No. But you've made me see something in my father I
never wanted to face before. Some meanness of spirit. I never
wanted to think of him like that. Even now."

"Even now?" Melanie looked confused. "What happened
between you two?"

"Nothing. You were mean to him, weren't you?"

"I guess," the woman admitted. "We had good times too,
though," she added. "In fact, most of the times were good. I
didn't even mind sharing him with your mother. Besides, he
was away so much, away from her. I traveled with him everywhere."

"How much did she know about you?"

"Who knows?" she said, as if to say, instead, Who cares?
"He could never understand that I didn't want jewels. Or want
anything. He thought all women wanted jewels. He kept wanting to give me things, but I didn't want anything. Finally I
took the Monet. But I don't think he understood women very
well. Were you close to him?"

"Oh yes," Abigail said. "Very." She stood up abruptly. "I
have to go. I really do."

"You want to have lunch sometime?"

"I'm going away."

"When you come back. Anytime."

"Thank you." She started backing away toward the door, columns of women moving.

"Did you get what you wanted?" Melanie asked.

"Yes." But she hadn't. Or had she? More than she wanted? Something hovering at the edge.

"Hope you get this figured out," Melanie said.

"Yes."

"Maybe you should let me help you. He did the same thing to me, in a way."

"He didn't do anything to me," Abigail said.

"Oh. I thought he had maybe. Something that never got resolved." She sounded sad. She paused, as if waiting for Abigail to talk, and then said, "Sometimes I wish I'd never met him. Let me give you my home number."

Melanie wrote it down and Abigail put it in her pocket, along with the list and the nugget, and left, lines of women following her out, same size, same shape, some young, some old.

Thursday, May 2

The next morning Abigail awoke unrested and troubled. Luke was beside her on the bed. On the plane she still couldn't get Melanie out of her mind. She didn't talk and neither did Luke. He was preparing for his Saturday meeting, a special gathering of partners of his new law firm, and she was reading something. She sat by the window. Luke had his long legs out in the aisle. She longed to talk, but she didn't know how to begin or what to say. "I wonder what he'll be like," she said finally. "Joe."

"Hard to know." He didn't look up from his papers.

"At least we'll know more then. . . ." But he wasn't listening, so she closed her eyes and tried to rest or sleep. Melanie kept coming back.

But why? All they'd done was talk. Argue.

The plane droned on. She stared at the crease in her gabardine pants where the line ran off the edge of her knee and plunged down. She said she was cold and pulled a sweater out of her sack beneath the seat. Luke helped her put it on over her head and went back to reading.

She watched him turn the pages—depositions, files. It had been there before. A memory. Wafting in and out. But she didn't look at it. She'd sensed it at the boathouse and then again with Melanie.

Just a conversation. Nothing big. Nothing important.

Just Rush talking. He was drunk. It was the winter of Clovis Moran.

The timing was right. Four years ago, a will to write.

But it wasn't important. He just said why didn't she look at things the way they really were. That was all. Nothing to feel bad about.

Then why did she feel bad? Why did she keep remembering it? The snow. The smell. His smell. The rancid smell of sweat and drink. The sound of bullets hitting the water. Light and dark. Ping.

It had been their last conversation before the will.

That stopped her. She stiffened.

"Try and relax," Luke said. "We still have a long way to go."

She stared out the small window of the plane.

It happened the day Moran was caught. The week he wrote the will.

She looked at the blues and pinks of the world below and began to feel hot. Her armpits were stuck to her sides and the back of her neck throbbed.

Forget it.

It was nothing.

"Why don't you look at things the way they really are?" At the boathouse. And then he leaned over and pushed himself up off the slip by his hands, fanny out, up first, the only way a drunk could get off the floor and then . . .

The memory was unclear. The boathouse, water light and dark slapping against the wood. It was still, no birds, no sound, only his canoe riding on the water. And the smell. For the first time she had noticed his smell. That was the very first time.

Her insides were knotting up.

The boathouse, old pine and black water. A girl with a camera and old clothes, casual garb, in fashion then. She was bored. Restless. And ambitious. Her career on the brink of change and recognition, but she didn't know that. Didn't know it was coming. Coming tonight, in fact, on its way even now, for Clovis Moran must have left his cave in the woods and started coming down, bringing with him recognition for her of a larger scale than she had ever had before.

Her father was the same as always. Monotonous, boring, and drunk. Oh, I'm the greatest guy in the world. I got a raw deal. Grace would tie anyone in knots. Not my fault. Not my fault about writing either. World's full of people don't know their ass from a hole in the wall. What's the point of writing if publishers are fucked up?

Abigail stared at the blue outside and wished Luke would talk, but he didn't, and so she went back inside again, back down through the years, one, two, three, four, to the fourth year, and Abigail Boarchards was not a daughter or an heiress, but a worker, sent north on a national story. A manhunt.

Two syllables. Manhunt. First a hunt for Clovis. Then a hunt for Rush. Now a hunt for Joe.

Manhunt.

Hundreds of pictures and phone calls, messengers to take her film to the airport, helicopters and dogs, all looking for Clovis Moran, and all the time more killings and more snow. Clovis Moran: the first time she'd heard his name. Police and roadblocks. She stayed at the inn, journalists and minicams, talk about expense accounts and how you couldn't put in for cabs here and how they had to find him sometime, didn't they, and she went to Weather Tree when things got slow. For a night or a day or an afternoon. Drive in, drive out. "Simon, any messages for me?" Rush didn't have the cane yet, but he walked from chair to chair, reaching out with one hand to grasp the next before he let go of the last, and when he sat his head bent over so much he made a shape that was almost round, his head bending out over his knee, bobbing like a flower too heavy for the stalk. And she told him everything, chatted about this and that, because that's what they did, Rushing Boarchards and his only daughter. She, his heir apparent, she talked and he listened. They had to fill the silence somehow, and what had worked once, a method of intimacy, had turned to format.

Only now something was different because this visit (for the first and only time, she thought, staring at the high blue sky out the plane window), he talked. He talked and talked, and she was the one who wasn't listening now. He said he'd started a new book and she said "Oh," because he'd started a hundred books and finished none, he hadn't finished a book in years. And so she paid no attention now when he said, oh liquid tongue, that he'd started another, almost finished and how good it was. And so, he talked; she, sassy, strong and indifferent.

Then, just before the end, she came in with her friend Josh, and for two days they waited at the icehouse. Tonight, the last night, he would come, Clovis Moran, all covered with snow and ice and look at her and say, "Didn't your father tell you about the cave?" "What cave?" And they would wake Rush and Diver and later the posse would head up into the mountains to the caves and even later she'd get a professional prize.

But she had no way of knowing that. She was at the boathouse now and she was bored and he smelled and ranted about Clovis Moran.

But he'd been doing that for days. About how he, Rush Boarchards, was the only person in the whole world who knew the woods well enough to find Clovis Moran. He spent the mornings upstairs writing the book, he claimed, then came down, so drunk he could barely walk, talk about delusion, got in the jeep and drove out to look for Moran. Wouldn't have anything to do with the posse because they were a bunch of fools, didn't know the woods from their assholes. He was the only one who knew the woods, knew the weather, knew how to find Moran. Had to find him. Sure, Pop. And he took just about every back road or logging trail he could find, as if the killer were just waiting out there for Rush Boarchards to come and catch him.

He got so obsessed that when Jackson called, Simon told him he'd have to hire a nurse if this didn't stop. Then Jackson showed up and said he for one thought they ought to humor him.

Abigail said that was absurd. She was short-tempered and irritable. Simon said he'd never seen her like that, and she said Pop turned everything into a way to prove himself. And how many years were they going to go on humoring him? How many? But Jackson paid her no mind, Simon neither. He just said Rush needed to get it off his chest.

She said bullshit. But she said it to herself. She didn't speak up. Because for years, ever since she first saw him sneaking a drink in the shed, she'd done the same thing too, pampered him, protected him, flattered him. But right now, then, that moment at Weather Tree, she realized for the first and only time—because afterward she sent it away, things in the ozone, buried, forgotten, drifting in the ozone—for the first time, she realized it didn't work. Nothing had worked—not pampering, not flattery. The distortions and the drinking continued. And, to make matters worse, she realized it had left her angry and disgusted, because he was fooling no one but himself, and what was the point of that? Wasn't anybody ever going to talk sense to him and tell him what was what?

The situation had gotten so absurd that Simon had even started following him out the road, discreetly, so as not to hurt his feelings, because several times he just didn't come back. Then they had to remember where he said he was going and find him. And that was no joke. Finding him stuck in a snowbank somewhere or asleep with his car angled off the road, engine running. Sometimes he might have frozen but for the liquor, and they had to pile him into the jeep, cover him over with a tarp and bring him in. The day before, Polly had found him. Asleep at the wheel, the jeep half on, half off a little bridge back in the woods beyond old Frank's house. And when they came in, Simon had him by the legs, Polly by the arms, and they had carried him upstairs to his room like a sack of coal.

He opened his eyes once, just long enough to see her watching, and then he tried to turn belly down and hide his face, but instead he barfed all over himself and the landing.

She wouldn't even have come back in at all after that, except for Josh. For what she and Josh were doing. A couple of days before, Josh had driven one of the old trucks deep into the snow outside the icehouse near where Licking River angled down through the meadow. The truck looked stuck for good and abandoned, and then they had spent the night in the cab. Twice now, two nights, motor off, no heat, wrapped in sleeping bags, holding hand warmers, with camera, gun and flashlights ready. "Everyone knows about the icehouse," Josh had said. "Everybody's cut ice in here one time or another. Moran's got to know." The icehouse full of food—cheese, steaks, butter and bread. No people, just food to lure him there.

Last night they finished two thermoses of cocoa, sitting in the cab, four hamburgers and two boxes of cookies. Simon said they were "plumb stupid," what they were doing. Polly didn't say anything, of course, and Rush took their plan to catch Clovis as a personal affront to his capacity to find him first.

But this morning Rush had been so bad he couldn't have sat at his desk if he'd been roped in, and when she peeked in around nine, he lay on the bed, face in the pillow, arm hanging to the floor. The room stank, a mixture of sweat, smoke and booze, all the weird stench of his body. But she didn't really notice or remember the smell until several hours later when she saw him at the boathouse and the smell rose up off him like a huge cloud enveloping her.

She left his room, got her cameras and drove out to Licking River. There she listened on Diver's shortwave to the posse talking back and forth. She took a look at the extra dogs brought in from Albany. They were locked up in the back of the tiny jail, dark and snarling. One was sitting on the bed.

Diver looked tired. He called her Abby, as he always had. Said he sure was surprised about Clovis. He always thought the guy was "just slow." But he left no tracks. Nothing. Goddamnest thing, he said, the guy just disappeared, nothing left but somebody dead or hurt and the clear unbroken line of the snow where Clovis, like a bird, had gone. Diver shook his head. "Must be more to the guy than I thought."

Then he asked, did she ever know Joanne Moran, and she said no, and he said he'd met her once, just once. And when Abby asked why he wanted to know, he kind of shrugged and said it was long ago. But he looked troubled. She had ignored it. The family had had a lot of trouble, he said and she ignored it, because she was all wrapped up in herself and thinking of getting back to New York, and because she wasn't really interested in Diver, or Joanne Moran either, except for the fact that she was dead.

And besides, Diver went on, he was tired of all those reporters asking about Clovis. What was there to tell? A veteran. A sorry, miserable veteran. Nobody knew the Morans. They stuck to themselves, but so what? What was the point of bothering everybody with questions? He wasn't a bad guy at heart, Clovis, just sick. He probably didn't even know what he'd done. They had to catch him, that was all, poor son of a bitch. Put him away.

Abby stared at the map on the wall behind his head. Licking River Township was marked in red and the place where Clovis lived and the places where he had come out were marked in red as well. Pen marks slanted in different ways showed where the posse and the soldiers had searched, the marks looking like an ever-growing splotch of water spreading in a vaguely circular pattern away from the town of Licking River. Weather Tree, not marked on the map, but present in the form of lakes, ridges, mountains and rivers, loomed to the north and the west, largely untouched by the hunt.

Josh's map was different.

It was an old Forest Service watershed map with no markings for roads or towns or anything. It just showed high ground and low ground, with lines for swamps and marks for every river, stream, lake, brook, spring or inlet there was. Water. It was a water map, and all Josh had done was trace one particular network of water, Licking River itself. The river stretched like a vine almost directly north–south. It started high up in a spring not too far from the western boundaries of the Weather Tree tract, came down under the old railroad tracks that intersected with the road to Weather Tree on their way to the old mines up in the mountains. Then it proceeded down through the length of Weather Tree, across the meadow and the clearing and then on toward the general vicinity of Licking River Township.

Along the way, five smaller streams fed into the river, coming from the right and the left, and what Josh had done was put a red mark on the map for each of Moran's targets. Each, it turned out, was alongside Licking River or one of these connecting streams, and of all the sections of the river as yet untouched none was as big as the one that angled through Weather Tree—came down out of the mountains and the forests and into the open land of the clearing and went right past the icehouse full of food.

"The only place he hasn't come so far is Weather Tree," Josh had said. "He uses Licking River like a road. God knows where he's holed up back in there, but this is how he comes out. I'm sure of it. He uses the river. He follows it. He knows these woods like the back of his hand, better than he knows himself. He's been roaming out there ever since he came back from the war. Now he just follows the river straight to whatever he wants."

They had told Diver, but Diver said everybody had ideas, and besides, it didn't tell them where he was now.

So now, on the very last day, she said so long to Diver and picked up Josh for another night of waiting. They drove back in, he went up to see Simon and she took the back stairs up to find Rush.

But he wasn't there.

She sneaked a look at his desk, but there was no manuscript in sight. She hadn't really believed there was one anyway.

Then she heard the gunshots.

She followed the sound and picked up his tracks outside in the snow where they led down to the lake. She found him in the boathouse sitting out at the end of a slip with a rifle in his lap. The water licked at the boards and his canoe floated alone, rising up and down on the currents, bumping against the wood with a hollow sound.

Out at the end, wind had brushed the snow away, and when she came, he looked up at her and, for a second, he seemed happy. As if he'd sort of wondered if she'd show up, hoping that she would, and was happy now that she had. He smiled at her but when she didn't return the warmth, his face fell into a sullen look. "Never expected to see you," he muttered.

He was sitting with his legs splayed out in front of him and his back propped up against the wall. He looked like a rag doll or a drunk. Cigarette ashes had dropped on his jacket, and under its bulk, on the boards, two quart bottles of vodka were barely concealed. One no longer had a top and the other was almost empty. Beside him were dozens of cigarette butts.

"Where've you been?" He put his head up against the wall to steady it so he could look at her.

"With Diver." She sat down beside him.

He dropped his head and fumbled on the dock among the boxes of ammunition shells for a bullet. He finally managed to grasp one and then, still fumbling, tried to load it in the casing.

"What are you shooting at?"

He didn't answer.

"What are you shooting at?"

"People."

She looked. There was snow everywhere, white land, white mountains, but the lake, wind across it, was a million shapes of black and white, moving, light and dark. She could hear Licking River, here where it was headed toward the sea.

He lifted the rifle and, lurching, tried to get himself in position to shoot. He wedged the gun into the small of his shoulder and, still lurching, pulled the trigger. Zing. The shot sounded as if it went straight up. Never did hit the water.

Tried again. Zing. Each time he reeled back as he aimed and the shot went high.

She brought out her camera and a couple of lenses.

He kept the rifle up, his chest heaving, as if the gun weighed a hundred pounds, and kept pulling the trigger. Zing. Off in the air.

Then, suddenly, ping, it hit the water. He did it again, ping, quickly, ping. "Don't think I can get him, do you?" he said triumphantly.

"Who?"

He kept shooting at the water, as if it was a thing to destroy, but it was coming closer, closer, he holding it at bay.

"Get who?" She looked through the lens, turning it from fuzzy to clear.

But he didn't answer. He dropped the gun down and said, "Why don't you leave if you're so bored?"

"Can't. It's work."

"So? Leave anyway. Show them who's boss. Who gives the orders."

"Sure, Pop."

"These are big times for me," he said abruptly, but then he heaved forward, as if following the words out of his mouth, and so she didn't think about the words at all. "Big days," Rush said again.

Clicking with the camera, mountain face-to-face against itself in the water. Click. Click.

"Never felt better," he said. "I'm on the up and up now. Everything's falling into place."

"Sure."

"He can do it," Rush said. "I can do it."

"Sure." Click. Click.

"He can do it. I can do it," he said again.

"Who?"

"Moran."

"Oh." She got down on her belly, elbows up for more shots.

"You know what he's doing, don't you?"

Click. Click. She didn't even pay him any attention.

"Somebody's got to help him."

"Right."

"Book's gonna be good, Abby."

"Uh-huh."

"And I'm gonna find Clovis. Help him."

"He's going nowhere but jail."

"You'll be proud of me. This book's going to be a real success." He lit a cigarette and stared out toward the mountains. Sun and bare snow. "He's out there somewhere, Abby. Fantastic. Keeping the fuckers off his back. We should have done it the first time."

She had no idea what he meant but all she thought about
was his smell. It assaulted her every time she breathed. She
hated it. The smell of decay. Self-induced, self-allowed, and she
hated it. Because wasn't life yours to create and control?
No, not always.
Yours to make?
No, not always.
"They're gonna kill Clovis, Abby, if I don't find him first."
His breath kept catching her. It was disgusting. He was dis-
gusting. And suddenly she glared at him until he looked at
her. And immediately averted his eyes. She went on glaring.
He shrank back against the wall, shoulders falling, as if he was
trying to disappear. And get away from her.
"You're disgusting," she said.
He began to pick at his pants, his eyes tiny watery things.
She'd never seen him like that. Seen him squirm, or be quite
that drunk.
He was sweating profusely.
She went on staring.
He lifted up his arm and tried to wipe his face clean, but it
still shone like a layer of grease, and as soon as his hand was
gone, sweat reappeared on his forehead.
"You are really disgusting."
His eyes glazed over. "You just don't think I can save him.
But I'm gonna, Abby," he pleaded. "You'll see. I'll find him. I
promise."
"Stop it."
"I'm gonna finish the book. Dedicate it to you. You'll see
I've turned the corner."
"Stop it."
"You'll be proud of me."
"You can't even walk."
"What do you mean?"
"You can't even walk and you won't admit it."
"What d'you mean?"
"You're disgusting. Look at you. Oh, Pop." She softened a
bit.
He looked around, at the bottle, cigarettes, the debris and

frowned. "So?" he said, confused, as if he'd found nothing wrong.

"You're a mess. Why don't you take a good look at yourself?"

"You just don't want to listen to what I have to say."

"You're right, Pop. I don't want to listen to you. I want you to listen to me. I want to help you. I want to talk to you. Please listen and hear me. You need help. Somebody has to tell you. Somebody has to get through to you."

"Pretty high and mighty."

"But look at yourself, Pop. You can't walk. You can't drive. You can't write."

"I'm doing a lot right now."

"You just drank two bottles of vodka. Is that your idea of a lot?"

"I'm trying . . ."

"You're trying to kill yourself."

He flinched.

"You even smell." She shouldn't have said that.

"Smell?" he asked.

"Yes."

"Is that what everyone thinks?" His head fell.

"Of course, Pop. You're in bad shape. I'm worried. Everyone's worried. You don't have to be this way."

"And so they all talk?"

"Of course they do."

"You've heard them?"

"Yes."

"They all say I smell?"

"But you do smell, Pop. You can barely walk. You expect people not to notice? Polly had to carry you in."

"Polly too?"

"But you can change."

His head was down, his beard lay against his chest, and it looked as if he was barely breathing.

"All you have to do is stop drinking and start taking care of yourself. You just have to take care of yourself. Pop, please, won't you do that?" Her voice was more real and pleading and loving than it had ever been before. It was the first and only time she ever confronted him. "You haven't turned a corner! You're not 'on the up and up.' You're killing yourself, Pop. It's as simple as that."

But he wasn't listening. He just sat there for a long time, like a balloon with a leak. He didn't say anything. Neither did she. She stared at him, he stared at the floor. She knew she'd done a terrible thing, attacked him when he felt full of hope, but she thought it was necessary. Somebody had to tell him the truth. Maybe it would help.

Her hands gripped his arm tight. "I'm trying to help you, Pop. I love you. I want you to be happy and whole and not depressed. You can, Pop. You can do anything, anyone can. That's what we're here for, people, to set our sights and go, and you can too. You can do anything. Just pick a path and follow it, like a river, follow it. I know you can do it, because you taught me to do it. Remember how you always told me to do what I wanted to do? But to be sure and do it? To find it and do it? Now you can do that too. You just have to take the first step and then the second and begin. The same as you always told me."

A breeze came up and blew ashes over his legs. His eyes were still down and she gripped his arm, feeling her presence alone would fill him with life and hope. But the skin on his face seemed to hang lower every second.

"There's a lot you can do, Pop," she whispered. She put her arms around him. "You can go to Connecticut. Get help."

"You don't understand . . ." he said.

"Then tell me. I want to understand."

"You'll make fun of me."

"I'd never do that."

"Maybe I haven't always told you the truth," he said warily. "What if I tell you and you don't like it?"

"I'd like anything from you."

He paused. Took a breath. She waited.

"Things have been harder than you think," he said.

She wished he hadn't said that.

"They have," he whined. "You just don't know. I'm not what you think I am."

"Please don't say these things, Pop. Self-pity isn't the way out. Face up to things."

"Maybe I am and you just don't want to hear it."

"Then tell me."

"I've had a lot harder time than you think."

"Money. Inheritance."

"You won't even listen."

"All right. I'll listen." But then she hadn't. "Tell me how hard it's been."

"You only see what you want to see," he said.

"Don't you know how much I want to help you?"

"But maybe I don't want help! Ever think of that? Maybe you've got me all boxed in nine ways from Sunday."

"I'm trying to get you to see yourself."

"You're not letting me be who I really am," he said. "I'm a coward, a failure. Look at all you've done and then look at me," he whined. "Four books. Three were trash and you know it, I know it, and the critics know it. I never had what it took. For anything. But now it's different," he slobbered. "I'm on the up and up. Everything's going to be different, Abby. New book. Find Clovis. You'll see, Abby. You'll be proud. I used to think I'd be like you. Fuck the family and make it on my own. Well, now I'm on my way again."

She started to interrupt, but he reeled on.

"I'll do it, too," he said. "This book is about the real world. War. Cowardice. I'm going to tell it all."

"How, Pop?" She flared up. "Are you going to do it vomiting? On three bottles of vodka? Drunk in the back end of a truck? What are you going to do about your smell?"

"Please don't, Abby."

He was moaning and she thought he was about to cry but she still didn't relent. "I want you to face the truth about yourself."

"Don't, Abby. I can't take as much as you can. I'm not strong like you. You don't know how hard I'm trying. It may not look like much to you, but—"

"You're every bit as strong as I am," she said, "and I want you to listen, goddamn it. I'm waiting for you to change and start taking care of yourself. You're a drunk. Who smells."

He flinched.

"And sweats."

"Stop it," he said.

"Face it."

"No," he exclaimed.

She got up.

"Where are you going?"

"I don't like being around people who smell and don't take care of themselves."

"Wait."

"I'm going."

"Listen. I'm trying . . . Please," he pleaded.

"I'm waiting for you to tell me you're going to take care of yourself." She took a couple of steps. "Will you?"

He started to push himself up.

Hands out, fanny up, fingers on the boards for balance, trying to give himself the final push. "You're the one with the pretense," he said, heaving, pushing to straighten the legs and get an upward thrust. Swaying. Trying to get up with nothing to lean on, no crutch, no chair, nobody. "You're the one doesn't see things the way they really are."

Fanny up, fingers on the boards, knees still swaying, and normally she'd reach out and provide the handle necessary to do the deed and prevent the humiliation. But now she waited, arms folded, and watched, thinking . . .

Actually thinking . . .

. . . maybe this'll show him.

And all the arms and legs swayed out in different directions and he fell down.

And rolled over.

And she watched.

He saw her watching.

She didn't move.

He tried to get up.

"Well, what do you think, are you a drunk?"

And she had turned and headed up the hill past the spot where the weather tree had lived and died, never dreaming that something else had just died as well, an aging man's self-respect and love for her.

Torn up, they were, shreds all over the boathouse floor. But she never meant it to go so far, and heading up the hill, snow and shreds around her everywhere, she never dreamed that behind her in the windy slip of an empty boathouse was a Will and a wish, Four Quarters and Nothing More.

And saw him next, this new father of hers with a secret in his heart, hours later, in the middle of the night, rubbing his eyes, as Josh was telling him about Clovis and the cave. And two weeks later, after he tried to shoot the man with one ear, when he called and said he wanted to go to Connecticut. And she drove him to Connecticut and thought everything was all right, over, the boathouse forgotten, forgiven, past. Winter and snow and water lapping, the sound of bullets and his smell coming out, dank and raw, puss and oil and sour smoke coming out of his mouth and pores, the smell like an octopus to get her. But the incident was over and forgotten, she thought. Him rolling on the boards, bottle falling in the water, and the crunch of snow as she walked back up the hill.

Hoping maybe this would help, honesty and truth for once, and that hope was what had made her speak and made her walk away, leaving him behind. The afternoon sun hit her in the eyes, and even then Clovis would already have started down from the cave, walking his way along Licking River toward Rush Boarchards and Rush behind her thinking of a will and the greatest thing he had to deny her, not money or even the land, but himself. And Clovis heading east to the railroad tracks, then west along the tracks to the river that would take him south to intersect once again with Rushing Boarchards and his family, and Rush thinking he could deny her everything, land and money, family and a past.

And himself.

But if Rushing Boarchards' life stopped then, save for melancholy and revenge, hers was still getting underway. Clovis, with his big old fur-lined rubber boots, was stepping into Licking River, the power of its water up around his calves, its power taking him south to her, water winding its way through the woods and the hills to the clearing and beyond.

That night she waited in the car for Clovis and her future. Poor Clovis, he was just hungry and looking for his son, although she didn't know that then. Then she had given no mind to him at all; this was work, not a man at all. But all along, had she but known, he was just hungry, wanting his boy, lost in the woods, or so his distorted mind believed.

She saw him first, not Josh. He was coming across the pasture, more like a tree than a man in the moonlight, and she watched and didn't say a word, because suddenly something about him just looked so sad she couldn't move. If she hadn't seen the sadness in her father only hours before, she saw it here and couldn't say a word, thinking, how could a killer look so sad? But he did. In the bright light of the moon, arms down, snow all over, scarves, mittens, jacket, face so small, covered with growth and icicles. And she nudged Josh and they waited. He came closer, toward the icehouse. He didn't even have a gun. Why didn't he bring his gun? He had the other times. And they got out, Josh's gun not even raised, but her camera up, getting it ready, putting it into focus. And she saw him, closer, closer in the crosslines at the center of the camera, his eyes alarmed now and frightened, snow around his face and his hands waving, waving her away, and she coming closer and closer, and suddenly she put the camera down. And Clovis stopped, held by her eyes.

"Who are you?" he asked.

"I'm Abby Boarchards."

"I know you."

"Are you hungry, Clovis?" Camera down.

"Watch out," Josh was saying.

"Are you hungry? Where've you been, Clovis?" His eyes so sad and frightened, but she not frightened at all, a boy here, a child only, and she working, not thinking that she'd been with another boy at the boathouse that very afternoon, someone sad and lonely too.

"Don't you know me, Abby?"

"Did you think Joanne was going to take you away?" All nice, as if she could help. "And put you in a hospital? Is that what you thought? Are you cold?" To get him to trust her, to dispel the fear and get more sadness and lostness in that incredible face.

"Didn't he tell you about the cave?"

"Who, Clovis?" Camera down, but ready, waiting for more of that look, the vulnerability, sad but still, sad and lost. "Are you all right?"

"Didn't he tell you what happened in the cave?"

"What cave?"

"I have a boy too." His arms out now, eyes getting sadder. "Didn't Rush tell you about my boy?"

But she only waited. Moving. Getting ready.

"He's not very old."

Bringing the camera up.

"What are you doing?"

"It's all right, Clovis." Flash. Flash.

"Abby." Betrayed. "Don't take me away," he shrieked.

Flash. "It's all right." Flash. Flash.

"No."

It was perfect. He was crying, hurt, lost, betrayed, his face everything she had wanted, the torment, even sweetness of someone thought to have nothing sad or sweet, only murder and rage. He turned. Flash. And she moved. "Don't go," she cried, sweetness again, and he turned back, hopeful maybe. But flash, flash, relentless now.

"No," he cried, his face covered with hurt and ice.

"Yes, come back. Tell me more."

He tried again. He turned. "The cave?"

But the camera met him again, flash, flash, success and a prize within her grasp. And she never knew it, of course, or thought of it quite that way, but she was propelled by ambition, to get what was extraordinary here, to get that feeling she herself had felt: How could a killer look so sad? As if he were the victim, not the dead. And when, out of nowhere, had come the chance, that spell, "Abby Boarchards, I know you," she had used it, followed it. "Where've you been, Clovis?" Played it, single-minded. "You all right, Clovis?" knowing instinctively it would bring vulnerability and trust and get her exactly what she wanted, the look of betrayal and hurt, pictures and her work all that counted now, no matter what it did to him.

And there he was, frightened now and running. Josh ran after him, but Clovis was better, faster, going through the field, back up alongside Licking River, going through the field as if he knew exactly where to put his feet and Josh didn't. Josh didn't even have his gun now. He had dropped it. And Clovis a figure in the pasture running away. She wished he'd go forever and not get caught, just as Rush had said, not get caught.

But he did get caught. She told Rush what Clovis had said about "the cave" and she told Diver.

And the posse found him lying in a sleeping bag in the cave, with Sterno and a can opener, frying pan, batteries, flashlights and every single belonging he had, stacked up all around him. He was wide-eyed, sitting up and waiting, when the posse came.

Someone shone a light in through the mouth of the cave and caught him in the eye.

She looked down at the sands of the desert far below and felt the snows and cold of that winter years ago. The shreds of love on the boathouse floor seemed as clear as his bottles and cigarettes. She looked at Luke. "I understand what happened," she said aloud.

"What?" He glanced at her, preoccupied, papers in his hand.

"I think I understand what happened."

"About what?"

"Why he disinherited me. You were right."

He put his papers down.

"Remember you asked me if I ever had a fight with him and I said no? I must have pushed it completely out of my mind. But I was horrible to him. Just before he redid the will. I didn't mean it. It was all to get him to stop drinking and face the truth, but I couldn't have picked a worse time." She turned and stared out the window. "I guess he was full of hope then.

It's hard to believe, but . . ." She shivered. "No wonder he blamed me. Have you ever done that?"

"What?" Luke took her hand.

"Do you think he envied me?" she asked then. "Independent. Working. Everything he wanted to be, and I bet he thought I'd never keep it up. Some mothers are jealous of their daughters' looks. But I never even guessed."

"We're descending now," the stewardess said. "Fasten your seat belts for landing."

"He wasn't competing with Jackson or Polly. He was competing with me."

They rented a car and took the highway that headed north toward the mountains. Abby looked around. Rushing Boarchards wasn't here. Joe Algodones was, and people of Spanish descent, one-time conquistadors who'd eased down through the centuries to little more than beans and poverty, their little villages grim reminders of what time can do. She thought about three old men, each linked to her through time and deed, good and bad. Three old men. Only one remained.

"What do you think Joe's really like?"

"To be honest, Abby, I don't care that much."

"I do. I really think I do. I never knew Clovis and I misjudged my father. Maybe I'll get a chance with Joe."

The air was cool and pleasant, touched with the smell of piñon and pine. Luke was driving. The land stretched away from the road flat and dry, with occasional sage or mesquite. She opened her windows.

"Have you thought about what to do if he is dangerous?"

"Yes," he answered.

She looked across the desert, Joe out there somewhere, Luke in here, in the car, and Boarchards far away for once, more where a father belonged.

"I feel good," she said aloud. "I really do. For the first time I think I understand why he did it." She stretched her hand out the window, as if grasping the freedom in the air, and stared at the bareness and the enormous sky. Its bigness seemed to match her own, none of the decay and overgrowth of Weather Tree. She looked at her watch. Three more days. See Algodones, Victoria, Sam and Bostrine. Then it was over. And maybe Jackson was right. Maybe it didn't matter which way her decision went.

Just make a decision and live with it. Without looking back.

But in Pescadero there was no truck outside the house, no '72 Chevy truck, and her heart sank. "Goddammit," she said. "I want to find him. One minute I think I understand Pop. The next minute it all comes crashing down because how on earth can . . ."

"Calm down."

". . . I understand him if I don't know what this Algodones is all about and now he's not here after all."

"Calm down. Maybe he's coming. Maybe we can at least get his address."

She stared at the sherbet-green house with a picket fence. It looked like a joke. Then the front door opened and a little gray-haired woman was running out to meet them.

"You must be Abby," she cried.

Abigail got out and took the woman's hands, hiding her confusion over this odd little creature who wore a brown dress and big black shoes. She had gray curls and bright eyes and seemed more like a chipmunk than a grown-up.

"Is Joe here?" Luke asked, surveying the rest of the neighborhood, other pastel houses built in a time when color was thought to compensate for age or roots.

"Come on, come on," Sue Ann was singing.

Luke went inside first, and when the floor mat chimed under his feet, the woman started to laugh. "Sometimes I walk back and forth just to hear it play," she said.

"Joe," Luke called.

The house had one floor and plenty of rooms and windows, but there was no sign of Algodones. "Is Joe around?" Abigail asked. "Do you think I'll like him?"

But Sue Ann darted ahead toward the kitchen.

"I'll go see." Luke headed in another direction.

Abigail followed Sue Ann through the living room, and the

dining room. It had eight chairs and cabinets full of china that looked unused. "Where is he?" she asked.

"Come quick."

"Where did you say he is now?"

Sue Ann opened the kitchen door and rushed over to the table to show her an array of cheese. She pointed to one. "There," she cried. "I remembered. Tell Mr. Boarchards I remembered."

"Is Joe coming?" Abigail persisted, wondering if the woman was retarded.

"Not right now."

They picked up the tray of cheese and went back out to the living room. Abigail let Luke know Sue Ann thought her father was alive, but he told her to let it be, and so they listened to Sue Ann talk. She talked and talked, as if Abigail and Luke were the only people in the world who knew or understood her cousin, and maybe, Abigail thought, they were.

Their grandfather was Irish, their grandmother Spanish, and of two daughters, she said, one, her mother, married "an Anglo" and the other, Joe's, did not. The only children were Joe and Sue Ann, and when the parents died, they latched on to one another. "Joe takes care of me," she said. "We always lived in the desert, but when he came into money, he said we should move to the city and so I said, 'Whatever you want, Joe.' "

She showed them Joe's collection of books, including Rush's four and Abigail's two, but they all looked unread. Then she took them into a small room almost taken over by a big short-wave radio set. "Mr. Boarchards bought it for him once," she said proudly. "He listens to it all day long."

Back in the living room, Abigail kept listening for someone at the door. "Joe's mother died in the street," the woman was saying. "In an accident."

Maybe she's a little crazy, Abigail thought, with a glance at Luke.

"I told Joe God had his reasons, but he said he didn't need God's reasons."

"I want to see him," Abigail pressed, her voice rising with tension. "Please tell me where he is."

"He says other jobs stop at five," she sailed on, "and some people don't even work at all, but he never stops."

"Please tell me."

"He says your father should do things with his money, but I tell him, 'That's not for us to say.' But he says somebody has to watch out for these things, and if he doesn't, who will, and when he puts it that way, I suppose he's right. Otherwise, he says they're going to take over, people like that. He says they own oil wells and railroads and airplanes and hotels, and he says he doesn't like Whitaker Rushing."

"Whitaker," Abigail repeated dully.

"He says he's gotten away with murder, and I said, 'Oh Joe, murder?' And he says, 'Well, not exactly murder.' Joe knows a lot of things like that. He can talk to people like you and Mr. Boarchards. He knows what's really going on."

"Where did he meet my father? Tell me, please."

"On top of a rocky hill." The woman smiled as if the memory were hers.

"But was it in the war? I have to know."

"Oh yes."

"Do you think Joe will come?"

"It is getting late," Sue Ann admitted. "Do you know he reads four newspapers a day?"

"Where does he get them?" Luke asked.

"He says it's the biggest newspaper store in the world."

"On Times Square?" Luke pressed.

"All I know, it's New York."

"So he lives in New York?" Luke asked.

But she looked away. "They even save them if he's away."

"Maybe he was away in January," Luke said to Abigail.

"He's not here, is he," Abigail cried at last. "He's in New York, isn't he?"

"But I didn't want to tell you."

"But why not?" Abigail exclaimed with desperation. "This is Thursday already."

"Thursday?" the woman asked, confused.

Luke took Abby's hand and squeezed it.

"I wanted you to come," the woman was saying. "I wanted—"

"You must have been happy when the war was over," Abigail interrupted, putting her voice in a monotone, trying now to keep her mind on the facts she had and those she wanted to get. "He must have come home full of stories."

Sue Ann looked at her blankly. "But he didn't come home," she said. "He called from New York and I said, 'Joe, when are you coming home?' And he said there was nothing for him here. And I said, 'But, Joe, what is there for you there?'"

"What did he say?" Abigail asked.

"He said he had things to do and people to look after, and I said, 'But, Joe, what about me?' He told me not to worry, he had that all figured out. He said he was going to take care of me, that I would get the best."

"But what was he doing with my father?"

"When he was little he wanted to go to West Point, but I told him only rich people went to West Point."

"What was he doing with—"

"He got mad and wanted to know why and I said, 'I don't know everything, Joe.' When he called from New York, I asked him if he was going to stay in the Army. He said no, he couldn't, but it didn't matter anyway. He said he had something else more important to do. Do you know you look just like Mr. Boarchards?"

"What happened to his ear? What happened to his unit on Bataan? What happened with my father?"

"He had a girl friend too," Sue Ann said. "And he never told her either. He just stopped writing. He's been alone ever since. He doesn't have anybody."

"Except my father. And Clovis."

"That's right," Sue Ann said. "And Robbie too, of course."

"Yes. Robbie."

"But, truthfully," she added, lowering her voice and bending in closer to Abigail. "I don't think Joe really likes people. What do you think?"

"I think you're right."

Sue Ann wrote down his address: 531 West Seventeenth Street, New York City. "It's a wonderful neighborhood. Near the waterfront, he says, with ships and things. Big houses."

That did it. Abigail didn't think she could stand it anymore. She got up to leave.

"Restaurants and stores and . . ."

And winos and old men and rooming houses and factories where they made box tops.

"And he says his house has high ceilings and a garden and lots of birds."

"Squirrels too?" Abigail said.

"Oh yes. And squirrels."

They drove back out of Pescadero, back past the all-night burrito stands and the truck stops. Finally the desert opened up again and Abigail looked out at the darkness and wondered where out there Joe and his cousin had lived and died.

They spent the night in a motel, but after Luke fell asleep, she lay there, with a window and the night only inches away. She held him in her arms, and stared out at the blackness. There was a butte far away and a path where a road went and she watched each new light, a truck or a car, and tried to figure out what first her father and now Joe was doing to her mind.

Friday and Saturday, May 3 and 4

There's a possibility Algodones is more fanatical than dangerous," Luke said to Alvah on the phone from the airport the next morning. "But no one ever said fanatics can't be dangerous. This is all getting to Abby," he went on. "Can you go with her tomorrow to find Joe? I've tried to cancel my meeting with the law firm but I can't. It's been planned too long. It couldn't have come at a worse time, it turns out. Means I can't go down there looking for him until tomorrow night. Can you go with her in the morning?"

Abigail watched Luke with a dull expression in her eyes. He was shaking his head. "Alvah has to be in Washington," he told her. "You'll have to wait for me."

"It's all right," she mumbled. "I'll wait. I don't care anyway."

"You want to look for him when we get back to New York tonight?" Luke asked when he hung up.

She shook her head. "I'm exhausted."

"You sure you're not thinking about finding him by yourself?"

"No."

"It wouldn't make a lot of sense."

"I know," she said impatiently.

"Promise me."

"Yes."

Back in New York, Luke spent the night at her apartment. There were notes from Alvah and Melanie in the mail and a lot of telephone messages. "Call me," Melanie had written. "We'll have lunch."

Abigail dropped the note on the bed and read Alvah's. Someone at the Salvation Army had seen the ad about Joe and called. Algodones had been a cook there, but two months ago he'd told the manager he was under terrible personal pressure and quit.

The answering service reported that Solomon Irving had left his home number, Phoebe had called, and Jackson had left a message saying, "Sam's in the hospital with the Big C."

Abigail didn't call anyone back.

They had hamburgers and champagne in the kitchen.

"Are you going to see Sam and Victoria tomorrow?" Luke asked.

"How do I know?" she replied irritably. "And don't ask me about the will."

"You're depressed."

"I'm depressed."

As soon as Luke left the next morning, Abigail jumped out of bed. She got dressed in blue jeans and a sweater, took the nugget, the list, Joe's address, and was almost out the door when the phone rang. "Hello," she answered curtly, looking at her watch.

It was Phoebe. "What happened?"

"Where?"

"New Mexico."

"Nothing. He wasn't there."

"But what happened? Calm down. Tell me."

"I can't now, Phoebe. I'm in a hurry. I have a lot to do." But then she briefly described Sue Ann and her plans to go look for Joe with Luke that night. "But I feel like going to see him right now," she said.

"That probably doesn't make much sense. What if he did something? You never know."

"So what? I'll worry about that later. Right now I want to get this over, finished and done with. I want to get on with my own life without this hanging over me."

"You sound kind of desperate," Phoebe said.

"No. I'm exasperated. I can't stand it. I really can't stand it, Phoebe. I've done the whole investigation, done almost every single thing I set out to do and found out everything about my father, myself, why he did it. Everything except this one thing. This one thing at the core of his life: why all the connections lead to Algodones. If I get that, I know I'll be able to decide about the will and decide easily, and everything will be over. But I can't get it, Phoebe, and it's so frustrating. It keeps being one step away. I can't find Joe. . . ."

"You'll find him tonight. . . ."

"But I've had it," she rushed on. "Besides, I want to find him by myself. It's between him and me. It has nothing to do with Luke. I don't even care if he is dangerous. I just want to get on with it."

"You mean you don't like Luke?"

"I'm not saying that. I love Luke. But this has nothing to do with him."

"But . . ."

"It's about Joe and me and my father and Clovis and Robbie and . . ."

"But . . ."

". . . and I have to deal with it. Not Luke. Not Alvah. Like the will. They can't decide that either. I have to. Same as I have to face Joe and ask him what's going on. Not Luke and me. This is my life, my past, my . . ."

She hung up.

She took the West Side subway south. She never looked behind or over her shoulder and she didn't feel the slightest bit anxious or afraid. Instead she felt impervious to everything, numbed by all that had happened. I'm on automatic pilot, she thought grimly.

At Times Square she got out and walked across to the International News Supply. "Do you work here?" she asked a man inside. "I'm interested in one of your customers. He gets the papers from you every day, and when he's away, you save them for him."

"So?"

"Any reason he could have missed the papers?"

"I don't follow."

"Is there any way something could have happened and he wouldn't get his regular supply? Say he went out of town?"

"Never. We keep the papers until they get back."

"But what about January?" she asked.

"January the same. No. Wait a minute. Gas heater exploded in the back and took the whole place apart. Fire. Boss shut down for a month."

Walking back to the subway, Abigail looked into the windows of the cheap cafeterias around Times Square and pictured Algodones reading his papers. Maybe he had missed the most important story of all.

The subway was a long time coming. Grace said once she'd never been in a subway in her life, but Victoria said she had and she didn't mind it one bit. As long as they were clean.

At Fourteenth Street, Abigail got out and started walking west. The people on the street began to look like Rush. Drinkers. There were bars and diners, doorways everywhere, and strays going in and out, old men who couldn't stand up straight, women shaped like barrels carrying grocery bags. There was no life here, no community, just little outposts among the warehouses, and Abigail felt some pity for the people, but not much.

Someplace, sometime, she was thinking, they had had a choice.

She was beginning to feel a bit of anxiety about what was ahead, but not much.

The building at 531 West Seventeenth Street was four stories high, no different from the others—dirty stones, a stoop, and a door that didn't shut. Inside the tiles were stained and the light bulb was dead. Her eyes got accustomed to the dark. She saw three closed doors, but no mailboxes or list of residents.

She was about to knock when a door opened and an old man came out. "Do you know where Joe Algodones is?" she asked.

"Haven't seen him." He smelled of liquor and kept walking. He reminded her of Rush.

"Know where his room is?"

"Three. Back."

She climbed the stairs. It smelled of urine and wine. At each level, there was a window, but the glass was so dirty it looked as if it was covered with paper. By the time she reached the third floor, she started to have a stomachache. It was nervousness. At the landing, she turned left past the bathroom.

She knocked at number three.

No answer.

"Hello?" she called. "Joe?"

She turned the doorknob. It moved a little. She rattled it and tried again, but it still didn't open. "Damn," she said. She reached her hand up along the shelf on top of the door, but there was no key. She glanced at the hall window, but it was out of reach.

In the bathroom she felt under the sink and, going down on her knees, looked under the tub. The stench was overpowering. She felt along the pipes and the drain, then came to the toilet. It was layered in filth, but she found the key—taped to the back of the bowl.

With a quick look down the stairs, she slipped the key into the lock and opened the door.

Whatever she'd been expecting, it wasn't there. No lonely, drab place, this. No emptiness. Instead it was as cluttered and full as an attic. A gallery of life but impenetrable, in total disarray, as if a storm had come through and overturned everything.

It was crammed end to end with cartons and files, like something of Rushing Boarchards', but if her father's basement had seemed untouched and forgotten, this one had been assaulted in some rage or frenzy. The boxes had been tipped over and ripped open. Their contents were flung at random in every direction. There were papers, books and magazines all over the floor, and everywhere there were things that leaped to Abigail's eyes, totally familiar. Photographs of her entire family were tacked to walls all over the room, and her pictures, her work, torn from books and magazines, lay like confetti on top of everything—floor, table, bed.

Abigail stood in the doorway, too stunned to move, all her restlessness of the last few hours gone. Half of what was here was hers. Her eyes took in everything. She couldn't believe it. She felt drained and tired. He had pictures of her, her father and Clovis Moran, her father getting the award from General MacArthur, she getting awards, even the one of Clovis Moran, all icicles and snow, getting caught by her.

Abby reached down and picked up a photograph off the floor. Victim of an earthquake, taken by Abigail Boarchards. She picked up another, a campus demonstration; another, a presidential aide going down some steps to jail. She dropped them, pieces of her life, on someone else's floor.

She turned over a box and spilled out its contents. The label read "Boarchards." But inside there were just copies of magazines, old newspapers and books with titles like *The Rich, How to Live on a Thousand Dollars a Day, High on the Hog and What It's All About, The White Power Elite.* There were other boxes, one marked "Abigail," but as far as she could figure out, all it had were multiple copies of her books. Others labeled "Astor," "Rockefeller," "Ford," "Kennedy" were the same. She thumbed through the contents—newspaper stories, Xeroxes of excerpts from books, with the names circled in black ink, again and again, so that the pages looked like odd designs of circle art.

Some of the papers were different. She picked up a handful, strewn on the floor. They were typewritten, words covering every inch of space, leaving no margins at all. They had long strings of exclamation points and capital letters. "THEY are going to destroy US," he had written. "The RICH own everything. THEY control Politics, Money and Foreign Policy. All they want to do is protect THEMSELVES. But what about the rest of the PEOPLE? What about Hispanics, veterans, prisoners, welfare mothers, blacks? What about them? Boarchards says he understands, but I don't know. I don't TRUST him at all. NOT ONE BIT. NOT EVEN A LITTLE BIT!!!!!!!!!!!!"

Abigail looked at the snapshots of the Rushings and the Boarchards. They were shown riding horses, swimming, Florence twirling a parasol, Bostrine painting in the meadow, Max and a group of chums on the veranda. Lots of pictures of Rush —driving cars, boarding airplanes, walking with his little daughter on his shoulder. There was even one from a tabloid of him and Melanie, dancing at El Morocco.

Then she saw one other picture, so small she almost missed it in the profusion. She went closer to look. It was in color, a little boy. He was smiling. He had freckles and a cowlick and he looked friendly. He also looked just like Clovis Moran.

Abigail stared at him for a long time. Then she sat down on the bed and looked some more. It was little Robbie Moran off the cliff. The boy in the kitchen, a face she'd never seen that night, but it had to be: the resemblance to his father was too striking. My father says you owe me. What boy? There was no boy. And here was his face tacked to the wall along with hers. Abigail was stunned. The face was little Robbie Moran, but it was also someone else. It was the boy in the reform school, the boy in the red brick building, the one she'd looked for all her life. "Are you from Licking River?"

He had looked at her for a million years, blue eyes along the walls, because he had known even then what she only learned today: that they were already connected.

Abigail looked about the room. She thought it was the saddest, most wretched place she had ever seen, a storehouse of other lives and a man's obsession; but his obsession was hers, his history was her history. She felt like crying, or succumbing to the sadness of it all, but instead she stood up. She knew Joe had reached out and taken hold of her as strongly as if the obsession all along had been hers, not his. She knew she had to find him, but if she had known that all along, now she knew that what she wanted was to try to be his friend. They were the two survivors, already linked. But she also knew that she was still no closer than she had been all along to knowing what had brought Joe and her father together in the first place, or created a bond between them strong enough to last for thirty years.

She searched in the drawers and under the bed. She found dirty clothes, shaving equipment, the typewriter and, finally, to her astonishment, she found sheets of paper listing her movements for the past few weeks.

She stared at them in renewed anxiety, even disbelief. "Returns apt., 6:50. Wait. No sign. 9:15, home." He had followed her to the Rushing Mansion, to the subway when she went to see Bud Krajewski, and to the airport when she went to Washington to Isabel's. He had even been outside Wednesday when she went to Melanie's, watched her look for a taxi and followed her through the subway.

Abigail's heart was pounding and she held her breath, listening for someone. One moment she had wanted to befriend him, now she was terrified he'd walk in. Biting her lip, she hurriedly continued searching the place. She pawed through boxes, opened drawers and looked under the mattress. She didn't know what she was looking for exactly, just more. Something more.

She found letters from her father and raced through a few, struck by their intimacy. "Dear Joe, no news except Sam's now head of the board of trustees at the opera—I know what you'll think about that—and Abby got her first job. Of course her thing about photography will never last, but she's a good girl. No one's going to push her around."

"Summer's come," said another. "It's so bloody hot you can see yourself sweat. The place is jumping with people, and so it's impossible to work."

The next was even more nondescript. "Got your note about the medical bill. Will take care of it right away. Caught a cold too. Don't know how, except Polly and I took a walk over to Bush Meadows and on the way back it rained. Stuff like that never used to bother me."

But the last letter was different. "I'll leave the money in the kitchen. I don't want to see you. Seeing you makes it worse."
"But what? Why?" Abigail muttered. "What's the 'it'?"
Finally she pulled a box out from under the bed. It was heavy. She pried it open.
The box was full of thin gray sticks with little red wicks. They looked like candles. They were dynamite.

Outside on the sidewalk she wondered where to wait. There was an orange crate up the block and she headed for it to sit there and look for him, but the minute she reached it, she saw him. She knew immediately who he was. She stopped dead in her tracks and stared.
The diner was almost empty and he was right behind the window. He had thick dark hair and a growth of whiskers. He was wearing a white shirt and a three-quarter-length brown-checked coat with fluff on the insides. She noticed right away how much younger, more vital and healthy he seemed than her father. She didn't notice the ear, just the pinched look on his face. He was intent, so locked in a world of his own that she never doubted for a second who he was.
As he paid the bill, he suddenly looked up and she was caught in the hold of his eyes. At first he just stared at her, obviously surprised to see her, but then his lips began to curl up, fold away, and a look of pleasure, or relief, came over his face. He seemed almost ecstatic.
Then abruptly he averted his eyes, put the change in his wallet and looked up again, as if knowing she'd be exactly where he'd left her. Abigail started to move, but couldn't. She was paralyzed, by fright and confusion. He was even stranger than she'd expected. Then he walked out the door and straight toward her. He came closer and closer, and when he suddenly stopped, not two feet away, her head jerked back as if she'd been slapped.
"Got ya, didn't I?" he said triumphantly. "I knew you'd come." The lips curled up in disgust. "Knew he couldn't take it."
The weirdest thing about him was his ankles. They showed.

He wore black pants that were about three inches too short, white socks and black shoes that had laces but almost no soles; they tilted down in back.

"What's he want?" he asked. "Thought he'd get away from me, didn't he? So what's he up to?" He sounded harsh and mean and her heart beat faster. She stared at his lip. Blood had caked on it where he had picked the skin.

"So what's he up to?" he repeated loudly.

Abigail felt herself riveted by the power of his personality. That's what surprised her the most. He was confident, commanding and controlled, and she didn't have a doubt in the world that he could have sustained a hold on her father for thirty years. Or Rush on him, for that matter.

Suddenly he pounded his foot on the pavement in frustration, and that frightened Abigail even more. But he can't do anything here, she thought. She heard a truck go by, but she couldn't take her eyes off his face. He was controlling her with his eyes.

He took out a pack of cigarettes and lit one. "Know what I think?" He sounded sly. "You two are up to something." He blew the smoke away from her. "Two peas in a pod. That's what you are."

Abigail shook her head.

"I knew what to do. He thinks nothing can get at him up there. But I know him better than he thinks. You. I can get you. The only thing I can't figure out is what he thinks he's doing." He tilted his head and looked at her out of the corner of his eye again, as if she was going to tell him. But the wind caught her hair and blew it around. "Just like him, aren't you?" he sneered, crushing his cigarette impatiently against the pavement. "Same snooty air. Both looking down your noses at people. Think you're better than everyone else."

For a second Abigail was confused. Rush Boarchards hadn't looked down at anything. He'd barely stood up for years. But then she remembered the pictures and the medals, the way he used to be, and she realized that Algodones was back there too, tacked to a wall thirty years old, stuck in a time when Boarchards was tall and Joe wasn't.

Then she saw the ear. She had expected his head to be flat there, but instead an intersection of scars was punctuated with knobs of bunched-up flesh, sprouting all over the place, as if the knife had left seeds behind and, in the middle of everything, a hole.

"You think he's really planning to cut me out?" he suddenly asked.

At first she thought he was talking about the will or the ear. He cocked his head uneasily. "You think so?"

Suddenly Abigail knew she understood the bond between Joe and her father. It was dependency. Two isolated men, making their lives together. And of course, she suddenly remembered, Joe still didn't know Rush was dead! She almost blurted it out right then, but instinctively she drew back the information to give herself more time. "Why don't you ask him?" she said, finding her voice for the first time.

"I don't need to ask him. I got him just where I want him." He took out another cigarette. A truck passed by, headed uptown, but the wind, ominously, had stilled abruptly. It was calm. Rain was coming and the air seemed expectant, the clouds heavy.

In the vacuum Abigail felt something collapsing inside her. "What are you trying to do, Joe?" she whispered.

He stopped lighting the cigarette and looked at her.

"What are you doing, Joe?" She leaned toward him. "Did you just want to hurt him all these years? Is that it? Do you want to hurt me too? Is that why you're following me? Sending me those letters? What did I do to you?"

He hung his head like a little boy. She was stunned. All she had done was change her manner and he had transformed. "I don't know," he mumbled. "I got my work to do."

"But what happened, Joe?" she asked urgently. She sat down on the orange crate. "I don't understand."

He came a little closer to her, she the shorter now.

For the first time she liked him a tiny bit and forgot his weirdness. "I don't understand what's going on," she said. "I don't understand him and I don't understand you. What did he do to you?" They were only a few feet apart. She looked up.

He didn't answer, but something in his face had softened. "So you live here?" she asked.

"Over there." He met her eyes for a second, but then looked away, almost shy.

"You used to be a cook."

"He told you a lot about me, huh?" He sounded proud. "He says I'm a good cook."

"What else did he say?"

Joe shrugged. "Anything. Everything. He says I'm an ugly son of a bitch." He grinned for a second. "Guess I am. He told me I should wear hats. You want me to put a hat on? I have one in my pocket. I always have one."

"You like him, don't you." She watched him, fascinated.

"I just know him, that's all."

She remembered he still didn't know Boarchards was dead. "Tell me what happened. Was it before or after your squad was hit by the Japanese?"

"They put me in a camp."

"I know. They cut your ear too. Was he there?"

Algodones looked confused. "Not in the camp."

"Was he there when they took off your ear?"

He nodded.

"What did he do to you? Please tell me." She sounded kind.

Joe looked at the ground.

"I know he did something bad."

He nodded.

"But what?" Suddenly she knew why he didn't tell her. It was all he had, some secret knowledge that had become a link to intimacy. "Was it very bad?" she pressed.

He nodded.

"Were you in the cave when he killed that Japanese soldier?"

Tell me, she wanted to scream.

He looked confused, but he said, "No."

"Was Clovis?"

"Clovis was just a kid." Voice almost inaudible. "We were all just kids."

"So you were there too? In the cave?"

"He was crying," Algodones said.

She remembered the manuscript: Hooper, Hupper, Melvin, Clause, crying.

"And he was frightened." Joe hunched his shoulders over and, imitating, started moaning like a baby. "He was crying."

"Poor Clovis." She thought he meant Clovis.

"No."

"You didn't feel sorry for Clovis?"

He stood up straight.

Suddenly she felt anxious again. She stared at him. He had transformed all over again. He bared his teeth and her heart started thumping. What had happened? She stood up. She realized the street was empty, no people, no cabs.

"There he was," Joe said nastily. "The cave's so hot you can't breathe, and he had a gun." His eyes narrowed, got mean. "He said he was the best shot. He said he—"

"Who? Who are you talking about? Clovis?"

"You know who. Your father. He said he should stand watch. I said he was too tired. He said no, so I let him. I got them that far, three days—no food, no water."

Just like the hero in the manuscript.

"Clovis was almost dead," he was saying. "I had to carry him. Rush no better, and all the others had enough to take care of themselves. But Rush and Clovis were my buddies." Joe was holding her with his eyes. "They were my best buddies. So I let Rush stand watch. I went to sleep and suddenly I woke up. I don't know why. If I hadn't, I'd be dead with the rest of them. And I saw this Jap in the entrance, no more than fifteen years old, but I didn't see Rush. I couldn't find him. Why doesn't he shoot, I'm thinking, but then I saw him way over on the side, hiding behind some rocks. He could see the boy, but he didn't move. He didn't even shoot. 'Shoot,' I yelled"—Joe suddenly screamed—"but he didn't. I reached for my gun and shot the Jap myself, but even before he went down, eight more of them came, and the last thing I remember is Boarchards sliding down into a crevice. I didn't even know he was alive for five years."

"You mean he didn't kill the Jap?"

"They got my ear," Joe shrieked, "and they took Clovis and me, and Boarchards got away."

"You mean he lied? He didn't kill that Jap?"

"He didn't do anything. He didn't even try. He just hid behind that rock."

Abigail started to back away. "You mean he lied about everything?" she mumbled.

"Ask that trapper. He knows everything. He's the only one your father told. You think he's so great. A big hero. But what about me? What about the others? Seventeen men died because of him."

"You can't say that for sure," she said, backing away. "If you couldn't kill all of them, what could he have done?"

"I made him pay. He was scared the truth would get out. Him a coward. I'll get him," Joe muttered. "He thinks he can cut me off."

Abigail stopped abruptly and glared at him. "You lost your chance. He's dead."

"Don't kid me."

She didn't say anything.

"What do you mean?"

"He's dead. He shot himself. January fifth."

Joe's eyes opened wider.

"You missed it. Remember January? You were away. You didn't get your papers."

"That fucker!" he yelled. "That goddamned son-of-a-bitch coward thinks he can buy me off! 'Here, Joe, take this.' 'Take that.' Thinks that's all I want. Money."

Abigail was spellbound, his connection to her father so deep, their dementias so linked.

"He didn't like it one bit when I showed up. Took me months to find that place, then he wasn't even there. I finally found him by reading the papers. Reading the papers," he screamed. "I had to hang around outside nightclubs waiting to see if he came out. When I finally found him, he pretended he couldn't remember. 'Let me give you a fiver for some coffee, chap.' 'Look at my ear,' I yelled at him. 'You did that, five years ago.' But he acted as if he knew nothing about it. 'Five

years is a long time,' he says and walks away. Next time I find
him, he says, 'How can I remember? I was only in the Philippines a couple of months.' This time he says, 'Come on, let me
buy you a drink.' And he finally says, 'Oh yes, I vaguely remember. Weren't you on Bataan?' Bataan," Joe screamed.
" 'Weren't you on Bataan?' " he mimicked in rage, his face con-
torted. "He never said he remembered. He never even said he
remembered."

Abigail stared in fascination, this is a third Joe, neither cold
and dangerous nor meek and vulnerable, but enraged with
memory unleashed.

" 'Here, let me buy you another drink!' " he continued quoting her father. " 'Didn't we ride in a jeep or a truck?' 'But I
didn't recognize you, you've changed so much.' 'Recognize me,'
I yelled. 'What about the cave? Don't you remember the cave?'
And all he said, calm as could be, was, 'What cave?' " Joe fell
silent. "But I knew," he said, looking at Abigail, "if I didn't get
him to admit it one way, I'd get him another. And I did. He
paid me good. He paid me real good. I had him. He was afraid
of me. Afraid of what I could say."

"He needed you, Joe," Abigail said. "That's what it was. He
needed you because you were the only one who knew the truth.
He wasn't afraid of you at all. If anything, he was afraid of
himself. I have to go," she announced abruptly. "I can't stand
this anymore." She started to walk away.

"That's not true!" he yelled after her. "He was afraid of me."

She kept going. She was too bewildered by everything to stay
any longer.

"He hated me. I'll get you," he added threateningly. "Can't
get him, I'll get you."

"Yeah?" she yelled back, suddenly furious too. "What for?
What'd I ever do to you? Why bother me with everything? It's
not my fault. It's his fault."

"I'll say it's his fault," the man ranted behind her. "But he
never admitted it. He never said he was sorry. And it was my
ear. My ear."

She had looked for a cab, but there was none. The subway
lay in the opposite direction, and there were no buses. She

heard him breathing, heaving almost, as he followed her, and she walked faster, looking back over her shoulder. Suddenly she'd seen a cab ahead, run for it. Algodones started running too. "Don't go, damn you," he had yelled angrily. "I want to talk."

But she had jumped into the cab and sped away. She slumped down in the back, Boarchards' naked life yawning before her, a lie at the center—a stupid lie, a secret no one shared but Pollibeaux, when the truth wasn't awful at all. It was the stuff of war, she thought, of life and death. He certainly could have killed the Japanese kid, but not the other eight. He never could have prevented the slaughter. Much more likely he'd have ended up dead or captive too, just like the rest, and that was the point: he knew it, she thought. He had known it as he slid down into the crevice. He'd seen the future ahead himself —death or torture or captivity, nothing else, and so he slid down into a crevice, along with vomit and fear, and clung to some thread of hope. And waited for the others to leave. And then crawled out over the bodies, a future of another sort ahead, but it no more than a thread right then. Just a tiny little thread, but slowly, through the years, it wrapped itself around his neck, so that he got more and more confused whether he was really Frank, Mark, John, Julius, the hero, or the other, Hooper, Hupper, Melvin, Clause, hero or a coward, victim or accuser, and if Algodones blamed him for everything, Rush blamed her. But the thread got tighter and tighter around his neck until it destroyed him, no one ever knowing about the cave but Pollibeaux, when all along, someone else, another kind of man, a man of a different history and a different background, might simply have forgotten it. Seen it for what it was, the stuff of war and life, and not let it ruin him.

Suddenly she leaned forward in the cab, barely aware she'd made another decision. "Hurry, driver," she said. "I have a long drive ahead." Pollibeaux, she thought. I have to ask Pollibeaux about it. Her destination now all of a sudden not the apartment, but the garage and a final, last, but brand-new leg to her investigation. Another journey, unexpected, but the last one. Back to Weather Tree to find Pollibeaux—her father's best friend and the only one he had ever told about Algodones and the cave, the only one who knew for sure he remembered. Polly, five miles in at Camp Four, where Cloe had said he'd gone till June. Polly, who'd look at her with disregard, but tell her what Rush himself had said about Algodones and the cave.

And then, Abigail knew, then she'd make her decision about the will. With the picture of her father finally complete, she'd know what to do. There at Weather Tree. There, where her father had made his decision about her.

But as the taxi neared the park, without even thinking about it, Abigail told the driver to go to the East Side. She took the list out of her pocket—"Victoria, Sam and Bostrine"—and clenched it in her fist.

At the apartment, Morris the butler took her to the library and asked her to wait. When he came back he took her down a long corridor to a sitting room half a block away.

"Darling," said Victoria, rising to give her a quick kiss.

"How is he?" Abby asked, the list still in her hand. "Uncle Sam."

The woman shook her head. "You know how to face things," she said unexpectedly. "You're so strong. You always know what to do."

"Are you all by yourself?"

"Yes."

Morris brought her sherry, but Abby put it down on a table untouched. "Is there something I can do to help you?" she asked. The room would have been quiet except for the mumble of voices from a radio in the wall.

"Just love him," Victoria answered, looking at her urgently. "Forgive him. Everybody's sent flowers, of course," she rushed on, glancing away, "but I'm the same. I never want to visit hospitals. Nobody likes to see bad things, and why should they? But he needs friends, Abby," she said, urgent again.

"But he knows so many people."

"They're busy," she said vaguely. "I've arranged everything else for him, you know. Parties, balls, birthdays. But I don't know how to arrange a death."

Abigail didn't say anything. The woman didn't realize what she had said.

"I've arranged everything else for him," Victoria persisted.

"What can I do?"

"It's so good to talk to you. I've missed you. You always know what to do, what you want. You're so lucky. But I don't know what my responsibilities are. I've done everything, but I can't get people to stay with him. He needs people. To take his mind off things."

"You keep talking about 'people.'" She'd never seen her aunt distraught like this.

"Because I can't find enough of them." Victoria pointed to her address book by the telephone. "He's alone and I have to fix it. Now. While there's still time." She sounded hysterical.

"Relax, Victoria," Abigail said, going across the room and taking her aunt in her arms. "You are taking care of him," she said, holding her close. "You're doing everything."

"But he's alone," the woman said, breaking away to pick up her address book on the table.

"There's nothing you can do about that."

"But nobody deserves to die alone, Abby. Whatever they've done. He doesn't deserve this. He loved you, Abby. He did."

"Maybe, once." She was surprised at how bitter she sounded.

"Rush only did it to teach you a lesson, Abby. I'm sure of it. None of us cares about money. You know that. It was just to teach you a lesson."

Outside she called Luke, first at her apartment, then at his, but there was no answer. She thought of interrupting him at the meeting, but she called Mary instead. "When's Alvah coming back from Washington?" she asked.

"Tonight," Mary said.

"Will you tell him I found Joe and I've gone to Weather Tree?"

Mary started to ask her more, but she hung up.

At the garage she got the car and drove toward the hospital. The rain had started. It was pelting down. She looked at her

watch. What had Victoria said? ". . . while there's still time."
Victoria, Sam and Bostrine. I have a whole lifetime to face
things, Abigail thought, but I want to do it all by Monday. Because then she'd have done everything. Gone to hell and back.
Faced everything she could think of facing, broken the family
pattern of isolation and retreat. And then she'd call Solomon
Irving and say something. Anything. It didn't matter.

At the hospital she parked in front of a hydrant and ran in,
her coat over her head. In the elevator, she suddenly realized
that by doing this, by doing every single thing she had done the
last three weeks, she'd done all the things her father had never
been able to do. He was right. They were different. Opposites.
He'd told one lie once about a cave and then it had started, lies
on top of guilt, and he ended up running forever, facing nothing. He'd gone to hell, but never come back out.

She got off the elevator. The night lights weren't on yet and
the storm had darkened the windows. There were no atten-
dants in sight as she went down the corridor, her boots oozing
from the rain. At least Sam had been honest with his dislike of
her, she thought, not like Rush, who'd hid it until too late.

She found his room, pushed the door open. Tiny lights from
a bridge flickered outside the window. Flowers had been
pushed back against the wall, roses, mums, and others. Sam was
in the bed, but he was almost invisible, a bald head poking out
from under the sheet. Machines were lined up around him,
connected to his body through his arms and nose and belly,
tubes sprouting off him everywhere. He had obviously had an
operation, and his companions now, the machines, had dials instead of eyes, and big bags of blood hung around him like
skinny people with weird heads and no mouths.

He was lying on his back, his arms flat at his sides, eyes
closed. She had never seen him asleep. She went over to the
bed, but then she didn't know what to do. He looked so thin.
She had assumed they'd talk, fight, but instead, he was barely
even there. She wondered whether to leave.

Then she realized he wasn't asleep after all. He opened his
eyes and looked at her, little tiny peek holes, and then closed
them, exhausted. Then suddenly he opened them again, frown-

ing now, and turned his head as far away from her as possible. He was straining to get away from her.

Abigail gripped the metal railing by the bed. Goddamn you, she thought. None of you ever fight. You hide and sneak.

She turned to leave, but suddenly, in the silence, she heard the tiny whistle of his breath, whistling in and whistling out. Whistling in and out, as if the passage for air or life was the tiniest little thing in the world. She stared at him, aghast, as if he'd come alive, as if he was a tiny insect or a tadpole, grasping for birth.

His eyes were closed and she watched, as if waiting for something to hatch. She listened to the tiny breathing, a will to survive. The room seemed so empty—tubes, metal, nothing to help a lonely person die. Then, not even knowing what she was doing, she reached out her hand and laid the top of her fingers on his face, and then quickly pulled them back as if they'd been burned.

Then she did it again, lightly, and it was like touching the newest form of birth.

She did it again, again.

And the next time, she placed a tiny bit more of her fingers down near his eyes, and slowly moved them back over his forehead and around the roundness of his bald head. Then she did it again and again. She looked like him too, she supposed, because he looked like Rush. But Rush's death was different, she thought, his an act, a deed. If only it could have been the beginning, she thought, rather than the end, his ability to act, because with one success behind him, perhaps he'd have gone on to more. Paralysis over.

She put her whole hand on Sam's head. It was hard at first, but then it got easier. She kept smoothing the skin. It got warmer. She breathed with him, in and out, fingers on his skin, something to help a lonely person die.

Then his head moved. It turned in slowly toward the middle. He was watching her. It rolled slowly over past the middle to the other side, until it was turned toward her. Then he stared at her, tiny spots of blue, and frowned. She could tell he was trying to ask her a question, but then the look faded, from exhaustion more than anything, and he went blank, staring up at her, no trace or hint of what he was thinking.

Then something panicky crossed his eyes; she saw it, something changed in the blue, and she felt the silence was awful, too much. No one else to help or comfort him. Leaving one hand on his forehead, she put the other on his chest and started to stroke it softly.

He moaned.

She went on stroking and he went on staring at her, looking the way a baby looks. He moaned again.

"Hello, Sam," she whispered.

He blinked.

"Hello."

He blinked again, a blink the only signal he had left to give. She bent down and rubbed her cheek against his. Then he let out a deep, enormous sigh and closed his eyes.

She thought he had drifted off to sleep, but then he opened his eyes again, as if to make sure she was still there, taking her in again, and then he closed them. She went on stroking, rubbing. Every now and then he opened his eyes and looked at her and blinked.

Once she leaned over and kissed him on the cheek, and once a nurse came in and told her she had to go. "I'm his daughter," Abigail said and the nurse nodded and left.

Downstairs she tried Luke again, but there was no answer. It was dark now. She called Max, but Foster said he'd gone out. "Is everything all right?" he asked.

"Yes," she said, and hung up.

She drove north in the rain, stopped once to get gas and call Luke again, but there was still no answer. She called the answering service and told them to give him a message. "I saw Joe," it said. "I'm going to Weather Tree."

She kept driving, but just before the turnoff that headed over the hills to the river and Bostrine, she pulled into a gas station and called Luke again. This time he was home.

"Where are you?" he cried. "I've been worried."

"I saw Sam. I've been at the hospital. Did you get my message?"

"Yes. What happened with Joe?"

"He's completely different than we expected. He's been terribly mistreated."

"Yes, but what happened?" he asked. "What's he doing?"

"Nothing. He was waiting for my father."

"Waiting?" Luke asked in disbelief. "What happened in the war?"

Abigail told him. "But I wasn't nice to him," she rushed on. "I meant to be. But then I upset him."

"Where is he now?"

"At home, I guess."

"No, he isn't," Luke said. "I just came back from there. I went down looking for you hours ago. I asked people where he was and they said he'd gone out. He said he had to send some telegrams."

"Telegrams?"

"But he never came back. Where are you?"

"I wish I'd been nicer to him, done what my father should have done. Treat him right. Repay him with respect, not money."

"That's not up to you," Luke said.

"But maybe I can help him. I'm going to see him again when I get back. He doesn't have anybody, Luke. But I don't know how to get through to him. He's complicated. He flies off the handle. One minute you hate him, but the next he's almost sweet. He's strange, but there's something a little marvelous about him too."

"Sure."

"No, there is."

"How much did you upset him?" Luke asked.

Before she could answer, someone started knocking on the door of the telephone booth. "I have to go," she said.

"But why are you going to Weather Tree again? We just came back from there."

"I want to see Polly."

"You said you'd be finished when you found Joe."

"I want Polly to tell me about it. Tell me what my father said. About Joe, Clovis, the cave, everything. Then . . ."

"But you don't need that," Luke argued. "You don't even like Polly. You said you were never going to ask him for one single thing."

"I know," she said hesitantly. "And I meant it. But I need him now. For this."

"Seeing Polly isn't going to make you different from your father, you know. That's what this is all about, Abby. Breaking the pattern. And you don't have to feel responsible for Joe, either, just because Rush didn't."

"But maybe I do, Luke," she said.

The man outside came back and stood near the telephone booth. "I only know when I've been to Weather Tree once more, everything will be clear. Please understand."

"I do understand, darling. I do," Luke said, gentle all of a sudden. "But I also want to take care of you a little . . ."

"Then just . . ."

". . . and not let anything happen to you."

"Nothing's happening to me."

"And you don't want me to come with you, do you," he said, relenting.

"I have to do this by myself, Luke."

"Then call me tomorrow."

The man outside knocked on the door.

"I really have to go," she said.

"You never told me about Joe's room," Luke said suddenly.

"It was a mess. Pictures everywhere. Robbie Moran. I have to go."

"I love you."

She hung up.

Bostrine's driveway was broad with towering trees and a lawn that spread down to the river. Abigail passed the tennis courts and a pool that twisted and turned like a lake. The house itself was grand, a palace preserved, and its chimneys rose up into the storm like fingers of defiance. She shifted down to first gear and stopped. There were lights on inside. She got out and ran through the rain. She rang the bell. She felt calm and her face was shining. You tried to cut me down, Pop. It almost worked.

Harrison opened the door. "My goodness," he said, rain splattering in his face.

"I want to see Aunt Bostrine."

He took her coat and led her down the middle of the grand hall. "She never goes to bed anymore," he said over his shoulder. "She stays up later and later." He knocked on the door of the drawing room.

"What is it?"

"Miss Abby. She wants to see you."

There was silence.

"Send her in," Bostrine said.

Harrison opened the door. Abigail stepped ahead a couple of feet and her confidence dissolved. Her heart started pounding and she started to turn back, but Harrison had shut the door.

Bostrine was sitting across the room at an elaborate table inlaid with gilt. She rose, her face inscrutable, and stared at her niece. Abigail didn't move. The room was rich with antiques and art. Double windows looked out on the lawn and the river, and on the table in front of her little picture frames spread out in arc after arc.

Abigail wondered if there were pictures of Nicer there, watching over her.

"What's happened?" the old woman asked. She wore a long gown with fur at the collar and brocade descending to the floor. "What's the matter?"

"Nothing. I just wanted to see you. I saw Sam. I have to decide about the will by Monday."

"Then you're all right?"

"Yes."

Bostrine picked up the phone on her desk. "Harrison, bring tea and something to eat. She needs a towel for her hair."

She sat down, Abby sat too, wondering how many people wore jeans and boots in here. "I stayed with Sam awhile," Abby said.

"This rain is just like Florida."

"He's dying."

"I know," Bostrine said.

"I felt so sorry for him." She paused. "That was the only time I've ever been drunk, Aunt Bostrine. I want to apologize for calling in that condition."

Harrison brought the towel. "The rest is coming," he said.

Abby started wiping her hair.

"You really are too unpredictable," Bostrine said wearily. "I don't hear from you in years, and then all of a sudden you call up in the middle of the night. And now this. You are so very confusing. Is there something you want?"

"I wanted to see you." She paused. "To tell you something about Rush. You loved him. I know you did."

"Is that what you were doing up there at Weather Tree?"

"It has to do with Joe Algodones."

"Nasty man. He sent us letters."

"I found him and he told me a lot about Rush."

"What does he want?" Bostrine asked.

"He doesn't want anything. Not from us. He just wanted Rush to . . ."

"Don't be naive, Abigail. People like that always want something. Money. Help."

"He's different." She told Bostrine about the cave, the shooting, the three men who lived, and the cover-up that followed.

The old woman sat down heavily. "Poor boy." She let out a deep sigh. Harrison came in with tea. "Can we have a brandy?" she asked. He brought it to her and she held it in her hands, neglected then to drink. "He should have told us," she said, when they were alone. "He thought he could do anything, and then when he couldn't, he didn't understand. You're the same, Abby, your father's daughter."

"Because I think people can do anything they set their minds to?" she asked, taking some brandy.

"No. Because you don't care what you do to them. He had a kitten once and he kept throwing it in the water. Marcel got furious. Said it was cruel and that cats hate water, but Rush said they didn't have to. But after that it was people. He never understood them. He never understood they couldn't be perfect either. Take Andrew."

"What about Andrew?"

"Rush hurt him terribly. Did you know that?"

Abby shook her head.

"Your father convinced Andrew he had to be good at everything, sports, debating, school. He never accepted that Andrew just wasn't cut out for that. You're the same. You made your father's life miserable and you never even knew it. Doesn't that bother you?" she asked, suddenly intent.

"Of course it bothers me. But he did everything he could to hurt me, Aunt Bostrine—the will, those letters. 'You think you're so damn hot, well, take this.' Well, I am going to take it, Aunt Bostrine. He left me one thing, one inheritance: the specter of being like him. And I'm doing everything I can to learn from it."

"Don't you care about any of us?"

"Can't you understand? Do you think I wanted to be like my mother? Or my father? Or Sam or Victoria? Why should I want to be like any of you?" Her voice was rising. "You're all unhappy. He committed suicide. My mother threatened to commit suicide. No one will visit Sam in the hospital because he doesn't have any friends. Is that the way I'm supposed to be, just because I have the same last name? Why didn't you all clap and cheer? And say, 'Yea, Abby, keep it up.' "

"Don't talk like that."

"I'm being honest," Abby said. "I tried to carve out something for myself that was me, not my family, but all mine. So I could be somebody."

"So you want to be famous?"

"That's not it at all. I just want to be strong and happy and myself. . . ."

Bostrine turned away.

"Why didn't you tell anyone you were in love with Nicer?" Abigail demanded.

"What?"

"Why didn't you tell anyone you were in love with him? You didn't even tell him, did you?"

"That's none of your business."

"Then why am I your business?"

"I don't understand a word you're saying."

Abigail got up and walked across the room toward the empty marble fireplace.

"You know," Bostrine began, "if I tell my friends anything, you name it, they understand. But if I tell them you're a photographer, they don't know what it means."

"Do you?"

"Of course I do. You run around, work all day, all night, and always put yourself first."

"That's not true."

"If you're supposed to photograph something at seven o'clock, but you're also supposed to have dinner with me, what comes first? Me or the work?"

"The work."

"Then that's what I mean."

"But that's not the heart of what I do."

"To me it is."

"But it's not. . . . You're not even listening," Abby said. "You don't even care."

"I'm listening perfectly. You're saying I never understood your work and I'm saying I did. We all did. But from our point of view, and you don't like that one bit. I'm an old woman, Abigail, and if I told you I didn't understand this disco dancing, you wouldn't think that so very strange. So why should I understand you or your work?"

"Everybody was always saying what was wrong with me. I was fat, awkward, too ugly; I asked too many questions. Instead it was always, 'Charley,' 'Charley,' 'Charley.' "

"Well, of course," Bostrine said.

" 'Of course' what?"

"Well, it's so much more important what happens to a boy. And besides, which is more the point, you were such a mess. We all worried dreadfully about you."

"I wasn't a mess. I was just different."

"But they're the same thing, darling," Bostrine said.

Abigail sat down again. She didn't know what to say. They were silent. A clock was ticking away somewhere. She looked at her watch.

"Is your hair dry?" Bostrine asked. "I don't want you catching cold."

"I won't."

"There's a hair dryer in the guestroom."

"I'm not spending the night."

"Nobody's used it in a long time. I'll tell them to make pancakes in the morning. Children like pancakes. I was young once too, you know. I had a lot of beaux. They were happy times; or at least, they seemed happy afterward."

"You were very beautiful."

"Not like Florence."

"But at least everyone loved you," Abby said. "You've spent your whole life taking care of people."

"But nobody really cares. Just like you." Bostrine traced her hand along the shelf behind her, rows of gold-embossed appointment books stretching on the wall like the years themselves—luncheons, teas, dinners and deaths. "This is the only time anyone's ever come to me in the middle of the night."

"My father cared."

"Not really. He was more like you than you think. All children are self-centered, and they all feel like you, unloved and unwanted."

"But Pop didn't make me feel unloved. At least not until he died. That's why the will hurt so much. Because I thought we were so close."

"Don't mention the will. I dread to think of what trouble you're going to start. I'm too old for that. I just wish we could all forget the will. Forget all the bad things and go back to simpler things. But you're like Florence. You always were. You always had to know what's what. So did she. If she was foolish as a child, she wasn't afterward. She learned. I could have married Nicer, you know," she went on without a pause, "but I never told Father that's what I wanted, and so he didn't know, and then suddenly it was all set up the other way. Sara-Fey was so happy. Nicer must have thought I didn't care. He courted me first, but I didn't know how to say the things girls were supposed to say then. I was too shy . . ."

"Shy?"

". . . and Sara-Fey was such a sweet little thing. Simple, really, she never had a mean thought in her head. And then, when June came, we all went to Weather Tree, and that's when their courtship began. He had awfully small hands, you know," the old woman went on, so quietly Abigail could barely hear. "He was a tall man, but his hands were short. I always thought he was a little embarrassed by them. But he always seemed to know what he was doing. I like that in people."

"You're the same way."

She shook her head sadly. "People only think I am because I make a fuss and scare them."

"You don't scare me."

"I scare Sam. Poor Sam. And I scared your mother. But your father was good to you, Abby. For a long time he was. He loved you more than anything. I never scared him either. I suppose that's why I loved him so much. He never did anything he didn't want to."

"Then why can't you love that quality in me?"

But Bostrine wasn't listening. "When I had Sara-Fey and Nicer with me, things were much better," she said. "We had lovely times, but there was always that moment when everyone went in another direction and I went to my room alone. Don't let that happen to you, Abby. Work isn't worth it. Sometimes I used to stand in my room and listen to the water running in the house and know it came from their room. Or hear the pipes jiggle. The pipes make such a lot of noise here in this old house. In Hobe Sound I could hear Nicer snore." Bostrine sighed. "What am I going to do with all these things, Abby?"

"What things?"

"These." Bostrine gestured around the room and suddenly she looked helpless. "What am I going to do with them? I have so much. I don't know why I let it happen. I thought I wanted it all, and I suppose at the time I did, but now there's no one who cares. No one wants it. They just want my money. Sometimes, can you imagine, I say, 'Talk. Talk to me.' And I'll be looking at a chair and wanting it to say something. Can you imagine, Abby? But is there something here you want? Something you can take home?"

She looked at Abigail and Abigail suddenly felt their past falling away and the old lady's eyes, blue and big, reaching out across the abyss. "Is there, Abby? I have a nice Fragonard."

Abigail started shaking her head.

"There's an awfully pretty Renoir. I keep it in the dining room. You could sell it and get some money. Get something you wanted. I wouldn't mind if you did that. Or took a trip."

Tears welled up in Abby's eyes.

"Is there anything else? Please let me give you something."

Abigail shook her head. The tears were sliding down her face.

"Then do it for me. Let me give you something. I know I don't have very much that's modern. But . . ."

"I like old things," Abigail said through her tears.

"You do?"

"And I like pieces of sculpture, broken pieces."

"You do? I never heard of that."

"And photographs, drawings."

"I have lots of drawings. . . ."

"I love drawings." Abigail got up and in one flowing movement crossed the room and knelt in front of her aunt. She gripped her knees and looked up, her face wet from tears.

Bostrine reached out and took her head in her hands. "I got the Renoir in Paris. Florence said it was inferior, but I liked it anyway . . ."

"I saw your egg."

". . . and I still like it now."

"The Fabergé egg."

"You did?"

"I went in your bedroom because I wanted to know more about you." She wiped her nose with her hand. "I opened the drawer and saw the book Nicer gave you. And his picture. He looks so wonderful. I bet he loved you too. I know he did." She was kneading her aunt's hand, blue and gnarled, in hers. "He just wanted to protect Sara too. Like you. But he really loved you."

Bostrine looked down, her face intent.

"All those years, I bet he loved you and tried to take care of you the best he could, by taking care of Sara too."

"He did tell me once I made him very happy," Bostrine whispered.

"Did he mean he loved you?"

"I don't know. Sometimes I think yes. Sometimes no."

"What did he say?"

"He said, 'You've made me very happy, Bos. I want you to know that.'"

"Oh, Auntie," Abigail giggled. "How formal."

Bostrine laughed too. "It must sound funny nowadays."

"Oh no, it sounds wonderful. What else did he say?"

"He said, 'You look so beautiful, Bos. You always look beautiful.'"

"Did he know what you were feeling?"

Bostrine suddenly hung her head. "I don't know, Abby, and that's the worst thing of all. Sometimes I think yes. Sometimes no. We were in Hobe Sound and I was staying with them because Nicer was dying. We opened the windows so he could hear the waves. I was holding his hand, I remember that, and he was very pale, but he looked just like he did when he was young, his eyes were just as clear as ever. But then the doctor came in and I thought, I mustn't go. I must stay with Nicer. I mustn't leave him alone. But I left and went downstairs, and the butler, he was Foster's cousin, he said I had a telephone call. So I took the call. Then the butler came rushing in and said Sara wanted me upstairs and I hung up. I just hung up. I knew what had happened and I thought, Why did I have to leave the room? I could have been with him. But why did he have to die, Abby? I loved him. I really did. But I never told him and I can't bear it," she whispered. "That's the worst thing I ever did, Abby, not telling him. Because what if he didn't know?" She stopped and stared at her niece, as if to allow her time to contemplate the dimensions of that possibility. "You mustn't ever do anything like that. Even if your father did and I did. Never saying the important things. Don't be like us."

"I won't."

Bostrine clutched the girl's hands. "Don't be like me, Abby, don't. But you won't, will you. Rush gave you that terrible spirit. I used to tell him he was ruining you, letting you be so independent, and he said never mind, he knew what he was doing. And I guess he did. He wasn't ruining you at all." Bostrine found a handkerchief in the pocket of her gown and blew her nose. "But you do look just like him."

"I know."

"Did you ever see a good picture of Nicer?" Bostrine picked up one on the desk. Set between dozens of seed pearls, the exposure was clear and gray. It showed him looking out, eyes and hair and face. "At least I fell in love," she said. "I did do that."

"Yes."

"Your father never could, Abby. Not really. Have you? This man you took to Weather Tree?" She put her hands on the girl's face. "But don't be afraid of it. Don't hold back. Just give everything you have. But you won't be afraid. I can see that all over you. You're much too sure of yourself as it is."

"Oh, no, Auntie. That's not true at all. Really. I'm just like you. Inside I'm scared and insecure."

"Is that true?"

"Yes."

"Then come and let me hold you," the old woman said, and pulling Abigail up, she stood and put her arms around the girl and held her tight. "Let me hold you and make you better," she said, starting to cry.

Abigail felt her aunt's arms tight around her back and smelled the scent of something in her hair.

"Was your father wrong, Abby? Or have you been this way all along and I just didn't know? I tried with your father, darling, but he just wanted to be left alone, and it never occurred to me you were any different."

The road to Weather Tree was worse than ever. The mud was thick and bottomless, sucking up high on the wheels, and she had to drive on the edge of the road the whole way in to find traction. By the time she reached the clearing the rain had stopped. At the courtyard she got out. The trees made a sound, moving in the night, and rain dripped from the branches.

Inside it was cold and dark, and even downstairs she thought she could smell the smell. Her father's smell, decay oozing from the pores.

Too tired to light a lamp, she found a flashlight in the kitchen and started down the hall. The big room yawned in front of her, dark and empty. Exhausted, she lay down on the couch, Whitaker Rush on one side, the moose on the other, Navajo rugs on top of her, and fell asleep immediately.

Sunday, May 5

She never heard a noise.

She woke up and there he was, not six feet away, sitting in a chair with his socks showing. Her father's antique steel hunting rifle was slanted upright in his arms and he was looking straight at her. His right hand was on the detonator and the box of dynamite was at his feet.

She didn't move. More dynamite was taped up the wall to the moose and across the room, up the stairs to the hall.

His eyes were wide like saucers and he didn't say a thing. He just looked at her, the knobs on the side of his head pulsing.

Abigail froze the inside of her mouth to keep from screaming. She was stunned. It had never occurred to her he'd do anything like this. "Joe . . ." she began, then stopped.

He didn't move; he didn't blink. "I didn't know you were here," he said.

"Then stop this, Joe. Leave." She sat up on the couch. "I liked you yesterday, Joe. I did."

"Shut up." He aimed the gun in her direction.

"But I want to tell you something," she stuttered in fear.

"I don't want to hear it."

They sat in silence, but he didn't move. He just stared at her, like nothing was happening. Her eyes glazed over, fixed on the barrel of the gun. It seemed as big as a cannon. "But I liked you," she stuttered finally. "I did."

"Shut up."

"I was going to come see you again."

He blinked.

"Because I liked you. And I felt bad about how he treated you. I wanted to make it up to you."

"With money," he snickered, his finger twitching on the trigger.

"No," she said angrily. "By talking. By having a cup of coffee."

"I like tea."

"Okay, then. Tea."

"He told you about me," he said flatly.

"No, he didn't, Joe. He had nothing to do with it. I found you. I've been looking for you for three weeks. I even went to New Mexico looking for you. I saw your cousin."

Joe's eyes gaped in amazement.

"I hired a private detective to find you," she rushed on. "I put ads in the paper."

He slowly lowered the gun, but his hand still rested near the detonator. "Why?"

"I wanted to talk to you about him. He didn't send me. He never told me about you. He protected you. It was me. I wanted to meet you."

"You want me to put a hat on?"

"Why do you always say that?" she exclaimed.

"He was always telling me to wear hats."

"I don't mind how you look. I don't care if you have one ear or six ears. I just want this to stop. All of it. Everything. You stalking me. The sadness. The dynamite. Everything. What do you think you'll get out of blowing up this house? You'll get in a lot of trouble, that's what."

Joe pulled a bunch of papers out of his pocket and handed

them to her. They were telegrams. "I sent them to everyone," he said. "Your uncle, your aunt, your . . ."

She started reading. They were all the same. One was even addressed to her. "Now it's my turn," they said. "I get the last word and I say if I get the house, I get you all. I'm going to blow it up and you'll be too late to stop me."

"They'll be here to stop you," Abigail exclaimed, her heart leaping in hope.

"But maybe they don't know yet," Joe said slyly.

"Why?" she cried. "When did you send them?"

"It's not when I sent them. It's when they're going to be delivered."

"When?"

"Sometime this morning."

"But when this morning?" she asked frantically, looking at her watch. It was almost nine.

"Worried, aren't you."

"Of course I am. I'm only human."

"No need to be mean," he said sullenly, his face falling.

"The first thing they'll do is call Simon. He'll stop you." Joe smiled eerily at her.

"What'd you do to Simon? If you hurt him, I'll—"

"I didn't hurt him," he whined. "I didn't. I promise."

"Then what did you do to him?"

Joe shrugged almost apologetically.

"What'd you do?"

"Nothing."

"What?" she insisted.

"I just tied him up, that's all," he said.

Abigail glared at him. He averted his eyes and they sat in silence a long time, the barrel of the gun pointed vaguely in her direction. She kept looking at the detonator, wondering how hard a push was needed to set it off. She didn't think he wanted to kill her, but she didn't know if in his determination to destroy the house, he might not get her as well. She thought frantically about how to get away from him or deactivate him. But at least she had figured out what was motivating him, she realized. He had lost everything and he knew it. His obsession about Rushing Boarchards had been the only thing that gave his life meaning, and with it gone, in the vacuum left, he had flipped over the edge. He had to do something. Anything. He was coming apart and he had simply followed his anger for guidance and ended up here with the dynamite.

Her presence had confused everything, she knew, and he was in a holding pattern again, just as he had been the last three weeks, the last thirty years. Waiting. Waiting to see what Boarchards would do. Only now the Boarchards was she. She, the heir apparent to everything, she thought ironically.

Suddenly Abigail sat up and started to pull her boots on. "Come on," she said. "Let's go see Pollibeaux at Camp Four. That's why I'm up here. You told me he knew everything."

"Why do you have to see him?"

"Because."

"Because why?"

"Because he knew my father better than anyone and because he knew you. He's the only one who knew you."

"But I never liked him," Joe said, pouting a bit.

"Neither do I."

"Then why do you want to bother with him?" Joe frowned and cocked his head, sitting there looking like a funny child with his socks showing and a play gun in his hands.

"He's the last person on my list."

"List?"

"Never mind that, Joe," she said lightly. "Come on. Let's go."

"But I don't want him to see me." He didn't budge from the chair.

"Then stay outside the cabin."

"We'll get lost in the woods."

"There's a trail."

"You don't believe me, do you?" he exclaimed with sudden harshness. "You think by sweet-talking me, I won't blow up the house. Well, I didn't trust Rush, and I don't trust you. Look at this." He moved the rifle to his shoulder, aimed at the window across the room and fired.

"Stop it," she ordered as the glass splintered and crashed on the floor.

He aimed at another window and fired.

She threw her hands to her ears. "What are you trying to do?" she cried.

The next bullet hit the end of a moose antler with a thud and went into the wall. Joe smirked and returned the gun to his lap.

"You make me so goddamn mad," she exploded, her eyes blazing. "I like you. I even liked your cousin. I tried to find out everything I could about you. I went to a lot of trouble and I've tried to be decent with you, but if I'd treated you badly, like everybody else did, you wouldn't even know the difference."

Joe's head fell. "I know the difference," he mumbled. "Come on. I'll go see Pollibeaux, if that's what you want. I don't want to make you mad."

She stared, spellbound by his change.

He averted his eyes and looked embarrassed. "Finish putting your boots on."

"Then you put boots on too," she said sternly.

He looked down at his black shoes with no soles.

"You can't wear those in the woods," she said. "Go in the closet and get some boots. I won't move."

Taking the gun, he went up the stairs to the landing and around the corner to the closet.

Abigail let out a deep sigh and tried to think. Joe peeked around the corner to make sure she hadn't moved. What's going on, she thought urgently. What's this all about? She couldn't figure out what he needed in order to stop.

"I'm ready," he said in a minute.

She got up and followed him down the hall. She glanced at her watch again. Ten minutes had passed. When would the telegrams be delivered? Outside the sky was blue, and all signs of the storm were gone. "Where's your truck?" she asked.

"I hid it."

They got in the jeep and she drove, but instead of heading toward the trail to Camp Four, she went straight to the farm.

He didn't say anything. At the farmhouse, she heard the dogs barking inside. Joe still didn't intervene. He followed her up the steps and inside he just jostled her with the gun and pushed her across the kitchen.

Simon was on the floor with a dishtowel wedged in his mouth, his arms and feet tied behind his back. She knew he was all right because he glared at her angrily.

Suddenly the phone started to ring.

"Let me answer it," she pleaded.

Joe just raised his gun at her. "What'd you come here for anyway?" he asked as the phone kept ringing.

"To see Simon," she muttered. "To make sure he was all right. Joe, I can't stand this," she said, and abruptly she slid down the wall to the floor with a thud and sat there. "I really can't. I'm sorry for all you've been through. I wish it hadn't happened, really, I do. But . . ."

"I tried to help Robbie too," he said unexpectedly.

She looked up at him. "My father never visited Clovis, did he," she said, remembering the letters from the basement.

Joe shook his head again. "I did. Somebody had to. Somebody had to sit with him. Bring him chocolate. He always liked chocolate. And Tootsie Rolls. But Tootsie Rolls were getting harder to find, and so . . ."

"And my father?"

"He made out like he didn't know Clovis. He just wanted to go on pretending nothing ever happened back there in the Philippines."

"He wrote you a letter to say good-bye," Abigail said from the floor. She could see his anger had ebbed. "It was a nice letter. He said you should go home. Spend time with the short-wave." She watched him closely. She could tell he was listening hard. "He knew your work was finished too, Joe." Behind her Simon kicked his feet against the counter. "He was concerned about you."

"Why do you care what happens to me?" Joe asked sullenly.

"I don't know how much I do care, to be honest. But what's going to happen to Sue Ann? If you hurt us or blow the house up, they'll put you in jail. You won't get away. You think the rich are powerful—well, they'll really get you for this. Why can't you just stop? Go away?"

"Because. I want him to apologize," he pouted. "That's all."

Abby felt herself starting to cry, not tears of sorrow, but of exhaustion and frustration. They were pouring out of her eyes. She tried to wipe them away.

Joe cocked his head, watching her. "You really want me to go?"

She nodded.

He stood looking at her, as if he didn't know what to do. Then he picked up a towel on the counter with the tip of her father's rifle and handed it to her. "Wipe your face."

She took the towel and blew her nose.

The phone started ringing again. They waited in silence until it stopped.

"Can I still come with you to see Polly?" Joe asked meekly. "He'll tell you that I'm right."

She saw Simon listening and was relieved. That's what she'd wanted: to let him know where they were going. "If we do that, Joe, then will you leave?"

Joe didn't answer. He reached out his hand to help her up. She took it. It felt warm and a little moist. She wondered suddenly if he was anxious too.

"I have to go to the bathroom," she said. She went off to the little room by the kitchen and afterward got a pillow in the living room for Simon. Back in the kitchen she bent down to put the pillow under Simon's head, but he glared at her some more and squirmed toward Joe, trying to kick him with his legs.

"I'm sorry, Simon," she mumbled.

"Come on," Joe said. "Let's go."

Leaving, Abigail suddenly realized what Joe wanted.

He wanted to be with her. Now she was all he had. She and his cousin, and she was the only one who understood or knew the past.

She drove across the meadow to the place where the trail to Camp Four headed down into the woods. There wasn't a cloud in the sky. At the edge, she stopped and got out. The ground was soggy. Joe didn't move. He sat inside holding his gun, looking out at the forest through the dirty windowpane.

"Come on," she said. "It's all right. There's a trail." She opened his door. "We won't get lost."

He stepped out, gun in hand, and looked up at her for reassurance. Abigail looked back at his brown eyes and hole for an ear and realized she was doing with him what she hadn't done with her father: she was working it out. Working out a relationship with him. "We won't get lost," she repeated kindly.

"But I've never been in the woods," he said.

"It's all right," she answered. "Nothing will happen. I promise."

They set out. It was midmorning. The woods looked like a wall, green and wet, and Joe stared at them with trepidation. Abigail went first, he followed. It was like going underground. The sun was gone in here, shade now, only patches of light. The trail opened up in front of them, but the trees laced overhead and around them on all sides. Joe walked skittishly, as if the trees might jump him, but after a while he seemed to notice that the space around him moved too, moved as he moved, and never came any closer or went farther away. He seemed to relax.

Abigail thought about Camp Four and the lake ahead. It was a long walk, and she realized she might miss the deadline altogether, but she was beginning to realize she didn't want to contest the will anyway. She was just too tired.

"I've been to lots of funerals," Joe said abruptly. "Rockefeller. Astor. Lots of them. And I spent two days at Bobby Kennedy's funeral. Rush got me a pass so I got to stay inside the church the whole time, didn't have to go through in line."

"Why do you go to funerals?" she asked over her shoulder.

"You see a lot of people. All kinds. I followed one man out of the Kennedy funeral and know what he did? Went across the street to a bathroom and changed his clothes. Went in in a suit, came out in a uniform. He was a janitor."

"What else do you do?"

"Lots of things. I like stockholder meetings. He gave me his proxies, so I tried not to miss them."

They kept going. It was moist and green. The land squished and water rushed in to fill their tracks. The path was narrow, an indentation in the ground with markers on the trees every now and then to show the way. But she knew the way, just by the look of the land and the line of the sun. They passed one lake, another, marshes and a swamp where beavers had dammed a stream. Gray trees surrounded by water stood naked and dead at the roots, silent things dead amid the life. Birds swooped down, darting at the water. They stood and watched.

"I couldn't find him at first," Joe said.

"Who?" She looked at him and realized she had stopped being afraid of him. That something had changed.

"After the war," he was saying, "I knew he was up here somewhere, Clovis had told me that much, but I didn't know where. And he wasn't in the telephone book. Anywhere. Not here or in New York."

"Why didn't you just ask someone? Everyone knew him."

"I did. I asked a few. But they looked at my ear and wouldn't tell me. Sue Ann said why didn't I look in the library; libraries had everything. So I did, only I didn't know there were so many of them."

"Who?"

"The Rushings and the Boarchards."

The trail twisted and turned. The sun went up and over the top of the sky and she felt in the pocket of her pants for the nugget and the list. She was thinking hard and clearly about the will. For the first time now, it was easy.

"He talked about you all the time, you know," Joe said after a while. "Except the last few years, I guess, when he didn't talk at all. You know how we worked it?"

"How?"

"January, April, June and September. That's when I came up to get the money. Only this last time, he said not to come in January. Said he'd be someplace else by then. But I didn't believe him. He never went anywhere. He made me spend the night, cooked me breakfast. When I left, he came out to the truck. Told me to take care of myself. Asked me if I knew you. I told him of course I didn't know you, and he said, 'Well she's better off than I am.' "

"What did he mean?" she asked, holding her breath.

"He meant money," Joe said. "That's what."

"But I don't have any money."

"Sure you do."

"He left it to Charley."

"What'd he give you?"

"Nothing," she said.

Joe shrugged his shoulders. "Who cares?" he said over his shoulder, he in the lead now. "What's the big deal? If he left it to a hospital, you wouldn't mind. That's what they all do. Leave everything to hospitals, churches, cats. He was always saying how you wouldn't take money, wouldn't take a car, so why do you want it now? Charley's different; he can't live without the money."

"But you don't understand. I was disinherited."

Joe shrugged. "They leave it to museums all the time. I told you that." He sounded exasperated with her inability to catch on.

"You don't leave land to museums," she argued.

"You never owned it before, so why should he saddle you with it now?"

"It's not exactly 'saddle.' "

"It never did him any good. If he wasn't rich, he never would have lied to me. He never would have lived a lie. If you had all this stuff, you'd end up just like the rest of them."

"That's not true."

"Maybe not. But how was he to know? You ever think of that? Think of the peace of mind it gave him to know for sure you were safe. You know."

"No. What?"

"Protected from the money."

"But he got angry at me. He hated me."

"Even I know better than that," Joe said with disgust.

"But he did," she argued.

"Well, so what if he did. Didn't you ever get angry?"

"Not like that," she said.

"Well, maybe you're just different than him."

"That's true," she said.

"Sure," he said knowingly. "It made him feel better, that's all. I yell and scream all the time. I don't mean it. It just makes me feel better. Don't you understand anything? Just doing it, just saying those things about you made him feel better. That's all. Doesn't mean he meant it one bit." He paused. "And he didn't mean it," he said. "Not for a minute."

"But I was mean to him."

"So what? He was protecting you. He didn't want you to fall into the same trap as him."

"Maybe you're right. But how do you know? How can you be so sure?"

"One good thing about knowing as many people as I do," he said confidently, "is that I get to understand human nature."

Walking on, she turned Joe's words over in her mind. Was it possible he was right? That Rush really hadn't hated her and that disinheriting her was a perverted act of protection? There was still a mile to go when she remembered something else: one time Rush had given her advice. Only now she couldn't remember exactly what he'd said. The lake opened up below, stretching far in one direction, less in the other. Suddenly she turned off the trail and headed into the woods.

"Hey," Joe called. "I don't want to get lost."

But she kept going until she came to a great big rock and started climbing up.

"What are you doing?"

She reached the top and wedged herself into a position so she could lie down and see the sky, the trees and the lake. Joe watched her and then, following suit, found another rock and sat down too. Abigail closed her eyes. She knew she was on the brink of a decision. A final resolution. She could feel the land stretching away on all sides, north, south, east and west. Sun, shadows, trees, leaves and birds. Everything growing, dying. She loved it, the sound of wind, the feel of air. She heard branches move and sway, sounding as if they had a thing to say.

"War is always awful." Gradually it came back to her. Pop had said that long ago on the lake below, disinheritance and the will still years away. "And that's something you just have to accept," he said.

"I don't think anybody ever has to accept anything," she replied.

"There's a lot you have to accept. That's how life works."

"But I hate that idea."

"That's because you're young and full of piss and vinegar. You'll learn."

"I don't ever want to learn that."

"But you will," he had said, growing serious as he paddled across the lake. "Someday something will happen and no matter how much you don't like it, there won't be anything you can do about it. You can't fight everything, Abby. I know. I've tried. I know you think you can, and so far you've done a pretty good job at it, but you can't do that forever. You can't overcome everything and you can't undo anything. One day you'll think about this," he said. "Something will happen to you and you'll just have to accept it and live with it, for better or for worse."

Back on the rock with the birds calling and the wind blowing, Abigail replayed his words over and over in her mind, and made her decision. It was easy when it came. It seemed natural, obvious, the only thing to do. She was going to leave Weather Tree for good and not contest the will. As Max had said. Let the act be done. His act of disinheritance was part of the past and now she was going to leave it in the past where it belonged. She lay there listening to the birds and the leaves, the rustling and whistling, and after a while she stood up and started down the rock. "Come on, Joe," she called. "Let's go home."

"What about Polly?"

She shook her head. "There's no point anymore. I'm finished. There's no reason to see him. I don't need him."

Abby reached him and they walked toward the trail. "Why didn't you just accept what my father did to you and forget it?" she asked him. "Why didn't you just tell him 'You're a bum and I don't want to do anything with you'?"

"Because he wasn't a bum," Joe said shyly.

"But you tied yourself to him for thirty years," she said.

He didn't answer and she let him be. They reached the trail and set off single-file toward home. They had four miles to go.

"You should forget what I told you about Rush and the cave," Joe said after a while. "You don't want that hanging over your life. You don't want to be like me. Do you? Hung up on the past?"

"No, I don't, Joe," she said softly.

"I didn't think so."

The sun had moved around the sky and was headed down the other side. Abby looked at everything intently, thinking she would never see it again. The woods were colder now, and she pulled her woolen jacket tight around her neck. It was getting darker, too, and at a pond ahead loons were calling, once, twice, sounds as beautiful as sounds could be, and she listened, knowing they were saying good-bye to her.

Suddenly, through the trees ahead, she saw two men walking along the trail heading in their direction. She grabbed Joe's arm, pulled him to the ground and scurried off into the woods. They hid behind a rock and peered out, the men coming closer. It was Josh and Diver. They had guns and were walking fast, almost at a run. When they disappeared, Abigail got up and headed deeper into the woods, away from the trail.

"We'll get lost," Joe whispered.

"They're looking for you. Just like I warned you. Do you want them to catch you? We'll go home this way. Come out the other side of the clearing, where they won't be looking," she said, running along, "away from the farm. Where did you hide your truck?"

"At the edge of the clearing."

"Can they find it?"

"No. I drove it off the road. You don't want them to catch me?"

"What would that prove, Joe? I ask you. After all we've been through, what would that prove now?"

They went at a slow run, stopping often to catch their

breath. The sun was starting to set behind their back and they stuck close together. Abigail heard an owl, a sign of night coming, and affixed the knowledge of the sunset at a spot behind her right ear and kept going in as straight a line as possible.

"What are you doing?" Joe asked.

"Just what Clovis did. I'm heading for Licking River. It'll lead us through the woods and we'll follow it down to the clearing. You don't like the woods much, do you, Joe?" She grinned and gripped his arm for a second.

"What if they find me on the road? What'll I do then?" he asked.

"I'll drive out with you."

"But why?"

They kept going. Darkness came. It was after eight when they finally heard water ahead and came to the river. It was about fifteen feet wide, rushing over the rocks, white water that glowed in the night like phosphorescence. It looked beautiful and strong, endless. She wanted to stand and watch it, but she veered quickly off to the right and followed the shore downstream, going as fast as she could in the darkness. The river went through narrow ravines and around the bottom of Licking River Mountain with its caves high above. The sound of the water licking was loud, then soft, but constant, always there. Like acceptance, Abigail thought. It was just there, water flowing, flowing to the sea, like life, she realized, knowing the thought was not new or even old, but ageless. You have to accept life. That's what Rush had meant, and that acceptance like that was glorious and wonderful, not a fearsome thing.

"He was a complicated man, wasn't he?" she said aloud.

"That's for sure," Joe said with vigor. "He even wore socks that didn't match."

Finally the lake opened up ahead of them and across the black expanse of the water they could see the farmhouse far to the right and the Big House opposite, both ablaze with lights. There was noise too, cars, voices, a police siren somewhere, and jeep lights up in the pasture positioned near the trail to Camp Four.

"My God," Joe muttered.

They even heard the sound of a helicopter warming up, but then it reversed and the engine died down.

"He kept a canoe here somewhere," she whispered anxiously. They ran along the shore and, finding it, turned it over and slid it out into the water. "Get in, and sit down," she said. "Don't move. I'll paddle."

She held the boat steady while Joe, frightened, crawled down the middle to the bow, and then, getting in, she pushed off and the canoe glided out into the water. She paddled strongly. Suddenly the lights went off in her father's house and it stood huge and black against the sky.

"What's happening?" he whispered.

"I don't know."

Floating now, they listened while first one jeep, then another started up in the courtyard and headed up the road. At the crossroads the jeeps turned toward the farm, leaving in their wake silence at the end of the road where Rushing Boarchards had lived.

She started paddling again, going the long way around, passing Back Bay, where Rush Boarchards lay at the bottom of the lake. But suddenly she turned the canoe and headed out into the middle.

"What are you doing?" Joe asked. "They'll see us."

"Hand me the gun," she said when she reached the middle.

"Why?" he asked as he gave it back to her.

"I want to get rid of it." She took it in her hands. It was cold to the touch and heavy. She thought of the night in January when Rush had sat with it in the dark in the kitchen. "Quick, Joe. This is a little ceremony," she said urgently.

"What ceremony?" He was looking back at her from the bow as the canoe floated in the breeze.

She held the gun up in her arms. "Let's pretend the gun is the past. Your past, his past, me, the cave, the will, everything, and when I drop it in the water, it's all over."

Joe frowned. "That doesn't make sense." He glanced hurriedly over his shoulder toward the shore line and the Big House.

"Sure it makes sense," she said, looking at the shore too. "But only if we believe it enough. All we're doing is burying it. Okay? Putting an end to the whole thing."

"Oh, I get it," Joe suddenly exclaimed. "It's a funeral."

"That's right," she said patiently. "Ready?" She held the gun over the water.

"Ready."

Abby paused. "This is the end," she mumbled to herself. "I'm letting go of the past, the money, the land, and the hate."

"You don't want to be bitter either," Joe piped up. "And that too."

"And bitterness. I'm letting go of that too."

With that she dropped into the water of the lake the antique steel-and-wood hunting rifle Whitaker Stylus Rushing had given his littlest grandson half a century past. It splashed long and flat against the surface, gurgled a bit as liquid rushed up the barrel, and disappeared from sight.

With one last look at the spot where it had gone, Abby took up the paddle again and headed for the boathouse.

"Know what I think?" Joe whispered from the bow as they got closer.

"What?"

"I think he'd be proud of you."

Abby felt a rush of warmth. "Do you really think so?"

"Only he'd take credit for it," Joe said confidently. "Say it was his doing because he had the sense to disinherit you."

Nearing the boathouse, they floated, listening for voices again, but there were none. It was quiet. Abigail brought the canoe in and they set out through the meadow to Joe's truck.

They kept wide of the house and the road until they reached the top of the clearing, where the road headed toward town. She waited while Joe went into the trees to get his truck. She heard him start the engine and, looking across the meadow, saw lights in the farmhouse and the pasture, but no sign of any automobiles on the road.

The truck came out, its lights off, and she jumped in the passenger seat. Driving in the dark, they set off toward the highway. They were silent, intent, Joe driving carefully.

"What will you do now?" she asked after a while.

"Go home."

"New Mexico?"

He nodded.

She noticed something on the dashboard and picked it up. It was two photographs, back to back, the one of little Robbie Moran off his wall and one of her from an old yearbook. She had braces and bangs. "Joe . . . ?"

But he didn't answer.

They drove on in silence. Then suddenly he began to sing softly to himself. "Swing low, sweet chariot." He had a nice voice. "Coming for to carry me home . . ."

Abigail shook her head, his choice of music as incongruous as everything else. Then she saw he was beaming. "Why are you so happy?" she asked, happy herself all of a sudden.

"Why? Because."

"Because what?"

"Because this is fun," he said.

"Fun?"

"This is an adventure." He paused. "Isn't it?"

"Oh yes." She laughed. "It certainly is."

"I bet you sing too."

"A little."

"And I bet you're a good dancer," he said proudly.

Abigail smiled to herself. "I guess so, but right now I'm tired."

"Not me. I never felt so good."

When they reached the highway, tension returned. "You're not going all the way with me," he said sullenly. "Are you?"

"I can't, Joe. I have to go back. They're worried about me."

"Will you come to Pescadero?"

"Sometime."

"You promise."

"Yes."

He brought the truck to a halt by the garage and turned off the engine.

She opened the door but didn't get out. "Take care of yourself," she said reluctantly.

"Okay."

"You helped me a lot, you know," she said. "You helped me understand everything. Him. Me."

"By telling you about the cave?"

"No," she said. "By everything." She took his hand on the seat and clutched it. "By everything you did." Her voice cracked with emotion.

He heard it and looked at her face, their hands, then back at her face. "You look just like him," he said. "Did you know that?"

She nodded. "I guess I should go," she said, but she still didn't move.

"I've got something for you," he said suddenly. "It isn't much, but it's all I have right now." He leaned forward and took the picture of Robbie off the dashboard. "Maybe you'll like it. Seeing as how you think and all." He handed her the small, dog-eared photograph of the little boy. "Robbie," he said. "Seeing as how you knew his father too, of course."

"Yes," she said. She looked at the face. Two boys, one boy; the reform school and the kitchen. "What boy? There was no boy." And there wasn't after all. He wasn't growing old like her. He had stopped, over a cliff. "Thank you," she said. Then she grasped his hand once more, got out and shut the door.

Joe started up the engine. She went over to his side. He rolled down the window and looked at her.

"Be careful, Joe."

"I will. You don't have to worry about me." Then he pulled out into the road and headed down the highway.

She waved, and he waved, and gulping back tears of emotion and fatigue, she stood in the middle of the highway and watched until he was gone.

Then she headed toward the garage, found the key to the door under a brick, got a jeep and left.

The drive back in was faster and quieter. She watched the lights push back the darkness and looked at every tree and turn in the road, to fix it in her mind forever. When she reached the clearing, she looked at all the lights at the farm and wondered who was there. Diver, Josh . . . But abruptly she turned off the headlights and, at the crossroads, headed down toward the courtyard alone. She had one more thing to do.

She had to face Rushing Boarchards. The only name not on her list.

The house was dark. She opened the front door, listened, and went inside. Then she started down the hall at a slow run, up the back stairs two at a time and down the corridor to Rushing Boarchards' room.

The smell came closer and closer, stronger and stronger. In the doorway she stopped, the smell so palpable it was real. She tried not to breathe, but finally she took a breath and the awful smell washed over her. She gulped and drew it into her body. She found a flashlight on the mantelpiece and turned it on. The narrow beam of light picked out the files, skulls and bones, skeletal faces glowing in the light, eye sockets, black and peering. The salad bowl was still filled with ashes, the bed unmade, just as he had left it. She shivered. It was a terrible thing you did to me, she thought. Even if you didn't wholly mean it. Even if in some odd way you were trying to protect me.

She took the crumpled list out of her pocket and laid it on the skinny black keys of the old typewriter on his desk. "There," she whispered. "I did it. I did everything I said I'd do, Pop, and I'm not coming back. But I love you and thank you for all you've given me the last three weeks, as much as all the years before."

She shone the light around the room again, skulls and empty eyes, and then, moving quickly, she took first a bear skull, then an antler, then some little bird skulls and the head of something that might have been a fox. Her arms full, she looked one last time at his desk. Even in the half-light she could see the thin coating of cigarette ash. It seemed to have settled on her list already.

She went back down the hall to the balcony and the front stairs. She glanced across at the moose and shone her flashlight down along the fireplace. People had taken the dynamite down and the detonator was gone. She looked at the painting of her great-grandfather, Whitaker Stylus Rushing, and even at the floor itself, Rushing Boarchards down below in the basement with his files. Then, almost running now, she went down the hall and out the door.

Outside she was confronted abruptly by the lights of a jeep coming toward the house. She waited, fixed in the glare. The jeep honked once, twice, again. It sounded excited, and almost before it had fully stopped, the door sprang open and Luke jumped out.

"Abby," he cried, running over. "You're all right."

She beamed and held up her arms full of skulls and bones, as if they were precious trophies, but Luke just took her in his arms and held her to him as best he could. "Where is he?" he rushed on, looking over her shoulder.

"He's gone. I drove him out. It's all over."

"But you're all right? We've been looking for you everywhere, Abby. Max, Alvah . . ."

"I'm not going to contest, Luke," she interrupted, stepping away. "But I'm sorry I caused so much trouble. How's Simon?"

"He's fine. And that's Max behind me." They turned and looked up the road, more headlights coming across the clearing.

"Do you think he'll understand?"

"About the will?"

"No. About Joe. Me taking him out?"

"It's not hard to understand. Me, I was hoping that's what you were up to. You couldn't help your father, but you could help Joe and you wanted to very much. That's all there is to it." He looked at her, with her arms piled high with her father's things. "You certainly look happy," he said with a grin.

She nodded and beamed down protectively at all her bony possessions, as if they were still furry and alive, in need of maternal warmth. "Do you hear Licking River?" she asked suddenly, listening to its sounds in the night, water flowing to the sea to mingle with bigger things.

The car lights were coming closer. Abigail smiled into the glare now and tried to wave with her cluttered arms. "I like Uncle Max, don't you?"

"Yes."

"And Bostrine too."

Luke put his arm around her back, but she started moving

toward the jeep. It stopped and Max got out on one side, Alvah on the other.

She went up to Max, and he looked down at all the things in her arms. "Well, it looks like you're all right after all, aren't you, old thing."

"I'm sorry I caused so much trouble."

"What trouble? No trouble. But I guess you're ready to come home now, aren't you?"

"Yes."

"And you're finished?"

"Yes."

"You sure?"

"Yes."

"No more questions in that funny little head of yours?"

"No."

"And you're not going to contest the will, are you?"

"No."

"Hear Licking River?" the old man asked.

"Yes."

"I never do get tired of hearing that sound."

"Me neither."